Also by Diana M. Hawkins

Lumpy the Elephant
(A children's picture Book)

SHADOWS ALONG THE ZAMBEZI

A NOVEL

Diana M. Hawkins

iUniverse, Inc.
Bloomington

Shadows along the Zambezi

iUniverse books may be ordered through booksellers or by contacting:

iUniverse
1663 Liberty Drive
Bloomington, IN 47403
www.iuniverse.com
1-800-Authors (1-800-288-4677)

ISBN: 978-1-4759-5470-8 (sc)
ISBN: 978-1-4759-5469-2 (hc)
ISBN: 978-1-4759-5468-5 (e)

Library of Congress Control Number: 2012918605

Printed in the United States of America

iUniverse rev. date: 10/24/2012

Dedication

I dedicate this book to my husband, Scott, my champion throughout its creation.

Acknowledgements

Without the love and support of my husband, Scott, this novel might not have been completed. During its creation, he accepted my lengthy periods of seclusion, without complaint. Whenever I completed a chapter, he willingly stopped what he was doing to read it and provide me with constructive feedback. In particular, his help in developing my male protagonist's character was invaluable, as was his suggestion for the title.

I owe much to Johnny Rodrigues, chairman of the Zimbabwe Conservation Task Force for his unflagging support. He generously gave of his time to go over the entire manuscript, and answer my countless questions.

Chris Duckworth, in Johannesburg, South Africa, reviewed an early version of the manuscript, edited it, and provided me with many useful suggestions.

My four daughters also contributed to "Shadow's" creation: Margaret gave me the incentive to tackle the mammoth job, Joanna assisted me with aviation terminology and procedures, Lori helped with editing and put forward some excellent plotting ideas, and Heather helped proofread many chapters.

To add a measure of realism to the novel, my nephews in Zimbabwe helped me include selected lines of dialogue in the Shona language, and assisted me in depicting actual veterinary procedures commonly performed on wildlife.

In addition, I salute my fellow members of "Thee BPC Book Club," who constantly gave me encouragement throughout the writing of the novel.

My grateful thanks go to each and every one of them.

Disclaimer

Some well-known, public figures and many place names in this work are real and certain historical events mentioned in it may have actually taken place. However, this is a work of fiction and the characters, events, incidents, organizations, and dialogue in this novel, are either products of the author's imagination or are used fictitiously.

Contents

Prologue Tuesday, April 3, 2001 1

1. Monday, June 30, 2008. 9

2. May through July 2008. 18

3. Sunday, August 03, 2008 25

4. Monday, August 04, 2008. 32
   Descendants of Nkosikaas (Chieftainess) *33*

5. Monday, August 04, 2008. 35

6. Monday, August 4, 2008 45
   Descendants of Nkosi (Chief) *51*

7. Tuesday, August 05, 2008 57

8. Tuesday, August 05, 2008.. 62

9. Tuesday, August 05, 2008 70

10. Thursday, August 07, 2008 76

11. Thursday August 14, 2008 86

12. Friday, August 22, 2008 95

13. Tuesday August 26, 2008 106

14. Saturday, August 30, 2008. 110

15. Saturday, August 30, 2008. 120

16. Monday, September 1, 2008 127

17. Monday, September 08, 2008 135

18. Monday, September 08, 2008 145

19. Tuesday, September 09, 2008 156
    Descendants of Chembere (Old woman) *158*

20. Thursday, September 25, 2008 159

21. Friday, September 26, 2008 169

22. Friday, October 3, 2008 182

23. Friday, October 3, 2008 187

24. Saturday, October 4, 2008. 191

25. Tuesday, October 7, 2008 205

26. Saturday, October 11, 2008 216

27. Monday, October 13, 2008 232

28. Saturday October 25, 2008 240

29. Friday, October 31, 2008 250

30. Tuesday, November 4, 2008 261

31. Tuesday, November 4, 2008 272

32. Wednesday, November 5, 2008 279

33. Thursday, November 6, 2008 283

34. Thursday, November 06, 2008 294

35. Friday, November 7, 2008. 304

36. Friday, November 7, 2008. 312

37. Friday, November 14, 2008 328

Afterword 335

Glossary 337

Author Biography 345

Endorsement for Shadows along the Zambezi 346

Map of Zimbabwe 348

PROLOGUE
Tuesday, April 3, 2001

Sandie van Rooyen was angry and upset. Her husband should never have left her and the children alone on their Zimbabwe farm. Robert Mugabe's brutal land invasions were on the rise.

Why did he take the Cessna and fly off to Harare, just to collect tractor parts? If he'd waited, they'd have been delivered by the end of the week. Surely a delay of one or two days in the plowing didn't matter that much. She thumped the dining room table with her fist, hurt by his obvious disregard for his family's safety.

Before he left, he'd pulled her into his arms. "You'll be fine," he had assured her with his usual air of confidence. His kiss had lingered long, and for a brief moment or two, it seemed to erase all her fears. Then with a spring in his step, he walked away.

"Don't worry Sandie," he called out, as he turned to wave goodbye. "I've left a shotgun with Shoriwa and I'll be back tomorrow afternoon; before you know it. You've got the emergency radio, remember."

"Don't worry?" Sandie scoffed under her breath as she watched him disappear. "That's easy for you to say."

Several hours later, she felt somewhat more composed. Nonetheless, the possibility of an impending attack still bothered her. In the sewing room, she found her nine-year-old daughter, Bernice, hunched over the Singer, trying

1

to sew a straight seam. Sandie realized her daughter was frustrated since a wiggly line of stitches was the best she could do.

"Mummy, I can't get it to stay straight." Bernice frowned, tossing back a head of blonde curls. "The silly machine keeps pulling the material crooked."

"Sweetheart, the secret is to guide the fabric, using the lightest touch. You aren't in a tug-of-war with the machine, you know." Sandie lifted the Singer's sewing foot. She snipped the thread, and lined up the fabric. "Here, try it again."

Moments later, her son, Brian, entered the room.

"Mum," the eleven-year-old whined, "I'm bored. Can I go fishing down at the dam?"

"Brian, with Dad gone it's not safe. I don't want you going outside the security fence."

Her son rolled his eyes, stamped his foot, and headed for the door.

"Not fair! It's the school holidays, and instead of having fun, I'm stuck inside all day!"

"I'm sorry Brian, but that's the way things have to be. Perhaps Dad will take you fishing after he gets back tomorrow."

Brian kicked out at some invisible foe and stomped from the room. Sandie shook her head. He was such a handsome boy, with the dark hair and facial features so like his dad.

Wanting something to calm her nerves, she retreated to the kitchen to make a mid-morning cup of tea. She put the kettle on the Aga coal-fired stove, and waited for it to boil. Outdoors, the dogs were creating a commotion. They had three: Ali, a boxer; Russ, a feisty little Jack Russell terrier; and Jock, a Rhodesian ridgeback named after the ridgeback in Percy Fitzpatrick's novel, *Jock of the Bushveld*. Penned within the tall security fence encircling the farmhouse, all three were excellent guard dogs, alerting the family whenever a vehicle drove up or a stranger passed by. For some reason their barking sounded more frantic than usual.

Sandie rose from the kitchen table and walked to the window overlooking the farm's vehicle yard, with its garages, workshops, and storerooms. Through the grenade screen, she spotted a group of Africans standing outside the security fence. One of the men stood head and shoulders above his five companions. Parked in the driveway was a black Mercedes she had never seen before. At least half of the men carried rifles, slung carelessly over their shoulders. Her stomach tightened. Balanced on the shoulder of a man in the rear, was a long-barreled weapon with a pointed end. She recognized the firearm as a hand-held, rocket-propelled grenade launcher. She gasped and her breaths quickened.

The tall man had a head of closely cropped, gray hair with a deeply receding hairline. In contrast to his rag-tag companions, he wore an expensive pinstriped suit, a light-colored shirt, and a silk tie with diagonal stripes of gray, black, and white. A patina of red dust covered his stylish, highly polished leather shoes. Compared to his henchmen, he was far too well dressed. She wondered if his togs were the ill-gotten gains from an earlier farm invasion.

Their farm workers, usually visible at this time of the morning as they attended to their various tasks, were nowhere around. Over the barking of the dogs, the group's leader shouted out, shaking his fist.

"Mr. van Rooyen! Mr. Pieter van Rooyen. In the name of your country's president, Comrade Robert Gabriel Mugabe, I am taking your farm!" he hollered. "You must leave immediately!"

Through the burglar bars, Sandie retorted in the loudest, fiercest voice she could muster. "Go away! You're trespassing on private property!"

With his lips tightened in an evil grimace, the man yelled back, "You stupid whore! I am Chenjerai Hitler Hunsvi, chairman of the Zimbabwe Liberation War Veterans' Association, and this is our farm now. Get off! Go! Unless you leave today, you will be very, very sorry."

Sandie's outraged response, "Go to bloody hell!" exhibited far more courage than she actually possessed. Where in the heck was Shoriwa with the shotgun, she wondered. Her gut clenched. What had Piet been thinking? A gun that fired birdshot was hardly any defense against an AK-47.

She backed away from the window and rushed off to find Brian and Bernice. She found her daughter in the sewing room, still struggling with the sewing machine. Sandie's voice shook. "Wh... Where's Brian?"

"I think he's in his room, Mummy. What's the matter?"

"I'll tell you in a minute, darling. First, we must find Brian. It's urgent!"

Sandie darted out into the corridor with Bernice at her heels. She found her son sitting on his bed, playing a hand-held video game. She plopped down next to Brian, and pulled both her children close.

"Darlings, there's a problem. I need to get on the radio and call for help. Go into Dad's and my bathroom and keep out of sight."

Ever since the terror attacks began during Rhodesia's bush war, the family's designated, safe room had been this windowless bathroom with its small, overhead skylight.

"Lock the door and keep it locked. Unless you hear my voice, don't open it for any reason," she said, squeezing them tightly. "You two have to stick together. That's very, very important!"

"Mum, what's happening?" Brian's voice had a tremor.

"No time for long explanations. There's a man outside who wants to take our farm." She hugged them again and said, "We're not going to let him, but

I must get on the radio to get us some help. In the meantime, lock yourselves in the bathroom. Run!"

The children hurtled out the door to their parent's room. Sandie followed them out into the passage, where the farm's high-band radio sat on a wall-mounted shelf. She turned the dial to Channel 20. It should summon their neighbor. She picked up the microphone, took a deep breath to fight down a rising feeling of hysteria, pressed the transmit button, and began to speak.

"Glengarry Farm, Glengarry. This is Kigelia Farm. Angus, are you there? Glengarry, this is Kigelia, over."

The radio crackled and her heart lifted when she heard Angus's deep, resonant voice. "Glengarry here. Good morning, Sandie. Over."

Angus McLaren, the great-grandson of a Scottish immigrant, had farmed next door to the van Rooyens for the past eleven years. The families were close.

"Angus, there are some armed men outside our security fence. They say they're here to take the farm. Over." She felt a lump in her throat and fought back tears.

Angus's voice was consoling. "Sandie, just hold on, hey. Dave Packer and I are coming. We'll be there as soon as we can. Meanwhile, go to your safe room and stay there. I know Piet's away. I saw him fly over this morning. Don't panic, my girl. We'll be there soon. Do you copy? Over."

"Roger. I heard you, Angus." Her voice trembled. "Please hurry. Over and out."

As she replaced the microphone, a flood of relief washed over her, but the feeling was short-lived. Outdoors, amidst a chorus of frantic woofs and yaps, came the crackle of automatic fire. Chills ran down her spine as the multiple whelps and whines, dwindled into a solitary howl. Had those monsters shot the dogs? Her eyes filled with tears, and her shoulders convulsed from the sobs escaping her throat.

She pressed her cheek against the cool, plastered wall and wept, fearing the unknown terrors that awaited them. Would her family meet the same cruel fate of others who had died? In recent months, Robert Mugabe's vicious thugs had brutally murdered eight white Zimbabwe farmers, many of their black workers, and hundreds of his political opponents.

As she turned to enter the master bedroom, Sandie heard scraping sounds coming from down the hallway. Through the arched doorway leading into the living room, she caught sight of the ridgeback, leaping up at the grenade screens outside the French doors. He was barking frantically, begging to come in. She opened the door and Jock bounded inside, circling her legs in delirious joy. Weak with relief, she bent down to pet him, running her hand along the ridge of hair along his back. The dog's coat felt wet, and after examining her red, sticky palm, her initial feeling of relief turned to dread as she realized it was blood. Was it his, or had it come from one of the other dogs? She hurriedly inspected Jock all over, and after finding no injuries or open wounds, she murmured a quick prayer of thanks and grabbed him by the collar, leading him into the hallway.

Moments later, she cringed as a deafening explosion rocked the house. Sections of corrugated iron roofing, shattered rafters, and chunks of ceiling board tumbled down through a cavernous opening in the roof above the living room. Clouds of dust swirled about and flames licked the edge of the carpet against the back wall.

In the hallway, Sandie and the dog had fortunately escaped the blast. Determined to protect herself and the children, she pulled Jock towards the bedroom. Once inside, she released his collar and wiped off her hands. From the walk-in cupboard, she grabbed her husband's FN rifle off a gun rack mounted on the wall. Afterwards, shaking with fear, she seized another, the Browning automatic, and filled her pockets with boxes of ammunition for both weapons. With Jock at her side, she tapped on the master bathroom door.

"Let me in! It's Mum."

The door opened and Jock leapt ahead of her, almost knocking Brian to the floor. Sandie slipped in after the dog, locking the door behind her. The children reached out for her, white-faced and trembling. She forced a smile as she hugged them

"There's good news. I spoke to Mr. McLaren on the radio. He and Mr. Packer are on their way over, right now, to help us."

"What was that terrible bang?" Bernice whimpered. "We were so scared!"

"They shot a hole in the roof above the living room. Not a big thing. We're not expecting rain this week and Dad can fix it as soon as he gets home, tomorrow."

The dog's arrival was a welcome diversion for the children.

"Brian, before you pet him, wipe him down." She handed him a wet washcloth.

He ran it along the dog's back and sides. "What's this, Mum? Where did it come from?" He held up the bloodstained cloth.

"I'm not sure. Just wipe him down all over." She was not about to tell the children she suspected the other dogs had been shot and it could be their blood.

The terrifying sounds of automatic rifle fire resumed. She cringed.

"I wonder if Mr. McLaren's arrived yet." Brian's voice quavered. "I… I… I hope he comes s… s… soon."

"So do I."

Sandie's hands trembled as she loaded the FN rifle with two magazines taped together. Piet had taught her this trick. It allowed her to shoot forty rounds in less than a minute, before reloading. There were six more magazines in the box. She also loaded the Browning twelve-gauge shotgun, which was capable of firing five shells per magazine. She knew Piet had been teaching Brian how to use the shotgun. If necessary, she could press him into service.

Inside, Sandie grieved. What was the world coming to that she had to count on her eleven-year-old son to fire a weapon to protect his sister and mother?

*   *   *

Within fifteen minutes of Sandie's alert, her neighbors, Angus McLaren and Dave Packer were on their way. They were racing towards the Kigelia Farm homestead along the single-lane, dirt road, which intersected off the main Karoi thoroughfare. Approaching them, at great speed, was a large, black Mercedes, throwing up a billowing trail of dust. Angus slowed his pickup and steered to the left to let the Mercedes go by. As they passed, Dave got a good look at the driver.

"Damn! That was Hitler Hunzvi."

Angus groaned, his face contorted with worry. "Bloody hell."

Both men were intimately familiar with the exploits of Chenjerai Hunzvi, the man who had adopted the *nom de guerre*, Hitler. He openly referred to himself as the biggest terrorist in Zimbabwe, and his name was synonymous with Zimbabwe's breakdown of the rule of law. Everyone knew Hunzvi had initiated the violent invasions of white-owned farms, along with supporters of Mugabe's Zimbabwe African National Union – Patriotic Front (ZANU-PF). Hunzvi was likely coming from Kigelia Farm. Fear knotted Angus's belly.

After passing the Mercedes, he floored the accelerator. With its rear wheels spinning, the truck hurtled towards the homestead, three miles away. Moments later, he and Dave heard a loud explosion up ahead.

"Oh, bloody hell! We've got to hurry, *kurumidzai*," Angus yelled.

*   *   *

The house had been strangely quiet after the first blast tore a hole in the roof. Sandie presumed the RPG, she'd seen earlier had caused the explosion. A terrified Bernice sat on the bathroom vanity, weeping softly. Sandie wrapped her arms around her daughter, whispering words of comfort. Brian had stretched out in the bathtub, using towels to pillow his head. He had his arms wrapped tightly around the large dog lying beside him. Sandie wondered if Jock sensed her son's fear, since the dog was feverishly licking Brian's neck.

In a shaking voice, the boy asked his mother, "How long do we have to stay here?"

Sandie could tell her traumatized son was fighting back tears. "Honestly, I don't know, Brian."

A second thunderous explosion shook the walls of the house bringing sounds of splintering glass. Bernice let out a shrill scream and Brian hugged the dog even tighter. Sandie bottled up her own fears, continuing to reassure her children their neighbors would arrive soon.

Soon they heard voices coming from somewhere inside the house. Filled with terror, Sandie realized their attackers had gained entry. They were speaking in Shona. She recognized a few words. Covering her face with her hands, she prayed silently. She begged the Lord to save them. Dear God, she prayed, please save my children even if you see fit to take me now. I know I've often failed you, but Brian and Bernice are innocent children and deserve to spend more time here on this beautiful earth you created for us. If you want to spare my life, I promise I will do everything I can do to...

An explosive sound of gunfire cut short her prayer as bullets blasted through the bathroom door. One struck Bernice, and Sandie saw her daughter's limp body tumble off the sink top onto the floor. Another bullet hit her on her left shoulder. She ignored the burning pain and dropped down to check on her daughter. Bernice lay motionless, face down, on the linoleum floor. With only one functioning arm, Sandie grasped the girl's pink sweater and pulled her over. She saw that the bullet had left a small hole in her child's left temple and a gruesome, bloody exit wound above her right ear. Overcome with grief, she let out a bloodcurdling wail.

"Oh, my God! No! Not my baby girl!" she screamed. Disregarding the searing pain in her shoulder, she gathered Bernice up in her arms and rocked her back and forth, sobbing inconsolably.

Stretched out in the heavy cast iron bathtub, both Brian and the dog had escaped the initial volley of gunfire. The ridgeback jumped out of the tub and circled Sandie and Bernice, while whimpering piteously. Brian sat up, preparing to climb out.

The motion caught Sandie's eye and she screeched, "Brian, get back in the bath. Lie down, and be still in case they start shooting again."

He sank back into the tub, choking. Tears formed rivulets down his face. "Is Bernice okay?"

"No, Brian. She's not okay." Sandie sobbed.

The voices were louder now, and moments later the door burst open and slammed against the sink with a deafening crash. Two of Hunsvi's bedraggled foot soldiers stood in the doorway, their weapons leveled at Sandie. Jock curled back his lips, baring his teeth and a threatening snarl rumbled from deep in his throat. As one of the men stepped forward, the dog let out a bloodcurdling howl and leapt at them, knocking both men backwards. Their rifles clattered onto the tiled floor.

Sandie lowered Bernice and reached for the FN. Before she was able to aim it and pull the trigger, however, one of the men was back on his feet and had retrieved his weapon. He fired at Sandie, knocking the rifle out of her hands, almost severing her wrist. Blood gushed from her mangled, lower right arm. The pain was excruciating and her shoulder felt as if it was on fire. She slumped back against the bathtub, Bernice's lifeless body stretched out at her feet. She draped her left arm over the edge of the tub to grasp Brian's hand. She found it, and gave it a squeeze.

The ridgeback, meanwhile, was attacking the gunman's prone companion, snapping, snarling, and tearing at his exposed flesh. After disarming Sandie, Hunsvi's remaining triggerman turned his weapon on the dog and Sandie and her son saw their beloved Jock flop lifeless onto the floor.

Brian let go of his mother's hand, and Sandie turned to look at her son. His eyes widened in terror. She saw him reach for the shotgun he had concealed in the bathtub. As he lifted the barrel of the Browning automatic, the armed man approached. Time seemed to stand still as Sandie watched her beloved, courageous son face off against his sister's killer. He fired several shots that went high, peppering the wall above the door with birdshot. Seconds later, explosive rounds from the AK-47 hit Brian in the dead center of his chest. As he fell backwards, Sandie let out a piercing scream.

One or more of the bullets boring through Brian's chest, ricocheted off the cast iron bathtub, and slammed into the gunman's hip. He bellowed in pain, staggering backwards through the door. His fall caused his AK to pump two rounds into Sandie's chest. She felt no pain. A huge sense of relief surged through her. God had chosen not to separate her from her children. He was instead bringing all three of them home to his kingdom. With that final thought, her world clouded over and turned a brilliant white.

Chapter 1

Monday, June 30, 2008

Pieter van Rooyen hung up the phone.

"Wonders, upon wonders!" he exclaimed, throwing up his arms up elation. "Moses listen, this is the best news we've had in months!"

Moses Mafunda was busy stocking shelves in his employer's Titambire Bait and Tackle Shop. He stepped forward with a smile. "What is the good news, Baas?"

"Moses, I'm going to be speaking at the Harare Rifle Club's annual dinner in August. It's good news because it's going to give us a chance to do some decent fund raising," he said, vigorously shaking Moses' hand.

The nonprofit he had founded in 2003, the Zimbabwe Wildlife Protection League, or ZWPL, was sorely in need of a major influx in donations. It needed funds to continue saving the thousands of wild animals in national parks and safari areas across the Zambezi Valley. He thought back to when he first discovered the need for such an organization.

He remembered those miserable days, seven years before, when the government seized his farm and invaders murdered his family. Homeless and practically destitute, he had headed for Lake Kariba where, for several years, he frittered away his time until he managed to buy the bait shop for a song. Not long after that, he witnessed the beginnings of the wholesale slaughter of his country's wildlife. That was when he decided to take action to stop it.

*　　　　*　　　　*

It was Friday night, August 1, a little more than a month later and van Rooyen was getting ready to speak at the Harare Rifle Club's annual dinner. In the city's swanky, Meikles Hotel, he would be addressing a room full of hunters and outfitters, the ZWPL's largest and most important consumer groups. His goal—to inform them of the critical work he and his volunteers were accomplishing in the eastern Zambezi Valley, and how it benefitted the hunting and outdoors communities.

Rifle Club Chairman Moses Sibanda stepped up to the podium. He was a short, balding, portly man, in a formal, black, dinner suit. Glancing around, van Rooyen noted that most attendees were wearing dressy attire of one kind or another. At some point in his life, he might have felt uncomfortably under-dressed, and out of place at such an event in his gray suit and maroon, old-school tie. It didn't bother him tonight, however. Since he rarely attended such events, he had seen no point in investing in an expensive tuxedo. Rather than hobnobbing with strangers at functions like this, he would ordinarily have preferred be out in the bush, fishing on Lake Kariba, or flying down the Zambezi in his Cessna 150. Tonight however, he knew he must set aside his personal preferences for the benefit of the country's wildlife.

The dining room was packed. When he arrived, organizers told him that more than 150 club members and guests had shown up. As he looked around, it was evident the hotel had gone all-out in setting things up. Covering each circular table was a starched, white linen tablecloth, and at its centerpiece a slender, crystal vase with single, red rose. Place settings included expensive Irish Waterford wine and water glasses, Wedgewood dinnerware, and several sets of Sheffield, sterling silver knives, forks, and spoons. Standing sentry at each place was a rolled, starched linen table napkin. He hoped he wouldn't embarrass himself by using the wrong set of silverware.

Scanning the crowd, he recognized fewer than a dozen people. There were a couple of farmers and their wives from Karoi; former neighbors he hadn't seen since 2001, when he lost his family and farm. Although seven years had passed since the murders, his grief was still raw. Would he ever be able to forgive himself for leaving his wife and children alone that fateful April morning?

Sitting at a nearby table was National Parks Superintendent Hector Kaminjolo and his wife, and immediately to his right, a Scotsman, professional hunter and outfitter, Blair Nisbet. The Glasgow native and he were friends and they frequently ran into one another up in the Zambezi Valley, where van Rooyen led his league-sponsored, anti-poaching patrols. Blair took his clients there on organized hunting safaris and fishing expeditions, and they often frequented his bait and tackle shop on the banks of Lake Kariba.

As soon as van Rooyen sat down, Blair leant over and whispered in his unmistakable, Scottish brogue. "Piet, *afore ye* leave tonight, we need to talk. I have some information *ye* might be interested in." Van Rooyen's lifted brows registered his surprise. Blair nodded to him, but said no more.

Tonight's guests of honor included Zimbabwe's Minister of Tourism Victor Sebakwe, the Director General of Zimbabwe Parks and Wildlife Management Authority Nelson Zanunga, and their wives. Sebakwe was Zanunga's boss, having executive oversight over the National Parks. Zanunga, in turn, was Hector Kaminjolo's superior.

Van Rooyen was relieved that neither Zimbabwe President Robert Mugabe, nor his opposition leaders, Morgan Tsvangirai and Arthur Mutambara, were here tonight. Earlier that week, the three men had established a power sharing government. Nonetheless, their acrimonious negotiations, over the actual division of power, had been making headlines for weeks. In van Rooyen's opinion, their presence would have injected too much unnecessary drama.

Sibanda stepped up to the lectern, putting on a pair of heavy, horn-rimmed, reading glasses. The buzz of conversation hushed. He peered over his lenses towards the audience and nodded towards the table of special guests.

"Good evening Mr. Sebakwe, Mr. Zanunga, ladies and gentlemen. It is with much pleasure that I introduce tonight's keynote speaker, Mr. Pieter van Rooyen, Kariba businessman, private pilot, wildlife conservationist, and chairman of the Zimbabwe Wildlife Protection League. We invited Mr. van Rooyen to join us this evening, to talk about the important work he and his volunteers are doing to help save our wildlife in the eastern Zambezi Valley."

Kaminjolo caught van Rooyen's eye and winked. The two men frequently crossed paths and van Rooyen considered him an ally, particularly when he found himself butting heads with bureaucrats in the Parks and Wildlife Management Authority. Appreciative of Kaminjolo's encouraging gesture, van Rooyen returned his smile.

"Mr. van Rooyen formed the Zimbabwe Wildlife Protection League in 2003," Sibanda continued, "and since then, he and his team and their supporters have helped to save the lives of thousands of animals in our national parks and safari areas all across the Zambezi Valley. For instance, during a long drought several years ago, many of the man-made, waterholes in the Hwangwe National Park dried up. Around them, hundreds of animals were dropping like flies."

"The bore-holes dried up for two reasons." Holding up two fingers, he pointed to each in turn. "Firstly—because of broken-down pumps with no spares; secondly, fuel shortages—no diesel. However, thanks to Mr. van Rooyen and the league, this story had a successful conclusion. His call for help, broadcast worldwide over the Internet, brought spare parts from overseas donors, and hundreds of gallons of diesel fuel came in on lorries from South Africa. Soon, the pumps were back into business again, saving thousands of animals."

The audience responded with an enthusiastic round of applause.

"That was just one of the ZWPL's many good deeds. Piet will undoubtedly have much more to tell you, so I am happy to turn the microphone over to him." Sibanda stepped down.

As the applause waned, van Rooyen rose from his table, tugged at his shirt collar, and strode up to the podium, carrying a large paper bag. Well here goes, he thought, as he retrieved his notes and arranged them on the lectern. Stroking his chin, he reminded himself to temper his remarks, particularly in reference to many of the current political regime's past actions. If he spoke too candidly, he knew Mugabe's secret police would likely be banging on his door tonight. Aware conditions in Zimbabwe's prisons were beyond appalling, he certainly didn't want to risk ending up in Chikurubi, Harare's most infamous lockup. He'd heard that fifty or more intakes shared a tiny, dark, lice-filled room with nothing but a concrete floor covered in human waste to sleep on.

Smiling, he looked out towards the crowd offering the usual obligatory greetings to those assembled.

"Thank you Mr. Sibanda, for your kind introduction. Prior to giving you the rundown on what we've accomplished since we created the league in 2003," van Rooyen began, "I'd like to provide you with a little background information."

"As we all know, eight years ago Zimbabwe was a prime international destination for hunters, wildlife photographers, and tourists. People came here in droves from across the globe to hunt, visit our game reserves, and take in our country's world-famous sights, including the Victoria Falls, Lake Kariba, the picturesque Eastern District, and the Great Zimbabwe Ruins. We should all feel very proud that five of our national parks have been designated by the United Nations, as world heritage sites – places that have outstanding, universal value."

The crowd agreed with whistles and applause.

"Unfortunately things have changed and today Zimbabwe's once pristine environment has been ravaged by poachers who have slaughtered huge numbers of our wild animals."

Van Rooyen knew the audience was aware Zimbabwe's bankrupt economy and its crumbling infrastructure lay squarely in the lap of Robert Mugabe's chaotic land reform program, instituted in 2000. Consequently, thousands of innocent people were dying daily from starvation, AIDS, malaria, and cholera. Nowadays, few well-informed Zimbabweans accepted Mugabe's claims that the country's failures were due to severe droughts or the evil foreign policies of Great Britain and the United States. He saw no reason, therefore, to re-hash stuff the audience already knew.

Instead, he spoke of the legacy of Zimbabwe's game ranches and wildlife conservancies, which he credited with protecting many endangered species— the black rhino, cheetah, leopard, elephant, and the African wild dog. Despite the possibility of incurring risk to himself, he blamed the government for breaking its promise to the Zimbabwean people when it failed to exclude these lands from its controversial land reform program. He wondered how many people here tonight, beyond the dignitaries, knew that high-ranking government officials and their supporters had seized most of the conservancies in question.

Stepping back from the lectern, van Rooyen scanned the faces before him.

"Wildlife management requires specialized knowledge and those who seized game ranches and conservancies had no expertise in caring for the animals. In most cases, they simply opened up the lands to poachers. Aerial population counts, conducted in 2004, revealed they had slaughtered almost eighty percent of wildlife on the larger conservancies and forty percent of the supposedly protected animals in Zimbabwe's national parks."

Van Rooyen's passion moved many in the audience, but at the special guests' table, Tourism Minister Sebakwe sat stone-faced.

"Prior to the government's taking over some 4,000 commercial farms," he continued, "Zimbabwe had an unparalleled reputation for protecting its wildlife. Officials issued hunting permits to local game hunters, safari operators, and sportsmen from all over the world. From these, they collected detailed lists of the animals they shot. Based on these figures, the authorities controlled the number of permits issued to guarantee healthy game populations in the future. A generous portion of incoming local and foreign currencies went directly to National Parks. Fees collected allowed parks to properly maintain their facilities and operate them efficiently. The hunting reports also helped officials to keep an accurate running tally of the number of animals in the country."

A voice from the rear called out, "Good show!" Others clapped. Van Rooyen gave the man a thumbs-up and continued with a deep frown.

"Sadly, there are few if any controls in place today. The Parks and Wildlife Management Authority is bankrupt, and the once well-run system is in total chaos."

Whispers created a low buzz, parks' superintendent Hector Kaminjolo's expression turned glum, and Sebakwe feverishly scribbled notes on a pad.

"That was the situation, five years ago, when we founded the Zimbabwe Wildlife Protection League. At the outset, we established the league's four primary goals. First—to regularly patrol wildlife habitats and remove snares from surviving animals; second —to relocate those in danger; third—to assist Zim Parks with anti-poaching patrols, and lastly—to expose all illegal hunters and those who were assisting them."

The crowd applauded with enthusiasm. It gave van Rooyen a huge boost. However, when he saw Sebakwe whispering feverishly to an aid, he felt a prickle of fear. For a moment, a taste of bile flooded his mouth; he swallowed, and turned again to the audience.

"As it stands now," he said, "accurate wildlife counts haven't been conducted for years, so there's no way for us to know how many animals are left. Our rough estimates are based only on reports from volunteers, legal hunters like yourselves, and from the few tourists who still visit the parks. For this I want to thank you," and he saluted the crowd.

"Nonetheless, these results show us a mind-boggling, eighty-nine percent decrease—yes decrease—over the past five years, in the size of Zimbabwe's wildlife population. You must agree these are devastating statistics," he said with a grimace, his hands clenched into fists. His anger was burning like a low fire in his gut.

A loud buzz of conversation followed his last statement, and many in the audience were nodding their agreement.

"We believe poaching is largely responsible for these incredible losses." His eyes narrowed, and from behind the lectern, he retrieved the brown paper bag. From it, he pulled out a loop of barbed wire. He held the strand above his head, and gave it a menacing swing. The audience looked on silently.

"This harmless-looking piece of fencing material is used to create the cruel, capture device that we call a snare. I have no doubt many of you have run across strands of wire just like this, out in the bush. Believe me, it's an evil contrivance!" His lips tightened, displaying his feeling of contempt.

"With this instrument of torture, more animals are maimed and destroyed every year, than are killed by floods, fires, old age, disease and even guns—all added together!"

Sharp intakes of breath came from some in the crowd, and the room fell silent. Glancing over at the special guest's table, he noticed Mrs. Sebakwe raise her eyebrows, but saw no visible reaction from her husband.

"Snares are cruel, and they kill indiscriminately."

He went on to describe how poachers used them to snag wildlife species— from the tiniest rodent to the largest bull elephant. He spoke of the many years he'd carried out anti-poaching patrols in the Zambezi valley, coming across thousands of dead and dying animals, all with snares wrapped around necks, legs, torsos, or trunks.

"One of those we saved was a giraffe, whose neck was caught in a snare set high in a tree. Fortunately, we got there soon enough and one of my scouts climbed the tree and cut her loose. Our team once saved a black rhino with a snare imbedded in a hind leg. But I've got to tell you, saving the more dangerous animals is very challenging," he said. "We have to anaesthetize them just to get close enough to cut away the snare and treat any resulting wound. Then, if the injury needs surgery, we have to call in a vet. That's expensive, and the drugs used to tranquilize the larger animals, M99, and its antidote M5050, cost a lot of money. That's assuming we can even get them."

Van Rooyen told the diners that during their anti-poaching patrols, his team picked up hundreds of snares from trees, bushes, and along the countless game trails, which crisscross the Zambezi Valley.

"And we haven't even scratched the surface yet."

He explained snares were a method of hunting that dated back to ancient times. They were inexpensive devices and simple to create, using stolen pieces of telephone cable, barbed wire fencing material, even metal strands salvaged from burst tires left on main roads.

"Poachers also use nylon fishing line, rope, and even steel winch cables to make them."

He wrapped up his presentation, with an appeal.

"I call on everyone here to do their bit for game conservation. Pick up every snare you might run across in the bush and turn them all in to your nearest national park office."

Van Rooyen wished he could be brutally honest and spill all Zimbabwe's dirty little secrets. How there was no way to control poaching because Zim Parks had neither the money nor the resources to carry out regular anti-poaching patrols. In addition, because of the country's foundering economy, the government lacked funds for rangers' salaries, vehicles, equipment, and fuel. Without law and order in Zimbabwe, it was also impossible to control illegal hunting. Authorities rarely apprehended or prosecuted any poachers. To make matters worse, some officials responsible for maintaining law and order were themselves involved in poaching.

Then there were foreign hunters who were able to bribe Zimbabwe game scouts into violating the already lax hunting quotas. He did not believe Blair Nisbet was one of them, but could he be sure? Some questionable big game hunting concessions rewarded scouts handsomely in exchange for the special deals they negotiated with new owners of confiscated game ranches and wildlife conservancies. They often paid up to U.S. $50,000 to shoot as much game as they could carry away. Was Kaminjolo aware of this chicanery? Were his scouts making deals without his knowledge, van Rooyen wondered.

Van Rooyen spoke for another ten minutes, then invited questions from the audience. He concluded his talk with a brief, but heartfelt, appeal for donations. Before stepping down, he thanked the audience for their attention and directed them to tables set up in the hotel corridor where volunteers were on hand to accept their contributions. He hoped, meanwhile, contributors would give in American, British, or South African legal tender, rather than Zimbabwe's worthless currency. Local banks were pegging its current, official exchange rate at almost 1,800 Zimbabwe dollars for a single U.S. greenback.

As the crowd filed out, van Rooyen retreated to the back of the room. People approached him, shook his hand, and thanked him for his efforts. Approaching were the Karoi farmers whom he had hoped to avoid. Angus McLaren and Dave Packer had not only been neighbors—they had been his close friends. Seeing them, however, brought back too many painful memories he really wasn't ready to deal with tonight.

Leaving the hotel, he walked briskly to his Land Rover, parked across the street next to Africa Unity Square. The park was once known as Cecil Square, named after the country's founder, British Empire builder Cecil John Rhodes. It was a historical site in the city, formerly named Salisbury. It was here, that white pioneers had first raised the Union Jack, in 1890, marking their arrival in Mashonaland.

It was dark. Streetlights were seemingly a thing of the past. Either hooligans had smashed them, or the City of Harare could no longer afford the electricity. Blair Nisbet stepped out of the shadows as van Rooyen slipped his key into the door lock.

"Hey Piet, let me in the passenger side."

"What's going on?"

"I *didnae* want our conversation overheard," Blair said in a hushed tone, as he walked around to the passenger door. Puzzled, van Rooyen climbed in and leaned across to lift the door lock. Blair Nisbet got in.

"I wanted to let *ye* know there's something odd going on, just east of the Chewore confluence. I have clients due in next week from America, so I was in the area several days ago, looking around for trophy-sized game. While I was there, I saw some blokes speeding up and down the river in three high-performance boats."

"What's so unusual about boats on the Zambezi?" Was his friend Blair going *penga*?

"Piet, they were identical. Each one was near forty feet from stem to stern. What made them look bloody odd wasn't just their speed, and that they obviously cost a pretty penny. The crowning glory was the bloody machine guns they had mounted on their bows."

"Jeez hey, I agree that does sound nuts. I'll definitely look into it! Thanks, Blair, for clueing me in."

"Not a problem, *laddie*. It's just that it smelled a bloody lot like poaching to me and I don't want any rotten bastards killing wildlife my clients pay me good money to hunt," he chuckled. He then climbed out, swung the door shut, and disappeared into the darkness.

Chapter 2

May through July 2008

A small herd of elephants rested in a clearing surrounded by tall mopani trees. It was four o'clock on that crisp May morning. A sliver of light on the horizon heralded the coming of dawn in the eastern Zambezi Valley. Two adult cows stood posted like sentries on either side of a circle of their slumbering kin. In the dim light, they resembled a collection of dark mounds protruding from the veld. Except for the hoot of an owl perched nearby, only an occasional muffled snort or the sound of intestinal gas broke the pre-dawn silence.

A young female stirred. She struggled to her feet and circled the slumberous group. Local tribespeople had named her Mafashama. Shortened to Shama, her name meant big water. They remembered the raging floods that tore at the riverbanks the year she was born, nineteen rainy seasons before. After circling the clearing's perimeter several times, she lowered her head dropping the tip of her trunk onto the ground. The calf moved inside her, and she felt sharp pains, down deep in her belly.

The morning's first light crept steadily across the hills to the south as the sun turned the clouds' lower edges a fiery red. The herd's two sentries moved about, stirring the remaining elephants—another two adult females, and seven offspring of varying ages. One by one, they rose awkwardly to their feet with stretches and yawns. Shama had moved away from the main group and stood alone at the outer edge of the clearing. She appeared discomfited and

18

dark stains appeared on her cheeks as secretions streamed from her temporal glands, a condition exhibiting her tension.

Too involved in their early morning ritual of rubbing eyes and ears with their trunks, the main group paid little attention to the cow whose behavior seemed to be so out of synchrony with their own. An old dowager, with a broken left tusk, finally moved away from the main group and approached her daughter. She rubbed her head against Shama's rump and with her trunk reached beneath her daughter's tail to touch her female parts. They hung lower than usual and the group's matriarch sensed the birth of a new calf was imminent.

The old cow, Muchengeti, whose Shona name meant leader and protector, had assisted her family through numerous births during her forty-eight years. She would step up once more to serve as midwife. Meanwhile, other family members spread out to feed on the leaves, fruits, and new shoots of surrounding bushes and trees.

Two young male calves began engaging in a mock battle. With trunks intertwined, they pushed against one another in a friendly shoving match. They moved back and forth as each, in turn, gained the upper hand. Engrossed in their game, they inadvertently slammed into one of the feeding adults. The cow squealed in protest and cuffed both offenders with her trunk. Chastened, they broke apart and moved off.

Twenty-seven-year-old Umsizi was Muchengeti's oldest living daughter. She had a noticeable scar above her right eye. She approached her mother and younger sister, greeting them both with a gentle rumble. The expectant mother paced back and forth, while her attendants looked on. Several hours passed before the bulge beneath her tail began to expand. Her mother and sister closed in and stood on either side of her, stroking her gently with their trunks.

Curious, one of the previously sparring young males stepped forward to investigate. The expectant mother's two attendants pushed him away. Shama's firstborn calf, a four-year-old male, also approached. He made a valiant attempt to nudge his aunt and grandmother aside, so he could rub himself up against his mother. His senior, female relatives unceremoniously shoved him aside and chased him away. With the two older cows at her side, Shama entered the final stages of giving birth. Back on her feet, she lifted her head, spread her legs, and strained.

The sun had risen above the surrounding treetops when she expelled the new calf, enveloped in a slippery, white, fetal sac, onto the ground. After the delivery, Shama stood for a minute or two then turned and touched the fetal sac with her trunk. Inside it, the calf kicked vigorously and Muchengeti stepped forward to assist her daughter in tearing open the membrane. Together the midwives pierced it, exposing a wet, wriggling, female baby elephant. In less than thirty minutes, the two hundred and sixty pound infant struggled to her feet.

Once upright, it became a supreme effort for her to remain standing. She would take a few tentative steps and fall. Undeterred, she'd get up again, only to topple over once more. She repeated these motions more than a half dozen times in the next twenty minutes. The adults foraging nearby paid scant attention to the little calf's troubles. They evidently had confidence she would soon gain the necessary strength.

Once she had mastered the ability to remain on her feet for more than a few minutes, Muchengeti guided her towards her mother's teats. She was barely two hours old when she started suckling. Assured the newborn was gaining strength, the old matriarch moved off to join the others. In time, the calf would receive the name, Shungu – the desired one.

Muchengeti customarily led her family in search of grazing by mid-morning, but on this day she kept them foraging close to the mother and baby, allowing Shama time to rest and her calf the opportunity to get stronger. The newborn and her mother remained in the shade of the mopani trees until early evening. After suckling until she was sated, the youngster practiced tottering around on her wobbly legs until exhaustion overcame her and then she'd flop down for a well-earned nap.

Like most baby elephants, Shungu was a perfectly proportioned miniature of an adult. Her shoulder height was a little less than three feet, and stiff black hairs sprouted from her forehead, crown, and back. The backs of her ears were bright pink and, as she attempted to touch and smell everything around her, her little trunk whipped about like an out-of-control vacuum cleaner hose. It would take her months to learn how to coordinate her thousands of individual trunk muscles.

It was early evening when Muchengeti, let out a deep, "let's go" rumble. She then set out northward, along a well-trodden game trail through the mopani forest. Her family followed her in single file. The new mother's older sister, Chirema, the lame one, trudged behind Shama and the calf to protect the rear of the column. At sunset, the elephants reached the riverbank. Their bodies cast huge shadows along the Zambezi.

Gathered along the river's edge in the Charara Safari Area, were herds of buffalo and wildebeest and small groups of antelope: impala, kudu, eland, waterbuck, and reedbuck. Flocks of ibises, herons, cranes and other water birds paddled in the shallows, creating a chorus of squawks and harsh nasal "urnk, urnk" sounds. Discretely, they all moved aside as the ponderous elephants stepped down to the water's edge.

Except for the newborn, all the elephants dropped the tips of their trunks into the water to draw in the precious liquid. Once they'd filled their trunks, they lifted them, threw back their heads, and squirted the water down their throats. Each one repeated the motion until they had drunk their fill. The calves, who finished sooner than their elders, waded knee-deep into the river and playfully swiped at the water to splash one another. Others sucked up trunkfuls, which they sprayed in all directions, sending clouds of shimmering water droplets high in the air. The newborn, afraid of the moving water, pressed close to her mother. Since she would obtain much of her liquid nourishment from her mother for the next two years, there was no need for her to drink from the river.

The sky darkened rapidly, and the old cow stepped back from the water's edge. She gave a deep rumble to summon her family, and led the way back along the trail into the mopani forest.

*　　　　*　　　　*

Almost three months had passed since Shama gave birth. It was now late July and temperatures in the valley climbed. There had been no precipitation for months and the seasonal rains, which came in late October, were still nine weeks away. At daybreak, the family group of fourteen traveled east, plodding almost silently along another well-worn game trail that led through a sparsely treed plain of tall dry grass and scrub bushes. They walked in single file, with Muchengeti in the lead.

To the left of the column, the plain gently descended towards the Zambezi. To their right rose the thickly forested hills and steep slopes of the escarpment. The evergreen mahoganies and the big leafy tamarind trees provided some shade, but the mopanis were bare. They plodded on in the cool of the morning, needing to cover as much distance as possible before the rising sun's searing heat scorched the valley. Their feet kicked up small swirls of dust, which hung motionless over the trail. By mid-morning, they had reached a turn in the trail and headed downhill towards the river.

The valley's heat and humidity had now become increasingly oppressive. The sun blazed overhead and clouds of flying insects filled the air. They emerged from the tall grass to swarm and buzz around the giant passersby. The elephants fanned themselves with their ears, as much to fend off the kamikaze attacks of biting flies than to cool themselves.

The column continued along the trail, their progress soundless except for the soft padding of their feet, the leathery swish of their ears, and an occasional grunt and snort. The grass on either side of their path became shorter and coarser as they descended, and an hour later, they reached the vlei, a marshy strip of land next to the river.

Here the group dispersed. Two adult females and several calves began to feed, snatching up clumps of the coarse vlei grass, growing in the ankle-deep water. Muchengeti and the others continued down towards the river. In another five hundred yards, they crossed a sandbank and reached a narrow channel.

Shama's three-month-old calf watched as her mother and others waded knee deep into the water to drink. She moved forward, evidently fascinated by the small waves that lapped around her feet. Then plucking up as much courage as she could muster, she dropped her trunk into the stream. Astonished by the coolness of the water, she jerked it out and the motion sent her immature trunk whirling like a spinning propeller.

Meanwhile, her four-year-old, male sibling, Mhiko, and Rufaro, her three-year-old female cousin, were playing in the water. They had already drunk their fill and the adults looked on indulgently, as the two youngsters chased and tussled with one another in the water. A short distance away, hidden behind a dense clump of reeds, a crocodile stretched out on a sand bank, lazily soaking up the midday sun. The sounds of the nearby activity in the water roused the reptile's curiosity. It quietly slithered into the stream to survey the scene, its bulbous eyes, and nostrils barely visible above the water's surface.

The adult elephants were spraying themselves with the cool water. The youngest calf was still poised at the water's edge, observing the antics of Mhiko and Rufaro. Shungu had abandoned any attempt to drink with her trunk and kneeled at the water's edge, slurping up the liquid into her mouth.

In the youngsters' game of chase, Mhiko took his turn as the pursuer. The sloshing sound of the crocodile's powerful tail, as it propelled itself forward, went unheard over the youngsters' playful splashing in the shallows. Suddenly razor-sharp teeth sank into Rufaro's left hind leg, and she let out a hoarse cry. With its jaws locked in an iron grip, the beast—a four-hundred-pound mass of muscle, flesh, and scaly skin—began dragging its catch into deeper water. Rufaro bawled in pain and fright.

Trumpeting loudly, Muchengeti and Umsizi raced to the young calf's rescue. Shama pulled her own calf away from the water's edge, gathering her close. A fearful Mhiko hastily escaped, clambering up the bank to join his mother and sister. Using her trunk, Umsizi grasped her three-year-old daughter around her girth to pull her away from her attacker, but the crocodile held on fast.

Unable to drag the young elephant deeper into the river, the reptile shook its head viciously. Rufaro let out more ear piercing shrieks. The water around the struggling calf turned red. In fury, Muchengeti struck the reptile a solid blow to the head with her trunk. The impact dazed the crocodile for an instant, but did nothing to weaken its grip. As the creature's strong, razor sharp teeth continued to rake and chew at the young elephant's leg, Rufaro's cries weakened.

Muchengeti beat the creature while Umsizi, bellowing loudly, continued pulling her calf away from the crocodile. The calf's mother finally succeeded in dragging both Rufaro and the reptile, still attached to the calf's leg, up onto the bank. Blood gushed from the gaping wound in Rufaro's leg, creating a widening stain in the sand at the water's edge.

Muchengeti followed the grisly retinue. She rose onto her hind legs, trumpeted with rage, and slammed a front foot violently onto the reptile's back. As she dropped her massive weight onto the crocodile, its jaws gaped, instantly freeing Rufaro. The old matriarch had flattened the creature's body and crushed all life from it. However, she was not finished. Afterwards, she stabbed the carcass several times with her single long tusk and, for good measure, grasped the dead crocodile by its tail and slammed it repeatedly onto the ground, until there was little left to slam. Terrified, the youngest calves cowered between their mothers' legs.

Blood continued to spurt from Rufaro's left hind leg. Bone was visible in the gaping wound, encircled with shredded pieces of skin and flesh. The young elephant's cries had now turned to whimpers. The entire family group milled around on the bank. Crowding around Rufaro, they stretched out their trunks to touch and comfort her.

A short while later, Muchengeti urged her family back across the vlei, towards the forested hills. Rufaro moved forward slowly with an agonized, three-legged gait. Occasionally she let out a whimper. Her blood, smeared across clumps of coarse vlei grass, marked her progress. Umsizi dropped back to walk alongside her badly injured daughter and periodically reached down with her trunk to caress and comfort her.

When they had left the vlei and reached dry ground, Rufaro's front knees buckled and she fell. Umsizi wedged a foot under her shoulder to help lift her back onto her feet. As the others continued on, Muchengeti turned back and went to her daughter's aid. No sooner had they propped the calf up onto her three good legs, than she flopped down again. At this point, Rufaro was now too weak to whimper. Only the sound of her raspy breaths indicated she was still alive.

At the top of the rise, the rest of the herd looked back, and after seeing something was amiss, they turned and trooped back down the trail. The young calf's entire family surrounded her, frantically trying to rouse her. An older cousin grasped her trunk and shook it gently. Others nudged her with their feet or tusks, and her playmate forced his way through the adults' legs to stuff some grass into her mouth. Shungu remained glued to her mother's side.

An hour after Rufaro's last labored breaths ceased, her family accepted her death. Still, they did not abandon her. For several hours, they encircled the carcass, touching it gently with their feet and trunks. The adults dug up loose sand and dirt from the trail to cover Rufaro's body. Imitating them, some of the youngsters joined in, ripping up clumps of grass to pile over their dead sibling and playmate. In twenty minutes, they had completely covered the carcass in dirt and grass. As the herd grazed nearby, Umsizi and Muchengeti stood beside the mound.

Even after nightfall, Rufaro's family maintained a vigil over her burial place. It was only at the first light of dawn that Muchengeti roused her group and they reluctantly ambled away. The last to leave was the grieving mother. Only after an hour of repeated callings from her family members, who had reached the edge of the mopani forest several miles away, did Umsizi drag herself away and walk off to join them.

Two days later, they reached the Zambezi's riverine paradise – Mana Pools.

Chapter 3

Sunday, August 03, 2008

At the controls of his Cessna 150, Van Rooyen headed east towards the Mozambique border. Buckled into the right-hand seat was his long-time, game tracker, Ananias Mangwende. The single-engine, light aircraft sported a white paint job with a pale blue and navy trim. Painted in black letters along the fuselage, forward of the tail, was its registration Z-WKB—Whiskey-Kilo-Bravo. The pair took off from the Kariba airport at two thirty in the afternoon. Their mission was to investigate reports of suspicious, possibly poaching-related activity in the Chewore Safari Area south of the Zambezi.

After taking off, they soared over Lake Kariba's shimmering blue waters, turning towards the slim, curved, concrete dam wall that held back the lake's more than forty-four cubic miles of water. Continuing northeast, they followed the curve of the valley. From the air, through the smoke and haze, he could see the mighty Zambezi River snaking down the center of the land basin.

"I'm afraid we started out late, so we won't have a lot of time." Van Rooyen said, having to shout over the roar of the plane's motor. "In another three and a half hours, it'll be too dark to see much."

He checked the altimeter, noting they had reached their planned 3,000 feet cruising altitude and set the controls for level flight.

"I got two reports of possible poaching, Friday night." He looked across at Ananias. "Blair Nisbet said he'd seen three suspicious-looking, power boats just east of the Chewore confluence. The other report came from Mr. Kaminjolo. He told me he'd received some bush intelligence concerning poachers from Zambia who were planning to cross over into Chewore Safari Area. I'm sorry, hey, for messing up your weekend, Ananias, but I thought we should check out these tips right away."

"That's okay Baas Piet. What are we looking for?" he said in his slow, carefully enunciated, African accented, English.

"Be on the lookout for any unusual people, boats, or encampments. I'll take us down to a thousand feet, for a closer view, before we get to the Chewore River."

"Good," Ananias said, adding, "How did the meeting go Friday night in Harare?"

"It went well. We took in more than fifteen thousand U.S. dollars, in donations. It'll help a lot. Mr. Nisbet coughed up almost half of it. Very generous." Even though van Rooyen appreciated the hunting outfitter's altruism, it did not mean in the future he'd curry his favor in any way.

"Phew," Ananias whistled. "That's lots of money, Baas Piet. *Mahorokotoi*, congratulations," he added in Shona, clapping enthusiastically.

"I'm afraid I didn't impress the tourism minister. Sebakwe's a big Mugabe fan and I know, for sure, he objected to much of what I said. Afterwards, when I was driving back to Kariba, I got a little nervous about the headlights in my rear view mirror. After they'd turned off onto side roads, I felt much better."

"Eh Baas, it's not a bad thing to watch out for those powerful people." Ananias leaned forward in his seat. "My cousin's friend was working for Mr. Tsvangirai before the election and he was killed near Mutoko when his car ran off the road. The police told his friend's mother that it was an accident. But my cousin saw the car and there were bullet holes all over it."

"I'm not surprised. Many of the president's political enemies have died under some very suspicious circumstances. How do you think the power-sharing negotiations between Mugabe and Tsvangirai are going to end up?"

"Eh, eh. If Mr. Mugabe is still in charge of the treasury, and the army, and the police, then he is not sharing power, is he? He will have all of it – just like now." Ananias said with some cynicism.

"I agree." Van Rooyen nodded as he scanned the instruments.

Thirty minutes later, they caught sight of the Zambezi flowing through the Mana Pools National Park. Here the river split up and reunited several times creating long, grassy islands, dotted with trees. Herds of buffalo and impala speckled the riverbanks while grazing on the lush, green grass along the water's edge. Elephants were also in the area—big bulls alone or in pairs, and family groups of females and calves.

"Lots of game down there." Ananias pointed down.

Van Rooyen nodded. "There's no water inland. It's all bone dry, so they have to stay close to the river."

Further east, huge evergreen mahoganies, and gray acacias lined the Zambezi. With Mana Pools now behind them, van Rooyen throttled down, adjusted the flaps, and Whiskey-Kilo-Bravo dropped to an altitude of a thousand feet. The aircraft leveled out and both men peered down to study the terrain. Soon they were over the Mupata Gorge where the river narrowed, bordered on both sides by tall, steep, granite cliffs. The lofty stone faces were home only to lizards, rock rabbits, and cliff-nesting birds.

Further inland, several miles south of the river, Ananias pointed to a dried-up waterhole, encircled by a wide border of cracked, hoof-pocked clay. Around the depression, lay shriveled carcasses of partially consumed zebra, wildebeest, and impala, splattered with white vulture droppings.

"They probably died of thirst, and predators got themselves a good meal," van Rooyen commented.

The time was now four in the afternoon. Below them, the cliffs receded and the river widened. Ahead van Rooyen spotted the Chewore River, flowing north from Zimbabwe's interior to spill into the Zambezi. At the confluence, the two men saw elephants and giraffe drinking at the river's edge. Across the river, on the Zambian side, a herd of impala moved through the trees like a stream of burnished gold.

The Cessna continued east, but the men detected nothing remotely suspicious. Finally, in the distance, van Rooyen spotted the tail waters of the Cabora Bassa Dam in Mozambique. He glanced at his watch again.

"It's getting late. Disappointing, but it's time to go home. We'll fly back along the river, just in case we missed something." He banked the plane steeply on a return heading for Kariba.

Within minutes, they were again flying across the eastern boundary of the Chewore Safari Area. Up ahead, a herd of elephants swam across the Zambezi towards Zimbabwe.

"What a sight?" Van Rooyen whooped in exhilaration. With the herd now mid-stream, he circled them in a wide arc, hoping to see the group complete the crossing without spooking them. Ananias counted fourteen elephants in all. Except for several smaller calves paddling alongside their mothers, the group swam in single file, trunks held high out of the water like a string of snorkels. Van Rooyen kept circling until he saw the last animal clamber up onto the southern bank. They'd made the crossing from Zambia at this point, west of the confluence, where the river narrowed to about 300 yards, he surmised.

"Eh, Baas Piet. Did you see the little baby swimming?"

"*Ja*, I did hey. It looks like it's only a few months old. What a sight! As far as I'm concerned, just seeing those jumbos crossing the Zambezi was well worth flying out here today, even if we never find the boats."

Before turning the plane towards Kariba, van Rooyen took one last look back at the small herd. Their wet hides glistened in the late afternoon sun. His feeling of elation lasted long after they were lost to sight. They had been flying west along the river for less than twenty-five minutes. The hills to their left, rising from the southern bank were dotted with Mopani trees while clumps of reeds, bulrushes and other aquatic plants sprouted along the river's edge.

"Look Ananias!" he called out. "See down there, in those *muchenjere*." He pointed to some watercraft moored in between bunches of aquatic grasses.

"I see them, Baas. Speedboats, three of them, next to the sand bank."

Van Rooyen swung Whisky-Kilo-Bravo into a tight turn, and looked downwards, to study the three long, slender boats equipped with powerful outboard motors, tied up in dense reed thickets at the water's edge. He saw their sleek, gleaming white hulls, trimmed with navy and turquoise stripes, and their bright, polished brass cleats, glinting in the evening sun. They appeared to be empty except for coils of rope stowed between the seats. Not a soul could be seen anywhere around.

"I see them," Ananias said as van Rooyen continued to circle. "Who has three boats all the same and why didn't we see them before, Baas? And what are those things on the front?"

"Maybe it was our angle of approach. We might have been flying a little further to the south. What things are you talking about?"

Puzzled, van Rooyen circled again to get a closer look.

"Ananias, I'm not sure what those things are," he said. "Wait. Hell! They could be gun turrets! Do you see that big upright plate? It could be a shield to protect the gunner and that round metal platform, behind it, is probably a machine gun mounting. Who in the hell would have powerboats like these tied up out in the middle of bloody nowhere?"

Ananias shook his head in silence.

Van Rooyen circled once more and straightened up, heading due west. As he flew across the mopani and mahogany woodlands, less than a half mile inland from the boats, he spotted a beige-colored utility vehicle parked beneath a stand of trees. Around it, not a soul was in sight.

"Look at that truck, over there."

Ananias' eyes followed van Rooyen's pointed finger. "I see it."

"For sure, hey, we've got to bring a ground team back tomorrow."

Van Rooyen maintained a return course directly to Kariba, and as they flew on in silence, he looked down at the Cessna's instrument panel. The paint, around many of the dials, levers, and buttons, looked scratched and worn. Whiskey-Kilo-Bravo was showing her age. His mind slipped back to when he'd first laid eyes on her.

He was ten when his father purchased the Cessna in 1978, brand, spanking new. Before it arrived, Koos van Rooyen had constructed a dirt runway on their Karoi farm. His son would never forget his excitement, the day his mum told him Dad was flying in that afternoon with a new plane.

Van Rooyen could still picture the scene. He and his mum had inflated blue and white balloons, fastened them to sticks, and stuck them in the ground along both sides of the newly cleared runway. Later they waited on tenterhooks, eyes glued to the horizon, expecting any minute to see that distant speck in the sky. Finally, the long-awaited dot appeared, growing ever larger as it approached. Magically, it took on the shape of a plane, touched down, and rolled down the runway towards them.

Afterwards, he experienced the joy of his father taking him up for rides and on family trips down to Beira, on the Mozambique coast, for a week's seaside holiday. Later still, his dad gave him flying lessons, which led up to the thrill of his first solo flight. Only after he turned sixteen and had earned his longed-for, private pilot's license, was that initial rush of adrenaline eclipsed.

He was sure his father would have been pleased to know his old plane, once registered by the former Rhodesian Department of Civil Aviation as VP-WKB, and now re-registered as Z-WKB, still flew, and now assisted in the protection of Zimbabwe's wildlife. He sorely missed his parents, both gone now – killed in a car accident, eight years ago.

These remembrances, however, invoked other memories of an even more devastating loss. The realization that his son would have turned nineteen this year, struck him a powerful blow. He wondered if Brian would have inherited his Dad's and his Grandpa's passion for flying. A renewed grief stabbed at his heart, but rather than allowing himself to succumb to the dark thoughts and feelings of the past, he banished this thought train from his mind—at least for now.

On their approach to Kariba, the sun appeared as a flaming ball as it sank slowly behind the Zambian hills. Microscopic dust particles danced in the atmosphere, suffused with color that turned the sky a blood red. Van Rooyen flew in over Kariba, a settlement spawned during the building of Kariba Dam in the late 1950s. Today, the town sprawled across the hills and lakeshore near the dam wall.

It was a quarter past six o'clock, when they touched down. After disembarking, van Rooyen turned to Ananias.

"We'll leave first thing in the morning. I'll meet you at the Zim Parks office at half-past-six, sharp. Tell Mathias and Godfrey."

Diana M. Hawkins

Ananias nodded.

Upon entering the terminal building, van Rooyen spotted Jessica Brennan across the main concourse. She was an attractive young American, who'd often attended the League meetings he chaired. She was in Zimbabwe, conducting a study of elephants in the eastern Zambezi Valley for some international wildlife foundation. She saw him and waved.

Ordinarily, he might have stopped to talk but he needed to make an early start in the morning, so instead he waved as he strode on towards the exit. She caught up with him in the parking lot.

"Piet, you look like you're in a hurry, so I'll be brief."

He found her American accent charming, but walked on.

Undeterred, she kept pace with him. "My sponsors are conducting an Africa-wide census of both the savannah and forest elephants. They want me to contribute figures for the eastern Zambezi Valley – from the Kariba dam wall to the Mozambique border. I believe an aerial survey would be my best bet, so could I interest you in flying me to collect data? You'd be well compensated," she added with an impish grin.

"Jessica, I'm in a bit of a hurry. Perhaps we can talk later, hey?" Realizing her proposal involved money, he questioned her. "When do you want to start?"

"Later this month, or early September." She was now jogging to keep up with him.

"Sounds okay. But don't forget, hey, after the rains come in November, they won't be sticking close to the river. Spread out, they'll be more difficult to find."

"That's a big consideration, of course," she said, while continuing to trot beside him.

He had now reached his Land Rover, where Ananias stood waiting.

"By the way," he said, "just for your information, I'm heading out with my scouts to the Chewore, tomorrow, to check out some suspicious boats. We saw them from the air today and it looked like they could be fitted with gun turrets. Who, but ivory smugglers, would need armaments in this area?"

"That sounds dangerous, Piet. You'd better be careful."

"I will. We can talk later about your elephant census."

With a frown wrinkling her brow, she turned and walked briskly back into the terminal. Her shoulder-length, auburn hair bounced from side to side.

He watched her retreating figure until she disappeared into the terminal. That she had a fine set of swinging hips was not in doubt, and as long as he had the necessary funds to keep Whiskey-Kilo-Bravo in the air, he suspected he would be more than happy to fly Miss Brennan up and down the Zambezi Valley for as long as she needed.

Van Rooyen unlocked the Land Rover and he and Ananias climbed aboard. Ananias had witnessed the subtle interchange between him and Jessica, and when van Rooyen glanced across at his tracker, he noticed his uplifted brows and knowing smile. He colored slightly, wondering if Ananias could read his mind.

"What's so bloody funny?" To cover his embarrassment, van Rooyen slammed the gearshift into reverse and backed rapidly out of the parking place.

Ananias chuckled.

Chapter 4

Monday, August 04, 2008

West of the Mupata Gorge, the steep, rocky canyon walls drop precipitously into the Zambezi, and the land flattens out on the Zimbabwean side, as the river widens. It was close to midday and on a sandy beach at the river's edge, a herd of fourteen elephants stopped to drink. They had swum across the river from Zambia, the previous afternoon, and overnight had trekked westward to the Mana Pools National Park. Now, having drunk their fill, the matriarch, Nkosikaas, signaled the family to move on.

They made their way south away from the river, across a ridge of small, sparsely treed hills. From there, she led them even further south towards the interior of the Chewore Safari Area, where they stopped to rest in a clearing beside a dry streambed. The younger calves lay sheltered from the afternoon sun between their mothers' pillar legs.

Suddenly, the deafening sound of automatic rifle fire shattered the hushed, late-morning hum of flying insects and the soft whisper of blowing leaves. Nkosikaas spun around to face the source of the terrifying blasts. She raised her trunk and spread her enormous ears out wide.

Emerging from the surrounding trees were at least a dozen men, three of them armed. Bullets tore into the matriarch's two oldest daughters. They slumped lifeless to the ground. Nkosikaas let out a deafening cacophony of bellowing trumpets as an expression of her rage and fear. Sensing her alarm, her remaining family members joined in the tumultuous chorus and those left standing immediately closed quarters, huddling together with the youngest ones drawn in beneath their mothers' bellies.

Sadly, the elephants' time-honored strategy of bunching up to protect the family group, played right into the hands of today's man-predator. Nkosikaas stood by helplessly as members of her family, one after another, were shot and silenced forever. As the spray of bullets swept across the entire herd, she too succumbed. The lone survivor, one tiny calf trapped unseen between two of her fallen relatives.

*   *   *

Nkosikaas's three-month-old granddaughter found herself trapped between the bodies of an aunt and a ten-year-old, male cousin. Death was not a concept known to her, thus she failed to understand why they were both lying there so still, pinning her to the ground. Out of the corner of her eye, she saw several perplexing, two-legged creatures through a gap between the bodies either side of her. They made high-pitched, mumbling sounds as they moved among the motionless bodies of her family. She tried to scramble to her feet but her aunt's leg was pinning down her left ear and foreleg, trapping her.

Descendants of Nkosikaas (Chieftainess)

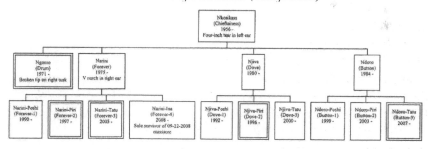

Single-frame box = female. Double-frame box = male.

For what seemed a long time, she wriggled and squirmed to free herself without success. After a while, screeching sounds assaulted her ears from several directions. This fearsome racket seemed to carry on interminably. Then it stopped and she looked up to see one of the two-legged creatures peering down at her. She froze in terror.

The ear-shattering noise began anew and came closer. The body of her aunt beside her began vibrating violently as a shower of red splatters filled the air and fell all around. The noise quieted for a moment and she saw the creature tugging at one of her aunt's tusks. For a split second, the motion shifted the weight off her trapped appendages and she was able to struggle to her feet. The creature eyed her with astonishment, but did nothing to hinder her escape.

All around her in the trampled clearing of red-stained grass, lay the bodies of her family members. She approached each of them, searching for the one whose scent she knew so well. Finally, she found her mother. She was motionless, and her eyes beneath their long lashes were glassy and staring in death. There were two small wounds on her huge forehead and deep, bloody cavities where once her powerful tusks had been rooted.

The calf rubbed up against her and burrowed her head behind her foreleg to reach her chest to suckle from one of her teats. Even in death, her mother's breast provided a few cups of lukewarm milk for her calf. Having sucked out all she could, she flopped down beside her and slept.

The sounds of the power saws ceased and the poachers loaded their plundered ivory into boats tethered on the bank of the river.

Chapter 5

Monday, August 04, 2008

At crack of dawn the next morning, van Rooyen and his team departed Kariba and four hours later, they reached Mana Pools. He stopped the Land Rover along the Zambezi's southern bank and Ananias and his two game scouts, Mathias Majoni, a veteran, and new hire, Godfrey Simeon, jumped out to stretch their legs. The journey so far, along rough, dirt roads had been long and uncomfortable.

The sight of the river, divided into separate channels by wide sandbanks, always took van Rooyen back to some of the happiest days of his childhood. He and his father had often camped and fished close by. His dad would reverse the boat trailer into the water and they'd launch the canoe and drift down the river's southernmost channel, always keeping a respectful distance between them and the hippos.

"Eh, Baas Piet, see that one over there," said Ananias, wide-eyed, pointing to an enormous, gaping mouth with tusk-like teeth, which had surfaced not far away.

"Damn! He must be the biggest daddy of them all, hey." Van Rooyen wondered why hippos appeared so calm in the water, yet were known to kill more people in Africa than the 'Big Five'—lions, leopards, elephants, rhinos, and buffalos—combined."

"*Hongu*, yes," Ananias agreed. "When I was a young boy, a hippo attacked my little boat just because he didn't like me in his part of the river."

"How did you get away?"

"Eh. I paddled to the bank and ran away fast. Very happy I wasn't hippo lunch that day."

Everyone laughed as Ananias clowned around, holding one hand between his knees, while reaching high above his head with the other, to demonstrate the size of the hippo's open mouth.

"I've never had a run-in with a hippo, touch wood." Van Rooyen tapped his forehead. "I'm told they're even more aggressive on land than they are in the water."

Van Rooyen scanned the deserted riverbank. It was the dry season, and at this time of the year, there'd normally be hoards of zebra, wildebeest, buffalo, elephant, and other game coming down to drink. Today, however, except for the hippos, there was not a beast in sight and along the shore, few if any game tracks. Poachers had obviously made inroads in this area, and if the government wasn't involved, it had to be turning a blind eye. Somebody was no doubt profiting from this. When he founded the ZWPL, he'd sworn to stop poaching once and for all.

"We'd better get moving," he said as he reboarded the Land Rover. Now wasn't the time to reminisce and admire the view. Everyone climbed aboard, and as they bumped along the road, the game scouts sitting in the truck bed bantered back and forth in Shona, occasionally lapsing into peals of laughter, or bursting into song.

Deep in thought, van Rooyen thought back to his conversation with Jessica at the airport yesterday. Had he been too short with her? He had been rather brusque, he recalled. Kaminjolo had introduced him to Jessica, three years ago, shortly after she arrived from America. Since then, she had attended nearly all his monthly League meetings and invariably had something useful to contribute. Someone had mentioned she had a master's degree. With just his high school O-Levels from St. George's in Harare, he knew he couldn't compete with her in that arena. Nonetheless, he couldn't deny with her figure and those auburn curls, she was a knockout. Maybe one of these days, he promised himself, he might actually get off his duff and ask her out. He hoped, meanwhile, he hadn't ruined his chances. The fact was he might have invited Jessica out on a date a long time ago, if not for his fears of betraying his beloved Sandie.

At three o'clock in the afternoon, they reached the Chewore Safari Area. A concrete post with the crudely chiseled initials C.S.A. marked the entrance.

"Let's look for vehicle tracks," van Rooyen said, pulling off on the side of the road. Ananias jumped out and reminiscent of an archeologist searching for old bones, he knelt down to examine the ground. He was sign cutting, a centuries-old technique to analyze and interpret footprints, tire tracks, or any other evidence of an earlier presence.

"There are fresh tire marks," Ananias said, slapping at an annoying cluster of tiny mopani flies that swarmed around his face. "The treads are sharp, looks like new tires." He pulled a steel tape measure from his pocket and calibrated the distance between the two tire tracks. "Wheelbase is 116 inches, Baas Piet. *Mukuru rori*, a big lorry," the tracker remarked, before pocketing the tape and climbing back into the truck.

Van Rooyen shoved the Land Rover in gear and the truck lurched forward. Ananias retrieved a pen and notepad from the glove box and jotted down some figures.

"For as long as we can see the tracks, I'll keep going," van Rooyen said, speaking in a hushed tone. He leaned towards Ananias. "I'll drive slowly. Tell them, in the back, no more talking."

Ananias passed on the order and as they crept forward, he kept his eyes peeled on the road ahead. They had covered almost five miles, when they heard in the distance the explosive sounds of rifle fire. Rolls of popping, automatic gunfire bounced off the surrounding rocky hillsides and echoed throughout the valley. Almost instantly, the frantic trumpets of panicking elephants resonated through the bush.

"Bloody hell!" Van Rooyen cursed, slamming his foot on the accelerator and veering off into the bush. He'd anticipated encountering poachers armed with snares, or at worst, single-shot, bolt action rifles – not military-style, automatic weapons.

The Land Rover ploughed through tall grass, tree saplings, and thick mounds of thorny, Jesse bush, before jolting to a sudden halt behind a rocky outcrop. The men seized their shotguns from storage lockers beneath their seats, leaped from the vehicle, and encircled van Rooyen to await his instructions.

"Don't shoot! Their guns are bigger than ours," he whispered to the now-somber group. "We don't want to get in a firefight with them."

While van Rooyen carried a rifle, loaded with deadly, .375 Holland & Holland Magnum cartridges, his men had considerably less-lethal, double-barreled shotguns.

"For now, let's keep out of sight; just close enough to see what's happening and to get some identification on the vehicle and the boats. Don't use your weapons except in self-defense. All we can do is document what's going on here and submit the report to the authorities."

Van Rooyen felt in his breast pocket for his digital camera. He signaled the men to follow him and, with weapons at the ready, they moved through the trees towards the source of the gunfire.

"There's no point in my trying to get Zim Parks on the radio. Before Mr. Kaminjolo can get his rangers assembled, these people will be long gone with the ivory."

The group exchanged some quick words, disbanded, and melted quietly into the bush. Rifle in hand, van Rooyen crept around the rocky outcrop. He moved fast, taking cover behind bushes and trees. The gunfire had ceased before he had covered a half mile. Now all he could hear were the faint sounds of men's voices, coming from behind a small *kopje*. He climbed the hill and the Shona speech became clearer. Moments later, however, the high-pitched screech of power saws drowned them out. When he reached the summit, he dropped spread-eagled behind clumps of tall grass. Setting his rifle aside, he raised binoculars hanging around his neck, parted the tall stalks of grass, and looked down. His gut wrenched as he surveyed the grisly scene unfolding below.

On a trampled, grassy field stained red with blood, lay the carcasses of thirteen elephants. Evidently members of a family group, they included adult females as well as adolescents and calves of both sexes, big and small. An overwhelming sadness constricted his throat. He, more than most, knew the devastation of losing an entire family. He pulled out his digital camera, adjusted the focus, and began pressing the shutter.

His anguish quickly turned into an intense, fearsome anger as he watched men wielding power saws, slashing the faces of these once-proud, majestic creatures to cut away their tusks. Evidently, tusk size was immaterial to these barbarians. One man had butchered a youngster, probably no more than three years old. The tusks, his plundered booty, likely measured less than four inches in length. He shook with uncontrollable grief and rage, powerless to do anything but continue to shoot images of the carnage.

The poachers worked speedily and efficiently, obviously well practiced at performing their gruesome tasks. Three four-man teams carried out the ivory harvesting, speedily and efficiently. While one man wielded the chain saw to cut away a tusk, the second removed the ivory and handed it off to a third, the runner, who carried the booty to the river, passing it to the fourth man, who loaded the plunder onto the boat. From his position, he could not see the boats, but he knew they were there.

Out of the corner of his eye, a movement on the field caught his attention. A young calf struggled to its feet. He judged the little one to be just a few months old. Once upright, the youngster staggered among the elephant carcasses, looking for its mother perhaps. The sight sickened him and for a moment, he considered throwing caution to the winds and racing down to save the calf. Sound judgment prevailed, however. Had he done so not only would he have risked his own life but the lives of his teammates as well.

Instead, he took a deep breath and continued snapping pictures. He followed the little chap's progress, expecting at any moment to hear a final rifle shot. Thankfully, none came.

For the past forty-five minutes, the sun had been beating down on him. His watch read half past three. Here in the valley, during the final month of the dry season, the heat and humidity was already stifling and his clothing soaked with sweat. He drank a few swallows of warm water from the canteen on his belt, thankful there was more to replenish it back at the truck. While there should be no scarcity of water so close to the river, he knew it was unsafe to drink. Africa's rivers and streams harbored water snails carrying a parasitic disease, Bilharzia or Schistosomiasis, which affected the kidneys, spleen, liver, and the bladder.

The sounds of power saws ceased. Down below the poachers were obviously wrapping things up. Less than an hour and a half had passed since he'd first detected the gunfire. He moved north along the ridge on top of the hill, crawling unseen through the tall grass, until the river came into view. The boats loaded with ivory were pulling away and he snapped a half dozen more shots. According to the camera's image counter, he had taken fifty-four frames.

Down below, he heard the poacher's vehicle crank up. He hoped his team had managed to get the vehicle's license plate number, its chassis ID, and registration numbers, if any, from the boats. When the sound of the departing vehicle faded away, he descended the hill making his way back to the Land Rover.

He sat on the tailgate waiting for Ananias and the two game scouts. They appeared fifteen minutes later. Looped over Mathias's arm were at least a dozen wire snares they had picked up along the way.

"Hey, Baas Piet," Ananias announced with a wide grin. "We got the plate number." From his trouser pocket, he pulled a wrinkled scrap of paper, which he handed to van Rooyen. Scribbled on it was, 'Zambia BAJ 4757, Nissan X-Trail 2.0, and Diesel 4x4.' "I don't know the year, maybe only one or two years old."

Van Rooyen slipped the note into his pocket. "Good job," he said, patting Ananias on the shoulder. "I hope this will help us to find the poachers. Now we have to go and pick up the calf. Did you see it?"

"Yes, Baas. But it's going to die. The baby has no mother." Mathias, whose face wore a sorrowful expression, shook his head.

"We might be able to save it," van Rooyen countered. "Come!"

Looking doubtful, Mathias and Godfrey followed him and Ananias to the Land Rover. After refilling their canteens and dropping off the snares, all four men hiked back to the scene of the massacre and spread out in search of the calf. Up close, the extent of the carnage was sickening. Van Rooyen looked around. He had never seen such a heartrending spectacle.

Behind a group of carcasses on the far side of the field, he caught sight of Godfrey leaping high into the air, an arm raised to attract his attention. The young scout beckoned him, and placed a forefinger across his lips to signal a need for silence. When he got there, Godfrey pointed down at a tiny calf, covered in blood spatter, nestled against the remains of an adult female.

"Still alive?" van Rooyen whispered.

"Yes, Baas. It is sleeping. But where did all this blood come from?" Godfrey's eyes were like saucers.

"Maybe it came from one of the others. Let's get a rope on it before it wakes." van Rooyen murmured. "Godfrey, you go back to the Land Rover and bring me the *tambo* from under the front seat."

While Godfrey was off fetching the rope, van Rooyen crouched down to take a closer look at the calf, a female only two or three months old. He surmised the bloody carcass beside her belonged to her mother. She was a large cow with a sizeable V-shaped notch torn from her lower right ear. If her breasts, now hidden behind the calf, were swollen with milk, they would know.

On the north side of the clearing, Ananias and Mathias viewed the dead elephants in deep, somber silence. Never before had they seen such horror. They started towards van Rooyen and he looked up and whispered, "Shh! Don't wake her." Placing an arm around Ananias's shoulders, he drew him aside.

"Godfrey's gone to get a *tambo*," he murmured. "When he gets back, we'll tie her up until I can get back with the truck."

"Then what do we do with her, Baas?"

"We'll check her for bullet wounds. If her injuries are treatable, we'll take her to Mrs. Precious Chitora's place." He chose not to voice the alternative – a brain shot to the head.

Under an unforgiving sun, the three men sat cross-legged in the grass just a few yards from the calf, awaiting Godfrey's return. They had all but drained their water canteens and the elephant carcasses were ripening fast. Thousands of flies buzzed around, before settling on the corpses. Van Rooyen knew the stink of decomposing flesh would soon attract Africa's scavengers; nature's cleanup crews—hyenas, vultures, even an occasional jackal.

Although the Land Rover was only a mile and a half away, the minutes ticked by. He watched the calf intently as she dozed and prayed Godfrey would return before she awoke. With a shoulder height of about thirty-six inches, he estimated her weight at roughly two-hundred pounds. The sight of her chest steadily rising and falling, he found comforting.

Short, stiff, black whiskers sprouted from the calf's forehead and back, and in the deep wrinkles of her hide, the blackened blood had solidified. There were no visible wounds, so he assumed the blood splatter had come from other elephants during the grim, de-tusking operation. Until they rolled her over, however, he and his team couldn't be sure. While admiring her long, sweeping eyelashes, he noticed her eyelids flutter and her eyes met his. Evidently startled, she struggled to her feet.

"Oh, hell," he shouted and he, Ananias, and Mathias tackled her to the ground. Clearly terrified, she struggled to free herself, uttering pathetic little whimpering sounds.

"It's okay, little girl," van Rooyen murmured in her ear. "We won't hurt you, I promise." He lay across her forelegs and chest, while Ananias covered her hindquarters and Mathias hung on to her tail.

"Godfrey, Godfrey, where are you Godfrey," van Rooyen grumbled, checking his watch. At 4:40 p.m., the calf was lying on her left side. She had managed to free her hind legs and was now kicking strenuously to get loose.

"Mathias, let go of her tail. Help Ananias hold down her legs."

With her right side now uppermost, they had an opportunity to search for more bullet wounds and were relieved to find none. The cow's breasts, now revealed, were indeed swollen with milk. Van Rooyen felt a strong pang of grief for the little, motherless calf.

"It looks like this baby girl is in fine shape," he commented. "Now, if we can just get her to Kariba, to Mrs. Chitora, she'll have a chance for a reasonably long life."

Van Rooyen breathed a sigh of relief when Godfrey arrived ten minutes later with the twelve-foot rope. They fastened it around the calf, using slip knots to encircle both her girth and neck firmly, and secured it to a nearby dead tree stump. Leaving Ananias and Mathias with the calf, van Rooyen and Godfrey departed to fetch the Land Rover.

To protect their young charge from the burning, hot sun and suffocating heat, Ananias proposed they move the calf towards the tree line. He loosened the rope from around the stump and he and Mathias attempted to guide her towards the trees at the southern edge of the clearing. The calf put up a valiant struggle, evidently unwilling to leave her dead mother. She fought the ropes and head-butted her handlers, knocking them both to the ground. Then she took to her heels, dragging her tethers behind her, and trotted at a fast clip north towards the river. Ananias and Mathias followed in hot pursuit, but before they could catch her, she slid down a steep embankment and disappeared from sight.

Meanwhile, van Rooyen and Godfrey had reached the Land Rover and were driving back to pick up the elephant calf and the remaining team members.

"Baas Piet, who is this lady, *MaChitora*?" the young game scout enquired.

"She operates a wildlife orphanage on her farm near Kariba. Her grandfather was a game tracker, who worked for National Parks in the 1950s, with Mr. Rupert Fothergill."

"Who is Mr. Fothergill?"

"He was the game ranger who led the world-famous wildlife rescue, Operation Noah. You've heard of Fothergill Island on Lake Kariba, haven't you?"

"Yes Baas."

"Well, they named the island after him. That was almost fifty years ago, when Zimbabwe and Zambia were called Southern Rhodesia and Northern Rhodesia."

"Eh. Baas Piet, too many years ago."

"Definitely long before you were born. Has anyone ever told you the story about the building of Lake Kariba?"

"No Sir." Godfrey shook his head.

Van Rooyen took a deep breath and began recounting the story his own father had told him, when he was just a boy.

"They started building the dam in 1955, long before even I was born, Godfrey," van Rooyen chuckled. "After they finished the dam wall in 1959, it blocked the Zambezi, causing its banks to overflow. Then the water spread all across the valley and it created Lake Kariba."

"What happened to the people who lived next to the river?"

"Well, they had to move their villages to higher ground. Some of them weren't happy about it, but the government sent lorries to help them. Afterwards the government saw that the animals were in bad trouble, too. While the lake was filling up, game rangers discovered the hilltops were turning into islands, trapping the wildlife. Without help, thousands of animals would have drowned, or starved to death."

"Not good, Baas," Godfrey said, shaking his head.

"You're right. Anyway, the government told Mr. Fothergill to go and sort it all out, so he and his trackers and game scouts sailed around the lake every day to catch as many animals as they could fit into their boats. Then they'd take and let them go into two new national parks, the Matusadona and the Chizarira."

"I know those places." Godfrey's eyes brightened. "How long did it take before the lake was full?"

"My Dad told me it took four years. And he said that, by 1963, Lake Kariba was famous for being the largest man-made lake in the world."

"Still the biggest?"

"Not anymore. There are bigger dams now in Ghana, Canada, and Russia. Anyway, back to Precious Chitora. Her farm's on the lakeshore and she takes in all kinds of rescued animals. She treats them if they're injured, and once they've healed, she releases them back into the bush. She's amazing Godfrey. She's taken in elephants, rhinos, lions, leopards, cheetahs, giraffe, zebra, buffalo, and more species of antelope than you can think of, hey. She tells people that if it has wings, or more than two legs and lives in Africa, she'll take it."

Godfrey laughed, clearly impressed. "She must be very clever to know about so many animals." He looked towards van Rooyen, wide eyed.

"*Ja*, that's for sure," van Rooyen nodded. "She's been to classes in South Africa and in America to learn about being a wildlife rehabilitator."

Up ahead, vultures were circling. Maneuvering the Land Rover close to where they had last seen the calf, van Rooyen and Godfrey clambered out and trudged down to the field of elephant carcasses. There was no sign of Ananias, Mathias, or the baby elephant. Now, in the spot where they'd left them, several hyenas were tearing at the mother elephant's flesh, and scores of squawking vultures were squabbling nearby, fighting one another over the remains of other members of the herd.

Van Rooyen was clearly annoyed. "Blast it! Where did those blokes go?"

"Do you want me to look for them over there?" Godfrey pointed to the river.

"No," he said curtly. "I don't want to lose you, too. We still have close to a five-hour drive back to Kariba. Stay with me!"

Circumventing the killing field, he strode purposely towards the river. Godfrey followed. When they reached the riverbank, van Rooyen began shouting out for Ananias and Mathias. He thought he detected a faint response coming from the west, so he and Godfrey jogged along a rocky trail paralleling the river. Ten minutes later, they came upon the missing tracker and game scout, but no elephant calf.

Seeing the scowl on van Rooyen's face, Ananias lowered his head. "Baas Piet," he began, "The sun was too hot! We tried to move the calf into the shade, but she got away."

"You did the right thing to move her out of the sun, Ananias. But what do we do now?" Van Rooyen threw up his hands in frustration. "We can't leave her here; there are hyenas back there."

"She's not far away, Baas Piet," Mathias said. "She's had no milk for a long time and is very weak."

For the next thirty minutes, the four men crisscrossed the area south of the river and eventually came upon the calf, sleeping in a stand of tall reeds.

"She needs water! Quick!" Van Rooyen handed Godfrey his canteen to fill at the river. When the young scout returned, van Rooyen moved the calf's trunk out of the way and poured its contents into her mouth and down her throat. Then another and another, Godfrey making repeated trips for refills.

After receiving the water, her glazed eyes finally showed the first signs of a sparkle. She still lacked the energy required to put up much of a fight, so she allowed the men to guide her towards the Land Rover. Van Rooyen, meanwhile, wondered how they were going to lift the two-hundred pound calf into the rear bed of the Land Rover. By the time they'd reached the vehicle, he had devised a plan. It required the use of the large, heavy-duty tarpaulin, stored behind the front seats. Following his instructions, the men laid it out on the ground and folded it in half, twice. Next, they guided the calf onto the tarp and, with each man grasping a corner, they successfully hoisted her aboard amid much groaning and straining.

"Good job!" Van Rooyen praised them afterwards and everyone beamed. Soon they were on their way back to Kariba with Godfrey and Mathias sitting on either side of the calf. They had secured her with a rope tied fast around her girth and looped through sturdy bull rings welded to the truck bed. While underway, van Rooyen radioed Mrs. Chitora to notify her of the calf's imminent arrival. Exhausted, the youngster slept during the rest of the journey.

Chapter 6
Monday, August 4, 2008

At the same time van Rooyen and his team were driving to the Chewore confluence to check on the mystery boats, Jessica Brennan was leaving her rented cottage on the hills overlooking Lake Kariba. It was 7:45 a.m. and she planned to spend the day checking on her elephants in the Mana Pools National Park and its adjoining safari areas. On her way out of town, she was going to call in on Hector Kaminjolo at the local Parks Authority headquarters.

She steered her 1998 chocolate brown, four-wheel-drive, Toyota Land Cruiser down the steep, narrow, winding road from Kariba Heights to the town's small business district. Under a bright, cloudless sky, the lake turned a shimmering, iridescent blue. Ten minutes later, she arrived at a low, brick building with a sign out front, which read Zimbabwe Parks and Wildlife Management Authority. Before alighting, she pulled down the sun visor to check her reflection in the vanity mirror, and ran her fingers through her wavy, still damp-from-the-shower, shoulder-length, auburn hair. A red, green, orange, and black striped, Zimbabwe flag fluttered in the breeze from a mast near the front entrance. She parked around the side of the building.

Inside, receptionist Violet Tomana greeted her. "*Mangwanani*, good morning, Miss Brennan," she said, smiling.

"Hi Violet. You're looking very spiffy today."

The young woman wore a bright, yellow hairpin in her short afro, complimenting her vivid, red, and yellow-striped shirtwaist dress. With a coy expression on her face, she lowered her head and giggled. "Oh Miss Brennan, you are very kind."

"Is Mr. Kaminjolo in the office yet?" Jessica said with a friendly smile.

"Yes, he's here, but let me find out if he's still on the telephone." She picked up the receiver and dialed an extension. "Sir, Miss Brennan is here." Words followed moments later by, "then I will bring her in."

"Don't get up, Violet, I know the way," Jessica said, proceeding down a short hallway. She knocked, and before entering Kaminjolo's office, she re-tucked her short-sleeved, white, cotton shirt into her belted, tan slacks.

As she entered, a clean-shaven, black man of medium height rose from behind the desk, and stepped forward to greet her. He wore the regular, khaki game ranger's uniform, embellished with three silver stars on his green epaulets, signifying his rank as a regional supervisory ranger.

"Good morning, Jessica." He smiled as he shook her hand. "Please sit," he said, gesturing to a chair facing his desk. "How can I help you? Are you having problems with your elephants?"

"Thanks for seeing me, Hector," Jessica said. "No problems. At least none I'm aware of right now. I bumped into Piet van Rooyen at the airport yesterday and he mentioned he'd just made a reconnaissance flight over Zambezi Valley east. He told me he was investigating some suspicious boats that Blair Nisbet had clued him in about, Friday night. He also said you'd received some bush intelligence about some possible ivory poaching out there. Did he tell you about those boats and the vehicle he'd spotted out there?"

"No he hasn't, but then I haven't seen him since last Friday. Thank you for letting me know."

"This concerns me, of course, because I've got elephants out there that are part of my study. I had to come by here anyway to pick up Patrick, so I thought I'd just check to see if you'd received any more information."

"No. Nothing."

"Well, I'm driving over there this morning to check on some of my elephants, so I'll just take a look-see," she said, rising from the chair.

"*Hokoyoi*, be careful," Kaminjolo cautioned her, as she left his office.

Game scout Patrick Sinamapande was waiting for Jessica beside her Land Cruiser. He saluted as she approached.

"*Mangwanani*, good morning, Miss Jessica. I've loaded the water cooler and the lunch bags," he said, as he climbed up into the passenger seat.

"Morning, Patrick. Thank you."

She pulled out of the parking space at eight o'clock and they headed east through the Charara Safari Area towards the A-1. The fifty-mile stretch of highway, from Kariba to Makuti on the A-1, twisted and turned through the hills of the Zambezi escarpment. In Jessica's opinion, it was a two-lane, excuse for a road. Her Zimbabwean friends claimed that prior to 2000, it had been a well-maintained, paved thoroughfare. She found this difficult to believe, however. Floods had eroded the edges of its tarred surface, creating steep drop-offs of up to twelve inches in depth. Moreover, the road was full of ruts and potholes, some deep enough to break an axle. Making matters worse, this busy highway was the scene of frequent accidents. Drivers forced to steer around the many road hazards, often crossed the centerline in the face of oncoming traffic, causing many collisions and fatal smashups.

What would her American family back in Lawrenceville, Georgia, think of driving conditions here? Conversely, she wondered, what would people here in Zimbabwe would think of the I-85 freeway and its sixteen lanes of traffic, running through Atlanta toward Hartsfield-Jackson International Airport, on the city's south side? The traffic there slowed to a standstill during weekday rush hours. She wasn't sure which was actually worse.

"Patrick, when do you think the government is ever going to fix this road?"

"Eh, Miss Jessica! With what?" Patrick laughed. "The government has no money. Mrs. Mugabe went shopping in Hong Kong in July and she bought a new palace there."

"A new palace? Where on earth did you hear that?"

"My girlfriend saw it on the Internet. She goes to the Internet café in Kariba every week."

"Ah, the Internet." Jessica sighed. "What would we do without the Internet?" It was online that she had discovered that Zimbabwe—despite all its problems—would be the ideal place for her to conduct the research she needed for her doctoral dissertation. The Internet was responsible for bringing her here—that, and her love for wildlife—elephants in particular.

Zoo Atlanta had introduced her to elephants, giving rise to her passion for the species. At least twice a year, her parents would bundle her and her younger brother, David, into the car for a trip to the zoo. Animals were a family passion. Growing up, she couldn't remember any time when their home wasn't supporting a menagerie. She and her brother constantly brought home injured birds, chipmunks, squirrels, stray cats and dogs; once even a baby opossum. If, by chance, she had found a stray elephant, she'd undoubtedly have tried to bring that home too.

For years, their father, Joseph Brennan, had operated an equine and large animal veterinary practice in Lawrenceville, northeast of Atlanta, where he treated horses, other domestic livestock, and even wildlife, on occasion. The fenced acreage and barn behind their house constantly served as a temporary home for a variety of ailing creatures.

After graduating from high school in 1992, she attended the University of Georgia and earned a Bachelor of Science in biology and a master's degree in Wildlife Management. David joined her later, following their dad's example, to study veterinary medicine. In 1998, Jessica began working for the U.S. Fish and Wildlife Service, as an assistant refuge manager at the Timberton National Wildlife Refuge in Tennessee.

Less than twenty miles from the refuge, she had discovered the Hohenwald Elephant Sanctuary, a 2,700-acre, safe haven for both Asian and African elephants. Jessica immediately signed on as a sanctuary volunteer, and from then on, devoted almost all her spare time to help care for its residents—the retired denizens, and performers from zoos and circuses, from all across America.

By 2004, having set her sights on working with African elephants in Africa, she began canvassing organizations that funded research grants for scientific studies of the *Loxidanta Africana,* the African elephant. She applied to Michigan State University's department of zoology for acceptance into their Ph.D. program, proposing to study the long-term effects of culling on wild elephants. After the university accepted her into the program, she contacted an international non-profit organization, the Global Defense Force for Wildlife (GDFW), who awarded her a five-year grant, renewable for up to ten years. Finally, she applied for and received a permit from the Zimbabwe Parks and Wildlife Management Authority, to conduct elephant research in the Zambezi Valley.

Permit in hand, she bade farewell to family and friends, and boarded a plane bound for Africa. When she arrived in Harare on June 1, 2005, she purchased a used, Toyota Land Cruiser, drove north to Kariba, her chosen base of operations, and rented a small cottage with a magnificent view overlooking the lake.

Jessica immediately got to work, making daily forays into the bush to locate herds of elephants. Traveling with her was a game scout, assigned by Zim Parks to accompany her on these field trips. She was responsible for paying his monthly salary and among Zim Parks employees, these positions were highly sought after, primarily because they guaranteed a reliable paycheck.

Enos Gasela was her first assigned scout. He was a short, bow-legged man, with an infectious laugh and the widest, toothiest smile she'd ever seen. Jessica was saddened by his departure, a year later; even more so when she learned of his death, soon afterwards, from HIV/AIDS. She later learned that more than four million Zimbabweans had succumbed to AIDS between 2002 and 2006. She mourned Enos's death, crediting him with teaching her a huge amount about African bushcraft, the ways of the Zimbabwe people, and introducing her to many of the valley's elephants.

His successor was Patrick Sinamapande, a member of the BaTonga tribe. At age twenty-two, Patrick was more than twenty years younger than Enos. While he had completed high school and had a more advanced formal education than his predecessor had, Patrick did not have Enos's vast knowledge of the local wildlife and its environment.

Jessica began her study by photographing individual elephants and family groups, identifying each one; using a system developed by renowned researchers, Iain Douglas-Hamilton and Cynthia Moss. These experts had followed the lives of certain elephants for many decades in Tanzania's Lake Manyara National Park and in Kenya's Amboseli National Park.

Jessica entered information about each elephant into her laptop computer. As the data accumulated, however, she limited her subjects to members of just three matriarchal families of cows and calves, together with a half dozen bulls – approximately fifty animals in all. She gave each elephant a meaningful name in the local Shona or Ndebele languages, fitting their appearances or personalities. Some of the older elephants already had names given them by local tribespeople. These she had learned from Enos.

Her study elephants included the families of three matriarchs: Muchengeti, Nkosikaas, and Chembere. The bulls she followed included Nkosi, Fundisi, Mukuru, Ngomo, Chimuti and the youngest, Chiripi-poshi, Chembere's grandson. Muchengeti's family happened to be the first matriarchal group she encountered, so she named each one of her descendants. By the time she came to name Nkosikaas's and Chembere's families, however, she had run out of suitable monikers for their many descendants. She therefore devised a new naming protocol—their mothers' name with a hyphenated number, in Shona, indicating their birth order. For instance, the sons and daughters of Nkosikaas's daughter, Narini, were called: Narini-poshi for Narini-One; Narini-piri for Narini-two; Narini-tatu for Narini-three; and so on. Their genders, meanwhile, were clearly identified in the database.

Nkosi became registered as the oldest of her study bulls. She had pegged his age as being in the high sixties, based upon visual estimates of his tusk circumference. Thanks to Enos, who had collected tons of historical information from local tribespeople, she had been able to piece together much of Nkosi's life history. According to old-timers, he had fathered both matriarchs, Muchengeti and Nkosikaas, making them half-sisters. They might have also shared the same mother, but a DNA comparison would have been required to confirm this. Such a test was costly, however, and the results were not critical to her study. With the old bull, Nkosi, on her mind, she reminded herself she hadn't seen him in several weeks.

"Patrick, we haven't seen Nkosi for a while. Wasn't he missing from the bull herd, when we came across them last month?"

49

"Eh. Miss Jessica. I think he was at Mana Pools with Nkosikaas and her family two months ago. Maybe we'll find him today."

They finally reached the A-1 highway at 11:15 a.m., and Jessica turned left, heading north. The road to Mana was another twelve and a half miles further. Fifteen minutes later, they reached the turnoff and drove east along a gravel road through the Hurungwe Safari Area, their wheels churning up plumes of dust behind them. The deafening clatter of gravel, striking the underside of the Land Cruiser, drowned out all further conversation for the next eighteen miles.

Would they encounter Piet van Rooyen today? She had run into him at the airport last night and he'd mentioned coming out this way. Privately, she considered him rather good looking, in a Hugh Jackman kind of way. He seemed friendly, but she'd found him a little aloof. She rarely ran into him at any of Kariba's social gatherings. Did that mean he had a secret girlfriend tucked away somewhere?

After they crossed into the Park, Jessica pulled the Land Cruiser over to the side of the road and she and Patrick climbed out to stretch their legs and top up their water canteens from the cooler in the rear. Now, she needed to decide whether to drive directly down to the river or take one of a network of game-viewing roads. At almost half-past noon, the temperature had risen.

"Let's go take a look around the southeast side of the park," she told Patrick, as she climbed back into the cab.

They drove along winding roads, weaving around wooded hilltops strewn with gray, granite boulders. While edging their way down towards the river, they passed troops of baboons, small herds of eland, waterbuck, zebra, and wildebeest. Around a bend, they surprised some thirty impala that snorted in alarm and vanished into the trees, but they found not a single elephant. Ahead, the road took a sharp turn around a tall rock formation. Rounding the corner, a procession of the mammoth gray beasts suddenly confronted them. They had stepped out of the bush, less than thirty yards in front of them. The sound of Jessica's sudden braking caused their huge heads to turn as they eyed the skidding vehicle. Patrick beamed and clapped his hands in excitement.

"Oh, wow! Look at them!" Jessica exclaimed. She instantly recognized the group as Muchengeti's clan and began to check off each individual, mentally, as they came into sight.

Descendants of Nkosi (Chief)

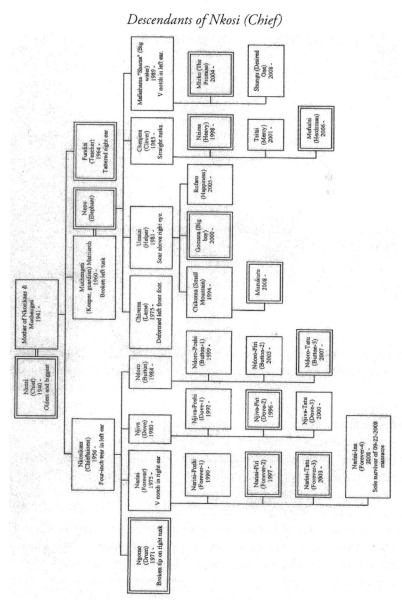

Single-frame box = female. Double-frame box = male.

Leading the way was the matriarch with her broken left tusk. At age forty-eight, Muchengeti was the largest cow in the herd. Behind her, traipsed her youngest daughter, Shama, with her two calves, three-month-old Shungu, and four-year-old Mhiko. Next came fourteen-year-old Chikoma, walking in step with her mother, twenty-seven-year-old Umsizi. Trailing Umsizi was her eight-year-old, male calf, Gomana.

Where was Rufaro, Umsizi's three-year-old calf, Jessica wondered. Perhaps further back in line, with the other three-year-old, Mufudzi, Chenjera's youngest. However, when Chenjera came into view with her male calf, Mufudzi, and her two female calves, ten-year-old Nzima and seven-year-old Tsitsi, Jessica realized Rufaro was indeed missing. Bringing up the rear, as she limped along, was Chirema, the thirty-three-year-old cow with a twisted, left front foot.

Jessica had long wondered why Chirema, Muchengeti's oldest living daughter, had never borne any young of her own. Was it because of her deformed foot that nature had left her barren? Despite her injury, she ably fulfilled her role as the family's aunt and protector. During their travels, she was almost always at the back of the column, to ensure that none of the easily distracted juveniles was ever left behind. From the looks of her impairment, Jessica believed a snare had probably caused it.

After crossing the road, the elephants remained in sight as they wandered through the trees in search of acacia pods and other delicacies garnered from the woodland floor. Jessica killed the engine and she and Patrick looked on in silence. All was quiet, except for the low buzz of flying insects, the cooing of doves in the acacia trees, and the crackling and snapping of dried leaves and branches underfoot, as the elephants moved about. They also heard the sporadic snort and the rasping sound of huge ears brushing shoulders. Occasionally a calf squealed in protest when challenged by a playmate, or if disciplined and pushed aside by an adult.

Jessica looked at her watch. It now read three thirty. She and Patrick had been enjoying the peaceful, pastoral scene, when suddenly all hell broke loose. The elephants put out an ear-piercing chorus of trumpeting, and deep rumbles resonated all around. Then suddenly, all twelve animals took off. There were sounds of crashing trees and splintering branches, as the herd stampeded south. This unexpected turn of events stunned Jessica. The ground trembled so violently beneath the herd's pounding feet, that she could feel the pulsations through the steering wheel.

She was aghast. "What set them off?"

"Eh. Miss Jessica, I don't know. I never saw such a thing before." Open mouthed, Patrick stared at Jessica in astonishment.

Since they had now seen Muchengeti's family, surprising as their encounter turned out, Jessica decided to delay going down to the river. Instead, she told Patrick, they'd head east in hopes of seeing Nkosikaas's or Chembere's families. They drove for ten miles, before heading over to the northeastern side of the park, where they stopped under a large mukwa tree for lunch. Yellow, trumpet-shaped blossoms smothered the tree and beneath it lay a thick carpet of spent blooms. With a new crop of green leaves likely to emerge, Jessica knew it would soon attract foraging elephants.

Lunch consisted of cheese and tomato sandwiches with fresh fruit—a guava and an orange. While they ate their meal in silence, they heard muted explosions of rifle fire in the distance.

"Sounds like there could be hunters north across the river," Jessica remarked, her chest tightening. She detested the sound of gunfire – it never boded well.

Lunch consumed, they stowed the empty sandwich containers in the back of the Land Cruiser, topped off their water canteens, and continued northeast. Now at four o'clock, the orange sun dropped lower in the western sky behind them. They had traveled another twenty miles when Patrick pointed to a flock of vultures circling to their left.

"Let's take a look," Jessica said, stopping on the side of the road. They disembarked and trekked into the bush. A hundred yards ahead through the trees, they spotted the big birds spiraling downwards. Jessica and Patrick doggedly pushed through thorn thickets and shoulder-high, dried grass, until they reached a small hill. They climbed the hill. It overlooked a dry, streamed and below them, just a hundred feet away, stood Nkosi.

With his rear end facing them, he stood unsteadily. He appeared to be ailing; his massive head hung low, and his thick, wrinkled hide hung loosely over prominent spine and hipbones. With the wind in their favor, Jessica and Patrick crept on down the hill. They watched the vultures descending one by one. At age sixty-eight, Nkosi was a behemoth – the largest elephant Jessica had ever seen up close.

The birds stood in a wide circle around Nkosi, awaiting the inevitable. Each bird's bluish-black head bobbed atop a long, sparsely feathered, sinewy neck with a white ruff at its base. Nkosi clearly disapproved of their presence. He watched them, swinging his trunk at those that came too close. They would briefly flutter away then return. After shifting position, he caught sight of Jessica standing less than twenty feet away, and turned to face her. Their eyes met.

Jessica felt a quick stab of fear. She looked around to plan a quick getaway, if necessary. Nkosi gazed at her with tired eyes swaying a little from side to side. Jessica maintained eye contact with him for almost five minutes. Then his huge body trembled, stiffened, and he collapsed. Falling forward, he stabbed his massive tusks several feet into the earth.

Startled, Jessica stepped back. The old elephant, however, made no attempt to rise. With his head propped up by his tusks, his forelegs pinned beneath his great chest, and his rear legs splayed out behind him, he remained motionless. He lay immobile for fifteen minutes and then let out a long, deep sigh, which reverberated along the full length of his outstretched trunk. A puff of dust rising at its opening signaled his final breath. Then he was gone, and the vultures rushed in.

Touched by the grand old man's passing, Jessica wiped the moisture from her eyes, and sent Patrick back to the truck to get a tape measure and a shovel. She needed to record Nkosi's particulars. She doubted anyone from Parks would perform a necropsy – an animal autopsy – so for her own records, she wanted to collect as much data on the old bull as she could. The removal of the old guy's tusks would be all she believed she could realistically expect from the local park ranger.

Patrick returned and together they chased off the carrion birds and shoveled away the dirt from around his tusks, so they could measure their length. They also took as many other available measurements. Because of the way he had fallen, they were unable to access his forefeet or measure his shoulder height. Using their combined strength, she and Patrick were able to shift his head just far enough to get a peek inside his mouth.

"Look how worn his teeth are," Jessica said, getting back up onto her feet. Patrick got down on his knees and peered into Nkosi's mouth.

"Miss Jessica, they are very flat."

"An elephant goes through six sets of molars during its life," she explained. "When Nkosi's last set were completely worn down, he couldn't chew anymore, so he literally starved to death."

"He was very thin."

"We can confirm he died of natural causes – old age, because he'd worn out his last set of molars," Jessica said.

She replaced her pen and notepad in her shirt pocket and started back towards the Land Cruiser. Patrick followed. Behind them, scores of vultures scurried in to partake in the feast.

"Patrick, those birds are the ultimate recyclers. They can strip a zebra carcass in just a few hours. With help from a pack of hyenas, it'll take them weeks to polish off Nkosi. Carrion eaters do a valuable job in keeping the environment clean and disease free."

They departed at five o'clock, heading south towards the park's office to give Mana Pools National Park Ranger John Chitsaru, directions to Nkosi's remains, to pick up the ivory. Ten miles down the road, they came upon a Zim-Parks Land Rover. Jessica pulled in behind it and she and Patrick followed the footprints leading into the bush. Two hundred yards from the road, they found the ranger with one of his game scouts beside a tall termite mound.

"*Masikati*, good afternoon, Ranger Chitsaru," she called out.

"*Waswera here,* how was your day? Miss Brennan," was his polite, traditional response.

As she came closer, she glimpsed the body of an elephant calf partially obscured by the termite mound. Was it Rufaro?

"Looks like a crocodile got her," Chitsaru said, pointing to the small carcass.

Jessica stepped forward and looked down at the dead calf. Dirt, dried vegetation, and white, streaked, vulture droppings covered parts of the carcass. A gaping wound on the calf's left, hind leg was surrounded by shredded pieces of skin and flesh. There were other, visible places on her back and side where the razor-sharp teeth and curved beaks of carrion feeders had ripped away chunks of flesh.

"I believe this is one of my juveniles from Muchengeti's family," Jessica said. "She's Umsizi's youngest, called Rufaro."

Chitsaru scratched his head. "Early this morning, I found the crocodile that may have attacked her by the river, near Vundu camp. Not much left of him," he said.

"We also lost Nkosi today," Jessica said. "He died of plain, old age. Patrick and I saw him take his last breath. It was sad, but he had a good, long life – sixty-eight years, according to my records."

"Yes, he was a *madala*, very old" the ranger concurred.

"He left some good ivory," Jessica said. "You'll find his carcass in the north-east section of the park. I'm sure the vultures will give you good directions," she added with a smile.

"We will go and pick it up."

"This poor little girl had only one-inch stumps," Jennifer commented, pointing to the dead calf. "Anyway, we've gotta go, Ranger Chitsaru. We'll catch you later."

"*Mazvita. Fambai zvakanaka,*" he said, thanking her for the information and bidding her a safe journey

Their trip back to Kariba turned out to be a grueling, eye straining, four-hour drive. The first hour, was spent driving directly into the setting sun. What a day it had been, Jessica thought, as she replayed its events in her mind. First, Muchengeti's and her family's strange behavior. What could have spooked them like that? Then the sad loss of Nkosi. Even though his time had obviously come, the death of one of her study elephants still came as a jolt.

For more than three years she had closely monitored his life. During the five minutes their eyes connected, was he conscious of the deep feeling of love and respect she had for him? Though she wished it were so, she doubted it. After all, during Nkosi's sixty-eight-year life, he had most likely received nothing but pain and grief from members of the human race.

Thirdly, there was the ranger's discovery of the missing Rufaro and earlier his discovery of the remains of the crocodile that had attacked her. This calf had been particularly special to Jessica. Rufaro had been the first baby elephant whose birth she'd ever witnessed. Umsizi had given birth to her only weeks after Jessica's arrival in Zimbabwe. She fought back sudden tears.

By the time they reached Kariba, the African continent was shrouded in darkness. Jessica dropped Patrick off at the Parks office, and drove home.

Chapter 7

Tuesday, August 05, 2008

Van Rooyen was sitting in Kaminjolo's office when the door cracked open and Jessica poked her head in. "Mind if I join you guys?" she said with a wide smile, her sparkling green eyes darting back and forth between the two men.

"Come on in, Jessica," Kaminjolo said, rising to his feet.

"There's a place for you right here." Van Rooyen patted the seat beside him.

Jessica entered and plunked herself down in the proffered chair. She wore a green, knit golf shirt with an elephant head emblem above her left breast. Van Rooyen thought she looked particularly good in green—the color accentuated her stunning eyes. He caught her looking in his direction, as she crossed her trim legs in a pair of sharply creased, tan slacks. When their eyes met, she quickly looked away.

"Actually, you couldn't have arrived at a better time," van Rooyen said smiling, "I'm getting ready to give Hector a report on my trip to the Chewore Safari Area, yesterday.

"Great! Afterward, I'll share some news which might be of interest to you both," she replied.

"Okay, let's get started," Kaminjolo said looking at his watch. "I've got to be at the airport to meet my boss at eleven o'clock."

Van Rooyen began. "Well, as I told you both earlier during my fly-over

Saturday, I spotted some unattended boats and a vehicle in the Chewore Safari Area, which I thought needed immediate follow up. So I drove out there yesterday with my game tracker and two scouts." The frown lines on his forehead deepened. "The bad news is we came across a poaching operation in progress and we lost a dozen elephants."

"Oh no! I don't suppose you recognized the matriarch?" Jessica blurted out, her eyes widening in dismay.

He turned to her, "No, I'm afraid I didn't." Then he shifted his gaze back to Kaminjolo. "First let me say this. My four blokes and I were totally out-manned and out-gunned! We faced at least a dozen poachers out there, and three had AK-47s. The elephants didn't stand a bloody chance, and neither would we had we injected ourselves into this fire-fight." Just the memory of the violence and his feeling of utter helplessness made van Rooyen's heart pound.

"There was nothing we could do," he reiterated. His face wore an expression of utter dejection. "All I had was a hunting rifle. No match for those AKs. And no way could I send my guys into the fray. All they had were double-barreled shotguns, for goodness sake. It would have been suicide for them to take on those machine guns."

There was an edge to his voice as he continued. "As you know, Hector, I've tried time and time again, quite unsuccessfully, to get the government to issue me permits for more modern, high-powered weapons to fight these bastards. This time, the only decent shots I got, and all after the fact I'm afraid, came from this camera." He pulled a small digital from his pocket.

He then turned to Jessica. "And in response to your question – did I recognize the matriarch? All I know is we counted twelve dead animals, among them five adult cows and I didn't recognize any of them. But if we plug this camera into your computer, Hector, we could take a look at some pictures."

Five minutes later, they were huddled around the monitor on Kaminjolo's desk. The first few frames displayed were too blurred to show much detail.

"Sorry, I'm not much of a photographer," van Rooyen apologized with a wry smile.

They viewed several more unclear shots and another showing a row of grass seed heads. Hector chuckled.

"I was on top of a hill, lying down in the grass. What do you expect, dammit?" A defensive van Rooyen laughed.

The next frame, a long distance shot, showed the trampled grassy field, stained red with blood, and dotted with elephant carcasses. Jessica gasped at the sight, her hand covering her mouth. Kaminjolo frowned deeply, shaking his head slowly from side to side. The next shots showed men with chain saws, cutting away the elephants' tusks. The gruesome scene forced Jessica to turn away and wipe at the tears welling in her eyes. Next came some close-up shots.

"As you can see, I finally figured out how to get the camera to zoom in." van Rooyen said without apology.

"Wait! Back up. I need to check that frame again," Jessica called out.

Van Rooyen pressed the back arrow on the camera, once, then twice.

"That's the shot. Wait up a minute. Let me see. Oh my God!" she said, "It's Narini, Nkosikaas's daughter. I'm positive, look at the notch in her right ear. Was there a calf? She had a newborn."

"We did save one little calf," van Rooyen said. "I was getting to that. She's the only one who survived this massacre."

"You did?" Jessica cried out in excitement. "Oh my God. You saved a calf. Wow! Where is it?"

"It's a she, by the way, and we took her straight to Precious Chitora's Rehab Center," van Rooyen said.

"Oh happy day!" Jessica joyfully threw her arms in the air. "Let's hope she survives."

Van Rooyen continued to advance the frames. "I have some shots of the calf looking among the corpses for her mother," he said. "While the poachers were carrying away the ivory, I saw this little one running around, in and out of the dead bodies. I kept waiting for one of those savages to take some pot shots at her, but thank the Lord, they never did. She had no tusks, of course, so I suppose they were just going to leave her there to die a long, lingering death from starvation. Bloody sods! Excuse the language."

"Thank God you saved her, Piet. At least now she has a fighting chance," Jessica interjected.

Van Rooyen stopped on a fuzzy frame showing a tiny calf standing beside the bloodied corpse of an adult female. The pitiful sight brought more tears to Jessica's eyes. She quickly brushed them away with the back of her hand. The camera's final shots showed three boats, loaded to the hilt with ivory, chugging eastwards along the Zambezi. After the last frame, van Rooyen let out a deep sigh and he and Jessica returned to their seats.

"Hector, I'll leave the camera with you, so your computer guy can download the photos. I'm sure you'll need them for evidence in your investigation," van Rooyen said. "Oh, I almost forgot this." He fumbled in his breast pocket and pulled out a scrap of paper. "My people weren't able to get any boat registrations, but they did get the license plate number from the poachers' vehicle—a late model, Nissan X-Trail, four-by-four, utility truck with Zambian license plate, BAJ 4757."

Kaminjolo took the crumpled piece of paper without a word.

"Well Piet, after what you've just told us," Jessica said, "the curious behavior Muchengeti exhibited yesterday, near Mana Pools, now makes a lot more sense."

"Why's that?" Kaminjolo asked.

Before responding, Jessica looked across at van Rooyen. "Piet, at what time did the poachers start shooting?"

"I'd say about three thirty in the afternoon – give or take a few minutes."

"Well, we first spotted Muchengeti's family a short distance north of the park headquarters at about three fifteen. Patrick and I watched them browsing for a while. Not long afterward, probably darn close to three thirty, the whole herd took off at great speed."

Both Kaminjolo and van Rooyen listened attentively.

"I'd never seen elephants behave that way before," she said. "But now it makes total sense. They were obviously reacting to Nkosikaas's infrasound alarm call. I also remember, immediately prior to that, hearing distant gunfire. At the time I just thought it was hunters."

Van Rooyen recalled Jessica telling him she had once assisted in carrying out experiments with elephant communications. She'd described infrasound, first discovered by American whale biologist Katy Payne, in the 1980s. The elephants' low frequency calls that other elephants could detect over great distances. People couldn't hear them because they were below the level of human hearing, Jessica had explained.

"You've told me about infrasound," van Rooyen said. Kaminjolo nodded.

"My other piece of news," Jessica continued, "is that Rufaro, a three-year-old granddaughter of Muchengeti's, Umsizi's baby, evidently died from injuries she received during a croc attack. I spoke to John Chitsaru at Mana Pools. He told me he'd discovered both her carcass, and that of the crocodile, that had attacked her. He believes Umsizi really took her vengeance out on the unfortunate beast, because the croc's remains were barely recognizable."

"And last, but not least," she added, "My oldest study elephant, Nkosi, died yesterday. Quite sad. I actually observed him draw his last breath. Afterward, I checked his molars and they were totally worn away, so the poor old man obviously died of starvation. He was in such poor condition, and at his advanced age of sixty-eight, his cause of death could only have been natural causes. I reported his demise and the carcass's location to Ranger Chitsaru, so he could pick up the ivory."

Kaminjolo pushed back his chair, stood up, and held out his hand. "Thank you Piet and Jessica for your reports. I like to be kept informed of what's going on in the parks. I will investigate that poaching incident in Chewore and I'll get your camera back to you, Piet."

Jessica rose to her feet and van Rooyen drew himself up to his full height of six feet, two inches. In turn, they accepted Kaminjolo's handshake, left his office, waved goodbye to Violet, and stepped outside, shading their eyes from the glaring sunlight.

"I'm going down to the rehab center to check on the elephant calf. Want to come?" van Rooyen asked, as they walked to their parked vehicles.

"Sure, I'll follow you," Jessica said, "I'd like to see her."

"No point in us taking both vehicles. Why don't you ride with me?"

"Sounds good," she said with a smile, dropping her car keys into her pants pocket.

Van Rooyen opened the passenger door to his old Land Rover, removed his wide-brimmed, bush hat from the dashboard, and slapped it back and forth on the passenger seat to remove grass and dirt particles.

"Sorry about all the dust."

"No problem. I've come to accept this as part and parcel of this magnificent continent. You should see my vehicle." She laughed as she climbed up onto the passenger seat.

Van Rooyen backed out of the parking space, and headed out towards the Chitora Wildlife Rehabilitation Center. For the briefest of moments while stopped at the first intersection, he looked at Jessica and smiled. Her presence gave him a warm feeling. It had been seven long years since he'd had any female companionship. Was it possible Sandie had forgiven him for not being there to protect her and the children, during that nightmare invasion? More importantly, had he forgiven himself?

Chapter 8

Tuesday, August 05, 2008.

Shortly after van Rooyen and Jessica left his office, Hector Kaminjolo pressed the intercom button on his phone. "Violet, would you bring me a cup of tea?"

"Yes sir! Right away,"

In less than an hour, he had to leave for the airport to meet his boss, Nelson Zanunga, the Zimbabwe Parks and Wildlife Management Authority director general. His plane was due to arrive from Harare at eleven o'clock. Kaminjolo had not been looking forward to this meeting. The man was a tyrant.

Violet knocked and entered with the tea.

"*Mazviita*," Kaminjolo said, thanking her as she placed the cup and saucer on his desk.

While Kaminjolo sipped his tea, he mulled over the myriad conflicting issues, which had bedeviled him of late. Firstly, there was the matter of culling—the killing of excess elephants. Zim Parks planned to eliminate 3,000 elephants over the next three years; the general had informed him of this on the phone last week.

Next on his list was the poaching issue. He frowned at the digital camera sitting on his desk. While nothing would please him more than to have those butchers brought to justice, he knew it would never happen. Should he even waste his time by attempting to mount an investigation into the crime? His superiors offered no support. In fact, the General's standing orders were to ignore poaching in the parks. People were hungry and needed to feed themselves, he said. The fact that elephants were slaughtered not to feed the hungry, but for their ivory, seemed immaterial.

Then there was the issue of the unnecessary death of Tusker in January. It irked Kaminjolo even now that he'd had to destroy this towering, fifty-year-old, single-tusked bull. For years, he had been a local icon and a favorite among visitors to the Charara camp on the Kariba lakeshore. A mob of New Year's Eve partygoers had victimized Tusker, senselessly abusing and provoking him. Witnesses described how the elephant finally vented his frustration on his tormentors, by trampling two unoccupied, parked cars before ambling away. In less than twenty-four hours, Kaminjolo received orders to destroy the 'rogue' elephant.

He fought hard for Tusker's life, trying to convince higher-ups the bull had no history of threatening people or damaging property. Nevertheless, Kaminjolo's pleas were not enough and his having to shoot the stately old bull had affected him profoundly.

To add to his trials and tribulations, he received frequent complaints from villagers, whose lands bordered the parks. They claimed elephants trampled and destroyed their maize crops—a serious matter for these subsistence farmers, since it meant they would be left with no food stores for the upcoming year. Conversely, however, he received repeated reports of squatters cutting down trees and building their huts on land set aside specifically for wildlife. Because wildlife, for decades, had been suffering the effects of habitat loss, he considered this a serious problem.

In the early 1990s, the Zimbabwe government made a serious attempt to deal with these kinds of dilemmas, by introducing a program designed to help both villagers and their local wildlife. Labeled CAMPFIRE, for Communal Areas Management Programme for Indigenous Resources, the plan allowed communities to manage their wildlife resources to benefit both animals and people. CAMPFIRE derived its income from leasing trophy hunting concessions to foreign hunters, who paid large fees to hunt elephants, buffaloes, giraffe, lion, kudu and other wild animals. Kaminjolo recalled the program enjoyed a particularly good year in 1993, when twenty-six districts earned more than US$1.4 million. Community leaders used the money judiciously to build and equip clinics and schools, drill wells, construct fences, build roads, employ tourist guides, and even fund local sports teams.

The plan had its problems however. Kaminjolo suspected that unscrupulous officials often pocketed the funds. District councils were not autonomous bodies and the government, through the National Parks and Wildlife Authority, had to approve their decisions. This, he considered, was a serious flaw in the system. Kaminjolo suspected that his boss, General Nelson Zanunga, who was no friend to wildlife, condoned the illegal use of these funds or likely misappropriated them himself. The fact he insisted that people address him by his previous military rank, spoke volumes about his character. His army career had spanned three decades, and he was widely suspected of helping lead the feared Fifth Brigade, during Mugabe's *Gukurahundi* in the early 1980s.

Gukurahundi, a Shona word referring to "the early rain that washes away the chaff before the spring rains," was the name given to the infamous military crackdown in Matabeleland, Zimbabwe's southernmost province. During this period, government troops slaughtered an estimated 20,000 people, throwing them down abandoned wells, or executing them. Most victims were civilians and members of the Ndebele tribe. People also suspected Zanunga of the simultaneous, wholesale slaughter of livestock and game in the area. Kaminjolo remembered when the President announced Zanunga's 2005 appointment as the Parks and Wildlife Authority's Director, and that the news left most Parks employees with a feeling of dread.

Violet poked her head around his office door asking, "Sir, do you want another cup of tea?"

He looked at his watch. It read almost half past ten.

"Violet thanks, but no. I'm going to meet General Zanunga's plane." He grabbed his uniform beret off the top of the bookcase, and raced out the door.

Kaminjolo found his boss briefcase in hand standing in the terminal's main concourse, impatiently tapping his feet. His flight had arrived five minutes earlier than scheduled. This had to go down as a first in Air Zimbabwe's history books, Kaminjolo thought sardonically. Air Zim flights were almost always late—sometimes cancelled altogether, when the President needed an aircraft to take him on one of his jaunts. Nonetheless, Kaminjolo suspected he was about to catch hell.

"General Zanunga, welcome to Kariba. How was your flight?" Kaminjolo hurried towards him, reaching out to take his briefcase.

"Kaminjolo, you're late! Let's get going!" The man scowled, clinging stubbornly to his valise, curtly dismissing Kaminjolo's assistance.

"I am sorry for keeping you waiting, Sir. My vehicle is parked right outside. Please follow me."

Kaminjolo's elderly green Land Rover, with its paint-chipped, Zimbabwe Parks logos on both doors, was sitting in front of the terminal ahead of a line of taxis. He held the passenger door open, as Zanunga climbed in. After pulling away from the taxi line, Kaminjolo merged into traffic departing the airport.

"What are you doing driving this old wreck?" Zanunga growled. "The Parks Authority took delivery of eleven, brand new Toyota Land Cruisers last month. I went to much trouble to get these vehicles for our rangers in the field."

Kaminjolo had seen the new vehicles during a recent trip to Harare. He considered them unsuitable for fieldwork. The single cab, open-bed pickups, had room on the bench seat for only the driver and no more than two, slightly built passengers. Moreover, with its bright, white finish, rangers would have difficulty sneaking up on wildlife in the bush. Its only useful feature appeared to be the elevated air intake mounted on the left front fender, which allowed it to cross rivers and flooded areas without stalling out. In any event, even if he'd wanted one of these pickups, none was available – the Authority's big wigs in Harare had snatched them all up. He'd decided, therefore, to hang on to his cranky, old Land Rover.

"I'm sure there are other field stations needing those excellent, new pickups" Kaminjolo replied, giving the exterior of his driver's door a resounding slap. "Old 'Chipembere' here, will give me several more years of good service."

Having departed the airport, they passed dozens of hawkers at rickety, roadside stands, lining both sides of the narrow tarmac road. Their wares on display included soapstone statues, wooden carvings, leather and game skin products, basket ware, pottery, and crocheted table linens. Each itinerant merchant waved frantically at the passing vehicles, in hopes of attracting arriving tourists bearing foreign currency.

"Do you want to stop somewhere for lunch?" Kaminjolo asked, as they neared the town center.

"They served lunch on the plane," was his passenger's terse reply.

Lunch before noon? That was news to him. He glanced over at the General's deepening scowl, which discouraged any further conversation. They continued in silence.

His boss wore the Parks and Wildlife Authority uniform, identical to his own, except for a fourth silver star pinned to his epaulettes. The man's hairline had begun to recede and his dark brown complexion bore the scars of a long-ago, case of teenage acne. He had a thick mustache and wore a pair of gold-framed glasses, perched high on his nose. His long, angular face bore a perpetual expression of disdain.

Once back in his office, Kaminjolo pulled out a chair for his visitor. When Zanunga removed his green beret, Kaminjolo placed it on top of the bookcase next to his own.

"Would you like a cup of tea, General?"

Zanunga nodded.

"Excuse me for a minute," Kaminjolo said, stepping out to give Violet tea-making instructions. His stomach growled with hunger, but he realized he'd have to delay lunch for a while. He wouldn't feel comfortable eating his sandwich in front of his superior.

"Kaminjolo, I expect you've heard those damned CITES people will only allow us to put up three and a half tons of ivory on their special auction in November," Zanunga snarled. "We had proposed putting up ten tons, but they turned us down. I even made a special trip to Geneva to sort it out, but they wouldn't budge." Gesturing angrily with closed fists he continued. "They've also closed off the sale to all our big international buyers. Only those cheapskates from Beijing and Tokyo will be allowed to attend."

Fearful of further inciting Zanunga's wrath, Kaminjolo remained silent. He let his boss ramble on.

"In future," Zanunga thundered, "we must do a better job of inflating our elephant population figures so we will be better prepared next time."

"Perhaps, General," Kaminjolo ventured, "when we do our dry season, aerial counts in the Zambezi, Limpopo and Chobe river valleys, we should count the elephants on both sides of the river."

Zanunga contemplated Kaminjolo's proposal for a few seconds, then burst out, "Of course! That's a very, very, good idea, Hector." His supervisor's eyes gleamed and he gave Kaminjolo a rare, wide-toothed smile. "Who can say those elephants across the rivers in Namibia, Zambia, Botswana, and South Africa didn't just cross over from the Zimbabwe side? Make sure we also include all the elephants in the border areas of Angola that could enter from the Caprivi Strip."

Hector experienced a sense of relief. Perhaps his boss's visit would go easier than he'd expected. Violet rolled in the tea trolley complete with china teapot, cups, saucers, sugar bowl, small milk jug, and a large plate of cream scones. She set out two cups and poured the tea.

"Do you take milk in your tea, General?" she asked with a demure expression.

"Yes and two spoons of sugar." He spoke in a jovial tone.

After handing both men their tea, Violet turned to the General. "You should try the scones, General. They're fresh baked today."

Kaminjolo reached for a scone and took a bite.

"She's right, these are good," he raved, grateful for anything to stave off his growing hunger pangs. He must remember to thank Violet. Today, she was definitely a lifesaver.

Zanunga scooped up two scones, stuffed a whole one into his mouth, setting the second one on his saucer against the tea cup.

"Give this woman a raise in pay, Hector," he muttered between swallows. "Now, let us get down to business."

He opened up his briefcase and removed a folder.

"I have been working with some environmental scientists who are worried about tree damage in our national parks and safari areas. They recommend we cull 3,000 elephants over the next three years."

Kaminjolo was taken aback. Three thousand? Was this really necessary? One minute his boss was talking about increasing elephant population numbers, and now he was proposing to cull thousands of them.

"Of course, to those nuisances, the overseas environmentalists," Zanunga continued, "Culling is a dirty word and they will cause us a lot of trouble. But hunting sounds better. So I'm making arrangements for professional hunters and safari companies to do our culling for us," Zanunga chuckled harshly. There was an evil glint in his eyes.

"How's it going to work?" Kaminjolo felt uneasy, even though the General obviously appeared to be pleased with himself for having cooked up such a devilishly clever plan.

Zanunga had a quick answer. "The idea is to encourage commercial hunters to bring their clients to Zimbabwe to shoot elephants," he said. "I've been negotiating with some European hunting outfitters who are ready to bring groups of five or more hunters to shoot an entire herd of fifteen or more elephants for a reasonable price."

"How much?" Kaminjolo was unprepared for the response.

"They started off at US$6,000 per hunter, but I told them they were talking peanuts. They'd have to double that, at least."

"Those people have that much money?" Kaminjolo's lower jaw dropped.

"Of course! Their clients are surgeons, solicitors, directors of huge businesses – big money men."

"How much will you accept?"

"Nothing less than US$10,000. At that price it will be highly profitable for us." Zanunga continued. "Not only do commercial hunters provide the guns, the ammo, and the shooters, but in the case of the Americans, the British and those from other countries who stupidly ban the importation of ivory, we also get to keep the tusks. Those we can sell on the black market for as much as US$750 per kg. So, you see Hector, we win big either way," he beamed, excitedly rubbing his palms together.

Kaminjolo offered a weak smile of appeasement. What a pile of rubbish, he thought. Zanunga not only proposed to inflate official elephant population figures, but also planned to kill them off herds at a time. He wished he could just walk away from this job. Then he'd be free to tell Zanunga exactly what he really thought about his crooked schemes. He felt torn. Kaminjolo enjoyed his work and wore his uniform with pride. It gave him a measure of stature in the community and even though his salary barely sustained him and his family because of Zimbabwe's spiraling inflation, his job came with certain financial bonuses. For instance, he was able to take home venison seized from poachers. It wasn't strictly above board, because Parks' policy was to leave it in the bush to feed the carnivores, but it helped his family when his pay check was barely enough to buy a five pound bag of sugar. Even though he hated having to compromise his basically, honest nature, he recognized it was sometimes unavoidable.

Zanunga interrupted Kaminjolo's thoughts with another plan he had concocted, that would drastically ease restrictions placed on local hunters.

"I am calling a meeting of all licensed commercial hunters in Harare next month, to announce Zim Parks' decision to suspend all elephant culling operations for the next three years. I will tell them that we will not only increase substantially the quotas of available hunting permits for all game, but we'll reduce the government's surcharge, from two percent of the daily hunt and trophy fees to a much lower 1.5 percent."

"That's quite a drop in government revenue in the long term, don't you think?"

"Not at all, Hector! Just look at the gains! Culling operations are expensive. Think of the Parks' personnel costs, their salaries, and overtime. Then add the price of fuel, ammunition, and the added wear and tear on vehicles and equipment, including weapons. The list goes on and on."

"I suppose you're right. I never looked at it that way before. But what about permits for the smaller game?"

"You know as well as I do, Hector, rural Zimbabweans have been suffering from near starvation. These reduced permit fees makes hunting for food much cheaper and available to many more people."

Kaminjolo murmured vaguely. Was his boss going over the edge, *penga*. Did the man really believe that, by reducing fees for hunting permits, he would put an end to the countrywide hunger? Didn't he understand most rural Zimbabweans were penniless – they had nothing, *hapana*? What was a half percent reduction of *hapana*? It was still *hapana*! In any event, the rural folk couldn't afford firearms. Their weapon of choice was the snare.

"By the way, my return flight to Harare leaves at five o'clock. What time should we leave here to get me back to the airport by four?"

"If we leave at half past three, we'll get there in plenty of time, General."

During their drive back to the airport, Zanunga said, "I know you're good at keeping your ear to the ground, Hector. I need to ask you something. Have you been hearing any talk about some poachers who call themselves the Crocodile Gang?"

"No I haven't, General. Where have they been operating?"

"All over the place. Mostly they've been going after rhino horn, but they've been taking some elephant ivory too. They attacked the Imire Safari Ranch, sixty-six miles east of Harare, a little less than a year ago. They slaughtered three adult rhino, leaving a young calf as the sole survivor. After the Imire killings, I had the Herald publish a notice that the Parks Authority was offering a three billion Zimbabwe dollar reward for anyone with information leading to their arrest. No one has come forward and I am not surprised. Local people are very scared of the Crocodile Gang. Imire was just one attack. There have been others."

"Yes, I know rhinos are in big, big trouble. I heard last month on Short Wave Radio Africa that twenty years ago, there were thousands of black rhino on the continent, and now there are only 460. That's bad, very, very bad."

"Do you listen to that rubbish radio station, Hector?" Zanunga asked, his eyebrows raised.

"Sometimes," he confessed his eyes downcast. Actually, it was a lot more than sometimes, Kaminjolo admitted to himself. He and Margaret tuned into its news broadcasts almost every night. In their opinion, it was the only trustworthy local news source in Zimbabwe.

Everyone knew Zimbabwe had only one broadcaster - the Zimbabwe Broadcasting Holdings - whose four radio stations and two television channels had the blessing of Mugabe's ZANU- PF. Members of the Diaspora, who had fled the political meltdown in the early 2000s, operated this alternative short wave radio station from London. Its listening audience had been huge during that period's political and economic turmoil.

Chapter 9

Tuesday, August 05, 2008

Precious Chitora's six-hundred acre, Wildlife Rehabilitation Center occupied a small peninsula, jutting into Lake Kariba. It was a short five and a half mile drive from the middle of town. Van Rooyen and Jessica entered the manned entrance gate and drove down a well-maintained, gravel road towards a collection of brick buildings perched on a hill overlooking the lake. Along the way, they passed clusters of antelope, an eland, several impala, a kudu, several sable, and a number of small duikers. They were feeding from bales of wheat straw, scattered among the trees on the grassy hillsides leading down to the lake.

From the Center's wide, circular driveway, they spotted Precious Chitora waiting for them on the front steps of a low, brick building. A generously proportioned, black woman, she wore dark gray slacks with a colorful, West African-style, dashiki over-blouse, and matching head wrap. Her affable smile revealed a row of evenly spaced, white teeth.

"Welcome. Welcome." She spread her arms wide to beckon them. "Thanks for coming. Piet, I bet you're here to see our newest resident. She already has a name, by the way. We've named her *Nherera* – that's orphan in Shona."

Beaming, she turned to Jessica. "I'm happy you came, Jessica, and so glad Piet brought you. We've met before elsewhere but now I get to show you what we do here. I can't wait."

Jessica considered herself a pretty good judge of character. While Precious's

70

gushy manner might be interpreted as phony by some, Jessica had found her always incredibly kind, generous, and altogether likable. One just had to get accustomed to her style. Genial to the utmost, she escorted them on a tour of the animal infirmary.

In the first unit, cages of various sizes, held an assortment of birds, a young baboon, a warthog, jackal, and a pair of young lion cubs no bigger than domestic cats. In two larger enclosures, a baby giraffe lay on a bed of straw and a young zebra stood with a temporary splint on one of its forelegs. The Center was evidently treating these animals for a wide variety of injuries and ailments—broken wings, snapped limbs, cuts and scrapes, malnutrition, dehydration, in addition to any number of diseases.

The noise level was overwhelming with practically every resident calling out in its individual squeak, squawk, bark, yap, grunt, or growl. Jessica covered her ears. She wondered how people contended with this daily score sheet of chaotic disquiet. Precious and her employees certainly deserved much respect.

She led them over to the larger pens and had to shout to be heard above the general melee.

"This baby giraffe is a special boy. He's an orphan and we are bottle feeding him. We don't know if he was abandoned, or if his mother was killed by a poacher or predator. Nowadays giraffe skins bring in a lot of money. As you know, the hide is popular for handbags, furniture covers, cushions, picture frames, all kind of things. He's particularly special to us," she added with a smile.

"For any reason, other than giraffes are beautiful animals, indigenous to Africa?" Jessica asked.

Precious laughed. "For all those reasons, but also because he's the only animal here that's not making a sound. Giraffes possess no vocal chords, you know. However, with their long necks, they can produce infrasound to communicate with one another, just like elephants."

This was something she'd never known, Jessica admitted to herself.

Moving on to the next cage, Precious continued her commentary. "This baby zebra was found this morning with a broken leg. Our veterinarian is coming today to put a proper cast on it. He's so young we're having to bottle feed him."

"Do you think he was injured while the herd was running from a predator?" Van Rooyen asked.

"Possible, but he could also have tripped over something, or got his leg wedged in an ant bear hole."

In the next cage was a young baboon.

"This little fellow's arm was caught in a snare," Precious said. "He managed to free its anchor, but couldn't get the noose off his arm. Poor thing. He could have been dragging that log around for months. When they brought him in, the skin was already growing over the wire and our vet had to surgically remove it."

Precious walked up to the baboon's cage, scratched his head and gently stroked his bandaged arm. "Eh. How are you today, little boy? Maybe next week you can go outside." Excited over the attention, the small primate leaped up and down, emitting short barks.

The trio walked on and Precious led them into an adjoining facility. Along the exterior wall was a row of horse stalls, three times the usual size. Their stable doors looked out over the lake.

"This is where we keep the larger animals needing treatment," she said. They stepped behind the line of stalls towards one in the far corner, and Jessica could hear loud voices, thumps, and bumps emanating from it. Van Rooyen pressed forward to peer inside.

"The baby elephant?" Jessica asked.

"Yes! Nherera is having one of her many daily feedings," Precious explained. "She's fed every three hours. It only became possible to bottle-feed an elephant calf successfully in the late 1980s. Before that, no one could keep them alive. Nowadays we can, thanks to the research done by Mrs. Daphne Sheldrick in Kenya. She and her late husband, David, were co-wardens of the Tsavo National Park in Kenya from 1955 until 1976. She was the one who discovered a combination of things were necessary to keep elephant calves alive."

"What are they?" van Rooyen wanted to know.

"It's complicated. First, elephant milk contains a lot more fat than is available in cows' milk. Also, during the calf's first two years, the amount of protein and fat in the mother's milk changes to meet the growing needs of the calf. It took Mrs. Sheldrick years of trial and error to come up with just the right formula. Secondly, as you know, elephants form incredibly close bonds with members of their families in the wild. Their relationships with their caregivers, elephant or human, are therefore vital. Mrs. Sheldrick learned a calf suffers such extreme stress whenever it loses an important caregiver that it usually results in death. To make sure Nherera always has a caregiver she knows and trusts, we employ six keepers, who care for her consistently on rotating shifts. She's getting to know each one of them, and over time they'll become her family."

"Thirdly," Precious went on, "Even newborn elephants need lots of space and won't thrive if confined to small enclosures."

She then led them to the corner stall, where two keepers worked with the elephant calf. Peering through the open doorway, Jessica saw one of them lift the little elephant's trunk to fully expose her mouth, while the other squirted formula from a quart bottle, down her throat.

"She's certainly chug-a-lugging it down fast," Jessica said, noticing the number of empty bottles lined up against the wall.

"I must say she's looking much happier now than when I dropped her off here, night before last," van Rooyen added. "That ride in the back of my Land Rover must have been hard on her."

Jessica noticed that at the sound of his voice, the calf looked up at van Rooyen. She wondered if the little elephant remembered the man who had saved her. From the look on his face, there was little doubt the calf was special to him.

Precious spoke briefly in Shona to the two men, and then turned to her guests.

"Although there's still a long way to go, she seems to be doing better right now. I'm optimistic that she'll grow up and give birth to lots of babies, of her own, one day. However if we could find an elephant mother to adopt her, that would be best solution."

"I'll be on the lookout for a foster mother for her," van Rooyen said, as all three of them they returned to the office building and he and Jessica left the rehabilitation center at noon.

"Piet, we need to talk about the elephant survey. Why don't we stop at my place in Kariba Heights and I'll fix us both a sandwich for lunch," Jessica said, as they drove away.

"Well, my cook packed me a lunch and a thermos of tea, but there's no reason why I couldn't eat it at your place, while we talk."

"Great," she said. "Then turn left at Hippo Drive. My house is at the intersection of Hippo and Lakeview."

Fifteen minutes later, van Rooyen pulled into the circular driveway in front of 4964 Lakeview Drive. The house was a small, single-story, whitewashed, brick building with a roof of red, Spanish-style, clay tiles. Its front garden, edged with a low, wrought-iron fence, brimmed with the color and fragrance of a dozen mature rose bushes.

"Nice house," he remarked as he stepped out onto the gravel driveway.

"I was lucky to find it," she said, "Its front verandah has a beautiful view of the lake. The owners left and returned to the U.K. shortly after I arrived. I feel bad for them. They weren't able to sell the property and even though I pay a monthly rent to a local estate agency, they've never been able to get any of their money out of Zimbabwe. To make matters worse, they've been hit by inflation because all the Zim dollars they've accrued here are now totally worthless."

"Yup," van Rooyen acknowledged. "A tourist at the airport the other night told me that one U.S. dollar now fetches – wait for it – five hundred thousand Zimbabwe dollars and that's *after* the Reserve Bank chopped off ten zeros!

People need to go shopping for groceries nowadays with a wheelbarrow full of bags of money just to buy a loaf of bread. It's absolutely ridiculous."

Jessica unlocked both the wrought-iron burglar screen and the front door, ushering him into the cool, high ceilinged living room. He followed her into the bright, cheerful kitchen, complete with modern electric appliances. Because of Kariba Dam's close proximity and it's hydro-electric power capability, residents and businesses here were not affected as often by the frequent power cuts bedeviling businesses and households in Harare, Bulawayo, and other large Zimbabwe cities.

"Here, take a seat," she said, pulling out a bar stool from under the breakfast counter.

"Thanks." He sat down and placed his sandwich container and thermos on the counter in front of him.

While she prepared her sandwich, she spoke of the need for a Zambezi Valley elephant survey.

"My research sponsor, as you know, is the Global Defense Force for Wildlife. Ever since the African elephant was placed on the endangered species list in 1989, they've taken a keen interest in all issues involving the species. I received an e-mail from my contact, late last week. The GDFW is especially concerned about a couple of proposed dam building projects in the Zambezi valley. If either dam were constructed, they'd have profound effects on wildlife habitats, for elephants in particular. The projects they're examining are the Batoka Dam, proposed to be built below the Victoria Falls, and the Mphanda Nkuwa dam, in Mozambique, below the existing Cabora Bassa Dam."

"The Batoka Dam project was cancelled several years ago. The Zimbabwe and Zambia governments were unable to reach an agreement about its funding." Van Rooyen poured tea from his thermos flask into its cup.

"Here, let me get you a decent cup."

"No, no Jessica. This one's perfectly fine."

"Well, if you're sure?" She returned the cup to the cabinet shelf.

"And you're right about the Batoka Dam, Piet, but there's no guarantee the project won't be revived again at a later date. In any event, the GDFW wants to get some current, baseline, elephant population figures in the valley. What they're asking me to do is survey east of Kariba Dam. This includes the Charara and Hurungwe Safari Areas, Mana Pools National Park, and further east to the Sapi, Chewore, and Doma Safari Areas. They say it's a total of approximately 4,000 square miles. They have a Botswana survey company doing the Chobe National Park and the Zimbabwe parks west of here, including the Matusadona, Chizarira, and Hwangwe National Parks."

"That 4,000 square miles they've staked out in the eastern valley is a pretty big area. How do they propose we do it?"

"I don't have the exact details yet, but I'm anticipating they'll divide sections up using a grid pattern. Then, as we fly along transect lines running east and west, I'll record the habitat type and the number of elephants seen in that segment. I'm told it's best to hold the airspeed at eighty knots, while flying at an altitude of two hundred feet."

"Jeez, Jessica. Don't they realize there are some pretty steep elevations in these places?" Van Rooyen spluttered, between bites of his sandwich.

"I'm sure they realize you'll fly over them, not into them," Jessica chuckled.

"And what are they willing to pay me?" he asked.

"US$500 an hour, for both you and the plane. Is that enough?"

"Enough for me. But I'll need to ask Whiskey-Kilo-Bravo what her going rate is." He took a swig of tea and grinned.

"Well if she wants too much more, she can probably count herself out of a job." Jessica responded with mock disdain then she broke into a wide smile.

"No. Seriously, sounds quite doable to me. When do we start?"

"I'll check back with them, Piet. What's your schedule like and how many days a week could you devote to this?"

"One or two days a week, depending on circumstances, and of course the weather. We might even be able to kill two birds with one stone. While you're counting elephants, I can be on the lookout for poachers."

"I'll get back with them first thing tomorrow."

"Your rubbish bin?" van Rooyen looked around as he crunched up the left-over wax paper his sandwich had been wrapped in.

"Next to the refrigerator. Here, hand over and I'll toss it in for you. By the way, before I report our negotiations to the GDFW, perhaps we'd better take a test flight just so I can assure them you're a competent pilot."

Piet smiled "No sweat. How about first thing in the morning? I was thinking of flying down to the Chewore confluence anyway to take a look at the site where the poachers took out those elephants."

"Sure," she replied, setting her empty plate and glass in the sink.

"So let's go. I'll give you a ride back to your car. Tomorrow, meet me at the airport at seven? Sound okay?"

"Sounds great." She followed him out to his vehicle.

Later that afternoon, while going through her study records, Jessica thought about the hours she had spent with Piet van Rooyen that day. The man was definitely growing on her. About tomorrow's plans – while she was ready to check out his flying skills, was she up to seeing a field of dead elephants, especially if they turned out to be a herd she'd been studying for the past three years?

Chapter 10

Thursday, August 07, 2008

Aboard the Cessna at seven-thirty the next morning, Van Rooyen and Jessica buckled their seat belts in preparation for a planned over flight across the Chewore confluence. Nearby, on the apron in front of Kariba Airport's terminal building, passengers boarded a Zambian Airways Boeing 737, preparing to depart on a scheduled flight to Ndola. Behind the 737 sat an Air Zimbabwe, Xian MA60, a sixty-passenger, turboprop aircraft, with a dozen red, safety lanyards hanging from its engine components and undercarriage.

"That plane's almost new, but it's been out of service, for months." Van Rooyen pointed to the MA60. "It broke down a while ago, and Air Zim's still waiting for replacement parts to arrive from China. Rumor has it the manufacturer won't ship the parts, until they get payment in advance."

"Makes sense," Jessica said, "Zimbabwe's credit is shot to hell." She knew the country's economy had been in retreat ever since Mugabe had begun his seizure of commercial farms in 2000.

She looked on as Piet fine-tuned the controls, toggled the master switch, adjusted the throttle, and turned the ignition. The engine coughed into life and the single propeller began spinning faster and faster. He keyed the mike.

"Kariba Tower, Cessna one-five-zero, Whiskey-Kilo-Bravo. Request clearance for takeoff. Departure to the east."

The radio crackled and the air traffic controller responded, "Roger, Whiskey-Kilo-Bravo, taxi to runway zero-niner-zero, and hold short."

They taxied to the western end of the runway to await further instructions. During his pre-flight run up, Jessica watched him checking the aircraft's ailerons, horizontal and vertical stabilizers, and rudder. Van Rooyen certainly appeared to be thorough, she thought, and an unexpected warm rush of admiration, for the man sitting to her left, surged through her.

He peered down to the end of the runway, commenting, "Although the tower checks the perimeter fences constantly, I've seen herds of buffalo, zebra, wildebeest, and even elephants obstructing this landing strip." His eyes scanned the brush growing along both sides.

"Kariba Tower this is Cessna one-five-zero, Whiskey-Kilo-Bravo. We're holding short, runway zero-niner-zero. Ready for takeoff."

"Roger," the tower responded, "Whiskey-Kilo-Bravo, you're cleared for takeoff."

Van Rooyen taxied the Cessna into position at the end of the runway. As he pushed steadily on the throttle, the engine roared, and the aircraft surged forward, pressing Jessica against the back of her seat. They were speeding down the runway, and then they were airborne, climbing steadily to 5,000 feet.

Below them, the Zambezi snaked north through the narrow Kariba gorge. Above them, the brilliant blue sky was clear, except for a few puffy, cumulus clouds hovering over the Zambian hills to the north. Some forty miles downstream from the dam, they spotted the A-1 highway up ahead with its parallel bridges stretching across the river. On both banks, long queues of cars and trucks waited to cross.

"Why are those bridges so close together?" Jessica had to shout to be heard over the roar of the motor and propeller.

"The Chirundu Bridges, carry traffic between Harare and Lusaka. This section was once known as the Great North Road, part of the famous Cape to Cairo route, envisioned by Cecil John Rhodes in the late 1800s. The first single-lane bridge, built before World War II, became a bottleneck, so Zambia constructed the second one. It opened to traffic in 2002."

For the next thirty minutes, they flew on in silence, while Jessica gazed out of the window, following the course of the river. She was heartsick over the possible deaths of Nkosikaas and her family and dreaded the thought of possibly seeing their lifeless bodies littering the veld. With the Kariba gorge behind them, the valley opened up into a wide flood plain, where the watercourse slowed and divided into separate channels, forming a multitude of small ponds and pools.

"Mana Pools up ahead," van Rooyen shouted. "Soon we'll see the Kafue

River flowing into the Zambezi from those northern hills over there." He pointed to the left.

Jessica stared out her window, her eyes peeled for elephants along the river, but she saw none. Too early in the day, she realized.

"How far to the site where the massacre took place?"

"About five miles on the far side of the Chewore confluence. Just another forty-five minutes or so," he replied.

Jessica laid back her head and dozed off, lulled by the rhythmic throb of the engine. She awoke when van Rooyen reduced power and the aircraft began losing altitude.

He pointed ahead. "That's the Chewore. We should be getting close."

Jessica sat high in her seat and peered through the windshield. In the distance appeared a clearing with a collection of indistinct gray blobs scattered around. Drawing closer, each took on the unmistakable shape of a fallen elephant. She counted twelve, adults and calves. A dark stain blackened the ground around each carcass. Van Rooyen dipped the right wing to circle the scene. The engine's loud drone scared off dozens of scavengers, including several hyenas. They bounded into the surrounding trees. A large flock of vultures fluttered away from the carcasses to form a wide circle around the edge of the clearing.

"I can't believe this." Jessica gasped at the enormity of the sight. Holding her hand over her mouth, she shook her head sorrowfully. Was this Nkosikaas's family, she wondered. A faint odor of death and putrefying flesh seeped through the plane's air vents. She held her nose.

"Bad smell, isn't it? Imagine the stink down there on the ground," van Rooyen remarked.

"Before we leave, I need to confirm—know for sure—if this is Nkosikaas's family." Jessica continued to fix her gaze on the field below.

"Didn't you already identify them from the photographs?" He continued to circle.

"Yes, and no. When we looked at your photos in Kaminjolo's office, I said I thought I saw Nkosikaas's daughter in one of the shots. From that, I just assumed they were all members of Nkosikaas's family."

"Well then, what more proof do you need?"

"You've heard the saying, haven't you? Those who assume, make asses out of themselves, or words close to it. Well, I don't want to come off looking like a donkey," she offered with a wry grin. "Could we circle some more? Please."

"If you can stand the stench, it's okay by me." Van Rooyen dropped the nose and Whisky-Kilo-Brave dropped to two hundred feet, leaving ample room to clear the surrounding mopani and acacia trees. "Grab the binoculars from behind my seat," he said.

Jessica reached back and grasped them. Adjusting the focus, she scanned the clearing, searching among the twelve, inert bodies for the one with correct identifying features. Several circuits later, she positively identified the matriarch with the four-inch tear in her left ear.

"Yes, it's definitely Nkosikass." She sighed deeply as she returned the binoculars to the seat pocket.

"We'll head for home then." Van Rooyen banked, turning the Cessna on a westward course.

During the flight home, Jessica jotted down details of all they had seen in her notebook.

"It's a real bummer," she said. "Not just because I've lost twelve animals, an integral part of my study, but the earth has lost members of an incredibly wonderful species whose very survival, today, is so precarious. To me, saving the calf, Narini-Ina, as you did is the only saving grace."

"Good name, hey – Narini-Four. I like it, Jessica. Perhaps you should tell Precious what her name really is. Better name than Nherera. Was she Narini's fourth calf?"

Jessica nodded.

At five thousand feet, Whiskey-Kilo-Bravo maintained a level, though somewhat turbulent, return course to Kariba. In the valley, temperatures had risen and thermal currents abounded. Jessica instinctively clutched her seat belt and took her mind off the bouncing landscape by focusing her attention on some circling fish eagles, which were riding the warm updrafts.

"Whenever I see those raptors in glorious flight," she said, "I don't wonder that flight has always been man's dream." Turning to van Rooyen, she asked, "When did you first fly a plane?"

"My Dad taught me when I was sixteen."

"Sounds like a family thing."

"It was, kind of. We were on our Karoi farm, when my Dad bought this plane back in 1978."

"This plane? Thirty years ago? Really?" Jessica's eyebrows rose in astonishment.

"That's right."

"And this is the same plane?" Could she believe him?

"Properly maintained, thirty years isn't old for an aircraft," van Rooyen insisted. "There are DC-3s still in service today that were built in the 1930s and early 1940s. Air Rhodesia operated them as late as 1975 on their regular runs from Harare to Kariba, Hwangwe, Victoria Falls, and other short-range, scheduled passenger flights."

"Amazing. Your father—a farmer, right?"

"Yup."

"Why did he need a plane?"

"He was on the board of the Farmer's Co-op for several years, and needed to go down to Harare for meetings. Flying saved time. Besides, he'd always wanted an excuse to own a plane. My grandfather flew a Spitfire for the Royal Air Force in World War II."

"So the love of flying was passed down the generations?"

"You could say that."

"Was there an airfield near the farm?"

"Not at first. My Dad had an earthmoving outfit come out and build him a dirt strip."

"And your parents, do they still farm in Karoi?"

"No. When I finished school at St. George's, I worked on the farm with Dad, and took it over in 1999, after he and Mum passed away."

"I'm sorry." Jessica frowned. Realizing her goof, she added hastily, "Aw Shucks, that didn't come out right. What I meant was I was sorry about your parents, not about your taking over the farm."

He laughed. "It's okay. My folks died in a bad car accident on the Enterprise Road, in Harare. A drunk driver hit them. The only blessing was they died instantly, so they didn't suffer. The worst part was telling my kids. They adored their grandparents."

Jessica's heart flip-flopped. "You have children? I didn't know that."

"I did have. Not anymore," he said, as a shadow crossed his face.

Puzzled, she paused before continuing. "Oh my God, Piet. I'm so, so, sorry. What happened?" Her face fell. "Wait, wait. I apologize for being so rude. I shouldn't be asking you these things. It's none of my business."

"No. It's not your worry," he replied. Nonetheless, he told her about his ill-fated absence from the farm in April 2001. "In hindsight, I should never have left the farm," he said, lowering his head. Haltingly, he described what happened when he returned home the following day.

"When I flew in, there were vehicles and crowds of people, surrounding the house. I had no idea what was going on. My neighbor, Angus McLaren, met me at the strip as soon as I landed, and broke the news. He told me a gang of war veterans had broken into the house shortly after I left. He said my wife, Sandie, had been hiding in our designated safe room with the children and one of our dogs." He took a deep breath before continuing. "Suffice to say there were no survivors."

"Oh my God! How old were the kids, Piet?"

"Brian was eleven and Bernice nine." Van Rooyen's eyes had moistened. He hurriedly swiped at them with the heel of his palms and re-grasped the control column with a tight, white-knuckled grip.

"I don't know what to say, Piet. To say I'm sorry for your loss just doesn't seem adequate." Conflicting emotions had her mind in turmoil. While genuinely grieving his suffering, she was also relieved to learn there was no wife. She immediately felt a sharp stab of guilt, regretting her uncaring, selfish thoughts. Oh Jessica, she thought to herself, how could you be so self-seeking?

*   *   *

Van Rooyen's mind reeled in doubt. Was he an idiot for spilling his guts to her? More than likely, she'd think he was just plying for her sympathy. Until now, he'd shared his past with few people in Kariba. Perhaps clearing the decks prior to contemplating a deeper friendship was a good thing. But was he ready to embark on a committed relationship? He wasn't sure.

To lighten the conversation, he smiled and said, "Jessica, I brought us a picnic lunch. Hungry?"

"Wow! You think of everything, Piet. What did you bring?"

"Just sandwiches. They're in the cooler chest behind my seat."

After devouring a lunch of cheese and tomato sandwiches, Jessica collected the trash and stuffed everything back into the empty cooler.

"How much longer before we get back to Kariba?" she asked.

"We've just flown over Mana Pools, so it'll be another hour. We should get there around half past two."

"In that case," she replied, "there's time for you to finish your story. What happened to the farm?"

"I reckon it's now a weekend resort for one or more of Mugabe's *shamwaris,* his friends. I haven't been anywhere near the place for years. Before I left for the last time, I loaded up as much as I could fit on my lorry, and sold everything in Harare, including the lorry. Afterwards, I hi-tailed it up here to Kariba."

He continued, "Sadly, there's more to this tragedy. This didn't just hurt my family and me. There were probably three hundred other souls who lived and worked on the farm and called the place their home—farm workers and their families. Those ZANU-PF monsters, who drove us off, set fire to their huts, beat up the men, raped the women, and chased everyone off the property into the bush. A week later, I went back to the district to see if I could find any of them. I was never able to."

Van Rooyen felt a lump in his throat as he pictured the faces of his missing workers, many of whom he had grown up with. Many had been his childhood playmates and he had known them all his life.

"How terribly sad. Then what did you do?"

"I bought the houseboat and, for a couple of years, spent my time fishing or just sitting around with nothing to do but feel sorry for myself. Then a friend of mine, Jerry Fisher, who owned the Titambire Fish and Bait Shop, decided to leave Zim in 2003 and go back to England. He was selling out—bottom dollar. So I took over the business, lock, stock, and barrel."

"So you went from being a farmer to being a shopkeeper?"

"I had fun at first, shooting the bull and swapping fish stories with the customers. After a while, though, I just lost interest in it, especially when most of our regulars left the country because inflation had gobbled up everybody's bank accounts. Our business really plummeted when tourists stopped coming. At that point, I hired Moses Mafunda to manage it, and nowadays we open only on weekends."

"When did you become involved with the Wildlife Protection League?"

"About four years ago, shortly after I turned over the running of the shop to Moses. I realized not only were the people hurting here, but the country's wildlife was in terrible straits, too. That's what made me get off my rear end and actually try to do something about it."

"Do you think you're making a difference?"

"Hard to say. Based upon the number a snares we're picking up, we must be putting a dent in the small-time, tribal poaching, but it's difficult to know if we're having much of an effect on the larger operations like this recent incident at Chewore."

"Do you have any new strategies for stopping the big guys?"

"Well, you heard my conversation with Kaminjolo yesterday. Top of our list of priorities is to get the government to issue us permits for some higher-powered weapons."

"Sounds reasonable," she agreed.

"There's another thing we have absolutely no control over, and it's the continuing sale of ivory to Japan and China. I'm livid that CITES' approved another ivory auction in Harare, giving the government an opportunity to offload much of its ill-gotten gains. The sale's less than three months away, on November first." Van Rooyen snorted in disgust.

"Yes, I'd heard about it. CITES is also sponsoring sales of ivory in Namibia, Botswana and South Africa, aren't they?"

"They are. Here in Zim, the government claims its stockpiles come from legal sources of ivory, that they've accumulated since the last CITES' auction in 1999. That's crap, I don't believe it for one bloody minute. Even though some of the tusks to be auctioned might have come from elephants dying from natural causes, like Nkosi, and from legal hunting, there's nothing to prevent Zanunga's and Victor Sabakwe's poacher friends from slipping their illegal ivory into the sale?"

"That's a danger, I suppose," Jessica said. "How much ivory is going to be auctioned off? Do you know?"

"I've heard a figure of three and a half metric tons being bandied about."

"What does that mean, in terms of number of elephants?"

"Well, if the tusks on today's average elephant weigh around twenty kilos, then three and a half metric tons would be equivalent to about one hundred and seventy-five elephants."

"That's terrible," Jessica replied, her face somber.

Down on the ground, the dun-colored grassland was punctuated with dotted trees clustered along the banks of the Zambezi's many tributaries. The small rivers and streams, flowing from the highlands down to the river, were mostly dry at this time of the year.

*   *   *

Jessica tried to picture a herd of one hundred and seventy-five elephants ambling down the arid watercourses, as they made their way down to the river to drink and bathe—all eliminated—too sad. Up ahead, she could see the A-1, in the distance, headed south from the Zambezi. Tiny vehicles were traveling back and forth along it. Immediately below, she had a bird's-eye-view of a property with scattered buildings, stands of uniform-looking trees, and along its northern boundary a swathe of bare earth, which looked like an airstrip.

"Piet, what's the place down there?" she asked, pointing ahead. "It's a short distance south of the river and looks to be some kind of a tree farm. It might even have a runway. Look down there; we'll be directly over the airstrip in a second."

Van Rooyen looked down. "Oh, that place used to be one of the country's largest growers of avocados and citrus fruit. There was a huge packing facility on site. They boxed fruit for export overseas. It was an important foreign currency earner."

"Is it still in operation?" she asked. "Avocado's! Yum!" The thought made her mouth water. She could taste, even smell, the delicious guacamole dishes served at her favorite Mexican restaurants back in the States.

"No, I don't believe so." he replied. "The farm was once owned by the Fabrizios, an Italian family. The grandfather, Giovanni Fabrizio, was one of the Italian engineers who worked on the Kariba Dam. I read an article about him, years ago, in *The Rhodesia Herald*. He and his family loved the area so much that when the dam was completed he decided to stay, rather than go back to Italy. The family bought that land, about a thousand acres, I think. Then they cleared it and planted hundreds of avocado and citrus trees." He paused for a moment. "Fataran! I remember now. That was the name of the farm. As the story goes, the owners originally wanted to register the property as *La Fattoria Arancia*, 'Orange Farm' in Italian. The government said the name was too long, so the family shortened it to Fataran. War vets invaded the farm in 2001 and chased the family off. This happened shortly after I lost Kigelia."

"What a shame all their hard work, and yours, was for naught," Jessica said.

"It's what happened to so many farmers here I'm afraid," van Rooyen said, pursing his lips.

Jessica studied van Rooyen as he sat erect and alert at the aircraft controls. His eyes constantly scanned both the bank of instruments arrayed before him and the views outside through the windshield and side windows. She found him attractive. Still, her inner voice urged caution. Was she ready to trust a man again? Her last relationship had ended so painfully.

Just three years ago, she was engaged to a man, who later dumped her for another woman. Paul Hansen was a handsome, fair-haired man of Scandinavian heritage. She had met him in 2003, while volunteering at the elephant sanctuary in Tennessee, where he worked as a veterinarian. Within weeks of their meeting, she had fallen madly, crazily, deeply in love with him. They were kindred spirits, she thought, sharing a love of wildlife and nature. She was studying for her doctorate and, in 2005, a once-in-a-lifetime opportunity arose for her to go to Africa to research elephants in the wild.

Paul was adamantly opposed to her leaving the States for what he called, a 'Godforsaken, third-world country, in Southern Africa, particularly one that had driven itself into bankruptcy and starvation.' He relented only after she promised him she'd be home in two years.

During the first eighteen months of their separation, their emails sped back and forth between the two continents, creating a virtual pathway of digital fire. Then their frequency slowed and she received his final 'Dear Jane' message in January 2007. He wrote to say he was breaking off their engagement because he'd met someone else, and that he and his new love would be married in June. Jessica never even learned her name.

She knew her parents were disappointed at first. They had hoped her forthcoming marriage would assure her prompt return home to the States. After the breakup, however, she received a long, consoling, letter from her mom. In it, her mother confessed that neither of she, nor Jessica's dad, had approved of Paul's behavior after she left; so in that regard they weren't sorry the wedding was off.

After receiving Paul's last e-mail, Jessica locked herself away to hide her tear-stained, face from the world. Even though he'd given her less than the promised two years to complete her doctoral dissertation, at first she blamed herself for the breakup. Now, she knew better; convinced that he'd have left her anyway, even if she'd returned home on schedule.

Now here was another man, not as strikingly handsome as Paul had been, but kinder and gentler. The burning question was, however, should she risk heartbreak again?

Chapter 11

Thursday August 14, 2008

Muchengeti and her family had spent the previous night either browsing or resting high on the escarpment, thirty miles south of the Zambezi. More than a week had passed, since the old matriarch had sensed Nkosikaas's frantic distress calls. Since then, however, she had led her family on a search, crisscrossing the valley east of Mana, in hopes of finding her older sister.

That night her daughter, Umsizi, gave birth to a stillborn, male calf. After she delivered the newborn in a slippery, white, fetal sack, her sister Chenjera, who served as midwife, helped her to tear the membrane open. Inside was a tiny, motionless calf, considerably smaller than the usual healthy newborn. Muchengeti and her three remaining adult daughters gathered around the new mother in silence. For almost an hour, Chenjera repeatedly tried to assist Umsizi in lifting the calf onto its feet. But the infant collapsed each time in a lifeless heap. This was a devastating loss to a mother, who had only recently lost her three-year-old calf, Rufaro, to a crocodile. Nonetheless, life had to go on.

At daybreak, Muchengeti gave her group the "let's go" rumble and led them northeast. Umsizi set off with the family, but agonized over having to abandon her dead calf and plagued by indecision, she returned several times to stand over the pitiful, tiny, branch-covered carcass. Eventually her fear of being parted from the herd, drove her to leave the calf and rejoin her family.

As they moved through the bush, Shungu, the herd's newest addition, toddled along beside her mother. While still reliant on her mother's milk, she would soon begin sampling various kinds of vegetation. Another two or more years could pass before she was weaned, unless a younger sibling arrived sooner to take first dibs on its mother's milk.

With every passing day Shungu gained strength, and except for the time she spent sleeping or suckling, she studied the behaviors of her elders, often clumsily trying to imitate them. With great interest, she observed her older companions coiling their trunks around bundles of dry grass and ripping them up from the ground by their roots. They shook off the dirt before stuffing the forage into their mouths. Shungu tried to imitate them, and failed miserably. At her tender age, her immature, floppy little trunk could not encircle a bunch of grass, far less grasp it tight enough to pull it, roots, and all, from the ground.

A game she thoroughly enjoyed involved ramming her head or rear-end into one of her mother's legs. Afterwards she would escape on the double, squealing and flapping her ears in excitement. Her proud mother found the lark endearing, but later she would probably consider it annoying. Nevertheless, for now she indulged her youngest offspring.

Later, well-practiced at the game, Shungu began targeting her two-year-old cousin, Mufudzi. Not anticipating the force behind his younger relative's quick shove against his right foreleg, Mufudzi lost his balance and toppled over. Bellowing in righteous indignation, he righted himself and set off in pursuit of his wayward cousin. Shungu sneakily found protection, beneath her mother's belly.

That morning there was a sense of expectation in the air. Muchengeti raised her trunk to detect any new scents in the wind and spread her large ears to capture all incoming sounds. She gave out a series of deep rumbles, changed course, and strode eastward with her family in tow. They crashed through mopani woodlands and started up a rocky hillside. At the top of the ridge, they met up with Chembere's family and both groups celebrated their reunion, joyfully, with noisy fervor.

During the heat of the morning, the two groups rested together in the shade of a stand of mahogany trees, but by mid-afternoon, they split up and went their separate ways. Chembere and her family turned west towards Mana Pools while Muchengeti led her herd northeast, towards the Chewore.

They followed the dry Chewore River meandering northwards to the Zambezi. The herd needed water. Several days had passed since they last quenched their thirst. No rain had fallen here for four months and none expected for another three. Deep layers of sand and rocks covered the parched riverbed. There was no water here. Or was there?

The matriarch knew the Zambezi was a two-day trek away. With the herd already dehydrated, it would be an impossible distance to cover without water. The old girl, nonetheless, had a trick up her trunk, knowing how to reach seemingly invisible sources of water. She left the bank and stepped into a depression in the middle of the dry, sand-filled, watercourse. Dropping to her knees, she dug into the hard-packed sand and gravel with her single right tusk. Having loosened the top layers, she then used her feet to hollow out a cavity. Continuing to scoop away the sand and rocks, she excavated a hollow more than three feet wide and three feet deep. As she persistently dug even deeper, Chenjera with her two long straight tusks joined in the digging and scooped out a second depression a short distance away.

Muchengeti's cavity was now four feet deep, and the sand was taking on an ever-darkening hue. Within an hour, she and Chenjera had excavated two wells, to depths of more than five feet. Both began filling with water. Muchengeti sucked up several gallons and emptied them down her throat. Afterwards she stepped aside for others to take their turn. Chenjera followed suit, and then helped her youngest who was unable to reach that depth. Drawing out the well's precious liquid into her trunk, she poured it down his throat. Shama did likewise for Shungu.

After all twelve elephants had drunk their fill, there was sufficient water left in the underground aquifer for them to cool themselves. The elephants gleefully sprayed the liquid over their heads, chests, and necks, while fanning themselves with their ears.

At sunset, they departed, following the riverbed towards the northeast. Muchengeti lead the way with Chirema, as usual, bringing up the rear. The herd continued moving on well into the night. Under a crescent moon, they foraged along both sides of the riverbed ripping up dried grasses and reeds and devouring the acacia pods they found scattered under the trees. At midnight they rested and continued their trek in the early hours of the morning. By midday on the third day, they reached the Zambezi and ran headlong down to the water's edge.

Early the next morning Muchengeti led her family east along the river. By noon they reached an inlet lined with a dense reed forest. The matriarch sensed something was amiss. She lifted her trunk high to sniff the wind and let out a deep rumble. Her family members closed in, cautiously spreading their ears. As if on cue, they slowly advanced and on the far side of a small rise, they came upon the shriveled carcasses of Nkosikaas's massacred herd.

As one, the herd halted and tensed without making a sound. Muchengeti led the way down the hill and approached a dead cow stretched out on the ground surrounded by a dark stained circle in the sand. The skeleton was loosely cloaked in a torn, stiffened hide, copiously streaked with the white droppings of vultures. Muchengeti tenuously reached out with her trunk to touch the remains and take in its scent. As if in respect for the deceased member of her species, she moved her right front foot in a circular motion over above the carcass as if to scan it. Afterwards, she repeated the same motion with one of her hind feet before moving on to the next skeleton. She performed the same ritual with a number of the older members of her family.

In spite of the decomposition and some missing body parts, carried off by scavengers, Muchengeti recognized the dead as members of her sister, Nkosikaas's family. A deep anger welled up inside her. Before leaving the scene of the massacre, the family covered the carcasses with dirt and vegetation.

*   *   *

Jessica and Patrick had planned to patrol Sapi and Chewore Safari areas, today. They set out early, leaving Kariba at six in the morning. Passing a local bank as they drove out of the town, they noticed a long line of people had encircled the entire block. Hundreds of men and women of all ages sat or squatted on the sidewalk or leant against bicycles. They included mothers with toddlers, breast feeding their babies, or carrying swaddled infants on their backs.

Look at all the people," Patrick exclaimed, looking around. "The bank doesn't open until nine. What's happening?"

"The Zim dollar's been devalued again. I heard this on the radio last night" Jessica replied. "They must all be waiting to make withdrawals. From the length of this queue, they must have started lining up at sun-up."

"I know about this inflation," Patrick said, beaming with satisfaction. "I don't put my money in the bank anymore. I learned my lesson. Now, on payday I buy mealie meal and dried Kapenta fish; enough to eat for one month. Then if I have any money left over, I buy chickens. Lots of chickens."

"That's really smart, Patrick, but what do you do with all the chickens?"

"My mother keeps them for me at her village. She gives me some of the eggs, she sells some to other people in the village, and they give her mealie meal. She also has a garden and gives me vegetables."

"That's plain, old fashioned bartering," Jessica enthused. "Good for you!"

Today, Jessica planned to check out the northern sector of the Sapi Safari Area. After leaving the tarmac at Makuti, they turned east, and at ten thirty stopped to stretch their legs. To the east, the distant mountains, kopjes, and rocky ravines of the Zambezi escarpment cast long shadows over the valley. They climbed back into the Toyota and continued north until Jessica judged they were about thirty miles south of the Zambezi. For the next ten minutes, they crept along a ridge roughly 100 yards wide, running north and south.

On either side of the hill's crest, the land fell away into wide valleys. On their left, trees ran along both sides of a dried riverbed. It was either the Sapi or the Chewore, Jessica thought.

She brought the vehicle to a halt, facing north, under an evergreen mahogany tree. They alighted and with Patrick in tow, she walked towards the eastern side of the ridge.

"Look," she called out pointing down the hill. "I'm counting thirteen elephants. But from this distance I can't tell who they are."

Suddenly, from the opposite side of the ridge, came the rumbles of a second group.

"Oh my goodness," Jessica exclaimed. "Did you hear that?" She walked across and peered down into the western valley. A hundred yards ahead, she spotted another herd climbing the hill.

"Quick Miss Jessica, we'd better get back in the car," Patrick said in a quavering voice.

They hurried to the Land Cruiser. All at once, there were at least seven or eight elephants milling around on the top of the ridge. Less than a football field's length in front of them, Jessica recognized them right away.

"That's Chembere and her family," she said, excitedly. From the glove box she removed her binoculars, elephant identification charts and a notebook. Sketches of all her study elephants, showing their distinctive tusk and ear anomalies appeared on the charts. She counted thirteen elephants on the ridge and checked each individual against the drawing. With no tusks, Chembere's identity was simple to confirm. Jessica had learned an African elephant's lack of tusks was usually the result of an uncommon genetic glitch.

She also spotted Chembere's eldest daughter, Chiripi, whose right ear had a number of slits and holes. Then Chitatu, her second daughter, whose left tusk pointed upwards and China, her youngest, who had a broken left tusk. Accompanying them, were the three cows' nine offspring. She checked them all off on a list in her notebook.

Jessica had just made these notations when a cacophony of trumpets, rumbles, and squeals rent the air. Muchengeti's herd topped the ridge from the east, and both families greeted one another exuberantly. The matriarchs approached one another, clicking their tusks together, while other members of both families joined in with their own vocalizations. Moments later, the adults put on an unusual display, spinning around, flapping their ears, then intertwining trunks. They followed this behavior with much urinating and defecating.

"Incredible," Jessica said, breathlessly. "I never thought I'd ever get to see this, Patrick. Famous elephant researcher Cynthia Moss, called this performance an elephant greeting pandemonium. This appears to be exactly what was happening here."

To cool the truck's interior, she rolled down the windows, and they continued to observe the spectacle. Today was only the second time Jessica had ever seen Shama's calf, Shungu. There she stood, less than a hundred yards away. Jessica studied her through the binoculars. Glued to her mother's side, she had obviously never experienced such a reunion before and seemed unnerved by all the frenetic activity.

Jessica's eyes focused on Chitatu-Piri, Chembere's nine-year-old, grandson. He had found a playmate in Gomana, Umsizi's eight-year-old calf, from Muchengeti's group. The two paired up for a friendly sparring match. Chitatu-Piri head-butted Gomana and the competition was on. Though a year younger than his sparring partner, Gomana proved to be a formidable opponent, and with several thrusts, he sent Chitatu-Piri skidding backwards over the edge and part way down the hill. His rival followed him. In retaliation, Chitatu-Piri dug in his heels giving Gomana a mighty shove. Not only did he launch the younger calf on a long, backwards slide, but sent him careening into his aunt, Chimuti, foraging lower on the slope. Highly irritated, Chimuti thwacked the youngster on the head with her powerful trunk.

"Elephant families are not too unlike human families, are they?" Jessica commented.

"Except people don't go to the toilet while greeting other people." Patrick chortled.

Jessica laughed. "You're right about that. But wouldn't it be fun to be as carefree as these elephants are today?"

Almost immediately, a deep frown replaced her smile.

"It seems unimaginable that these majestic animals could all be destroyed in a single minute – simply because of man's greed." She grabbed the steering wheel with a white-knuckle grip.

"It's our job to stop that." Patrick said.

In the ensuing silence, they refocused their attention on the scene before them. While the adult elephants continued foraging, the youngsters played. After receiving the clout from his aunt Chimuti, Gomana hurriedly moved away to escape even further admonishment from his elder. In his haste, he lost his balance and tumbled at least twenty-five feet down the slope, coming to rest unhurt at the base of a stout sausage tree. At the top of the ridge, his younger rival, meanwhile, performed his version of a victory dance excitedly twirling his trunk over his head. Afterwards, he plodded down the hill to join his playmate. Amused by his antics, Jessica and Patrick smiled.

With the sun now directly overhead, the heat inside the vehicle was oppressive.

"Let's go on down to Mana Pools. Perhaps we'll find the bull herd near the river," Jessica said, stuffing her charts and notebook into the glove box. She started the Toyota, u-turned, and drove away. Despite her recent bleak thought, she was thrilled to have witnessed and recorded a rarely viewed elephant greeting pandemonium.

They found five bulls in a grove of acacia and mahogany trees near the Rukomechi Camp, on the western boundary of the Mana Pools Park. Jessica parked under an ancient mahogany tree and pulled out her charts.

"See the big guy over there?" she whispered to Patrick, pointing to a large bull elephant with massive tusks with crossed tips. He stood, head lowered, evidently taking a nap in the shade about 150 yards away. "His name's Fundisi," she said. "We've estimated his age at forty-four. According to his DNA, he's closely related to both Muchengeti and Nkosikaas. Based on his age, he's likely a younger brother. Mukuru is the other big boy over there," she added. "The one with the hole in his left ear. He's about four years younger."

"The smaller one, behind Fundisi, is he on your list, Miss Jessica?"

"Oh that's Chipiri-Poshi – Chipiri's oldest offspring. According to my records, he's nineteen. Young males leave their matriarchal groups between the ages of thirteen and fifteen. I imagine Chembere kicked him out four or five years ago."

"And the other two – do you know them?"

"That's Ngomo over there. See the tip of his right tusk is broken off. He's thirty-eight. He probably lost it in a scuffle with Fundisi, or Mukuru, or some another bull. He's Nkosikaas's first born. It's sad to think he's now the sole survivor of that family. The other younger bull with the tusks splayed outwards is Chimuti, Chembere's oldest son. He's about thirty-one."

"Miss Jessica, that one over there, the one you called Mukuru. Did you see the wire around his foot?"

"No I didn't. Let me take another look," she said, peering through her binoculars. "Oh, I see it. Just above his right rear ankle. Damn! It's a snare." She spat out the words and her eyes narrowed in anger. "The most infuriating part is if Mukuru was a horse or cow, we could just walk up to him with a pair of wire cutters and cut the snare away. But because he's a dangerous wild animal, the only way to remove it is to dart him, render him unconscious, and that's a hazardous and costly procedure. Also risky for the animal; too many things can go wrong."

"What things?" Patrick eyed her quizzically.

"Lots of things. The wrong dose of the immobilizing drug could kill him, or he could fall in a position that affects his breathing or causes him serious injury. It's so darn exasperating. If I could just get hold of the so-and-so, who set it, I ..." With closed fists, she pounded the steering wheel, too angry to say more.

Patrick looked stricken and said nothing. Not until the bulls had moved on, and she had restarted the engine did he speak again.

"Miss Jessica, do not let such things make you angry. I must tell you how pleased I am to learn so much about the elephants from you. This will help me a lot one day when I am Chief Ranger."

Amused by Patrick's clearly defined ambitions, her anger dissipated, and she replied with a smile. "Patrick, don't worry about me. I'm fine, and more than happy to pass on to you what little I know. I confess much of my information about these elephants came from your late colleague, Enos." Then eyeing her wristwatch, she exclaimed, "My goodness. Look at the time, Patrick. It's nearly four o'clock, we'd better get going."

She swung the Toyota around and drove west, back towards the A-1. Further down the road, she spoke to Patrick about Fataran Farm.

"When Mr. Van Rooyen and I flew over this way a week or so ago, I saw this place from the air. He told me it used to be an important avocado and citrus tree farm. He said the place was Fataran Farm."

"Eh, Miss Jessica, I have heard some very bad things about that place," Patrick said.

"Really? What things?" She stared at him, her eyes widening in surprise.

Patrick frowned. "My cousin, Elliot, told me they have guards at the gate there, and those guys have machine guns. He said that when his friend took him there to look for a job, the guard shouted at him, *Hapana basa* – no jobs. That's okay. But then the guard pointed a big gun at my cousin and his friend, and said if they didn't drive away, right now, he was going to shoot them."

"Wow. Not exactly a warm welcome. Did he see anything else unusual?"

Waving his hands about excitedly, Patrick continued. "He told me those people, over there, are not good farmers. Weeds everywhere! Elliot knows about those things. He worked on a tobacco farm for five years, and he told me the foreman was very strict about weeding. The foreman said weeds use up all the fertilizer, so the crop does not grow big, and the farmer loses money."

Jessica wondered what the new owners of Fataran Farm were doing. Growing avocados and citrus fruit didn't seem to be their main purpose. Discussing the place with Patrick started her thinking about van Rooyen. More than a week had passed since they'd flown over the massacre and she'd seen him only once since then, when they'd had dinner together, last Saturday night. It was more than maddening to have him invading her consciousness so frequently.

That evening, at home, she thought back to their first date. He had looked so dashing in his light gray slacks and striped maroon and gray knit shirt. On their way to the restaurant, they'd stopped by his fish and bait shop briefly—just long enough for van Rooyen to introduce her to his manager, Moses Mafunda, and for the two men to discuss a few business matters. Afterwards, they had gone on to the Kariba Breezes for dinner.

From the moment he'd invited her to dinner, she'd looked forward with tantalizing anticipation to seeing him. At the restaurant, her pulse quickened as he pulled out her chair and guided her into her seat with a gentle touch to her shoulder. During the meal, the eatery's ambience was romantic, the service impeccable, the food tasty, and he'd been congenial and attentive. Missing, however, were the unforgettable snippets of closeness, she thought they'd shared earlier that week. Had she just imagined them? Although her disappointment was palpable, she disguised the feeling with a winsome smile and amiable chitchat.

That had been five days ago, and she'd heard nothing from him since. Truth be told, it was probably a good thing because she had a mountain of paperwork and reports to prepare and didn't need any distractions.

Chapter 12

Friday, August 22, 2008

Early Friday evening Van Rooyen returned home from an anti-poaching patrol east of Mana Pools. The day had been long, but fruitful, since the team had collected more than seventy snares. The downside to these patrols was always the gruesome discovery of dead and dying snare victims.

He understood why tribespeople resorted to setting traps to hunt for food. Ever since Mugabe's land grab began eight years ago, hunger had stalked the land. What he couldn't understand or forgive, however, was the number of snares that weren't checked daily, leaving trapped animals to die slow, agonizing deaths. Worse yet, the meat, which could have fed the hungry was left in the bush to rot. Today, he and his team had managed to free a small duiker and a young giraffe, thus saving their lives.

He grabbed a cold beer from the fridge and stepped out on his houseboat's aft deck. From his lounge chair, he heard the relaxing sounds of small waves lapping against the sides of the houseboat. The sun had already dipped below the escarpment. Its afterglow reflected off the atmosphere's dusty haze, painting the sky with a brief, soft, rosy blush. Later it gave way to a sparkling night sky.

With the darkness came the emergence of night sounds—the chirping of crickets, croaking frogs, hooting owls and the yips, squeals and barks of hyenas. Nighttime also brought the drone of insects and the dopplering whine of mosquitoes.

"Damn the mozzies," he exclaimed, slapping his arm. After the second quick jab of a mosquito bite, he picked up his beer and retreated indoors. No sooner had he sat down than the telephone rang.

"Hello."

"Is this Piet Van Rooyen?" The deep, baritone voice sounded vaguely familiar.

"*Ja*, speaking."

"Piet, hey, Angus McLaren from Karoi. Howzit, man?"

"Hello Angus. Thought I recognized the voice. Good to hear from you, my mate. I'm doing fine. You okay?"

"Compared to many of our *shamwaris* these days, can't complain. In fact, Patsy and I consider ourselves damn fortunate to still be here on the farm. I've got to tell you, man, I was bloody surprised to see you at the rifle club do. Patsy and I haven't seen you in years. We thought you'd booked it, gone down south, or taken off to Australia or the U.K."

"Not a chance, man. I've got too much Zambezi mud between my toes to survive anywhere else," he chuckled, giving his friend a quick rundown on his move to Kariba.

"Well Piet, I'm just bloody happy you're still around, and hey, tomorrow's Patsy's birthday. She's celebrating her fiftieth. We've invited some friends over for sundowners and a *braai*, and we'd love you to come. Our old mates will be chuffed as hell to see you."

"Sounds good, Angus. I'll be there. What time?"

"Around five o'clock. Hey, it's bloody good to talk to you again old friend. See you tomorrow."

"Thanks Angus. I'll be there." Van Rooyen hung up, cheered by the short conversation with his old neighbor. Nonetheless, he wondered how he'd manage the onslaught of old memories that visiting his old farming district would resurrect.

*   *   *

The next day he pulled out onto the A-1, and headed south towards Harare. Karoi was just fifty-five miles down this major arterial route, now a potholed, two-lane, tarmac road without shoulders or breakdown lanes. He felt a deep sadness, seeing the untilled, barren fields pass by on both sides of the road. At this time of the year, prior to the land invasions, farmers would have already ploughed and harrowed their land, in preparation for the planting of maize, cotton, tobacco, peanuts, and other crops. But today, as far as the eye could see, the fields were infested with weeds, scrub, tree saplings, and shoulder-high grass.

When he reached Karoi, he turned right off the A-1 and drove through the town's dingy business district. Dilapidated buildings and vacant shops, with smashed windows, now took the place of what years ago had been a thriving commercial center. Less than a handful of establishments were still in business, evidenced by vehicles parked outside. He saw old men squatting on cracked, concrete pavements, where weeds and tufts of grass pushed through the crevices. The sight of his former hometown depressed him. At the end of the main street, he turned right on the road leading to a cluster of local farms.

Van Rooyen knew the district well. He'd grown up, and lived here for years on Kigelia farm. He steeled himself for the moment he'd drive past the turnoff to his old home. He hadn't been back since February 2001, when he returned after the funerals, hoping to locate some of his farm workers. Mugabe's people had evidently driven them away; he'd seen not any of them since. Had they survived?

He looked away when he drove past the old road sign, Kigelia Farm, wanting to push away the painful memories. Even after seven years, he still believed he was responsible for the tragedy. Had he been there, he could have protected his wife and children.

A mile further down the road, he arrived at the turnoff to Angus's Glengarry Farm. On both sides of the farm road, maize, and tobacco seedlings, just a few inches tall, formed neat rows between furrows in the rich, red-brown soil. Arching over the fields were huge irrigation gantries, and beside the dam, green pastures stretched into the distance, where herds of fat, Hereford and Black Angus cattle grazed. He drew in a deep breath, relishing the familiar scents emitted by a mixture of cow manure and rich, loamy soil.

It was five thirty when he arrived at the homestead. Typical of most farms operating in the 1970s, during the Rhodesian bush war, the residence was surrounded by a six-foot, chain-link security fence with a four-strand, barbed-wire topping. He pulled up to the padlocked double gates and hooted the horn. Two large dogs, a black Labrador and a Rhodesian ridgeback, bounded up to the fence barking excitedly. A gate guard wearing faded denim overalls appeared from a small building next to the house. The elderly African turned to face van Rooyen and his lips parted in a wide, gap-toothed smile.

"Baas Piet. We have not seen you for a long, long time."

Van Rooyen leaned out the Land Rover's window.

"Tobiwa! Yes, it's been a long time. I'm happy to see you, hey. You've worked on Glengarry, how many years now?"

"I came to work for Baas Angus in 1988, Sir. Twenty years, now."

"*Ja*, it's been a very long time."

As Tobiwa pulled open the gates, Angus appeared at the back door and the dogs rushed forward to greet him. As he fondled their heads, he looked towards the Land Rover and waved. Van Rooyen drove through the gate and parked beside several other vehicles on the left side of the house.

"Hey Piet, it's bloody good to see you again," Angus boomed, stepping forward, to pump his hand. Afterwards, they slapped each other on the back as the dogs sized up the visitor by sniffing van Rooyen's shoes, and nosing up his calf-length socks.

Angus made an imposing figure. He was tall, powerfully built, and with a full head of dark, brown hair liberally sprinkled with gray. His graying mustache and goatee were neatly trimmed.

"Thanks for the invite, Angus. I brought a small birthday gift for Patsy," he said, holding out a box wrapped in wax paper—his Titambire Fish and Bait Shop had been fresh out of gift wrapping. Van Rooyen had searched the shelves for a gift for Patsy, and had finally settled on a recipe book, entitled Wild Game and Fish Recipes. He hoped she'd like the gift.

"Come in and give it to her yourself," Angus said, leading the way back into the house as the dogs barked and scampered around them. "Quiet, Zimbo. Stay." Angus commanded, as he stroked the Labrador's head.

"Good looking dogs," van Rooyen commented.

"We like 'em. Zimbo's been with us for quite a few years. He must be at least seven years old now. The ridgeback's younger. We got Skellum from a farmer in the district who booked it to Australia a couple of years ago. We kept her original name, which she lives up to, once in a while," he chuckled.

Van Rooyen found the name amusing. Skellum, meant rogue in Afrikaans. The dog reminded him of Jock, the ridgeback he'd once owned. His eyes moistened, and he unobtrusively swiped at them.

"Outside. Stay." Angus barked orders to the dogs, as he held the door open for van Rooyen. Together they walked through to a screened verandah in the back, which ran the full width of the house. The homestead stood on a rise, overlooking the picturesque, Hunyani mountain range.

"What are you drinking, Piet? Angus asked.

"Beer's fine, thanks."

"Lion or Castle?"

"Lion, please."

"Coming up."

Angus's wife Patsy walked over to greet van Rooyen.

At fifty she held her age extremely well, he thought. Few strands of gray were visible in her shoulder-length, blonde hair. Although she'd added a few pounds over the years, with her height of five feet, ten, she carried the weight well. In a sleeveless, pink and mauve, light summer dress, she was still a splendid looking woman, van Rooyen thought.

"Hello Piet," Patsy said, approaching him with a friendly smile. "Thank you so much for coming. It's so nice to see you again, and I must say, you're looking as handsome as ever." She winked, and stepped forward to give him a quick hug.

The unexpected compliment brought color to his cheeks. "You don't look too bad, yourself," he returned with a smile. "Thanks for inviting me. I'm glad to be here, hey, and happy birthday!" He handed her the gift.

An attractive young, twenty-something, blonde stepped forward, eyeing him with a shy smile. She took the present from Patsy.

"Hello Mr. van Rooyen," she said. Then turning to Patsy, she added, "Mum, I'll put this on the table with the other gifts and you can open them all after supper."

"Piet, do you remember our daughter, Libby? She was probably only a schoolgirl, the last time you saw her." Patsy handed over the gift.

"My goodness, Libby." Van Rooyen's eyebrows arched in surprise. "I swear I would never have recognized you."

"You haven't changed a bit, Mr. van Rooyen," Libby said. "Nick's busy right now," she said, pointing outside towards the swimming pool area where a young man was stoking the cooking fire. "That's my husband, Nick Coetzee. I really want you to meet him."

"Good. I'd like that," van Rooyen replied, as Angus arrived with a tall mug of beer and guided him towards Dave and Joyce Packer.

"Here Piet, take a seat." Angus pulled up a couple of chairs.

The Packers had farmed next door to the McLarens for decades and van Rooyen knew them well.

"Damn Piet, it's good to see you again." Dave leaned forward to shake his hand.

"I'm happy to see you both, too." Van Rooyen shook their hands. "It's been a few years. Are you still teaching, Joyce? Brian loved having you as his teacher."

Although she had to be pushing sixty, clearly she was still vigorous in both mind and body. He hoped the mention of his late son, would not make her feel awkward. In contrast, her husband seemed to have aged significantly. Dave had lost weight and his hair had thinned. He was now very gray.

"I would have taught school longer, Piet," Joyce said, "if I'd had more pupils like Brian. I gave up teaching last year. The job became just too difficult. Too many AIDS orphans," she explained. "And without parents to guide them and pay their school fees, many stopped coming to school. A lot were recruited into the Green Bombers. In the end, I'm afraid I just gave up," Joyce admitted with a glum expression.

Van Rooyen was familiar with the Green Bombers, Mugabe's well-known youth militia, named for their green uniforms. The international community first learned of them through a BBC Panorama television program. The piece, broadcasted in 2004, contained footage of their training camp activities. Like many Zimbabweans, he had his first, behind-the-scenes, look at the Green Bombers on satellite TV. The program showed the government subjecting thousands of innocent boys to rape, brainwashing, and brutality—all designed to mold youths to be loyal to Robert Mugabe and ZANU-PF, by teaching them to torture and kill.

Patsy approached and van Rooyen rose to his feet.

"Piet I want you to meet a good friend of ours, Sylvia Rogers. Her parents, John and Elizabeth Rogers farmed in Darwendale. You may remember he was one of the farmers attacked in 2000. Tragically, John was bludgeoned to death and although his wife, Elizabeth, survived the invasion, she died shortly afterwards of cancer."

Van Rooyen vaguely remembered the name.

Patsy took his arm and led him towards a petite, dark haired, young woman who stood looking out over the Hunyani Hills. In contrast to the other guests who were dressed in casual attire, Sylvia wore a slinky, black dress with a low, sequin-encrusted neckline. The outfit seemed more fitting for a night on the town, than for an outdoor *braaivleis*.

"Sylvia, this is Piet van Rooyen," Patsy said. "He used to be one of our neighbors. Now he's in Kariba keeping an eye on the wildlife in the eastern Zambezi Valley. He gave a most fascinating presentation three weeks ago at the Harare Rifle Club."

"Well, hello Piet," the young woman intoned in a low, sultry voice. "I wish I'd been there to hear it."

She didn't come across as an outdoorsy type, and van Rooyen doubted she'd have any interest in anything he had to say. Nonetheless, he owed it to Patsy to be polite to her guest.

"Sylvia, it's nice to meet you," he said politely.

They spoke for a few minutes. Because they had both shared a tragic life experience, he forced himself to listen to her rambling and mundane discourse. But as soon as he was able, he devised an exit strategy. Since he and this woman were evidently the only unattached people at the gathering, he wondered if Patsy had been trying to play matchmaker. He cursed himself thoroughly for not having asked Angus if he could bring a date. He could have brought Jessica and sidestepped this dilemma. Oh well, he'd know better next time.

"Sylvia, excuse me," van Rooyen said. "I haven't met Libby's new husband yet, and in case they leave early I'd better go and introduce myself."

He escaped with a sigh of relief and exited the verandah through a screen door onto the fieldstone patio, which adjoined the swimming pool. Angus and his son-in-law were turning over the juicy, fire-braised steaks and *boerewors* sausages on the grill. The savory cooking smells made his mouth water.

"Hey, you blokes have got enough food here to feed an army. Can I help?"

"I think we've got things under control, Piet," Angus replied. "By the way, have you met my son-in-law, Nick Coetzee?"

"No, I haven't. Pleased to meet you Nick," van Rooyen smiled and shook his outstretched hand.

Nick was a tall man, well muscled, with light brown hair and a tawny mustache and goatee. Definitely good husband material, he thought. Meanwhile, around the side of the house, van Rooyen heard Angus's two dogs barking excitedly as they jumped up behind a wrought-iron gate.

"Piet, Angus has been telling me all about your interesting work with wildlife in the valley and your shop in Kariba," Nick said. Before van Rooyen was able to respond, Patsy announced the food was ready.

"Everyone, come outside and help yourselves," she called out.

"Never mind, Piet. We'll catch up later. Carry on."

Van Rooyen joined the line of guests, to pick up a paper plate. After Nick forked off pieces of meat from the grill, he joined other guests selecting accompaniments from a wide array of side dishes laid out on a long table. There were bread rolls, a lettuce and tomato salad, corn-on-the-cob, baked potatoes, and a myriad assorted spreads, sauces, and relishes. Afterwards, with plates piled high, everyone returned to the verandah.

Outdoors, the sun was sinking fast. Between mouthfuls, Angus's and Patsy's guests engaged in lively conversation. Outside, however, the dogs were creating a commotion. Isaiah, the house servant, appeared in the doorway and Angus looked up.

"Yes, Isaiah?"

"Baas, some people at the gate. They want to talk to you."

"Do you know them?" Angus asked, rising to his feet.

"No, Baas," Isaiah said, and retreated to the kitchen.

Angus followed, and in five minutes rejoined his guests.

"There may be a security problem here," he told everyone. "I'd be more comfortable if you'd all come back inside the house."

His request caused an immediate stir; everyone started speaking at once. Angus raised his hand to get everyone's attention.

"What's going on?" Patsy's eyebrows lifted.

"There are ten Africans outside the gate." Angus explained to the group. "One of them is holding up a piece of paper, which he claims gives him the ownership of this farm and he's giving us twenty-four hours to get off."

His words prompted a sharp intake of breath from the group, and Van

Rooyen's heart sank. Was this the way it happened to Sandie? That was seven years ago and it seemed unbelievable how so little had changed since then. Nonetheless, everyone in Zimbabwe knew lawlessness and unrest would continue as long as Mugabe remained in power.

"According to our gate guard," Angus continued, "they arrived about fifteen minutes ago in a decrepit, blue, Datsun pickup. They ordered him to open the security gate, but thankfully, he didn't. He told them the *Baas* had the keys. Smart chap. Anyway, I've got to go and sort it out with these people. So, in the meantime, everyone stay put."

"Angus, I'm coming with you." Van Rooyen got to his feet, remembering how his friend had responded to his own family's call for help, years ago.

The two men walked through to the kitchen, while everyone else streamed back inside to the living room. Patsy closed the door leading out on the verandah and locked it. From the ferocity of their growls and snarls, the dogs seemed to be freaking out. The rattling of the wire mesh indicated they were leaping up against the security fence. Van Rooyen felt a wrench in his gut.

Just seconds before he and Angus reached the back door, they heard a short burst of gunfire, followed by a yelp, then frantic barking from a single dog. As the two men approached the back gate, Angus felt for the gate keys in the pocket of his shorts. The time was now half-past six and the sun had already dipped below the horizon.

In the gloom, they saw a man they surmised to be the group leader standing at the fence with an AK-47 rifle slung casually over his shoulder. Three other members of his retinue also carried machine guns. One of them had his rifle barrel leveled at the house. The remainder of the group was armed with pangas or knobkerries. The leader wore a stained, yellow tee shirt, a pair of rumpled trousers, and a dirty stained Panama hat, decorated with a zebra-skin, hatband. On his feet was a pair of dirty Nikes, without laces. His rag-tag companions, some barefoot, were similarly attired. Van Rooyen detected a strong whiff of alcohol.

"Who are you?" Angus demanded through the fence. "And what do you want?"

"I am Comrade Disaster, and this paper is signed by the Minister of Agriculture and it says Glengarry Farm is mine," he shouted, waving a typewritten page belligerently in Angus's face. "You must leave right now," the man demanded.

Van Rooyen murmured to his friend. "The law says you need to receive an official extradition order, to be evicted."

"Who are you? A lawyer?" Disaster sneered, stepping closer and flapping the paper at van Rooyen.

Grabbing the document through a gap between the fence and the gate, van Rooyen held it long enough to read a few paragraphs, before the Comrade snatched it back.

Van Rooyen turned to Angus, his face flushed with anger. "This is not an official government, Section eight acquisition order," he said. "It's just an application for land tenure, completed by someone called Ishmael Gondo."

"Are you Mr. Gondo?" Angus demanded of the Comrade.

"That's not your business," Disaster snarled, folding the piece of paper and shoving it deep into his trouser pocket.

"Comrade Disaster, or whoever you are, this is private property. You and your friends had better get the bloody hell out of here, right now!" Angus's face was contorted with rage. "If you come back, I will call the police."

There was no response, bar a few snickers. Angus and van Rooyen turned back towards the house. Van Rooyen looked back over his shoulder. All ten men stood behind the security fence in the now-floodlit yard, poking their fingers through the wire mesh. They shook the chain-link, and began belting out political slogans in Shona.

"*Phasi ne murungu* ,down with the white man; *pambere ne ZANU-PF,* up with ZANU-PF."

"Piet, there's no point in entering into any further discussion with these buggers. Let's go inside."

Skellum appeared from the side of the house, her tail between her legs. Whimpering, she ran straight for Angus and sidled up against him.

"What in the bloody hell's wrong with this dog?" Angus said. "I've never known her to act like this before. Where's Zimbo?"

As the chanting continued, van Rooyen scanned the front yard, inside the fence, and his eyes focused on a dark shape lying in the shadow of the gate shed. He moved closer and saw the black dog's slumped body. He returned to Angus's side, nudged him, and pointed to the shed.

Angus walked over and knelt beside the dog, searching for signs of life. Van Rooyen joined him and pointed to the dog's multiple bullet wounds and the large bloodstain on the ground.

"He's gone," Angus said, rising to his feet. "I'll bury him tomorrow. Piet, don't say anything when we go back inside. I'll break the news to Patsy later. Zimbo was her favorite. She doesn't need to hear this on her birthday. In the meantime, I'll have Tobiwa take Skellum around to the pool house."

Before retreating indoors, Angus turned back to face the gate. "Bloody, fucking murderers," he bellowed, shaking a clenched fist at the men behind the fence. His face turned beet red. "That's all you are, fucking murderers! I hope you all rot in hell!"

"Come, let's go inside," van Rooyen said, guiding his friend through the kitchen door.

Angus found Isaiah in the kitchen and instructed him to tell Tobiwa to take Skellum to the pool house.

"Also get some stew beef out of the fridge, and tell him to give it to Skellum." Turning to van Rooyen, he added, "Poor dog. She needs a nice treat after seeing her buddy shot."

The conversation hushed as the two men returned to the living room. All eyes were fixed on them. Angus plunked himself down on the settee next to Patsy.

"I've told them to get the bloody hell out of here." With a deep frown, he scanned the glum faces of his family members and friends. Noticing Patsy's trembling lips, he wrapped an arm around her. "We'll fight this, Hon," he reassured her. "We're not going to let them take away everything we've worked so hard for these last thirty years."

Van Rooyen's heart went out to his friends. Although Angus was putting a positive spin on the situation for Patsy, he knew they would soon have to confront the inevitable. Like many hundreds of Zimbabwe farmers before them, robbed of their land and their livelihoods, they'd eventually discover that where there's no law, there's no hope.

Van Rooyen knew the guests at Patsy's birthday celebration realized the uninvited visitors were members of one of Mugabe's paid gangs, dispatched to farming districts to terrorize the country's white farmers and chase them off their land. While these terrorists called themselves war veterans, it was widely known that almost all of them were too young to have fought in Zimbabwe's war for independence, which ended thirty years before, in 1979. In reality, most were unemployed radicals, recruited by ZANU-PF.

Outside, they heard bursts of automatic rifle fire. From the homestead's southeast side came thuds from bullets, as they hit the brick walls, and the shattering of broken glass. Van Rooyen prayed Isaiah, Tobiwa, and Skellum were safe.

"Quick, turn out the lights so they don't know what part of the house we're in," Angus said, before striding back into the kitchen to peer out the window. Libby and Patsy leapt up to switch off the interior lights.

Van Rooyen followed Angus into the kitchen and they were joined by Dave Packer. They discovered a terrified Isaiah, cowering under the kitchen table. Chagrined, he emerged to assure Angus he'd given the meat and instructions to Tobiwa. Outside the shooting stopped, and the four men observed through the window as the gang reappeared from the darkness into the floodlit yard. Except for the Comrade, they all piled into the blue pickup. Their leader approached the gate.

"We are going now. But we'll be back!" he yelled. "And, if you are still here, you and your workers will be very sorry!"

He climbed into the Datsun's front passenger seat, and the small pickup, straining under its load, pulled forward slowly, backfired, and then turned down the hill, gathering speed.

As van Rooyen's eyes followed the vehicle's single, red taillight as it disappeared into the night, he hoped its occupants wouldn't take pot shots at Angus's cattle as they drove by the pastures.

Dave Packer sighed. "I wonder when they're going to show up at my place, if they haven't already." Wearing deep frowns, Dave, Angus, and van Rooyen returned to the living room.

"Phone me when you get home, Dave, and keep me posted," Angus said. "I'm going to contact all the farmers in the district, tonight, and schedule an urgent meeting tomorrow."

"Will you phone the police?" van Rooyen asked him.

"No, but I'll go down to the station and file an incident report tomorrow, not that it'll do any good," Angus muttered.

"There's no point in phoning them tonight," he said. "They'll just tell me it's political and they can't do anything about it. Or they'll say they've got no petrol," he continued, his voice rising several decibels. "It just means I'll need to drive down to the police station to pick up a sergeant and bring him out here to investigate. Then after his investigation, he'll just repeat that it's political and they can do bugger-all about it. Damn it, it's all so bloody ridiculous, and it's not worth wasting my damn time."

Van Rooyen sympathized. He was all too familiar with typical, police run-around.

The occasion's earlier gaiety had been soundly doused and the mood was somber. Van Rooyen tackled the remains of his cold dinner, but after a couple of mouthfuls, he carried his mostly uneaten meal into the kitchen and left the plate next to the sink. His appetite was gone.

Libby and Joyce Packer made a valiant attempt to restore the earlier mood by rolling out Patsy's birthday cake and handing her gifts to unwrap. She seemed pleased with the cookbook and Van Rooyen breathed a sigh of relief. Afterwards, the party broke up and guests started to leave.

"Be sure to phone us when you get home, so we know you arrived okay," Patsy said, as she walked van Rooyen to the Land Rover.

Angus held open the security gate, and he and Patsy waved him a forlorn goodbye as he drove through. Van Rooyen's heart ached for them. He knew the anguish they'd be forced to endure in the upcoming hours, days, weeks, months, even years. In addition to being neighbors, he and Sandie had been close friends of the McLarens and the Packers. Tonight he felt guilty, selfish, and uncaring for having purposefully avoided them these past seven years.

Chapter 13

Tuesday August 26, 2008

Webster Kumale, a 30-year-old scout with the Zimbabwe Parks and Management Authority, was cycling along a dirt trail bordering the Hurungwe Safari Area. It was late afternoon and he was returning home to his village after a hard day's work.

Mukuru, a towering, 40-year-old, bull elephant was nearby, obscured by the tall grass and brush. He had been hanging out with the bull herd, but when they had moved on several days before, he was not able to follow them. A barbed-wire snare, coiled tightly around his right, rear ankle was causing him acute pain. Over recent weeks, the wire strands had become deeply imbedded in his flesh. His leg, now seriously infected, was swollen to almost twice its size, and the wound was oozing blood and pus.

Webster saw the lone elephant too late. He had already passed the bull's huge, tree trunk, legs when he detected some movement out of the corner of his eye. He looked back and realized his situation was dire. With adrenaline pulsing, he pedaled away as fast as he could to his village five hundred yards away.

Kumale was riding a brand-new bicycle he had recently purchased after saving every penny he could tuck away for the past two years. He was proud of his modern, mountain bike. Its wheels didn't squeak like those of cheaper bicycles. Its wide, heavy-duty off-road tires, hissed as he pedaled along in the soft, sandy dirt.

The hissing sound alarmed the elephant. Both the infection and pain in his leg had muddled his brain. It revived a long-buried memory of a fatal snake attack he once witnessed upon a one-year-old calf. His sibling's killer had been Africa's second most poisonous viper – the venomous, hissing, puff adder. Panicked, Mukuru's reflexes spun into attack mode.

He let out an ear-piercing, trumpet and took off in pursuit of his imagined aggressor. The pain in his right, rear foot, and ankle was intense. He was so consumed with revenge, it mattered not that he was pursuing a man on a bicycle, rather than the hated and feared reptile. The wet secretions dribbling down both sides of his face, revealed he was a bull in musth, overcome with aggression from the high levels of testosterone coursing through his veins. With ears spread wide, his trunk curled up against his chest, and his tusks bobbing ahead of him, he closed the gap in seconds and plucked Kumale off his bicycle with his trunk.

Webster's screams of terror began long before the bull reached him. His high-pitched wail stopped abruptly as his body hit the ground, raising a cloud of dust. Raw fear gave him the strength to scramble back onto his feet to keep running. Impeding his ability, however, were several broken ribs and a punctured lung. Mukuru trumpeted and again bore down on the young game scout. The beast was so close that Kumale could hear the raspy swish of its ears brushing against its sides. He felt a tug on his shoulder and he screamed, ripping off his torn uniform shirt to free himself.

It was too late. He heard a deep groan and realized it came from himself. Then all was silent, almost too quiet, and he knew his end was near. His hearing was gone, and his head battered. It felt as if a giant log had clubbed him on the head and split it open. Spit, blood, and teeth spewed from his mouth, staining the tall grass where he lay. Then his sight dimmed and the world disappeared.

*　　　　*　　　　*

On Thursday morning, Blair Nisbet was at his desk in the Harare headquarters of Nisbet Safaris & Hunting Outfitters, (Pvt.) Ltd., the largest hunting, and safari operation in Zimbabwe. As company CEO, he was poring over a recently negotiated contract between Nisbet Safaris and the Zimbabwe Parks and Management Authority. It called for the culling of three thousand elephants in the Zambezi Valley over the next three years.

The word 'culling' had attained such a negative connotation, worldwide, that Victor Sebakwe, Zimbabwe's Minister of Tourism, ordered the director for Zimbabwe Parks and Wildlife Authority, Nelson Zanunga, to turn the job over to local safari and hunting operations. From now on, local elephant population control would be called 'hunting,' not 'culling.'

A shrewd Scotsman, ever watchful over his company's financial transactions, Blair was satisfied with the deal his firm was offered. Terms of the contract stipulated that in return for the meat, hides, and tusks of all elephants killed, the Authority would issue preferred hunting permits to his clients allowing a single hunter to shoot as many as 10 elephants during a single hunt. The fee per elephant would be U.S. $1,000, fifty percent payable in advance, with the outstanding balance due at the conclusion of the hunt, prior to the hunter departing the country.

Blair's clients each paid U.S. $25,000 for a 14-day elephant and plains game hunting safari. It included transportation between the Harare airport and the Nisbet Safari Lodge in the Hurungwe Safari Area, meals, and accommodations at the lodge or in luxury, outdoor hunting camps, in addition to the services of a professional hunter with a team of wildlife trackers and scouts. Included was a camp chef and waiters to take care of the hunters' culinary needs. For each additional elephant, clients paid a U.S. $2,000 premium.

Five clients were flying in from New York tomorrow. Nisbet's hunt schedule was full until Christmas. While he perused it, the telephone rang. His receptionist told him Nelson Zanunga was on the line.

"Good morning General," Nisbet said.

"Blair I've got a job for you. There's a rogue elephant over in the Hurungwe. It killed one of our scouts, Webster Kumale, two days ago."

"I need a description of the culprit, so we can zero in on it."

"Get it from Kaminjolo," Zanunga barked and hung up.

Nisbet punched the intercom to get his receptionist back on the phone. "Carol, get Hector Kaminjolo on the phone."

While awaiting Hector's call, Blair stared out his fourth floor office window, which looked across Samora Machel Avenue to the Harare Gardens with its tall Cyprus and palm trees. A pretty sight, he thought, even though he admitted it couldn't compare to his beloved, heather-strewn highlands of Scotland. At times, he definitely missed his homeland. Moments later the phone interrupted his reverie.

"Carol, did you get him?"

"He's on the other line."

"Hello Blair. Kaminjolo here. You wanted to speak to me?"

"Greetings Hector. I got a call from your boss a *wee* while ago. He wants me to hunt down a rogue elephant of yours in the Hurungwe. He told me to get a description from *ye*. I *dinnae* want to end up, shooting the wrong bugger."

"I'm still trying to get the information, Blair. We've been talking to the victim's family to see if we can get a description from them."

"Well, as soon as you hear something let me know. I've got a group of hunters flying in from New York in the *morn*. You can get me on my cell phone if I'm not in the office."

*   *   *

Earlier, John Chitsaru, the Chief Ranger at Mana Pools National Park, had received a call from Kaminjolo directing him to investigate the elephant attack and provide a description of the offending elephant. With an initial report in hand, Chitsaru drove over to the village of Lalapanzi with his scout, Albert, to have family members guide him to the victim's body.

"*Masikati, makadini*" Chitsaru said in Shona, using a respectful greeting to wish the dozen-or-so villagers a good afternoon.

"*Ndiripo kana wakadiniwo,*" an elderly man replied with the traditional, polite response.

After identifying himself, Chitsaru asked the villagers to take him to Webster Kumale's body. The village headman nodded, gestured towards a footpath taking off into the bush, and stepped forward to lead the way. Chitsaru and Albert followed with the remaining villagers, with women and children, bringing up the rear. Mothers carried infants on their backs, while grasping the hands of other young children.

It was a short, five minute walk. The body, surrounded by tall grass, was splattered with dried blood. While officials looked on, Webster's neighbors and family members stood back shuffling their feet and murmuring softly, too afraid to come closer for fear of inciting angry spirits. Chitsaru and Albert stepped forward with a stretcher and loaded up the body.

Webster left behind a wife, three children, and a new bicycle. The latter being his family's sole inheritance, aside from a small amount in monetary compensation that his widow would receive from the CAMPFIRE program, in compensation for losses inflicted by wildlife.

A procession of mourners followed Webster's body back to the village. The women ululated, voicing traditional, shrill, wordless lamentations of grief. Back at the village, the officials placed the remains into the back of Chitsaru's pickup and after thanking the villagers and bidding them farewell, left for the local police station in Makuti, forty miles away. There, the district administrator would issue a death certificate and release the body to the family. Rarely was a post mortem performed, unless the deceased was a figure of national importance, which Webster was not.

Later, on Thursday, Chitsaru rounded up several scouts and headed back to Hurungwe to identify the elephant responsible. They began their search close to where they'd found Webster's body. They found footprints and a blood trail leading to where the Nyakasanga River flowed into the Zambezi. There they located the bull. Chitsaru reported it to Kaminjolo, informing his boss the animal was unlikely to stray due to a severely injured rear leg.

Chapter 14

Saturday, August 30, 2008

At six thirty in the morning, van Rooyen was relaxing on the rear deck of his houseboat, savoring his first cup of tea. The houseboat's anchorage was in a quiet inlet on Lake Kariba within the Charara Safari Area. He had found its location to be a mixed blessing. While he enjoyed viewing wildlife close up, he'd occasionally had to repair bullet holes in his home's exterior, the result of an errant hunter's misfired shot. Fortunately, he had never been home at the time.

From his rear deck, he had an unfettered view of a brilliant blue, inland sea that stretched for miles. Looking westward, the only visible shoreline was a distant promontory, which protruded from the Matusadona National Park. With a powerful pair of binoculars, he could watch elephants drinking and playing at the lakeshore.

He ran a hand through his tousled, dark hair and felt the day-old, stubble on his chin. Clad only in a pair of shorts, he briefly toyed with the notion of getting dressed, but was enjoying the quiet solitude and because he had no pressing plans for the day, he discarded the idea. It was still early enough for the sun to remain hidden behind the hills of the escarpment for at least another twenty minutes or so. The temperature was still a comfortable seventy-five degrees Fahrenheit, but he knew by lunchtime it would be in the high nineties.

In the week since the incident at Glengarry Farm, he had spoken to

Angus on the phone several times. His friend told him the gang returned the next day to hammer pegs all over the farm to claim their individual lots. Consequently, he had moved Patsy and the dog off the farm, sending them to stay with a relative in Harare.

Angus also reported that invaders had occupied the Packer's farm and several others in the district that day. More recently, he said, Comrade Disaster had stolen his tractor and trailer to cart his farm workers off to centralized, district re-education classes, presided over by ZAPU-PF. He said the thugs beat all who resisted, raped their women, and torched their houses, while Police refused to intervene. Van Rooyen felt a deep empathy for his friends and their workers.

He wondered how Jessica was doing. It was three weeks since their dinner date. He cursed himself for acting like such a cold fish that evening. Granted he was nervous. It was the first time in seven years that he'd taken a woman out on a date. But instead of relaxing and enjoying the evening, he spent the entire time imagining Sandy staring at him with an anguished look. If Jessica was hurt by his aloofness, she certainly hadn't shown it. Perhaps she was not as interested in him, as he hoped.

The phone rang and he went inside to answer it.

"Piet, this is Jessica."

His chest tightened in exhilaration.

"I apologize for calling so early, but I wanted to speak to you before you left." She sounded rushed.

"It's okay. I'm already up," he said.

"Something's come up. I urgently need to find a bull elephant before one of Blair Nisbet's hunters destroys him. Could you fly me over the Hurungwe Safari Area and Mana Pools to track him down?"

"I've got no commitments for today. What time do you want to leave?"

"As soon as possible?"

"What if I meet you at the airport at seven thirty? Is that too soon?

"Not at all. I'll be there, and thank you," she said and hung up.

Fired up at the prospect of seeing her again, he hurriedly shaved, donned a light blue cotton shirt, shorts, calf-length socks, and a pair of veldskoens. After running a comb through his hair, he was in the driver's seat, starting the Land Rover, all in the space of fifteen minutes.

He arrived at the airport with five minutes to spare, bounded upstairs to the tower to file his flight plan, and was back in the main concourse ten minutes later to find Jessica sitting on a bench in the departure lounge.

"Ready to go?"

She rose and they walked out to his Cessna, parked a hundred yards from the terminal building. He noticed in passing the Air Zimbabwe, MA60 turboprop still sat idle on the apron.

"What's going on?" he said.

"In brief, a Zim Parks' scout was trampled yesterday, and we must find the offending elephant before he's shot."

"Have they identified it?"

"Parks suspects it's one of my study bulls, Mukuru. He's the sole survivor of a family that was culled back in 1983. It's critically important, genetically, that we save him."

"Why? If he's a rogue elephant and man-killer, perhaps he should be destroyed."

She faced him, her green eyes flashing.

"I see," she retorted. "You obviously believe in execution without a fair trial!" Without giving him a chance to respond, she continued. "First of all, we need to find out what prompted his attack. Elephants, as a rule, rarely attack humans or other animals unless deliberately provoked. It usually happens when they're protecting a calf or family member, or under other extenuating circumstances. Secondly, there's his gene pool to consider."

"What about his gene pool – what do you mean?"

"Most of the remaining breeding bulls in the eastern, Zambezi Valley are related, in one way or another, to matriarchs, Chembere and Muchengeti. Therefore, without an influx of Mukuru's genes into the population, the descendants of these herds will become in-bred and, over time, weakened genetically."

"I get it." Her attention to the finer details impressed him. "So where are we headed?"

"I'm told Mukuru was last seen in the vicinity of the Nyakasanga River, west of Mana Pools."

"Then he shouldn't be too difficult to find."

During the flight, he told Jessica about his previous weekend's visit to Angus and Patsy's farm and described all that had happened to the Karoi farmers subsequently. As the story unfolded, her frown lines deepened.

"I've read a lot about these farm invasions since they began," she said. "But this is the first time I've heard the gritty details. How horrendous! These land grabs have been going on now for more than seven years. I just don't understand how such things can possibly continue this way. Did they call the police?"

"Jessica, you have to understand the politics here in Zimbabwe." He recounted all he'd recently learned from Angus.

"Oh my God, Piet, I just can't imagine such things happening in the States. I'd fire the whole damn police force."

"We can't blame individual police constables. They're in an untenable position. If they didn't follow orders, they'd be labeled as Mugabe's enemies and could be tortured and killed. It all goes back to the fact that, under Mugabe and his ZANU-PF cronies, this country has no rule of law. The politicians are corrupt; so are the police and the courts."

"Why does anyone stay here? Why do you stay?" she said, throwing up her hands in exasperation.

"I stay because, along with my partners in the Wildlife Protection League, I think I can make a difference and perhaps help put a stop to, or at least slow down, the wholesale slaughter of this county's wildlife. Other people, of all races, stay because they've simply nowhere else to go. Farmers and business owners who've lost everything have no capital to start again elsewhere; farm workers who've lost their jobs, their homes, and communities, where do they go?"

Jessica realized, for Piet, her question hit a raw nerve. He stared straight ahead with a grim expression. For several minutes, no one spoke. Finally he continued.

"The elderly have been hit the worst. Inflation has stripped them of their pensions and all their savings. I count it a blessing in many ways that my folks are in a happier place and never had to deal with this bloody mess."

"Before I came here, Piet, I'd never seen troubles like this. I think many Americans, myself included, tend to take our freedoms too much for granted."

"Maybe so, but let me throw the same question back at you. Why are you here? You could be back in America safe and secure, where I'm told your laws protect the people, instead of stripping them of their rights and possessions."

With arms folded and lips pursed, she contemplated the question. Then she responded.

"I'm here to work on my doctoral dissertation which, as you know, involves researching the behavior of African elephants. You do seem to have hundreds of specimens around here," she added with a sly grin.

"Is that it?"

"Pretty much."

At this juncture, however, Jessica wasn't sure if her newfound desire to get to know this man better could be another reason compelling her to stay.

*   *   *

The Nisbet Safari Lodge was perched on a granite hilltop, overlooked the Zambezi River. A natural stone façade covered the outer walls of the three-story, concrete structure. From a deck leading off the dining room, guests had a superb view of the river and, further north, a chain of mountains surrounding Africa's Great Rift Valley.

Emilio Sanchez and his son, John, visitors from Key Largo, Florida, were about to embark on their first African hunting safari. At five thirty on Saturday morning, they sipped coffee from Styrofoam cups, while awaiting the arrival of their hunting guide. While both men were accomplished anglers, this was their first trip to Africa and their first big game hunting expedition. Emilio owned and operated a successful, deep-sea fishing and boat rental concession on Florida's east coast. John would take over the business from his father one day.

For this trip, they booked an elephant hunt and three days of sport-fishing on Lake Kariba. They especially looked forward to their tiger-fishing excursion. Sport fishermen converged here from all over the world to hunt the elusive, hard-fighting, tiger fish that often reached a weight exceeding thirty pounds.

To date, the pair's actual game hunting experience had been limited to a few duck hunting forays into North Florida and Georgia. Emilio, however, an avid reader of Wilbur Smith novels, had harbored a life-long dream to hunt big game in Africa. While sitting on a Florida pier, six months before, looking east across the Atlantic Ocean toward the far-away, West African coast, he had decided now was the time.

Father and son were both stocky in build with nut-brown complexions. Only the graying spikes of hair, peeking from Emilio's baseball cap, and John's full beard, told them apart. As they awaited Blair Nisbet's arrival, dawn was slowly unfolding across the eastern horizon illuminating the sky with vivid swaths of fiery red, crimson, amber, and gold.

"*Guid mornin*," Nisbet boomed in his distinctive Scottish accent, as he strode across the deck towards them. "We've not met before. My driver, Dennis, picked you up at the airport. It's good to meet you Mr. Sanchez."

He and Emilio shook hands.

"Mr. Nisbet," Emilio said, gesturing to his younger, bearded double beside him. "This is my son, John."

"Please call me Blair. We *dinnae* stand on ceremony here," he said, as he reached to shake the younger man's hand.

Their host ushered them from the lodge and led them outside to his tan Land Cruiser, with the Nisbet Overland Safari logo painted in zebra stripes on both front cab doors. Its rear bed was fitted with two rows of elevated, upholstered seats.

"Emilio, would you like to sit up front?" Blair asked.

"Thanks, but no. John and I will be fine in the back – better view," the Floridian replied.

"Well, jump in lads," Blair said. "We're only going to drive for three or four miles and then we'll continue on foot. We have your water canteens, vests, rifles, and ammo in the cargo lockers under your seats. Oh, and packed lunches too."

"That's great! You think of everything." Emilio cheered, as he and John seated themselves.

"*Lads*, let me introduce you to our tracker, Sulemon, the most valuable member of our team." Blair pointed to the tall, black man who was approaching.

*   *   *

Sulemon wore a camouflage vest over olive-drab shorts and shirt and carried a long, wooden staff several inches taller than himself.

"Sulemon, this is Mr. Emilio Sanchez and his son John, from America."

"*Mangwanani*," Sulemon said, smiling up at Emilio and John, seated in the back of the vehicle. He studied the two men in their identical, safari-style outfits and chuckled inwardly. These two will need watching, he told himself. Then in response to their quizzical expressions, he said, "*Mangwanani* means good morning in Shona. Maybe you'll know a lot of Shona words before you go back to America?"

"Wonderful! And we can teach you some Spanish," was John's jovial response.

"That's good," Sulemon replied. "I want to learn it. How do you say *Mangwanani* in Spanish?"

"*Buenos dias,*" John replied.

Sulemon repeated the words, pronouncing them carefully.

Enjoying the banter, Blair chimed in with, "And in Scotland, we say, *guid mornin!*"

Everyone laughed.

With his boot propped on the running board, Blair looked up at his clients and with a serious expression said, "*Afore* we go, I need to give *ye* lads some strict safety rules. First, while *ye're* in the vehicle, stay in your seats at all times unless I tell *ye* to get out. Second: I understand that neither of you have hunted in Africa before, correct?"

"Uh ha," they both murmured in agreement.

"For *yer* safety, and ours too," Blair said, pointing to Sulemon and himself, "It's imperative that *ye* follow the rules."

"Of course," the men chorused.

"We hope each of *ye* will get to shoot an elephant today. I left some instructions in your room to describe how to aim your weapon, so that *ye* get a clean, lethal, brain shot. I hope *ye* took the time to read '*em.*"

Both men nodded.

Blair continued. "Rule number one is: only one hunter at a time can aim to shoot an animal. We'll have no Wild West shootouts here today! If that's what *ye're* looking for, *ye'll* find it back home in Tombstone, Arizona. Not here!"

Emilio and John laughed aloud, Sulemon chuckled, and even Blair's dour expression broke into a smile.

"How do we know who's supposed to shoot?" Emilio asked.

"*Och aye.* I was just *gettin'* to that," Blair said. "We'll toss a coin to decide who shoots the first elephant. Do either of *ye lads* have an American coin? Zimbabwe's currency is worthless nowadays, so we don't carry it around anymore."

"I've got a quarter," John said, leaning down and dropping the coin into Blair's outstretched palm.

"Okay, who's heads and who's tails?"

"I'll take heads and Dad will have tails," John replied, looking at his father with eyebrows raised.

"Good for me," Emilio nodded.

Blair tossed the quarter into the air. As it landed, he and Sulemon bent over to check the results.

"It's a bird," Sulemon reported. "So it's tails."

Blair scooped up the coin, showed its face to the hunters, and then turned it over to display the head of George Washington on its flip side. He tossed the coin back to John and announced, "Well, according to the coin toss, Emilio will shoot the first elephant. Everyone agreed?"

"We are," John replied.

"We'll be leavin' momentarily. We're goin' to start out searchin' for a particular bull Zim Parks has labeled as a rogue elephant."

"What's a rogue elephant?" Emilio said.

"It's an animal that's generally been making a nuisance of himself, pillaging crops and so forth." Blair chose not to frighten his clients unduly by telling them the bull was a known man-killer.

"We know he has an injury of some kind," he said. "The Mana Pools park ranger, who's been tracking him, told us one of his rear feet has left blood stains. We're going to be drivin' over to the area where he was last seen, and from there we'll proceed on foot."

The morning sun was already peeking above the horizon when Blair and Sulemon climbed into the cab of the Toyota. With Blair at the wheel, they drove south of the lodge, left the road, and ploughed through several miles of bush until they arrived at the dry, sandy-bottomed, Nyakasanga River.

Blair parked close to the riverbank, under a tree, and climbed down from the cab.

"From here we'll be goin' on foot," he said.

The two clients alighted and Sulemon pulled all the equipment from the cargo lockers. He handed everyone camouflage vests, web belts, canteens, rifles, ammunition, and packed lunches, leaving it up to his boss to demonstrate the proper use of the gear.

"This is how *ye* do it," Blair said, strapping on his web belt and attaching his canteen. After donning the vest, he showed John and Emilio the appropriate pockets for storing their ammo, rations and other personal items. Afterwards, he supervised the loading of the rifles, ensuring the men knew where the safety clip was located. Finally, Blair demonstrated the safest and best way to carry the weapon.

Sulemon, meanwhile, circled the area looking for elephant spoor. It took him less than five minutes to spot fresh tracks.

"Over here," he called out.

Blair approached and Sulemon pointed to the spoor, explaining it could be three days old. He also showed him the dried blood stains next to the nearby footprints.

"His injury looks bad. Maybe he hasn't gone far," Sulemon said. "We should follow."

"Everyone ready?" Blair called out.

"Ready," Emilio replied, slipping a roll of mints into a vest pocket.

"While we're on the move, maintain a strict silence," Blair instructed. "Too much chit-chat and we'll miss important sights and sounds and possible dangers. Remember, there are wild animals out here. Aside from elephants, we could run into lions, leopards, cheetahs, a rhino, or even one of those dodgy, Cape buffalos."

Once they set off, Blair and his clients trooped behind Sulemon, who followed the elephant spoor. Sulemon expressed confidence the tracks would lead them to their intended quarry—the 40-year-old, bull elephant. As the animal traveled south, away from the Zambezi, his footprints were clearly visible in the sandy, Nyakasanga riverbed.

For an hour and a half, they trod south. Along the way, they came across herds of impala, giraffe browsing from treetops, herds of grazing zebra and wildebeest, and the grisly remains of a lion kill denuded by scavengers of all its flesh.

As mid-morning approached, the temperature rose. Sulemon followed the elephant spoor where it left the river and headed into thick mopani woodland. Even though tracking became more difficult on the forest floor strewn with dead leaves, Sulemon ably continued the pursuit.

"This man knows his stuff," Emilio whispered to John, who nodded.

With rifles at the ready, the group made its way up several inclines. The leafless trees offered them little protection from the relentless sun, and sweat drenched their clothing. They entered an open, lightly wooded glade, and Blair sidled up next to Sulemon and murmured in his ear.

"I was sure we'd have run into the bull before now. We've gone almost five miles. How's your canteen? We may need to make a plan to get more water if canteens get too low. The Americans have been drinking a lot."

Before Sulemon had time to respond, a towering, dark mass filled his field of vision. An elephant crashed through a thorn thicket ahead and bore down on them.

"Take aim, Emilio," Blair shouted.

With shaking hands, Emilio aimed his rifle, released the safety, and trained his sights on the bull's forehead.

Mukuru was almost upon them.

"Fire," Blair bellowed.

Just as Blair gave the order to fire, Mukuru, already weakened by loss of blood, stumbled over a large tree stump and fell forward, impaling his tusks in the sandy soil. Emilio's bullet missed its mark, passing inches above the elephant's head.

At once, there was mass confusion. Everyone heard the shot and assumed Emilio's bullet had brought the elephant down. Mukuru lay prostrate fewer than five yards from Blair. From above came the drone of a low-flying aircraft. All four men looked up; unaware the elephant was struggling to its feet.

Now upright, the massive beast lunged at Blair and knocked him to the ground. Seconds later, he turned and scooped up the man's motionless body with his tusks. Emilio fired a second shot, which glanced off the elephant's massive shoulder, inflicting no more than a flesh wound. Filled with fury, Mukuru spun around to face his tormentors and with Blair lying suspended across his giant tusks, he let out a deafening trumpet and charged.

Too afraid to fire their weapons and accidentally shoot Blair, the men raced for the tree line. Due to the great pain in his leg, Mukuru was unable to give chase and instead lowered his head, allowing the man to roll down onto ground. He then limped away into the bush.

After the bull departed, the remaining members of the hunting party hurried back to check on Blair. Again, they heard an aircraft flying overhead. Their attention, however, was focused on the man lying unconscious at their feet. Sulemon checked his boss's vital signs. Blair was breathing, but had a barely detectable pulse. In all his years as a tracker, Sulemon had never before seen a bull elephant back away from a fight.

"Don't move him," Sulemon instructed. "Maybe his back is broken."

"What can we do?" Emilio asked. "Do you think the people in that plane up there saw what happened?"

"If they did, I hope they'll call for help?" John added.

"It is five miles back to the vehicle. Maybe I will run back there and drive to the lodge to get help," Sulemon suggested.

"No!" John's eyes were wide with terror. "What if that elephant comes back while you're gone? My father and I won't know what to do."

Knowing these inexperienced clients would be sitting ducks if the bull returned, Sulemon assured them he would not leave. He was also reluctant to leave his unconscious employer. He looked at his wristwatch. I was now ten o'clock. In two hours, the temperature would be well over one hundred degrees, Fahrenheit.

Chapter 15

Saturday, August 30, 2008

Shortly before the bull's attack, and unbeknownst to members of Blair Nisbet's hunting party, van Rooyen and Jessica had been flying one thousand feet above the Hurungwe Safari Area, and were closing in on their position. With her forehead pressed firmly against the glass, Jessica scanned the ground.

"I see Mukuru down there." She cried out, pointing downwards as they approached the Nyakasanga River.

Van Rooyen dropped the Cessna's right wing, forcing the plane into a tight, counter-clockwise turn. Below, Jessica spotted four figures walking along a trail in the mopane woodland.

"There's Blair and his tracker. The two guys with them must be clients."

Seconds later she squealed, her voice rising in agitation. "Oh my God, Mukuru's closing in on their position. I know they're going to start shooting the minute they see him. Oh Piet! Can we do anything to scare Mukuru off," she implored.

"We can't go any lower, Jessica. Not safe; too many tall rock piles. Look around."

"Wait! Oh my God, Piet, Mukuru's charged Blair!" With eyes glued to the scene, she watched the drama unfold. "Hey Piet, did you see that? Blair's down, and the others have scattered."

"I can't look, Jessica. For heaven's sake! I'm trying to fly this plane!" With eyes glued to the instruments, he was monitoring the Cessna's air speed, pitch, and altitude.

Spellbound, Jessica continued to look on. "The other guys are now going back to check on Blair. Lord, I hope he's okay. He's flat out on the ground and Mukuru's disappeared.

How badly was Blair hurt, van Rooyen wondered, his heart in his mouth.

"If he's hurt, we've got to pick him up and get him to hospital." Van Rooyen said, as he widened the aircraft's turning circle in search of a suitable place to touch down. He spotted a treeless stretch of ground a quarter mile to the southeast. Could he risk landing there?

"Jessica, I'm going to make a low pass over that open area over there," he said, pointing ahead. "Keep your eyes peeled for obstructions that could cause us problems."

"Right!"

The aircraft swooped down to fifty feet above the ground and, when they roared down the length of the field, the propeller's air blast flattened the tall grass.

"It looks like we've got about five hundred yards to work with—enough for a take-off and landing," he said.

Approaching the tree line, he pushed on the throttle, pulled back on the yoke, and they soared over the trees.

"See anything?" van Rooyen asked.

"No. But with the grass laid down flat, who knows what's underneath it."

"If you are, I'm willing to risk a landing here. The trouble is we don't know the severity of Blair's injuries. All I know for certain, is the sooner we get him medical attention, the better. If I attempt this I'm putting your life in jeopardy too, and you deserve a say-so."

"What are our alternatives?"

"We could radio air traffic control and ask them to contact Makuti for help. Unfortunately, cell phones are pretty hit-or-miss out here. Otherwise, we could fly straight to Makuti and alert the police and the hospital. Problem is there aren't many roads out here, so an ambulance won't get very close."

"That all sounds too iffy, Piet. I think we should just pick him up and fly him to Kariba. If necessary, we can take him straight to Harare."

"As long as you're okay with it, let's go," he said, whipping the Cessna around to approach the make-do runway.

"Brace yourself," he cautioned, as they swooped towards the ground. After the wheels touched down, Whiskey-Kilo-Bravo took several bone-jarring bounces, and slowed, bumping down the grassy field. Van Rooyen cut back the engine, they disembarked, and the pair set off on a quarter-mile hike.

*   *   *

Sulemon ran up to greet them.

"Thank you, thank you!" he said breathlessly, clapping silently in the traditional Shona gesture of gratitude.

"How's Mr. Nisbet?" van Rooyen asked, as he and Jessica fell in behind him.

"He is knocked out, but he is breathing and his heart is strong."

Both van Rooyen and Jessica heaved sighs of relief. When she reached Blair, Jessica knelt down beside him, took hold of his left hand, and spoke softly.

"Blair, this is Jessica. How are you doing?"

He was unresponsive.

"We need to get him to Kariba as soon as possible. He could have suffered brain damage, spinal injuries, or both," van Rooyen said, an urgent tone in his voice.

Emilio and his son stepped forward and van Rooyen greeted them before turning to Sulemon.

"We need a stretcher. Do you have a litter in your vehicle, a wide board, or anything flat we can use to carry him?"

"No Sir," Sulemon shook his head, explaining their pickup was a good five miles away, and while the Mana Pools office might have a stretcher; it was another eight miles further.

"But I can go there if you want," he said.

"No time for that. We'd be better off finding some materials around here to build one," van Rooyen said, glancing around for some suitable tree limbs.

"We can use my stick." Sulemon held out his seventy-two-inch staff.

"That's a start," van Rooyen said, eyeing the people around him. "Let's spread out and look for some straight, wooden branches. I've got an axe in the plane to cut them to size. While I go and retrieve it, Sulemon will you make us some *tambo*, for tying it all together?"

"I can do that," he said his lips parting in a wide smile.

"What's *tambo*?" Emilio asked.

"It's twine, made from the bark of the Mopane tree. There are plenty of them around here," van Rooyen said, adding that they could also use everyone's web belts.

Before jogging off towards the plane to get the axe, he stripped off his shirt and placed it over Blair's head and shoulders to shade him from the relentless sun. When he returned, members of the group had collected a number of usable tree limbs. Using Sulemon's staff to fix the length of the stretcher, John used the axe to cut four branches to size and he and van Rooyen laid them out on the ground. Then with eight cross braces cut to size, Sulemon used the *tambo* to tie the structure together, using two web belts to reinforce the framework. Once assembled, van Rooyen suggested they try out their contraption before lifting Blair into it.

"Who's going to volunteer?"

Jessica agreed and lowered herself on the wooden frame.

"Ooh! That hurts! It's awfully uncomfortable." She grimaced. "Can't we cover it with grass or something to cushion it a bit?"

"Great idea," Emilio said, and he and John ripped up armfuls of dried grass to create a thick cushion for the makeshift stretcher.

"Much improved," Jessica said, after her second try. As she rose to her feet, her companions doubled over with laughter at the sight of an extraordinary creature—part porcupine and part scarecrow. Tangled in her hair and poking through her clothes were zillions of tiny sticks and pieces of straw. With a wide grin, she slapped vigorously at the seat of her pants and ruffled her hair to remove the clippings. Van Rooyen looked on, marveling at her good humor.

Returning his attention to Blair, van Rooyen checked his pulse.

"Seventy-five. That's much better. Let's get going."

The four men lifted Blair onto their makeshift stretcher and carried him the quarter mile to the plane. With his friend still unresponsive, van Rooyen had become increasingly concerned. The likelihood Blair had suffered a brain injury now seemed disturbingly more probable, he thought.

"We'll fly him straight to Kariba. If the doctors think he needs to see a neurologist or brain surgeon, we'll fly him on down to Harare," van Rooyen said. Sulemon nodded mutely, deep worry lines creasing his forehead.

Before climbing aboard, van Rooyen inspected the plane's undercarriage for possible damage sustained on landing. It passed muster. He checked wind direction, holding up a moistened forefinger and then he and Sulemon jogged down the length of the improvised runway, looking for hidden obstructions. They located several soccer-ball-sized boulders and tossed them aside. Although the inspection delayed their departure by fifteen minutes, van Rooyen considered it a prudent move. His father had been a stickler for aviation safety and had drilled it into his son. He was always mindful of the words on a framed poster his father had displayed in their home.

'Aviation in itself is not inherently dangerous. But to an even greater degree than the sea, it is terribly unforgiving of any carelessness, incapacity, or neglect.' The sage words attributed to a Captain A. G. Lamplugh of British Aviation Insurance Group, London, dated back to the early 1930s.

Once he and Jessica were aboard, he turned on the ignition, checked fuel gauges, and started the engine. It coughed into life and the propeller whirled. He and Jessica waved goodbye to the men on the ground and the plane bumped over clumps of grass as it taxied down to the end of the field to turn the nose into the wind. Flaps set, van Rooyen pushed the throttle forward, and the engine roared, raising a cloud of dust sending Whisky-Kilo-Bravo surging down the grass-covered field. Fifty yards short of the tree line, he pulled back on the stick, the Cessna's nose rose skywards, and the wheels left the ground.

∗   ∗   ∗

After they leveled out at three thousand feet, Jessica released her safety belt and climbed back to take a closer look at Blair.

"I thought I saw his eyelids flutter," she told van Rooyen. "Blair, can you hear me? It's Jessica."

His eyes opened briefly and his pupils moved from side to side. This had to be a good sign, she thought.

"Blair, can you hear me?" she repeated.

"Where am I?" he replied, his voice groggy.

"Piet, he's regained consciousness," she shouted, slapping the side of his seat to get his attention. Van Rooyen leaned back, peering over his right shoulder.

"That's a good sign," he said. "But we must still take him to hospital."

"What's going on?" Blair grunted.

To Jessica he appeared dazed and confused.

"Piet and I are taking you to the hospital in Kariba."

"What for?"

"You've suffered a concussion."

"How?"

"You took quite a fall, and got a serious blow to the head. You also have a broken leg."

"What happened?"

"You were charged by an elephant."

"What?" He replied, shaking his head.

"Blair, an elephant charged you. Piet and I saw the whole thing from the air." Did he have no memory of the attack, Jessica wondered.

"Blair," van Rooyen broke in, "If that bull elephant had wanted to, he could have made mincemeat out of you."

"You saw everything?"

"We did. He lifted you off the ground with his tusks. Then he slowly put you down and walked away. It was the most incredible thing I've ever seen," he replied.

"I *cannae* remember a thing. I've never seen a bull elephant back away from a fight. Are *ye* daft? Or are *ye* making all this up, *laddie?*"

"Honest to God, Blair, I'm not. Ask Jessica. It was Mukuru, one of her study bulls."

"Piet's telling you the truth. We saw everything," she confirmed.

"He could have thrown you down and stomped you into the ground, but he didn't," van Rooyen added. "By the way we're taking you to the Kariba Hospital. How are you feeling?"

"Got a monster, bloody headache, but I *dinnae* need no damn hospital. How long before we land, Piet?"

"We should be there in thirty to forty minutes."

Jessica returned to her seat and for a while, they flew on in silence. Van Rooyen was the first to speak.

"Jessica, what's going to happen to Mukuru? Do you still want to save him?"

She responded instantly. "Of course! Nothing's changed. But I'm afraid Chitsaru and the Mana Pools scouts may hunt him down before I can get back to him."

"Do you want to go back on Monday to dart him, and treat his injured leg?"

"Oh definitely! But I can't do it on my own. I'm not a vet and I don't have the drugs, the equipment, or the people needed to pull off something like that," she admitted, frustrated by her obvious helplessness. "Are you saying you might be willing to help?" She turned to face him with a questioning look.

"Of course! Have you ever darted an elephant, before?"

"I've observed from the sidelines, but I've never actually done it, myself."

"Well, I have, so you're in luck," van Rooyen said, turning to her with a smile. "I worked with Dr. Kruger, from the Transvaal Veterinary Institute in South Africa on his elephant migration project four years ago. We fitted several elephant bulls and cows with GPS collars!"

"On the subject of GPS collars, why don't we kill two birds with one stone and fit Mukuru with one?" Jessica enthused. "But where do we get the collars?"

"I have a couple of spares Dr. Kruger left with me. We could use one of them."

"Fantastic!" Jessica said, her eyes lighting up like a pair of Fourth-of-July sparklers. "Thank you Piet. You've really made my day."

Van Rooyen called Kariba on the radio and arranged for an ambulance to meet the plane. It was waiting on the apron when they arrived. Two EMTs clambered aboard to remove Blair and the stretcher from the Cessna. As they deplaned, masses of fluttering straw fragments swirled around them like snowflakes before settling onto the tarmac.

"*Eh, amai we*! What is this?" The puzzled ambulance driver exclaimed.

Jessica and van Rooyen turned away to keep from collapsing in giggles.

Chapter 16

Monday, September 1, 2008

On Monday morning, Jessica and van Rooyen drove back to Hurungwe accompanied by Ananias, Mathias, Godfrey, and Patrick. They left Kariba around seven thirty in the morning after stopping at Kaminjolo's office to pick up the drugs needed for the immobilization of large animals.

Van Rooyen was at the wheel while Jessica examined the contents of the small cooler chest on her lap.

"Be careful," he cautioned her. "M99 is extremely potent. Even a needle scratch could kill you unless the antidote is injected immediately."

"That obviously explains why both drugs are in here," she said.

Packed in ice were M99 darts, syringes filled with the reversal agents, M50-50, Naloxone, and vials of antibiotics. Disposable syringes complete with needle guards, and supplies of surgical gloves, gauze, and cotton swabs were packaged in separate plastic pouches.

"There's everything in here but the kitchen sink. What are the syringes of Naloxone for?"

"It's the preferred antidote for humans," he replied.

"I am amazed Hector was able to persuade the government vet to hand over all this stuff," Jessica said.

"Kaminjolo's a good sort and very well respected. Of course, he'll probably catch hell from his boss for helping us to save Mukuru. The General was all for having him shot. I suspect he wanted to get his hands on those tusks, himself. There aren't too many 40-year-old bulls around anymore, you know. Mukuru's tusks would likely fetch two thousand U.S. dollars, or more, on the black market."

"Do we have a GPS collar on board?" Jessica asked.

"We do. It's in one of the cargo trunks in the back. Once fitted, we'll be able to keep close track of Mukuru's movements."

Jessica rubbed her palms together in excitement. "I can see huge benefits here, particularly for elephants like Mukuru who sometimes stray into rural farming areas. Instead of shooting crop marauders, Zim Parks can monitor their movements and send out scouts to shoo them off."

"Under normal circumstances I'd agree, but things aren't normal anymore. Parks' employees have gone without paychecks, sometimes for months at a time. Can we really blame them for occasionally shooting the game they're supposed to protect? I'm not suggesting for a minute we should condone poaching, but we have to consider reality."

"Piet, when it comes to game, other than elephant and rhino, I would agree with you one hundred percent, but I seriously doubt wildlife rangers and scouts shoot these endangered species strictly for food. Wouldn't you agree many of them are after quick riches from the sale of the horn and the ivory?"

"You may be right," van Rooyen conceded with a wry grin.

"So where exactly are we headed?" Jessica asked.

"Kaminjolo said Chitsaru told him Mukuru wasn't moving around much, probably because of his injury. He said he'd been seen hanging around a large tamarind tree near an inlet, three miles from the Nyakasanga River confluence."

"Then he shouldn't be too difficult to find him, right?"

"Right!"

Jessica was looking forward to spending the entire day with van Rooyen. Since they'd met, three years ago, she'd discovered in him a number of appealing personal qualities. He was clean cut, respectful, generous, decisive, conscientious, smart, and even quite sexy. While he didn't possess Paul Hansen's classic, movie star looks, she was frequently finding something new and intriguing about Piet. If he harbored any less-than-stellar tendencies, they had yet to surface.

He was wearing a pair of aviator sunglasses to ward off the glare from the rising sun. She studied him out the corner of her eye, as he focused on the road ahead. His fashionably cropped, dark brown hair revealed a few gray hairs at his temples. In profile, his features included a straight nose, prominent cheekbones, and a strong, chiseled jaw. His arms and the backs of his hands, deeply tanned from a life spent outdoors, sported a growth of soft, dark hair.

They bore a number of small scars; relics of past cuts and scrapes incurred in his line of work. His fingers, gripping the steering wheel, were long and tapered with neatly trimmed fingernails.

It was almost nine, when they reached the town of Makuti, where they turned left onto the A-1, travelling north. Before they reached Chirundu at the Zambian border, they left the tarmac and turned east on Mongwe Road. From here, they followed a rutted, dirt road through the Hurungwe Safari Area, passable only in the dry season. For miles, they bumped along a track strewn with boulders, broken tree trunks, branches, and piles of elephant dung.

They passed two hunting camps on the river, wound around thickets of bush, and discovered Mukuru near the Nyakasanga confluence, close to where John Chitsaru had said he'd last seen him. He stood less than fifty feet from a river inlet, shaded from the blistering noonday sun by a large tamarind tree. Van Rooyen braked, keeping a distance of about sixty yards between them.

His condition appalled Jessica. His head hung low and he bore the weight of his huge hindquarters on his left, rear leg while resting the other. His right leg was swelled to almost twice its size.

"He looks totally buggered," van Rooyen commented. "I think we got here just in time. I'm not sure he'd have lasted much longer."

Everyone piled out of the Land Rover and van Rooyen placed his index finger against his lips – calling for silence.

"We don't want to stress him out, so keep your voices low, and talk to a minimum," he whispered.

The crew silently offloaded the GPS collar and the day's needed supplies – water cans, ropes, and another box of medical supplies. Jessica took the GPS collar from Patrick and slung it over her shoulder. In her hands, she carried the small cooler containing the M99 and M50-50 immobilizing drugs.

Van Rooyen handed his loaded rifle to Ananias and passed Patrick a cigarette lighter and half a dozen firecrackers.

"I don't think Mukuru will charge us. He's too weak," he whispered. "But if he does, Patrick, you start setting off firecrackers to scare him off. Keep it up until he turns away."

He turned to Ananias, "If the firecrackers don't stop him, and it looks like someone's in serious danger, bring him down with a clean brain shot. Shoot only as a last resort!" Both men nodded.

Van Rooyen assembled the dart gun and Jessica brought him the immobilization drugs setting the cooler on the Land Rover's tailgate. He picked up a pre-filled M-99 dart and loaded it.

Jessica kept an eye on Mukuru. He stood quietly, rocking back and forth, while fanning himself with his large ears. He lifted his trunk, evidently inhaling their scent. When he turned to face them, she felt a prickle of fear.

Van Rooyen stepped forward, raised the gun, aimed it carefully at Mukuru's shoulder, and pulled the trigger. The dart hit its mark. The bull flinched, but made no move to charge or escape. Turning to the group, van Rooyen issued further instructions.

"Listen, hey. We've got to make sure he falls on his left side. If he falls on his right, we won't be able to remove the snare and there's that wound on his right shoulder, where Emilio's bullet grazed him. Someone bring the ropes, we may need them. As soon as we see him starting to wobble and it looks like he's about to fall, we've got to shove him over onto his left side."

As the group started towards Mukuru, his trunk dropped, his ears ceased their movement, and he began to sway. Everyone rushed forward, tipping him over onto his left side. Jessica stood next to his massive body, pausing for a moment to run her hand across his tough, wrinkled, hide. The skin in between the deep furrows felt surprisingly soft.

Van Rooyen issued more orders.

"Jessica, use something to keep his airway open and monitor his respirations. Mathias and Godfrey spray him with water and cover him with branches to help keep him cool. Make sure you protect his eyes from the sun. Ananias and Patrick, bring me the medical supplies and the wire cutters."

Everyone got to work. Jessica found an eight-inch, weathered stick, smooth at both ends, and fitted it into the opening of Mukuru's trunk to keep his airway clear. She could feel the rush of his breath being sucked in and blown out in tempo with the rise and fall of his huge chest. She knew a downed elephant loses its ability to moderate its body's temperature and she watched Mathias and Godfrey spreading branches across much of his body and spraying him with water. Afterwards, they helped Jessica hold the tape to measure the length of his trunk, tusks, body length, and the circumference of his feet. She recorded the measurements in a small notebook.

Van Rooyen and Ananias carefully severed the snare and removed it from above his right foot. After flushing the wound with water to remove dirt and debris, van Rooyen treated the wound with a first-aid spray and fly-repellent to prevent any infection and maggot infestation. The bullet wound on his shoulder turned out to be little more than a scrape, easily medicated with the first-aid spray. To treat the badly infected leg, van Rooyen injected Mukuru with a broad-spectrum antibiotic and took a blood sample for later analysis.

Their final task was to fit the GPS collar around Mukuru's neck. Godfrey scooped out dirt beneath the elephant's neck, through which to thread it, and Mathias helped van Rooyen fit it and secure the ends with heavy nuts and bolts.

Van Rooyen looked around. "Are we ready to inject the antidote?"
Everyone nodded.

"Then pull away the branches and Jessica, don't forget to remove the stick from his trunk," he said.

After a flurry of activity, Jessica and the crew returned to the Land Rover with their tools and remaining supplies. When everyone was safely seated in the truck, van Rooyen injected the antidote and walked away to join them. Everyone's eyes were on Mukuru, waiting anxiously for the bull elephant to awaken.

Minutes passed; nothing happened. They continued to wait, as Mukuru slept on. Jessica had a lump in her throat. Had they unwittingly destroyed this magnificent elephant?

"What do we do?" she called out to van Rooyen, who stood halfway between Mukuru and the Land Rover.

"I'm going to give him a second shot," he shouted. "Don't panic! This has happened before."

He returned to the truck to pick up a second syringe of M50-50 and jogged back to Mukuru's side. Jessica started to follow him, but he waved her back. She leant against the Land Rover and watched him, her heart thumping.

To check Mukuru's respiration, Van Rooyen stooped and placed his hand at the opening of his trunk. After signaling to the onlookers that all was well, he readied the syringe and injected a second dose of the antidote into a vein in Mukuru's ear. Van Rooyen stood beside Mukuru until he stirred. Then, to Jessica's relief, he ran back to the Land Rover. He started the engine, but the vehicle remained stationary until Mukuru regained his feet.

"We'll be on our way once he takes his first steps," van Rooyen said.

"Wonderful! Look, he's already putting a little weight on his hurt leg," Jessica said. "Now, with that snare gone, it must be such a huge relief to him."

"He's no doubt feeling hung-over; a side effect of the drug. But it'll wear off quickly and the antibiotic should have his leg right as rain in a week or so," van Rooyen said.

Five minutes later, Mukuru turned and took his first tentative steps down to the river inlet. Cheers and applause came from the Land Rover. The bull turned his head to look back at the vehicle as it drove away.

"I suppose we're on our way home," Jessica said.

"We're at least another hour's drive from Mana, so I'll phone John Chitsaru tomorrow and let him know Mukuru should be well on his way to recovery, and that he's now wearing a GPS collar," van Rooyen said. "Hopefully, once Kaminjolo's boss learns that wherever he is, his position can be viewed online, he'll rescind his order to have him shot."

"Ha!" Jessica retorted, "Let's wait and see."

*   *   *

They arrived home at 6:30 p.m., dropped off Ananias, Mathias, Godfrey and Patrick, and drove straight to the Kariba General Hospital to check in on Blair. At the front desk, an attendant told them he was in a room on the third floor. The moment they stepped out of the elevator, they heard his booming voice echo along the corridor.

He was sitting up in bed with his right leg, encased below the knee in a plaster cast.

"Well, look who's here?" he bellowed, "It's the *bonniest lass* in the whole of Africa, and my old mate, Piet."

Jessica smiled.

"Look at you, hey. You're looking pretty good, my man," van Rooyen said, as he approached Blair's bedside and shook his hand.

"Just a mild concussion," Nisbet said cheerily. "The doc said I was damn lucky. I suppose the elephant could have done me in."

"You're right about that," van Rooyen confirmed. "The whole scene was a first for me – just the way Mukuru let you down so carefully and then just walked away."

"Sulemon told me you went back there, today. What happened?"

"We found him, less than a mile from where he tackled you. He couldn't have strayed far the condition his leg was in."

"What was the matter with his leg? I *didnae* see anything when we first saw him."

"There was a barbed-wire, snare embedded just above his right foot. It was bad—seriously infected. By the time we got to him, it was badly swollen—looked almost beyond saving. I had to literally cut the snare out."

"Does the old boy still have a price on his head?"

"Not if I have anything to do with it," Jessica cut in. "To spare him, we've collared him with a GPS unit, so Zim Parks can follow him online and chase him off anytime he enters any tribal areas."

"That's smashing! I suppose," Blair said, pulling a face. "Especially considering he broke my leg, lost me my clients, an elephant hunt, and cost me a thousands of pounds, sterling."

"How so?" van Rooyen asked, his eyebrows raised.

"Sulemon said our American clients decided to cancel their hunt and go tiger fishing on the lake instead."

"Why? Couldn't one of your hunters have taken them out the next day?"

"Skip Bronkhorst was available, but those *lads* said they no longer had the stomach to take out an elephant."

132

Jessica understood why Emilio and John Sanchez had cancelled the hunt. After all, had they not witnessed, firsthand, Mukuru's walking away from Blair Nisbet, when he could so easily have trampled him to death?

A nurse wearing scrubs hurried into the room, announcing visiting hours were over.

"But they just got here," Blair blustered.

"It's okay Blair, we'll come back tomorrow," Jessica said.

"No need for that," the nurse said, as she effectively silenced her patient by inserting a thermometer in his mouth. "Under your tongue please, Mr. Nisbet." Then turning to his visitors, she informed them he would be discharged tomorrow.

"We've still got lots to talk about. Why don't the two of you come over to the Lodge tomorrow and have dinner with me?" Blair said, after the nurse removed the thermometer.

Van Rooyen turned to Jessica. "Okay with you?"

"Fine," she replied.

"Then we'll see you tomorrow, Blair," van Rooyen said, saluting his friend as he and Jessica exited the room.

* * *

They arrived at Jessica's house shortly after eight.

"It's late," she said. "Why don't you come in and I'll fix us a quick supper. Soup and a sandwich?"

"Sounds good. Thanks."

While she puttered around in the kitchen, van Rooyen sat on the couch browsing through a recent issue of National Geographic.

"There's a Castle in the fridge," she said. "If you want a beer. Help yourself."

He opened the refrigerator and pulled out a bottle. "Can I get one for you?"

"Sure. I'll drink it straight from the bottle. I don't need a glass."

Van Rooyen set the two bottles on the coffee table, opened one, took a swig, and continued flipping through the pages of the magazine. Before he'd skimmed a few paragraphs, Jessica arrived with a tray, laden with two steaming bowls of tomato soup and a plate heaped with quarter-cut, chicken sandwiches.

"Let's eat on the verandah?" she said, moving towards the glass door.

Van Rooyen rose, picked up the beer bottles, and elbowed open the door leading onto the screened porch. They set the food and drinks on the wrought iron table. Van Rooyen pulled out a chair for Jessica, and sat down across from her.

"Good soup" he said, nodding approvingly.

"Thank you."

Between mouthfuls, they studied one another furtively at first, avoiding the other's eyes for fear of inviting too personal a connection. Then they relaxed, sitting back to sip their beers and take in the sights and sounds of the lake. A multitude of night insects created an incessant, background drone. Above the horizon, the moon pulsed huge and silver in the black sky, its reflection shimmering across the surface of the lake. The only other lights visible on the water were those of the distant boats of kapenta fishermen.

"I've not seen this particular view after dark before," van Rooyen remarked, "It's truly magnificent."

"I've tried to capture it on film several times to send to my family in the States," Jessica said, "but I just don't know enough about setting f-stops and film speeds, etcetera, so my photos never come out right. You're not the only amateur photographer, you know."

He smiled. "That reminds me. I still need to pick up my camera."

"It's been a long day, Piet, but we accomplished a lot. You taught me a lot about fitting GPS collars. Thanks."

"No sweat. I'm glad I had that collar. I had fully intended to use it. It was just a matter of finding the right bull and having the impetus to do it. You provided both. Don't forget I have a second collar."

"Want another beer?"

"No thanks, Jessica. I'd better get going."

She filled the tray with the empty plates, bowls and beer bottles. He rose, took the tray from her, and followed her into the kitchen, setting the tray next the sink and turning on the water.

"Just leave the dishes on the counter, my maid will do them in the morning," she said.

He turned off the faucet and moved away from the sink. Then he gently turned her around to face him and embraced her.

Although startled at first, she sank easily into his arms. Then with her heart thumping, she lifted her lips to meet his. When they broke apart, he gave her a hug, smiled down at her, and moved towards the front door.

"Good night," he said putting his hand to his mouth and blowing her a kiss.

"Night Piet. I had a great day."

"Me too." Then he slipped out the door, closing it behind him.

Jessica peeked out the window as he climbed aboard the Land Rover. The engine coughed into life and her heart pounded as she watched him drive away. She wanted so badly to trust him, but could she?

Chapter 17

It was Monday morning in the Zambian capital of Lusaka, approximately seventy-five miles north of the Zimbabwe border crossing at Chirundu. The Tembo Travel and Tourism Agency occupied a suite of offices in the Holiday Inn on Independence Avenue.

Located off the hotel's lobby, the travel agency's glass-fronted entrance opened up into a large alcove. Two young women in green business suits sat at separate work stations. Embroidered above a Zambian flag appliqué on the breast pockets of their jackets was the agency's initials, T. T. T. Travel posters on the wall behind them promoted local sights and tourist activities – rafting, canoeing, and kayaking along the Zambezi between Victoria Falls and Lake Kariba, and game drives for viewing wildlife in Zambia's National Parks. Behind them, a rear door accessed a vestibule, leading to a storage room, an employees' break room, toilet facilities, and two private offices.

George Tembo, the travel agency's chief executive, occupied the largest of the private offices. Standing five feet, ten inches tall, he presented an imposing figure, powerfully built with shoulders that looked coiled, ready for a fight. His hairline receded deeply and what hair remained was wiry, gray, and closely cropped. Regardless of the weather, he invariably wore a tailored, dark gray, pinstriped suit to the office with highly polished, quality leather shoes.

Seated at an oversized mahogany desk with ornate, ivory inlays, he studied his appointment calendar for the week. In addition to owning and operating Lusaka's largest travel agency, he was an exporter of high repute. For years, he had been dealing in ivory and rhino horn and had long-standing, business relationships with several major Chinese ivory importers. These he had cultivated during the 1973-1985 slaughter of thousands of elephants in Zambia's North Luangwa Valley National Park.

In recent years, scientists had perfected techniques for tracing the origin of illegally traded ivory. DNA tracking of ivory seized from 1973 to 1985 revealed it came from savanna elephants originating within a narrow east-to-west band of southern Africa, centered on Zambia.

Tembo's valuable oriental contacts led to his being recruited in 1986 by powerful supporters of the Zimbabwe president to smuggle ivory out of that country. Five years later, however, the man who served as his Zimbabwe intermediary fell out of favor with Robert Mugabe and perished in a mysterious Harare house fire. During his five years in Zimbabwe, Tembo also assisted the government in finding overseas buyers for hardwood timber, diamonds, gold and other minerals that Zimbabwe Army officers were suspected of plundering, while fighting in the civil war in the Democratic Republic of Congo. Tembo naturally skimmed a generous finder's fee off the top of every transaction.

He later returned to Zambia and invested his ill-gotten gains in the travel agency, a legitimate business he used as a front for his smuggling deals with the Chinese. Later, when the United Nations' ivory ban took effect in 1989, his illegal enterprises in Zimbabwe, and later in Zambia, reverted to strictly clandestine operations. Only his trusted accountant was privy to details pertaining to his shady dealings.

Tembo's operations extended to a line of exquisite soap stone sculptures and woodcarvings of African wildlife. Talented artisans toiled in a rented warehouse on Los Angeles Road in Lusaka's light industrial park. The works of these underpaid artists were highly prized internationally; pieces selling for hundreds, even thousands of U.S. dollars.

Tembo had a meeting scheduled for Friday afternoon with Shubo Gu, an important client operating from within the Chinese Embassy just five blocks away. Officially, his dealings with the Chinese diplomat were confined to marketing Zambia as a tourist destination. In reality, however, Gu was Tembo's primary ivory buyer.

He was not looking forward to Friday's meeting. Unless he could turn things around speedily, he was at risk of defaulting on his contract to supply Gu with a total of 2,500 kilos of ivory by year's end. He needed to urge Raymond, his chief ivory supplier, to step up his deliveries. Kaseke maintained a base of operations on a Zimbabwe farm, near Chirundu on the Zambian border. His meeting with Kaseke was scheduled for two o'clock this afternoon.

He dreaded the seventy-five mile road trip down to Kaseke's Fataran Farm. He'd be travelling south along a crowded highway, which served as Zambia's single, most important trade route to Zimbabwe, South Africa and its bustling shipping ports. It was a nightmarish drive clogged with miles of snaking queues of trucks and buses. To arrive at his destination by the appointed time, he knew he must leave the office no later than nine thirty.

Not only was Tembo highly aggravated he had to make this tedious drive, but he was infuriated by Kaseke's failure to produce the promised product. Did the fool not understand how painstakingly he had negotiated this contract with Gu – a powerful man not to be trifled with?

A collection of large, intricately chiseled, Chinese ivory carvings were displayed atop the bookcase behind him. It included a three-foot-long, antique, train of eight elephants, two ivory carvings of Fu lions, and a statue of the Hindu goddess, Lakshmi, attired in flowing robes and scarves. He had received all of these valuable carvings as gifts from Gu at one time or another.

He glanced down at his diamond-studded, Rolex. He had less than an hour to review the ivory account his accountant had just delivered. He was horrified. The spreadsheet showed only two thousand and forty kilos of the agreed two thousand, five hundred, had so far been delivered—roughly the equivalent of 102 elephants. With less than three months to source the shortfall, he needed the tusks of at least another twenty-three.

Tembo wondered if Kaseke was double-dealing, selling ivory on the side. He was paying him a fair price—two hundred American dollars per kilo. For the entire two thousand, five hundred kilos contracted, he would be receiving five hundred thousand dollars, a huge sum of money. Was Kaseke also supplying others? The black market price for ivory had risen as high as U.S. $750, per kilo. At that rate, he could have grossed close to two million. It was certainly a most tempting proposition. Could the man be trusted? He stuffed the ivory account spreadsheets into his briefcase and walked out of his office, stopping briefly at Lucy Mukoko's workstation.

"Lucy, I have a business meeting and will be out for the rest of the day. I'll be back in the office sometime tomorrow. If you get any calls from the Chinese Embassy, reassure them that I will be there, Friday afternoon, for my three o'clock meeting with Mr. Gu."

Exiting the agency, he made his way through the hotel lobby towards the main entrance. He donned a pair of designer sunglasses and strode down the front steps to his black Mercedes parked in a reserved space in front of the hotel. At any other time, he would have flown down to Fataran Farm, but his Piper Seneca was out of commission, undergoing routine maintenance in South Africa.

At 9:45 a.m., he swung onto the main road leading south to Chirundu, his fuel tank topped up, and sandwiches and cold drinks on board. For the first ten miles, vehicles moved at a steady, sixty miles-per-hour. As traffic increased, however, they slowed. Over the ensuing ten-mile increments, his progress decreased steadily. Within five miles of the Zimbabwe border crossing, vehicles were crawling along at a snail's pace.

By two o'clock in the afternoon, when Tembo cleared the border inspection station, he realized he was late for his meeting. Irritated, he punched Kaseke's number into his cell phone. Although few remote rural areas in Zimbabwe had cell service, Fataran Farm benefitted by being within range of towers at the international ports of entry.

"Hello! Is that you Raymond? George here. I've just cleared the border post. The traffic was hell. I should be there in thirty minutes."

"I'll have the gate open for you," Kaseke replied.

"I'll see you." Tembo disconnected.

Cruising along in his Mercedes, he passed numerous curio stands set up along both sides of the road. They stretched on for more than a mile with local merchants and craftspeople hawking their wares to passing travelers. Their assorted merchandise was spread out either on makeshift tables or the bare ground. There were soapstone and wooden wildlife carvings, beadwork items, baskets of all shapes and sizes, tribal masks, cowhide drums, and *mbiras* the traditional Zimbabwean thumb pianos. Also displayed, hanging on lines suspended between wooden poles, were hand-crocheted linens and tablecloths. Around the stands, children danced and waved at the passing cars and trucks.

Tembo's nose wrinkled in distaste. In his opinion, these deadbeats and their stuff should be cleared out. Why wasn't Mugabe out here getting rid of them? He applauded the Zimbabwean leader's Operation *Murambatsvina*, his 'Drive out the Rubbish' campaign of 2004, when he sent in trucks and bulldozers to level all Harare's shanty towns. That the purge left thousands homeless was unavoidable, Tembo believed. Although it had created widespread international outrage, he considered the action well justified. In his opinion, Mugabe was within his rights to restore sanity to Zimbabwe's cities, which he claimed were being overrun by criminals.

Suddenly he caught sight of a child steering a homemade, wire-frame, toy truck across the road in front of him. He immediately braked and the Mercedes swerved violently and skidded to a stop, narrowly missing the boy. Tembo pulled off the road, got out of the car, and looked around. The child had vanished.

"Keep your fucking children off the road!" he bellowed hoarsely at some nearby vendors. They stared at him wordlessly.

"Next time I won't put my foot on the brake! Then what will you do?"

Angry and shaken, he climbed into the Mercedes and pulled back onto the tarmac. The engine roared as he slammed his foot down on the accelerator. The car took off, wheels spinning and tires smoking, as it deposited black, rubber tracks on the road surface. He drove two miles and turned left onto a dirt road marked with a signpost, Fataran Farm.

Five miles further down the dusty, dirt road, he reached a driveway leading to a property on the left, enclosed by a high fence. Two men pulled open a pair of gates and he drove through. He found Kaseke outside a large, windowless, brick building. He was a huge man, not only in stature but also in the size of his girth, which surpassed the thirty-six-inch waist of his ancestor, the legendary Ndebele tribal chief, Lobengula. Although his maternal grandfather had been a member of Ndebele tribe, Kaseke claimed Shona ancestry and was a card-carrying supporter of ZANU-PF. He wore baggy shorts and a sleeveless shirt, which accentuated his oversized, 28-year-old torso.

He stepped forward and tried the passenger door. "Open up, I want to take you to the house for some tea, you've had a long, hard, drive."

Tembo clicked open the door latch and Kaseke climbed in, wedging his large frame through the door.

"Welcome to Fataran," he said, offering his hand.

"Where to?" Tembo asked abruptly. Although he was still irritated at Kaseke, he gave him the traditional, African, three-part handshake.

"The homestead is in the center of the property," he said. "I'll direct you. Drive back behind these packing sheds, then turn right."

Tembo steered the Mercedes behind the row of sheds and followed a narrow tarmac road traveling east. He could see up ahead, a stand of tall, eucalyptus trees.

"The homestead's behind those gum trees," Kaseke said.

As Tembo drove towards the house, he glanced around. Beyond a large field of tall grass, on the left side of the road, were sizeable tree plantations.

"What are those trees?" he asked.

"Eh, avocado trees. They didn't have much fruit last year. Maybe because I was too busy with the ivory. We had no time to properly weed and fertilize them. Same with the citrus. Anyway, we picked enough for us, and we gave fruit away to the labor force and to our friends. They liked that. If you want, I can save some for you too after the picking."

Tembo ignored the offer. "How many workers do you employ here?" he asked.

"Twenty. Twelve of them go on elephant hunts with me and only work with ivory. The rest are house boys, gardeners, and mechanics to keep our vehicles and equipment in order."

They drove up in front of a large, white-washed brick house with a red, corrugated iron roof. Leading up to the front door was a weed-infested, brick walkway lined with overgrown, unkempt shrubbery on either side. So much for his gardeners, Tembo thought. He was certain in years past, this had been an attractive, well-manicured garden.

After alighting, Tembo scowled at the thick covering of dust on his once shiny, black, Mercedes. He followed Kaseke through the front door into a large, sparsely furnished, living room. Kaseke pointed to one of two shabby easy chairs squatting behind a coffee table.

"Take a seat. I'll arrange for some tea."

Tembo sank into the chair and looked around. The walls had chipped plaster, everywhere the previous occupant had once hung framed photographs or artwork. The Italian, marble floor, in shades of cream and beige, was badly chipped, and scratched, its former luster gone. He remembered Kaseke telling him the farm had once belonged to an Italian family and in 2001, he took over the property as part of Mugabe's land redistribution campaign. Kaseke was certainly fortunate to own such a valuable piece of real estate, Tembo thought. But it was shameful the man didn't have the foresight to care for its fine structures and the property's mature fruit orchards. With the wealth he was making from ivory, he could well afford to maintain it.

In Tembo's opinion, today's young people lacked good sense and failed to plan for the future. Didn't Kaseke realize that later on when he no longer had the youth or physical strength to traverse the bush for days hunting elephants, he could retire in comfort, living off his annual fruit harvest.

Kaseke returned and plunked his ample frame in the chair next to him. Tembo reminded himself to remain calm.

"Raymond, I'm worried that by the end of December we won't make the ivory quota I contracted to supply Mr. Gu. We still owe him another 460 kilos. What are your thoughts?"

"Well, George, I have another 260 kilos sitting in my warehouse, right now."

"How long have you had them?"

"Just a week," Kaseke said, looking away.

"How come you didn't tell me?" Tembo demanded.

Kaseke looked down. "*Handizivi,* I don't know. We were very busy, *ndakutadzira,* I'm sorry."

"I want to see those 260 kilos in your storage sheds," Tembo demanded.

"Okay" Kaseke said, lurching to his feet, "Let's go."

Tembo had been looking forward to that cup of tea, but more importantly, he needed to find out if Kaseke actually had the ivory.

They drove back to the largest of the three packing sheds. While climbing out of the Mercedes, they heard the drone of a low-flying aircraft. It barely skimmed the top of the gum trees, flying low enough for the men to see its registration, Z-WKB, clearly.

"Damn those fucking tour operators," Kaseke growled. "They're always buzzing us, just so tourists can see the damn hippos in the river." He unlocked the steel door's heavy padlock and they entered a large room lined with rough-hewn, wooden tables. Light streamed into the windowless building through eight large skylights. Tembo followed Kaseke to a table where twenty-six elephant tusks were arranged, largest to smallest.

"These belonged to the grandmother." Kaseke fondled the longest pair of tusks. "More than fifty years old, maybe?"

"Old for an elephant these days," Tembo commented.

"Nowadays it's hard to find the old bulls. Hunters from America and Europe are shooting them all. Then the government takes the ivory to add to its stockpile," Kaseke complained.

"A problem, I realize." Tembo shook his head sympathetically. He doubted Kaseke knew that Zanunga, head of Zim Parks, frequently funneled ivory from Zimbabwe's stockpile directly to him, receiving payment in Zambian Kwacha, British pounds, or U.S. dollars. Tembo, in turn, sold these tusks to his personal Chinese and Japanese contacts, bypassing Kaseke.

Tembo paid particular attention to the smallest tusks, less than twelve inches long. Until he'd learned from Gu, that these had great value as handles for daggers and the like, he had often wondered if the smallest elephants were even worth slaughtering.

"These ones don't weigh much, but the Chinese and Japanese pay premium prices for them." Tembo said.

"I know that. I always take the whole herd except for babies with no tusks," Kaseke said. "Sometimes there's a big female with no tusks. If we could chase her off, I would save my bullet. But those ones always stick around and cause lots of trouble, so they have to go too."

"My plane is down in Johannesburg getting a major rebuild. It'll be out of commission for months. How soon can you get this shipment up to Lusaka?"

"Taking it across the river, anywhere near Chirundu, is very risky. Crossing further down into Zambia's Lower Zambezi National Park is also dangerous and it would take time to get the ivory to Lusaka. But there's a man with an old plane," Kaseke said. "He keeps it parked in an old hangar at the

Chingozi airport in Mozambique. I've used him before and I'm sure I could get him to fly your shipment to Lusaka under the radar."

"Where's Chingozi?"

"Outside Tete."

"That's not far from here," Tembo noted. "Three hundred miles, as the crow flies. But how will he fly incognito into Zambia?"

Kaseke swaggered over to a large map of Southern Africa, pinned to the wall near the door, and pointed to a red pushpin south of the Zambezi, marking Fataran Farm's location.

"Best thing about those old Dakotas is they can fly low, under the radar. From here, he'll fly east back into Mozambique, and then turn north crossing unnoticed into Zambia."

He pointed to a sliver of blue on the map north of Zimbabwe's border with Mozambique. "The crossing's here, north of Cabora Bassa Dam. It's mostly just bush, no towns, and just one or two small villages." Running his finger due west to a spot south of Lusaka he continued, "Right here, there's an abandoned grass air strip, just thirty miles south of Lusaka. The pilot can land there, drop off the shipment, then turn around and fly back to Mozambique. There's just one thing. If he lands after dark, you'll have to put out strings of fire pots to mark both sides of the runway."

"Contact this pilot friend of yours, right now," Tembo insisted. "I need to know how much it's going to cost me." He had figured it would be well worth the money to have another 260 kilos delivered to Gu before their meeting Friday afternoon.

* * *

Kaseke walked over to a small, enclosed office in the corner of the warehouse, beckoning Tembo to follow.

"Come in and take a seat," he said, easing his bulk into a chair behind the desk and motioning to a seat across from him.

Kaseke fingered through a Rolodex, found the phone number for Manuel Chipenga, and dialed it on an old, black rotary-dial phone on his desk. The line crackled, and Someone picked up and spoke in Portuguese.

"Olá,"

"Is this Manuel?" Kaseke said.

"Yes, this is Manuel Chipenga."

"Manuel, this is Raymond Kaseke from Fataran Farm, in Zimbabwe."

"Oh, Raymond, how are you?"

"I'm well. I have a shipment to be carried special delivery, to Lusaka in a hurry. How soon can you do it?" Kaseke held his hand over the mouthpiece, whispering to Tembo, "special delivery is code for 'under the radar.'"

"How big is the container, and its weight, in kilos?"

"I have six containers – all are seven feet long, and thirty inches in width and depth. Total weight, including their contents, should be around 350 kilos."

"Well, the earliest I can do it is …" The voice on the line faded away.

"I'm sorry. This connection is rubbish, Manuel. I didn't hear what you said. Tell me again."

"I can do it Tuesday, September 30, at the earliest. Is that good?"

Kaseke looked at Tembo and mouthed the date.

He nodded, but a frown wrinkled his brow.

"Tuesday, 30 September is okay," Kaseke continued. "Now remember you can't land at Lusaka airport. There's an alternate landing site. I'll fax you directions and instructions. Give me your fax number."

"0-637555."

"Got it. I'll send the fax in a few minutes. Wait! Before you hang up, Manuel, what are you charging me?"

"You're a good customer, Raymond, so I'll give you… " His voice faded.

"Manuel," the line crackled again. "What did you say?"

"*Oh meu Deus!*" Manuel exclaimed in Portuguese. "When is your government going to fix your stupid phone lines? I said I'd give you a discount. Pay me US$750 in cash before I offload the shipment in Lusaka?"

Kaseke repeated the amount for Tembo. The Zambian trafficker's eyes widened. Then with lips pursed, he nodded.

"That's good, Manuel. We'll see you on the 30th. What time?"

"Five o'clock. One hour before dark."

"Okay, I'll fax you in a few minutes."

"*Obrigado,*" Manuel thanked him. "Phone me if you have any other questions, *tchau!*"

Kaseke hung up.

"Well, now that's all arranged, let's go back to your house and have that cup of tea you promised me," Tembo said.

After tea, Kaseke walked him outside to his Mercedes.

"Well George, it all sounds good. You'll be at the airfield to meet the plane and will have a crew available to set out fire pots? I'll send you a complete set of instructions."

"Yes, I'll be there and I'll have the cash in U.S. dollars to pay him. By the way, Raymond, I heard the other day about a band of Zimbabweans, who terrorize people. They call themselves the Crocodile Gang. Do you know them?

Kaseke let out a guffaw. "Yes, of course! Last year the boys and I took on the name just to scare people. There are some real *tsotsis* in Matabeleland, with that name, but they are not us. We just pretend to be them so the people around here will help us find the elephant and protect us from the police."

"Why do you do this?"

Kaskeke immediately dropped onto the floor beside his desk. Lying face down on his broad belly, he put his hands in front of his face and simulated the opening and closing of a crocodile's jaws. Tembo looked on, mystified.

"You see people in the Zambezi Valley are very scared of spirits and they believe the crocodile's spirit is very powerful. So powerful, that when we had the solar eclipse earlier this year, they thought the sun disappeared because the crocodile God bit a chunk out of it, just to show that he's angry at the people."

"So, because they're afraid of you, they'll cooperate and won't report elephant poaching to the authorities? My goodness, that's a clever trick," Tembo said, doubling over in a fit of laughter. Kaseke rose, and the two men cordially shook hands.

*   *   *

Tembo was still chuckling as he climbed into the Mercedes, waved goodbye, and drove off. He had to admire Raymond's cunning. He was satisfied that even though Gu would not receive this shipment of ivory prior to their meeting on Friday, he could at least inform him of the new plan. While the quota problem still existed, he was more confident now that Kaseke had a good chance of producing the promised ivory, in time.

Chapter 18

Jessica was at home eating breakfast when the telephone rang. She had not seen Piet in more than a week and her heart flip-flopped when she heard his voice.

"I was planning to fly up the valley today to see if I could catch any poachers red-handed. I need a spotter. Do you want to come?"

"Sure, I'd love to. Where's Ananias?"

"I gave him a few days off. It's a rather sad situation. His mother's dying of AIDS. He also lost his father that way last year."

"So sorry to hear that. But I'm happy there's a good reason for me to tag along," she added, her voice brightening.

"Hey, why don't we stop at Mana and spend the night at the Lodge," van Rooyen proposed with a wink. "We could have dinner there and check up on Blair."

"Great idea! I'll pack an overnight bag."

He arrived at a quarter past eight, and she hopped aboard with a small travel case and a paper bag.

"Tuna salad sandwiches and some fruit for lunch." she said jiggling the bag.

"Good job! We can pick up some cool drinks at the airport."

By nine they had climbed aboard Whiskey-Kilo-Bravo and twenty minutes later were airborne.

"I phoned Blair," van Rooyen said. "He's expecting us and said he'd send a driver to pick us up at half past four."

Jessica responded with enthusiasm, "I've never stayed at the Nisbet Safari Lodge before. I'm looking forward to it."

"By the way, I got some interesting information the other day from Hector Kaminjolo," van Rooyen reported. "He claimed it came from a reliable source—his boss, no less. He said Zanunga told him about a bunch of poachers knocking around who called themselves the Crocodile Gang."

"Well, if they're anything like the species they're named after, they sound downright scary."

Van Rooyen continued, "Hector said they'd been operating mostly in Matabeleland, going after rhino horn, but they've taken elephant too. Have you ever been out to the Imire Safari Ranch in Wedza east of Harare?"

"Yes. In fact, I was there two years ago. I heard about the Imire attack last November; just awful," she added with a deep frown.

"In this instance, investigators don't think the Crocodile Gang was responsible," van Rooyen said. "They interviewed a maid, who'd been assaulted and left tied up. She described her attackers as being men dressed in Zimbabwe Army camouflage fatigues and armed with AK-47s. She said after they'd captured her, they forced another farm worker to lead them to the rhino pens. It was there they shot two females and a male rhino. One of the females was pregnant."

"So terribly sad. Wasn't there a survivor?"

"*Ja,* yes there was, a four-week-old calf they'd named Tatenda."

"Do you think the suspected poachers were actually regular soldiers?"

"The evidence supports it, but we'll probably never know for sure. Hector had *The Herald* publish a reward notice, offering three billion Zim dollars for information leading to the perpetrators' arrests, but no one ever came forward, and it didn't surprise him because the locals were scared shitless."

"Can you blame them?"

"No, I can't."

Still headed east, they spotted the twin bridges up ahead, spanning the Zambezi at Chirundu. A minute or two later they were flying over the A-1 highway, stretching southwards towards Harare.

"Look ahead; we're coming up on Fataran Farm," van Rooyen said. "Such a crying shame that this beautiful property with all its potential should be laid to waste!"

Jessica gazed down on what appeared to be weed-infested fruit orchards and barren fields, below. "Did I tell you," she said, "that Patrick's cousin, Elliot, once went there to find work and was met at the gate by armed guards? Patrick told me they threatened to shoot him if he didn't leave immediately."

"No, I hadn't heard that before."

"Well, is it possible it's the Crocodile Gang's base of operations?"

"I doubt that very much," he chuckled, shaking his head.

"How can you say that, Piet? You can plainly see, they're not taking care of the fruit orchards, so what are they doing? Besides, if they're conducting some legitimate business, why would they need armed guards?" Behind her sunglasses, Jessica's eyes flashed.

"It's no secret, Jessica, that hundreds of Mugabe's *shamwaris* have taken over productive, commercial farms, all across the country," he replied, his knuckles blanching as he tightened his grip on the control column. "But, instead of growing badly needed, food crops, they've turned nearly all of them into nothing more than weekend resorts. I'd bet the guards are in place simply to keep journalists, snoopers, and other undesirables away."

"Sorry Piet, but I disagree. I'm convinced Elliot's correct and bad stuff's going on there."

Surprised by her emotional outburst, even his own reaction, he offered an olive branch. "Tell you what, before we land at Mana Pools later this afternoon, we'll come back here and I'll make a low pass over the farm and we'll take a closer look."

"That's fine," Jessica responded, jutting out her chin. "But I have to tell you it's going to take some real hard evidence to change my mind."

Below them the Zambezi widened and small islands popped up which increased in size and number the further east they went. They flew over the Lodge, the Mana Pools National Park visitors' center, and on towards the Sapi Safari Area. Except for the narrow strips of green lining both sides of the river, the surrounding hills and valleys, stretching all the way to the horizon, appeared to be tinder dry. The rains were still six to eight weeks away, and the heat and the lack of moisture were combining to produce dangerous fire conditions.

Van Rooyen cut back on the throttle and they descended to 1,000 feet. Flying on in silence, Jessica kept her eyes fixed on the ground searching for elephants, people, or any signs of illegal activity. In the distance, twisting spirals of smoke rose from small bush fires.

Close to the Chewore confluence, she spied a herd of elephants browsing on a hillside. She reached for the binoculars and focused in turn on each member of the group, hoping to find one she recognized. Finally, she spotted a large, tusk less female.

"Piet, look down there on the hillside. Chembere and her family—eleven of them," she said. "Oh, wow! Look, a newborn," she whooped. "It's with Chembere's youngest daughter, China. Her name means Thursday in Shona. I'd named her unborn calf, China-Poshi, Thursday-One."

*　　　　*　　　　*

Her enthusiasm was contagious and he felt a quick surge of excitement. They had shared their first kiss a week ago, raising his hopes that she might indeed have reciprocal feelings for him. However, he wondered whether it was a transient attraction on her part, or potentially a true and lasting love. Her mood could change very quickly, as he'd just discovered.

They consumed their boxed lunches at noon, and flew on until the tail waters of Mozambique's Cabora Bassa Dam came into sight. Here, van Rooyen turned the Cessna around on a heading back to Mana Pools. On the way, they flew over the remains of Nkosikass's herd. Scavengers had picked clean the carcasses, leaving behind only piles of bones. He was relieved to find no evidence of any recent poaching along their flight path.

At three o'clock, they once again caught sight of the mighty Zambezi, spread out across Mana's flattened, fertile, flood plain with its many pools and ox-bow lakes.

"This sight never fails to enthrall me," van Rooyen said, as they approached one of the world's most celebrated natural sites.

"We're still going on to take a closer look at Fataran Farm aren't we?" Jessica asked.

"Glad you reminded me," van Rooyen replied with a wink. "It's less than ten minutes away, but when we get closer I'll drop down to under one thousand feet."

Jessica pulled out the binoculars and stared ahead in search of the farm's familiar layout. With the plane's nose pointed downwards, van Rooyen watched the altimeter needle revolve until it registered nine hundred feet. Then he leveled out and reduced speed. In the distance, they could see the farm's eastern boundary. Jessica peered through the binoculars.

"Look, they have a dirt air strip over there. It must get a fair amount of use; otherwise, it wouldn't be so bare. There'd be some vegetation growing on it," Jessica said.

"I see it."

While flying along the farm's southernmost boundary, Jessica gave a running commentary of what she was seeing.

"On this side there are barren fields and the homestead looks to be slap-dab in the middle. Along the road, leading to the A-1, there are some larger buildings." As they closed in. "There's a black sedan parked outside one of them. I might be able to see its license plate when we get a little closer."

"Do you need me to come in any lower?" van Rooyen asked.

Again, she lifted the binoculars. "No this is fine. There are two men standing next to the car. It doesn't look like it has a Zimbabwe plate. Its number...wait. It's B...something, BAJ 74. Now I've got it—BAJ 7432. Can you write that down?"

Van Rooyen grabbed a ballpoint from his shirt pocket and scribbled the number on the back of his hand. From the air, Jessica noticed the two men looking skywards.

"One of them," she said, "the guy next to the driver's door, is wearing a suit and tie. The other heavier fellow is dressed in a casual maroon shirt and jeans."

Van Rooyen turned the Cessna towards the river. Its southern bank was less than a quarter mile from the farm. "We don't want to cause any consternation down there," he said, "particularly if they're friends of Mugabe's. If I fly back to Mana along the river, they'll think we're just sightseers."

"So you don't think there's anything going on here that we should be concerned with?"

"No Jessica, I'm afraid, I don't," van Rooyen said with a rueful look.

Fifteen minutes later, van Rooyen brought Whiskey-Kilo-Bravo to a jolting halt after bumping along the dirt strip.

"With the amount of traffic that flies in to Mana Pools, bringing with it all those tourist dollars, you'd think the government would tar this runway," van Rooyen remarked dryly.

They disembarked and a minivan sporting a Nisbet Overland Safari logo drove up, and a tall black man climbed out. He wore olive-drab shorts and a tan golf shirt with the company emblem, embroidered on its left breast pocket.

"*Masikati Baas* Piet *na* Miss Jessica." He smiled as he approached them.

"Sulemon, I'm happy to see you!" Jessica said, shaking his outstretched hand.

He turned to greet van Rooyen. "How was your flight Mr. van Rooyen? I hope you didn't see any more charging elephants," he said chuckling.

"No Sulemon," Jessica cut in with a laugh. "No more charging elephants. They're all keeping close to the river to keep hydrated. The entire valley is parched. Let's hope the rains come soon," she replied.

"The rain will come in seven weeks Miss Jessica," he assured her.

"I hope you're right," van Rooyen said, as he reached behind the passenger's seat, pulled out the overnight bags, and passed them to Sulemon. Afterwards, he removed three wheel chocks from the rear of the cabin, secured the aircraft doors, and placed a chock behind each of the plane's wheels. Van Rooyen wasn't necessarily expecting high winds, but ever cautious, he believed in being prepared.

He took Jessica by the hand and they followed Sulemon to the minivan. Fifteen minutes later, they arrived at the Nisbet Safari Lodge.

"This place is certainly impressive," Jessica said, gazing up at the tall, three-story structure with its natural stone facade.

"It is," van Rooyen agreed, as his eyes scanned the river below, where hippos floated like a string of fat, brown sausages.

They entered the foyer and Blair limped forward on crutches to greet them.

"Hey Piet, Jessica! A grand welcome to the both of *ye*," he said in his ever-noticeable Scottish brogue. "Your accommodations await *ye*. No charge. *Ye're* here as my guests and my head porter will take you to your rooms."

"My goodness! Thanks Blair," van Rooyen said giving him a friendly slap on the shoulder. Jessica echoed his sentiments.

"Would *ye* both be able to have dinner with me at seven o'clock?"

"Absolutely! We'd love to!" Jessica replied.

The porter took their overnight bags from Sulemon and marched towards the elevator. Van Rooyen followed and Jessica trotted after them.

The porter pressed the button for the second floor and the lift jerked twice before it began its slow ascent. They exited and followed the porter who led them down a short corridor to the left. He stopped between two doorways.

"You have rooms twenty-five and twenty-six," he said, opening both doors with a master key. He carried both pieces of luggage into Room 25, set them on the luggage rack, and threw open the curtains.

Out in the hallway, van Rooyen whispered to Jessica, "Do you happen to have a U.S. dollar or two for a tip?" She dug into her pants pocket and pulled out a creased, five dollar bill handing it to the porter.

"Thank you, *Medem*," he said beaming, then bounded back to the elevator.

"I think you just made his day," van Rooyen chuckled.

*   *   *

After the porter departed, van Rooyen followed Jessica into her room. It was a good size with a double, four-poster bed. Above it, a wrapped mosquito net hung suspended from the ceiling. Just part of the decor, he realized, since the windows were fitted with insect screens. Paintings of wildlife and local landscapes hung on the walls.

"These are adjoining rooms, Piet. Our room keys also open the interconnecting door." She slipped her key into the lock and tried the door. But it remained shut. "You'll have to unlock your side to let me in."

He entered Room 25, opened the adjoining door and Jessica went in to retrieve her overnight bag.

"We've got almost two hours to spare before we meet Blair," he said, plunking himself down on the edge of the bed. "Come; sit." He pointed to a space beside him.

*   *   *

She sat on the bed and he turned to her, taking her in his arms. His kiss was gentle, but delivered with the self-confidence of a man who knew what he wanted. Jessica stiffened at first, but found herself relaxing and savoring his embrace.

He was solid, hard as a rock, and pure male all over. It had been so long since she'd been kissed, really kissed. His mouth was firm, eager, but surprisingly gentle; not rough and demanding as Paul's had been. His scent was an exotic blend of manliness and the earthy aromas of the African bush. Over her blouse, his hand cupped her breast and she felt her nipple harden. He repositioned her and they lay together kissing hungrily. He drew her even closer and the growing evidence of his arousal pressed against her.

Torn between her body's needs and feelings of uncertainty, she pulled back. It was too soon, she thought, to introduce intimacy into their relationship. His dead wife was probably somewhere, hovering in the background. Could she compete with a ghost? Would he hurt her as Paul had done? Placing her hands on his chest, she gently pushed him away and sat upright. He didn't resist.

"I'm sorry Piet," she said, noticing the confused look on his face. "Although I'm sorely tempted – the time just isn't right." She bent over, gave him a friendly peck on the cheek, and hurriedly returned to her room.

Later, both freshly showered and changed, they trooped downstairs together to the hotel bar. Climbing onto bar stools, she ordered a brandy and Coke and he ordered a beer. Van Rooyen pulled out a credit card to pay for the drinks.

"Are you Mr. van Rooyen and Miss Brennan," the bartender enquired.

"Yes we are. Why?" van Rooyen enquired with raised eyebrows.

"Well, your drinks are on the house tonight – by order of Mr. Nisbet."

She and van Rooyen looked at one another, wide-eyed in surprise. "How nice of him," she said.

Ten minutes later, Blair hobbled in on his crutches.

"Good evening, Piet, Jessica. I have a table reserved for us in the dining room. Why don't *ye* bring your drinks and follow me.

They followed him to a circular table set for three. Jessica looked around. Mounted heads of antelope, buffalo, and other game were displayed around the room. It was a large dinner hall with seating for at least 100 guests, she estimated. This evening, there were only nine other diners.

*   *   *

After the waiter left with their host's drink order, they studied the menu. Van Rooyen noted it had many of the usual appetizers – soups, avocado wedges, barbequed meatballs, vundu pâté, samoosas, and sausage rolls.

"What's vundu paté?" Jessica asked.

"The vundu is a local catfish. It makes quite a tasty pâté," Blair replied.

"Perhaps, I'll try it another time. I think I'll stick to just an entrée, this evening," she said.

"Me too," van Rooyen echoed. "I like the sound of that Green Bean Bredie." He was familiar with this traditional, South African, lamb dish.

Asides from the lamb, the menu included a number of local delicacies including Guinea Fowl with Lychees; Ostrich Neck Stew; Crocodile Brochettes, marinated in honey, lime and ginger; Haggis the well-known, traditional Scottish dish; and listed at the bottom of the page an assortment of grilled steaks – rump, fillet, and T-bone.

Van Rooyen glanced over at Jessica. She was studying the menu with deep concentration. He realized she was having difficulty making a selection. Not wanting to offend her, he attempted to disguise his amusement. It was likely these local dishes might be a little too exotic for her American palate.

Blair offered a recommendation. "Jessica, you should try the crocodile brochettes. The dish is one of our customers' favorites." Then he looked up at the waiter. "I do think I'll have the crocodile."

Minutes crept by and Jessica continued to stare bleakly at the menu. No longer able to contain himself, van Rooyen hid behind his dinner napkin to stifle a guffaw.

Finally she declared, "I believe I'll have a rump steak medium-rare," and she returned the menu to the waiter.

Afterwards, she stared at van Rooyen with narrowed eyes, and he realized his amusement had evidently not been lost on her.

"How are *ye* both for drinks?" Blair asked. "May I order another round?"

"No thanks," said Jessica, who was still nursing her brandy and coke. She glowered at van Rooyen and he countered with a wink and a smile.

"I'll take another Castle," van Rooyen replied and Blair signaled for a waiter and placed the order.

"Did ye see anything of interest up the valley during your flight today?" He enquired.

Van Rooyen replied, "Nothing of significance, just a lot of parched earth. The game's sticking pretty close to the river. Let's hope the rains come before November."

"Blair," Jessica broke in, "we overflew a farm near Chirundu that I suspect could possibly be involved in some poaching activities. Piet doesn't share my suspicions, but have you ever heard anything untoward about Fataran Farm?"

"*Cannae* say that I have," the Scotsman replied.

"We've heard rumors about a gang of poachers, who call themselves the Crocodile Gang," van Rooyen said. "Do you think they were responsible for the attack on the Imire Safari Ranch, last November? Jessica suspects they may be operating from Fataran Farm, but I haven't seen any evidence to suggest it."

"These poachers are a serious problem nowadays," Blair agreed. "But as far as the Imire attack, didn't witnesses say those rhinos were shot by soldiers?'

"I think you're right," van Rooyen said.

"So far, thank heavens, none of us in the professional hunting community here in Zim have had to tangle with any of those blighters," Blair continued. "We may carry weapons powerful enough to stop an elephant in its tracks, but I'm afraid our regular hunting arsenal wouldn't put up much of a defense against an AK-47." He leaned forward and whispered, "I do, however, keep a few big guns under wraps for emergencies."

Van Rooyen nodded and changed the subject.

"By the way, Blair, how are you professional hunters managing these days?" he asked. "It seems the tourist industry, overall, has practically dried up. Foreign visitors are staying away because of all the worldwide publicity about our failed economy, the violence, and sicknesses, cholera, and AIDS."

"Hunters are a peculiar breed," Blair began. "We tend to take things in stride. When a buffalo, rhino, or elephant has charged you, that's real fear – primordial terror. Lesser things don't faze us too much. I *cannae* say we haven't been affected. Our usual number of bookings has certainly gone down some, but we're still getting a pretty, steady stream of clients. One thing's definitely in our favor – with this country's huge inflation rate, our overseas visitors are getting a huge bang for their buck."

Van Rooyen broke in, "By the way, I heard on the radio, Saturday, that the government has introduced a new, fifty thousand Zimbabwe dollar bank note to ease the public's burden of having to push wheelbarrows full of the smaller denomination notes just to buy a bag of groceries. Trouble is, this new note is barely enough to buy two loaves of bread."

Jessica added with a chuckle, "ZANU-PF, of course, says the country's money troubles are all the fault of the western powers, the U.S. and U.K., in particular."

"How stupid is that?" van Rooyen said. Everyone knew the Zimbabwe's downfall had been caused by one man, Robert Mugabe.

"Piet, how's your Fish and Bait shop doing?" Blair asked. "I know retailers have been clobbered by the government's order to lower their prices. Now shopkeepers complain about having to sell their goods for less than what they paid for them."

"They're not exaggerating, Blair. In fact, it's forcing many businesses to close their doors permanently. I'm keeping the shop open only on weekends, now. I have to tell you something quite amazing. My shopkeeper, Moses Mafunda, tells me that when overseas customers come in, they say everything is too cheap. They often hand over an extra couple of U.S. dollars, or British pounds, and refuse to take the change."

"The fact he tells *ye* this, and doesn't just pocket the extra cash, shows *ye've* got a bloody good, honest bloke working for *ye*," Blair said.

"That, I know," van Rooyen said.

"Consider this also," Jessica said. "The fact they don't want change could be because they no longer want to be saddled with any worthless Zim dollars."

Van Rooyen said nothing. Despite Jessica's cynicism, he had confidence in Moses's integrity.

"By the way," Blair announced. "I have it on excellent authority that the government is going to retire the Zimbabwe dollar soon. They've run out of bloody bank notes."

"Are you serious?" Jessica asked wide-eyed.

"Deadly serious. So if *ye* have any Zim dollars stuffed under your mattresses, *ye'd* better spend them now, because after the switch they'll be worth nothing. It's going to be announced on TV and on the radio."

"Wow!" Jessica said, "Now I understand your porter's amazing reaction, when we tipped him with an American, five dollar bill. Honest to God, the man's eyes lit up like a pair of sparklers on the Fourth of July."

By half-past-nine other diners had long since left the restaurant and they were alone; all except for one lone waiter who was hovering near the kitchen door. Blair announced he was ready to retire and Jessica and van Rooyen thanked their host for his generous hospitality. After he limped out on his crutches, they made their way towards the elevator.

Jessica laughed and poked van Rooyen in the ribs, "I can't believe how you were making fun of me over the Crocodile Brochettes. I don't care. Even if they happened to be the Queen of England's favorite dish, I wasn't going to eat no damn crocodile. What are brochettes, anyway?"

"I haven't a clue. I really wasn't making fun of you. It was just the priceless look on your face, when Blair recommended the crocodile," he said, wrapping an arm around her while they waited for the lift.

When they entered van Rooyen's room, Jessica noticed the huge riverbank mural on the wall behind the bed, with its crocodiles basking in the sun.

"Pete, I'm glad I'm not the one sleeping in this room. Those crocs on the wall would give me nightmares." Jessica said. She walked towards him, stood on her tiptoes, and wrapping her arms tightly around his neck, she gave him a lingering kiss. Afterwards, she stepped back, squeezed his hand, and whispered, "Goodnight, Piet. Thanks for the wonderful day – I enjoyed it so much. I'm going to my room, and I'll see you in the morning." Without another word, she disappeared into the adjoining room.

Van Rooyen's eyes followed her as she exited and closed the door behind her. He heard the lock on the adjoining door make an audible click.

Chapter 19

Tuesday, September 09, 2008

While Van Rooyen and Jessica slept, fifty miles to the west of the Nisbet Safari Lodge, an elephant herd stirred in the mopane woodlands. Near the banks of Lake Kariba, the sun's flaming, orange orb was yet to emerge behind the hills of the Zambezi escarpment.

An early morning symphony of chirping birds, droning insects and low elephant rumbles filled the balmy air. Sharp cracks, snaps, and splintering sounds of twigs and branches crushed underfoot by the great beasts, supplied a rhythm accompaniment.

Meanwhile on the lower grassy slopes, rotund, mud-encrusted hippos meandered about grunting as they tore up squeaky mouthfuls of turf. After daylight had arrived, they trotted back to the safety of the lake and submerged, leaving only their eyes, nostrils, and a pair of swiveling ears still visible in the water.

Chembere had led her family here, after parting company with Muchengeti's herd two weeks earlier. With her were her three daughters with seven offspring, ranging in age from newborn to fifteen. They were soon joined by Ngomo, Nkosikaas's eldest son, born thirty-eight years before within sight of the Kariba Dam. He had roamed the valley all his life. As a calf, he had remained with his mother until expelled from the family group at adolescence. Afterwards, he kept company with other male elephants of similar age and social standing. Their playful, mock battles primed him for success, one day, as a breeding bull. Over the years, he'd learned females coupled only with the most robust, mature, and powerful bulls. Only last year he'd discovered that he was now a serious contender. He attained this status earlier than normal for a bull under 40 years of age, primarily because hunters and poachers had taken out most of his competitors.

Two days before, he had sensed the onset of musth—a period of several months when his testosterone level peaked, bringing on a surge of sexual aggression. He had, therefore, left the bachelor herd and struck out on his own. In search of a mate, he had traveled west for miles along the shores of the Zambezi.

As he approached the A-1 highway, he heard the sounds of vehicles speeding north and south. He emerged from the trees onto a grassy verge on the side of the road, and stepped out onto the tarmac. Suddenly he heard a screeching sound as a vehicle skidded to a sudden stop right in front of him. The car was emitting loud, booming sounds. Its horn blaring, and the driver shook his fist at him. Unconcerned, Ngomo nonchalantly crossed the road and disappeared into a stand of trees.

By the next morning, he had reached the shores of the lake, where, in the distance, he could hear the repeated calls of a female in estrus. He took off eagerly in the direction of the sound. It led him to Chembere and her family. Recognizable to the group by the broken tip of his right tusk, he approached each of the adult cows who greeted him respectfully. He quickly zeroed in on the female whose calls had resonated through the valley. Chitatu, already a mother of three whose youngest calf was now five years old, was again ready to breed.

Their courtship ritual began with Chitatu leading him on a chase through the mopane woods, while her family members looked on with interest. He remained with her for two days mounting her several times. As her chosen consort, it was his responsibility to protect her from the unwanted attentions of other younger, itinerant bulls; a task he performed with much gusto, until he detected from her scent she was no longer ovulating. Then, it was time for him to depart in search of other females.

Descendants of Chembere (Old woman)

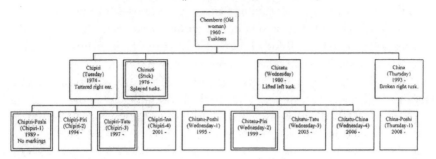

Single-frame box = female. Double-frame box = male.

Chapter 20

The Crocodile Gang was reputed to be the country's most ruthless, despised and feared band of thugs, predators, and poachers. Among Zimbabwe's deeply superstitious rural inhabitants, particularly those of the Zambezi Valley who held tenaciously to their ancient tribal beliefs, the gang was not only feared, but abhorred.

Raymond Kaseke and his band of poachers had been operating from Fataran Farm for at least a decade. While posing as the notorious Crocodile Gang, they had slaughtered many herds of elephants throughout the valley in search of 'white gold.' They were nothing other than charlatans, however, using the gang's fearsome reputation to secure the cooperation of local tribespeople. Failing that, their threats would coerce them to look the other way.

On Thursday morning, the telephone rang in Kaseke's office.

"Hello."

"Raymond, this is George Tembo here."

"Good morning, George. How are you?"

Ignoring the question concerning his health, Tembo continued, "Listen, my meeting with Shubo Gu is on Friday, October third. He postponed our earlier meeting because he had to return to China. Will your pilot will be delivering the ivory by next Wednesday?"

"Yes, George. It's all arranged."

"In the meantime, I have information about another elephant sighting. If you're able to take out this herd, it would double that shipment and put more money in your pocket."

"Tell me about it."

"Last night, a businessman flying in from Botswana told me he saw a herd with several bulls. Noon yesterday they were fifty miles west of the A-1, heading east."

"Good. I'll send out a team."

"Okay. Keep me informed." The line went dead.

Kaseke hurried from his office into the warehouse where his men were busy packing tusks cushioned in straw into cardboard coffins he had imported from China. He congratulated himself for this stroke of genius. Coffins served as a perfect shipping container. Not only were they affordable, but their importation raised few suspicions with the Zimbabwe customs officials. Due to the country's high mortality rate, caskets were always in demand. In addition, considering Africa's superstitions surrounding death, authorities would be less likely to open and search them for contraband.

"We are deploying on a mission first thing tomorrow morning," he announced to the men. "Report here for duty at five o'clock sharp with all your gear."

"Yes Sir," they chorused in union, saluting smartly, and stamping their feet.

Kaseke ambled over to the large map on the wall and lifted his meaty arm to point to a spot on the Zambezi's southern bank, east of Kariba Dam.

"Look here. Our boatmen will pre-position the boats at this bend of the river. It's one mile east of the Rifa Hunting Camp; only sixteen miles up-river from here."

"What time should they go?" his foreman, Stanley Matombo, wanted to know.

"It's nine o'clock now," he said glancing at the Rolex on his paunchy wrist. "Tell them to leave no later than two thirty, this afternoon, so they'll be in position before four o'clock. I'll have a driver waiting to pick them up."

By five o'clock that evening, Kaseke's men had moored both boats on the riverbank and his driver was returning to Fataran Farm with all four boatmen aboard.

*　　　　　*　　　　　*

Meanwhile, van Rooyen and Jessica were airborne over Mana Pools; returning to Kariba after completing an elephant count in the Sapi Safari Area.

"I was happy to see Muchengeti and her family this morning," Jessica commented. "I'll phone Precious first thing tomorrow morning to arrange to release the calf with Muchengeti's herd on Monday."

"What was your official count for Sapi?" van Rooyen enquired.

"Two hundred and sixty-five."

"I'd have expected a higher number," he said. "Especially since, at this time of the year, they are sticking pretty close to the river."

"Perhaps some of them have crossed over into Zambia because of all the poaching on this side," she ventured. "By the way Piet, I've been meaning to ask; have you heard anything more from your friend Angus McLaren?"

"We spoke yesterday," van Rooyen replied. "He's still on the farm, but he's sent Patsy and his dog, Skellum, to Harare to stay with relatives. He told me tensions on the farm are running high. Disaster, the so-and-so who showed up while I was there, has apparently been identified as a Clever Chitape, a well-known ZANU-PF rabble-rouser. Angus says he's in the pay of party big-wig, Ishmael Gondo.

"Who's he?"

"Gondo's the deputy minister for National Housing and Social Amenities."

"One of Mugabe's cronies?"

"Of course."

"Piet, how come these farm seizures are starting up again? Since the power sharing agreement was signed last month, between Tsvangirai and Mugabe, shouldn't they be trying to conserve the few productive, commercial farms that are still left?"

"Angus told me the Commercial Farmers Union believes top military officials, and other ZANU-PF hardliners, are going all-out to seize all the remaining, white-owned farms. Finishing the job before the country installs a new government, which could put a stop to it.

"Piet, how do you feel about all that's happened since independence?"

"There were, believe it or not, some 6,500 large-scale commercial farms when Mugabe first came to power in 1980. Admittedly, they sat on about seventy percent of Zimbabwe's best farm land. Farmers agreed there was indeed an inequity here and, after independence, most were willing to work with Mugabe to level the playing field. The farming community, including my Mum and Dad, were especially encouraged when we heard him say, during some of his earliest radio speeches, that he credited the agricultural community for most of the country's exports and foreign currency earnings. He then spoke out, encouraging white farmers to stay and remain a part of the new Zimbabwe."

"That must have been good news."

"Everyone breathed a huge sigh of relief. To begin with, a lot of white farmers, my dad and me included, supported his initial land reform program. It seemed fair, especially when the government began by suggesting that farmers with more than one farm put up one of their properties for sale. The policy then was to take farms on a willing seller-willing buyer, basis. In fact, one of our neighbors put up his six thousand-acre farm. Land values had plummeted by then, so although he didn't get as much as he wanted, it was enough to buy another smaller farm in Karoi."

"When did it all start to fall apart?"

"During his first twenty years in office. Mugabe did some admirable things, but he also perpetrated some unspeakable crimes. Under his leadership, for instance, Zimbabwe developed a top-notch educational system, available to all; Africa's best. Under white rule, I'm afraid, few black Zimbabweans got more than just a primary school education. Mugabe, however, made it possible for the smartest kids, of any race, to go on to become doctors, lawyers, scientists, and engineers. By 2003, Zimbabwe had the highest literacy rate in Africa; surpassing even South Africa's."

"That's commendable," Jessica said, noticing the look of pride on van Rooyen's face when he spoke of the positive things about his homeland. "You really love this country, don't you?"

"I do! I really do! But damn it, nowadays it seems I spend most of my time bitching about every bloody thing."

"You mentioned unspeakable crimes. What's that all about?"

"Unspeakable crimes. How about genocide for one," he burst out. "Haven't you heard about his *gukurahundi* – Mugabe's military operation in Matabeleland?"

"Only vague references to it," Jessica replied.

"Well," he began, "*Gukurahundi* is the Shona term referring to the seasonal rains that wash away the chaff of the previous year's crop. In other words, the purging of the old for the new; an act of purification. Mugabe is a member of the ethnic, Shona majority. Before independence, his strongest political opponent was Joshua Nkomo, a member of the Ndebele tribe that's centered around Bulawayo, in Matabeleland. There's always been a fierce rivalry between the Shona, a pastoral people, and the Ndebele, who are an offshoot of the warring Zulus. Before the white man came, the Ndebeles frequently attacked the weaker, Shona people to steal their cattle and women. This rivalry still exists, and Mugabe wanted to rid himself of his opposition. But rather than eliminate Nkomo himself, he decided instead to reduce the number of his supporters. That's why, three years after he became President, he ordered his North Korea-trained, Fifth Brigade to attack the Ndebele civilian population."

"What a hellish plan," Jessica exclaimed her eyebrows raised.

"In truth, the situation may have been more complicated than simple tribal rivalry between Mugabe and Nkomo. Anyway, the Fifth Brigade was deployed to Matabeleland in January 1983. The exact number of civilians – men, women and children – murdered by those soldiers is unknown even to this day, but it's been pegged it as high as 20,000."

"Oh my God, Piet, that's huge! How come the world wasn't outraged?"

"Because, for a long, long time, the world knew nothing about it."

"How come?"

"The media was tightly controlled and few Zimbabweans outside Matabeleland knew anything about it. Those who might have known were just too intimidated, too afraid, to breathe a word. It finally took an effort, years later, by a commission empowered by the Zimbabwe Catholic Bishops' Conference to open up that can of worms."

"It sounds a lot like the ethnic cleansing in Bosnia and Somalia. So sad," Jessica shook her head. "And the land reform debacle, what prompted that?"

Van Rooyen explained that after independence the government resettled some 140,000 people onto millions of acres of previously white-owned farmland; the undertaking accomplished with a portion of the £630 million that Great Britain had pledged to fund land reform.

"But because the government provided none of the new farmers with seed and fertilizer, they were hamstrung," he said, "unable to produce any food even for themselves, far less the entire country."

"Then, what happened?"

"When it later became apparent that Mugabe had not turned over most of the farms over to 'landless blacks,' but had instead given them to his *shamwaris* in return for political favors, Great Britain promptly withdrew its support."

"What a waste," Jessica commented.

"Oh, and before I forget," van Rooyen said. "Let me finish telling you what Angus told me. He said things were incredibly tense on the farm. Last week, when he and his neighbors met with a representative from Justice for Agriculture, the man informed them that of the original 6,500 white Zimbabwean farmers, they were among the fewer than 300 still left on their farms. Angus said Disaster is now permanently camped out on his front lawn, and every night he brings in drunken reinforcements to bang on drums and sing raucous songs until the early hours of the morning. Now, anytime Angus tries to leave the farm he's threatened by men armed with pangas."

Jessica listened, open-mouthed.

Van Rooyen continued. "They've herded off all his cattle, including the dairy cows, and have trampled his vegetable garden. He's now living off whatever canned food is left in his pantry. They've cut his phone line, and even though he still has his cell phone, he worries about keeping it charged, because of power blackouts. He knows the end is coming, so he's spending most of his time packing up valuables, and he's running out of boxes so I told him I'd bring him some tomorrow."

They flew west towards the sun. It hovered low on the skyline. Despite being filtered through a smoky, dust-filled, atmosphere, the sun would have been blinding except for a bank of clouds squatting conveniently on the horizon, shielding his eyes from the glare. They had yet to reach the Chirundu bridges. Van Rooyen scanned the river's southern bank in search of the three boats they'd spotted that morning. He wondered if they were the same ones, he and Ananias had seen prior to the massacre of Nkosikaas's herd.

"Jessica, keep an eye out for those boats we saw this morning. We're getting close now."

She craned her neck to see out his side window.

"I see something down there," she said. "But it looks to be only one boat not three. I'll have to get up to see down there," she said, unsnapping her seat belt.

"No Jessica," he said in a stern voice. "Put your seat belt back on. I'll circle so you can see them out your window."

Van Rooyen swung the Cessna into a steep turn. Momentarily, it rotated around the tip of its left wing as he brought it around for Jessica to get a clearer view.

"There's only one," Jessica confirmed. "It's a long speed boat, identical to the three we saw this morning. I've seen them before on TV. They're the kind that drug smugglers use in Florida; fast boats. In the States, I think they call them cigar or cigarette boats."

"They might use them to smuggle drugs in Florida," van Rooyen said. "But here I'm damned sure they're being used to transport poached ivory. I saw three of these boats moored here on the river, right before Nkosikaas's family was wiped out, almost eight weeks ago. After the slaughter, I saw the poachers loading the tusks. You remember the photos I gave to Kaminjolo? They were in those images."

"Was that less than eight weeks ago? It seems it was longer," Jessica said.

"The only difference, Jessica, is that then there were three of them. Now there's only one. Where are the other two?"

"What is that thing sticking up on its bow, Piet?"

"I saw them this morning. I thought they looked like gun turrets"

Jessica's voice hardened. "Really? Surely they wouldn't be shooting elephants from a boat?"

"Rather, I imagine they're employed for defense against an enemy; the authorities probably, or maybe even fellow poachers."

Van Rooyen pulled Whisky-Kilo-Bravo out of its turn and pointed the Cessna on a south-west heading for Kariba.

From 2,000 feet, he and Jessica saw the A-1 slip beneath them. They also saw wildlife heading down to the river—buffalo, wildebeest, zebra, and small antelope—to gather along the lush, green riverbanks. Also ambling towards the water's edge, were giraffes, long necked and graceful. At the bank, they reached to quench their thirst, heads down and forelegs splayed apart.

While the banks were lush with green vegetation, the grasslands and tree-spotted woodlands, that climbed the hills and rocky promontories on both sides of the river, were a dusty, brownish-gray and dry as a bone. In the distance, tendrils of smoke drifted skywards from dozens of small veld fires.

Less than twenty minutes after they spotted the boats, Jessica caught sight of a group of about a dozen elephants at the river's edge. Jabbing her finger downwards beside her window, she called out.

"Look Piet! Down there. Do you see them?"

"Where? I can't see anything."

"You'll have to turn around. We've flown past them."

"Do you recognize them?" van Rooyen asked, as he swung Whisky-Kilo-Bravo around.

"There's a big, old girl down there with no tusks. It must be Chembere. I see twelve of them; cows and calves. One of the calves is a newborn. Remember we saw them two weeks ago," she called out, gesturing in excitement. "I've now named China's baby, China-Poshi."

"That's good Jessica! But wait! Think about the two missing boats. They could have been positioned somewhere else to lay in wait for those particular elephants." Van Rooyen frowned deeply as he leveled out and turned back towards Kariba.

"Oh no!" Jessica cried out. "What are we going to do?"

"Whatever it is, we'll have to move fast, extremely fast. I'm thinking they already know about this herd and are planning to take them out. I'd swear they're the very same bastards that took out Nkosikaas's group. The only difference is, this time they'd better be prepared because we're going to be ready for them," van Rooyen barked, his jaw set in determination.

"What if they come tonight?"

"There's not enough time. It's already after six and the sun will be gone in fifteen minutes. They won't be able to do anything after dark."

"So what are we going to do?"

"As soon as we get back, we need to alert Kaminjolo and speak to Blair about getting some half-decent weapons."

*　　　*　　　*

At eight o'clock that evening, van Rooyen and Jessica sat in Jessica's kitchen, eating pizza when the doorbell rang. Jessica got up to answer it.

"Hector!" she said cheerfully. "Please come on in. Thanks for coming over at such short notice. I'm sorry we've had to cut in on your evening like this."

"No problem." he said as he stepped through the door.

"Come this way. Piet and I are in the kitchen. Would you like a slice of pizza?"

"No thanks," he said. "Margaret and I just ate supper."

"Hector, it's good of you to come," van Rooyen said rising to greet him and pulling out a chair.

"So, what's happening?"

"Hector, you remember the poaching incident last month in the Chewore Safari Area?"

"Of course."

"Well, I'm positive those same buggers are about to slaughter another herd. Twelve of them. Probably as early as tomorrow morning."

"Why do you think this?"

"Because I'm thinking they've tied up two of those long boats in the vicinity of the Rifa Hunting Camp – the very same boats they used to carry off the ivory last time. While we didn't actually see the boats there, they're definitely missing from their usual mooring. Also, this afternoon, when Jessica and I were flying in, we found elephants, five or six miles west of the Rifa Camp, and heading towards it."

"If I could, I would really like to get those *tsotsis*," Kaminjolo said, rubbing his hands together in anticipation.

"Well, with your help, Hector, I reckon we could take them on tomorrow. I've talked it over with Blair Nisbet, and I believe we could do it."

Kaminjolo's eyes brightened. "So, what's your plan?"

"We'll locate the herd first thing in the morning and set up surveillance. When the poachers come in for the kill, we'll surprise them and pin them down until you can get the police out to make the arrests. I would suggest you call the member-in-charge tonight and let him know in advance about what's going down."

A worried frown crossed Kaminjolo's face. "It's a good plan, Piet, but I don't believe we'll get any cooperation from the police. They'll just tell me they don't have the manpower, trucks or the petrol and that elephants are my business, not theirs."

Van Rooyen grimaced in disgust. "Damn! Same old story." Then his face brightened. "We don't need them, Hector. Your rangers have arrest authority. We'll do it without them," he declared emphatically, punching his right fist into his left palm. "Blair Nisbet's ready and willing to help and although he's not yet one hundred percent mobile, he's shed his crutches and says he'll be able to take up a static shooting position. But most importantly, he's going to provide us with some weapons to counter their AK-47s."

"How many people can we get who're already trained on these guns?" Kaminjolo said. "Very few of my rangers are qualified."

"I'll take one," van Rooyen said, jabbing his chest. "Then there's you, Blair and his tracker Sulemon, two of my three guys Ananias and Mathias. That makes six. Hector, what about your guy, Patrick?"

"Patrick's ambitious, he's served in the Police Reserve and I'm sure he's had training on automatic weapons," he replied.

Good old Patrick, Jessica thought to herself. Hector's right on about his being ambitious. She wondered if Hector suspected that Patrick planned to have his job one day, before stepping up to take Albert Kanunga's position as director general of Zim Parks.

"I'll get John Chitsaru, and he'll enlist three other rangers," Kaminjolo said.

"Well that makes an even dozen. Now, let's phone Blair and see if he can supply any more manpower."

Van Rooyen dialed Blair's cell phone. When it rang, he pressed the speaker button on his phone and laid it on the kitchen table. After five rings, Blair picked up.

"Blair Nisbet here."

"Blair, it's Piet. I have you on speaker and Hector and Jessica are here with me."

"And a very fine evening to *ye* all," he said cheerfully.

Greeting returned, Van Rooyen brought him up to speed on their discussion so far.

"Blair, Hector doesn't think it's likely we'll get any support from the Zimbabwe National Police. Do you have anyone qualified on automatic weapons?"

"Sulemon, of course, and I may also be able to bring Skip Brankhorst along, my other professional hunter. But I'm not sure if he has any clients booked tomorrow," Blair said.

"Excellent! To recap, we'll have a contingent of twelve, possibly thirteen. Jessica will be the lookout and will be in continuous radio contact with three of us. We'll take three vehicles, mine, Hector's, and Blair, do you still have that vehicle, you use for game drives with the rear seating for ten to twelve?

"*Aye* I do," he confirmed.

"Bring it if you would. The plan for tomorrow then: those of us in Kariba will meet at Hector's office at quarter past five, sharp. We'll depart no later than five thirty. Blair can you meet us at Rifa Camp at eight?"

"No sweat Piet," Blair replied. "Instead of taking the low road, along the river, we'll take the shortcut over to Rifa Camp, which should get us there easily by eight."

"Is there anything more we need to talk about?" van Rooyen asked.

"Yes," Jessica said. "Piet, you bring drinking water, most important. I know you have first aid supplies, shovels, ropes, and tarps in your truck, just in case we need them. Everyone should bring their own lunches. I'll make ours. Anything else?"

"I'll bring some guns and ammo," Blair added.

"That's good," Kaminjolo nodded his approval and added, "I'll bring the handcuffs."

"Then we'll see you tomorrow, Blair," van Rooyen said and hung up.

Jessica was excited; more than thankful action was being taken to save Chembere's family and proud, too, of the men willing to risk their lives to do it. She looked at van Rooyen and her chest tightened with love and admiration for him.

Kaminjolo rose. "Well, I'll be going then. We're starting early tomorrow and we all need some sleep."

"We appreciate your help, Hector," van Rooyen said as he walked him to the door. "We'll see you in the morning."

"Goodnight Pete, Jessica," Hector said, saluting as he turned and disappeared into the darkness.

"He's right, we need an early night," Jessica agreed. "I'll set the alarm for four thirty. Enough time for me to make the lunches."

They kissed briefly and then she stood at the front door watching van Rooyen drive away. How long would it take them to trust one another and themselves, she wondered.

Chapter 21

Friday, September 26, 2008

At five thirty the next morning, the sun had yet to emerge above the hills of the escarpment when two rugged, four-wheel-drive vehicles pulled away from the Kariba Zim Parks' office. Hector led the way accompanied by Ananias, Mathias, and Patrick. Van Rooyen and Jessica followed close behind.

After leaving the town, they veered off the tarmac road that continued on to Makuti, passed the dam wall, and turned towards the river. Jessica tensed as van Rooyen followed Kaminjolo steering the Land Rover down a narrow, twisting dirt track that took them down a steep incline to the riverbank.

When they reached the bottom, she glanced back to see the colossal concrete dam wall towering above them. No torrents of water surged through its six floodgates today; only trickles escaped which, over the years, had striped the concave wall with dark stains. Until today, she had never seen the wall up this close, or from this perspective. It was as tall as a forty-two-story building and with its flood gates closed, lake water was channeled through the underground, hydroelectric turbines of both the north and south power plants. From there, the water returned to the Zambezi through three massive outlets on both banks, and flowed another seven hundred miles to the Indian Ocean.

Jessica's musings were interrupted by a hard jolt as the Land Rover slammed into a gigantic pothole. For several miles, they had been driving along a treacherous dirt track, following a narrow, earthen ledge perched ten feet above the south bank. In places, last February's torrential rains had created deep gullies and drop-offs.

"This road is something else," Jessica commented as the Land Rover bounced over the uneven, rutted track.

"This is just a hunting trail," van Rooyen reminded her, "not a public thoroughfare. The Roads Department isn't responsible for its maintenance. Once in a while, if a section becomes impassable, Hector's people will move a fallen tree or fill in a deep gully."

Their progress eastward to the hunting camp, twenty-five miles downriver, was painfully slow.

"I'm keeping a distance of at least four or five car lengths behind Hector to give us plenty of room to react to any obstacles," van Rooyen said.

After several more miles, the narrow ledge gradually sloped away and they found themselves driving along a sandy beach beside the river. Ahead, Jessica saw groups of impala and other wildlife scrambling up the hillside to their right, spooked by the oncoming vehicles. Further on, downed trees, large rocks, or gullies too wide for the vehicles to traverse, occasionally blocked the road. To negotiate around such obstacles, both drivers had to shove their vehicles into four-wheel-drive and create their own deviations.

They had traveled approximately ten miles when they came upon a large bull elephant standing directly in their path. From the broken tip on his right tusk, Jessica recognized him as thirty-eight-year-old, Ngomo, son of Nkosikaas. The streaming temporal glands on both sides of his face were a clear indication he was in musth and likely to be temperamental, if not downright aggressive. Kaminjolo brought his vehicle to a dead stop some fifty yards short of where the bull stood. Van Rooyen pulled up another three vehicles' length behind him. Jessica was relieved Kaminjolo chose not press his luck by attempting to drive forward and challenge Ngomo.

Both vehicles remained stationary until Ngomo casually tramped down into the shallows to drink and bathe himself. As Jessica looked on, Kaminjolo restarted his engine and cautiously moved forward. She surmised he thought it was now safe to move. The bull, however, who'd been knee-deep in the river, more than thirty feet away, suddenly trounced back onto the trail and spun around to face Kaminjolo's truck, charging forward with an ear-piercing, trumpet.

Horrified, Jessica watched as Kaminjolo reversed rapidly, almost back ending their vehicle. Surprisingly Ngomo stopped short and then nonchalantly trudged back into the river. After drinking his fill, he sprayed himself with water and then mischievously blew a trunkful Kaminjolo's way. Afterwards, he stepped out of the river, stomped across the trail, climbed up the hill, and disappeared into the bush. Ngomo's show, Jessica thought, while both scary and entertaining, had delayed them almost twenty minutes.

After traveling several more miles, they came across a tall rock spire blocking their path. By the time van Rooyen and Jessica reached it, Kaminjolo had moved ahead of them and was already out of sight.

"How did he do it?" van Rooyen questioned. Undeterred, he thrust the vehicle into four-wheel-drive. "Hold on, Jessica," he cautioned. "The going looks steep. Just hang on tight."

"I'm fine," Jessica said, gritting her teeth and reaching out for handholds.

Van Rooyen accelerated, steering up the steep grade, coaxing the Land Rover forward as its motor roared and its wheels spun. "Come on! Dammit let's go. Let's do this!" he growled, as he slammed his foot down on the accelerator.

The truck's engine shrieked as the tires spun, ejecting small rocks, and churning out billowing clouds of dust. Finally, the wheels gained purchase and with a violent lurch, the Land Rover ascended the steep rise, ploughing over thorn bushes and young tree saplings. Jessica hung on for dear life, her face buried in her shoulder, silently blessing the person who'd invented seat belts and panic handles. Finally around the rock spire, van Rooyen brought them back safely to the river's edge. Jessica breathed a huge sigh of relief.

She looked at her watch. "Piet, it's almost six thirty. We've been on the road for nearly an hour."

"It's been slow going, I know," he replied. "But we should catch up with the elephants before eight o'clock. Hopefully Blair and company will already be there."

*   *   *

Earlier that morning at Fataran Farm, Kaseke's eleven-man team had reported for duty at precisely five o'clock as ordered. All wore their newly issued desert camouflage fatigues, of Chinese manufacture. The team's first order of business was to assemble outside the armory to receive a weapon.

Kaseke's right-hand-man, Stanley, signed out AK assault rifles to the men, selected one for himself, and an M4A1 carbine for his boss. The M4A1 was the semi-automatic now in use, by American forces, in Iraq and Afghanistan. Kaseke had acquired his on the black market. After issuing team members their weapons, Stanley led them over to the packing shed to collect their food rations. Kaseke's enormous, camouflage-clad frame stood at the entrance to greet them.

"*Mangwanani*, good morning, gentlemen," he boomed. "Today will be a good day, and tomorrow we can fill more coffins," he said in Shona, as he pointed back to the far wall where ivory-filled caskets were stacked in rows.

"You boys have done a good job of packing. Perhaps, tomorrow we'll be able to fill another twelve of these fine boxes." Pointing behind him he said, "Gladis, over there, has your rations for the day."

He explained the food packs contained a new kind of military ration that the Americans called MREs, and that he'd been able to procure several large crates of the 'Meals-Ready-to-Eat,' from his contact in Islamabad. This announcement brought cheers from the men and they stuffed the pockets of their fatigue jackets and pants with the MRE packs.

At precisely 5:45 a.m., Kaseke and his eleven-man team boarded two vehicles, a gray Nissan X-trail, with Zambian plates, and a blue Toyota Tundra twin-cab. The Nissan, on loan to Kaseke, was registered in the name of Olivia Tembo, George's wife. With its Zambian registration, he believed Zimbabwe authorities would be less likely to search it, during border crossings. They'd also find its ownership harder to trace. In the bed of the Toyota were three gasoline powered chain saws, ropes, and two full fuel cans. The weapons were stowed in the Nissan's trunk area, along with ammunition boxes and six-packs of bottled water.

Kaseke driving the Nissan, led the way through the farm's security gate to the A-1, five miles down the road. There, he took a right towards the Chirundu Bridges and after a mile turned left, heading west on a narrow dirt track paralleling the Zambezi.

It was a particularly hazardous stretch, where cyclists, pedestrians, and animals, both wild and domestic, weaved mindlessly all over it. Kaseke was forced to slam on brakes when a warthog sow with three piglets in tow suddenly ran out of the bush.

"Hey, why didn't you run over them, *VaKaseke*," asked the young man in the passenger seat. "*Ndinoda nyama*, I want meat." Others in the back guffawed.

"Pay attention!" Kaseke snapped, in annoyance. "When you are on a mission, you keep your mind on the job ahead. Not on your stomach!"

Suitably chastised, the youths fell silent. Then to ease their boredom, they began belting out contemporary Zimbabwean reggae and urban groove songs. To provide rhythm accompaniment, they clapped their hands, pounded the seat backs, and leant out the windows to beat on the truck door panels.

"Why do you sing these rubbish songs?" Kaseke bellowed over the din. "Our traditional ones are much better."

"You are too old-fashioned, *VaKaseke*. This is Zimbabwe's music of the future," a young man, in the back seat, called out.

A mile or two south of the river, they passed several villages with mud-daubed huts, topped with cone-shaped, thatched roofs. The tiny dwellings stood in carefully swept, dirt clearings alongside untilled fields. Seed for next year's crop had likely cost more than these families could afford. Besides, it was made available only to card-carrying members of the ZANU-PF. In the fields among the weeds in the parched soil, stood dried maize stalks leaning drunkenly at all angles – the remnants of a crop from several years before.

In one of the villages, Kaseke noticed a woman with an infant on her back pounding her few precious kernels into maize meal. Gathered around her were shirtless, barefoot children of varying ages with visibly protruding ribs. Kaseke knew Zimbabwe's rural folk had been hit hard by Mugabe's land reform policies, but he didn't consider this any of his concern. He had few complaints. He'd received Fataran Farm thanks to his uncle who was an important man and close friend and confidante of the President's.

The woman heard the approach of the two vehicles emitting the raucous singing. She looked up as they sped by, smothering her and the youngsters in clouds of dust. Her children leaped up, waving frantically, and chased after the trucks until their mother called them back. Kaseke eyed his watch. It was closing in on seven o'clock. They should reach the boats in about ninety minutes.

Meanwhile, unbeknownst to both Kaseke and Kaminjolo, the opposing forces were headed on a collision course that would bring them face to face in less than two hours.

*　　　　*　　　　*

Jessica took a deep breath. Now seven thirty, they had been on the road for two hours. After that terrifying detour around the rock spire, she was thankful to be alive, counting her lucky stars the Land Rover hadn't overturned, and rolled into the river, where she and Piet could have become a crocodile's breakfast.

Ten minutes later, they came upon Chembere and her family crossing the road. Kaminjolo slid his vehicle to a halt, with van Rooyen pulling up beside him. Tuskless Chembere, her three adult daughters, and their offspring ambled across the road, kicking up little puffs of dust with their feet. They had obviously been down at the river, because their wet hides glistened in the morning sun.

Jessica gazed at them through the trees lining the road as they milled about in a bare patch of ground. They scooped up the sandy soil, blowing it across their heads and over their backs to protect themselves from insect bites and the searing African sun. Afterwards they browsed for pods in a grove of acacia trees close to the trail.

The immediate area was dotted with rocky outcrops on both sides of the road. Kaminjolo pointed to a large hillock between them and the river. "We could park the trucks behind that big *gomo*, over there," he whispered.

"Excellent idea, Hector," van Rooyen murmured.

As the two vehicles moved off the trail, Blair, Sulemon, Skip Bronkhorst, John Chitsaru, and his three rangers arrived from the Mana Pools National Park and fell in behind them. With the trucks concealed and weapons dispersed, Jessica and the twelve men crossed the road. Not far away they could hear the elephants crashing around.

"They're back there in the bush," van Rooyen whispered to Blair, pointing to the tree line to the south. With the men shouldering their weapons and everyone toting supplies, they crossed the trail and slipped in among the acacia trees.

"Lads, we couldn't have found better country for mounting an ambush," Blair said. "We can conceal ourselves among these rocks."

"Wait, hey. Hold on a minute," van Rooyen cautioned the group, "Let's not get too carried away here. We're not fighting a war. We're here to support Hector in protecting Zimbabwe's wildlife."

Kaminjolo responded immediately. "He's correct, and I'm thankful to have your help. And because you are my good friends, I must tell you to be careful. When it comes to shooting poachers, the courts are not always on your side, especially if you are a white man. Some of my European rangers and game wardens should have received awards for their brave deeds while protecting the black rhino. Instead, they were arrested and put in jail. One ranger shot a poacher in self-defense, and was charged with murder. He's still in Chikurubi Maximum Security Prison."

"Did the police get the poachers?" Patrick said.

"No. The police didn't arrest any of them. It's a very bad thing, but nothing ever happens to the poachers."

"We appreciate your candor, Hector. Thank you," van Rooyen said. "Watch out everybody. None of us wants to spend a single minute in that hellhole they call Chikurubi. These weapons are only to scare them off. Remember to aim high over their heads. There's just one exception. If you're threatened, save yourself and then shoot to kill. But make sure you have a witness to testify in court. One more warning, don't any of you knock off a bloody elephant, or you'll have this woman to answer to," he said, reaching out with a wide grin and wrapping his arm around Jessica.

"For your information and her protection," van Rooyen added, "Jessica is unarmed. All she's armed with is a two-way radio because her job is to coordinate things and communicate directly with me and Hector."

"Blair, thanks for the use of your rifles," Kaminjolo said, adding with a chuckle, "I'm hoping with these guns and my bullhorn, we can scare those *tsotsis* into giving up."

Jessica's watch showed ten minutes past eight o'clock.

*   *   *

While Kaminjolo and company set up their defenses, Kaseke and his twelve-man band were less than five miles away, traveling west parallel to the river towards the spot where they had moored their boats. Kaseke drove the lead vehicle, with Stanley following in the Toyota. Kaseke kept his eyes peeled on both sides of the trail for any sign of the elephants. Based on George Tembo's information, he expected to find them not far from the boats. At fifteen minutes to eight, just two or three miles from the mooring, he stopped the Nissan, climbed down, and addressed the men in Shona.

"If anyone needs to urinate, do it here, now. We won't stop again until we see the elephants."

The men piled out of the vehicles and headed into the bush, making faces and joking with one another. After they had sauntered back, Kaseke addressed the group in hushed tones.

"From now on, we advance in total silence. There'll be no more talking, singing, or clapping."

"Yes, Sir!" they chorused.

Angrily, Kaseke swore at them, under his breath. "Don't you stupid people understand total silence?" he hissed.

Ten minutes later, they closed in on the boats tied up on the riverbank. The watercraft were over a rise and out of sight, less than a quarter of a mile away. Kaseke slowed the vehicle and they began crawling forward. Filled with anxiety, he wondered if. Maybe the herd hadn't been moving east as Tembo had assured him.

*   *   *

Three miles away, Kaminjolo, Piet, Jessica, and their group had left their vehicles parked north of the trail and were heading towards the elephants. They moved into the wind, so the herd wouldn't catch their scent. Creeping silently though the bush, they carefully stepped over dried twigs and branches. Chembere's family was foraging noisily in a stand of marula trees, some five hundred feet ahead. Closer now, Van Rooyen pointed to a circle of rocky outcrops and earthen ant mounds which surrounded the herd. He signaled the team to conceal themselves.

Jessica treaded softly towards tall, granite, balancing-rock formation to the west of the herd. It was higher than any other possible outlook in the immediate area. At its base, a few stunted trees grew out of the loose shale surrounding the pillar like rocks. Using the tree trunks as supports to pull herself up, she climbed to the first level.

From there, she scanned the boulders above her, searching for useful hand and footholds. Finding some, she hauled herself up onto the next level, six feet from the ground. Now for the top, she thought, as she spotted a broken piece of granite trapped between two large boulders. Pulling herself up, she squeezed her frame between the boulders, which were almost as tall as she was. Now perched fifteen feet above the ground, she had a panoramic view of the elephants and the surrounding bush.

The two-way radio in her pants pocket vibrated. Pulling it out, she held it to her lips. "Jessica, over," she said softly.

"It's Piet," van Rooyen responded. "Show us your location. Over."

She raised her arm.

"Good. I see you. Looks like you've got an excellent view. Over."

"Affirmative," she replied. "Where are you and Hector? Over." Jessica scanned the surrounding area and spotted van Rooyen, east of the herd. He was signaling from behind a large clump of Jesse bush.

"I see you. And Hector? Over."

"He's a hundred yards south of my position. Hector, show us your position. Over."

Through the trees, Jessica saw Kaminjolo's raised hand emerge from behind a pile of boulders closer to the herd.

"Jessica, Hector, everyone's in place around the perimeter. Blair, Skip and the rangers are in position. All we have to do is wait for the SOBs. Over and out."

Jessica's watch read half past eight. She took a sip from her canteen, stuck it back in its pouch, and wondered how long their wait would be. The sun was now well above the escarpment, and the temperature was climbing.

Minutes later, she heard the splintering sounds of broken branches as an enormous bull elephant crashed through the trees to join the cows. His arrival was heralded by excited, throaty rumbles from the older females Chipiri and Chitatu. They looked up, lifted their trunks, and spread their ears in greeting. Jessica's heart quickened at the sight of this magnificent giant who stood more than three feet taller than the adult cows.

From his gigantic, outwardly splayed tusks, she recognized him as Fundisi, the 44-year-old brother of Muchengeti and Nkosikaas. Even the family's younger members showed great interest in their visitor and trotted over to greet him.

Jessica was thrilled to see Fundisi. Since Nkosi's death, he had become her largest and oldest, study bull. In light of the anticipated arrival of the poachers, however, his appearance was most inopportune. Fundisi's tusks were enormous by today's standards. Poachers would consider them a rare find. She was keenly aware, therefore, that his life was in dire peril.

*   *   *

Kaseke and his team were close to the Rifa Hunting Camp. His most talented spotter, Mason Chikowore, was sitting up front beside him, smoking his ever-present smelly, newsprint-rolled cigarette.

"I'll go slow and you must look out on the road for fresh tracks. If you see any, tell me and I will stop," Kaseke said.

"Yes Sir!" Mason replied. His parted lips revealed a crooked set of tobacco-stained teeth.

The blue pickup crawled forward at a steady, five miles-per-hour, until it reached the boundary of Rifa Camp. Kaseke braked at the edge of a wide clearing. Here, the dried grass, normally chin high, had been cropped short. Scattered around the camp, beneath evergreen mahogany trees, were a number of well-appointed, brick chalets with thatched roofs. Kaseke looked around with relief. The place seemed deserted.

"I see nobody here, but I want no surprises," he said in barely a whisper. "Mason, get in the back and fetch four weapons. The ammo clips are also in there. Give two guns and some ammo to the boys in Stanley's truck and we'll keep two in ours." As a rule, Kaseke would not have risked placing loaded weapons into the hands of these impetuous, young men, especially whilst on the move. Who knows what would happen? But on this occasion, he believed they needed to be ready for the unexpected.

Mason dropped his cigarette, ground the burning end into the dirt with the heel of his boot, and stuck the *stompie* into his breast pocket. Then after retrieving the AKs and ammo clips, and handing them out, he clambered aboard the Nissan. The two vehicles drove through the camp and exited back onto the main road.

"I see elephant tracks," Mason reported. "But they are too old."

Ever since they'd left the villages closer to the A-1, they'd encountered no traffic moving in either direction. Kaseke was thankful. He'd feared the sight of two civilian trucks, filled with men in camouflage, and crawling slowly along the road, would pique someone's interest. Perhaps someone would report them to the authorities, or a pesky, good Samaritan would stop to render aid thinking they might have mechanical trouble. Either scenario could spell disaster.

They'd driven for thirty minutes since departing the hunting camp. Kaseke's watch read almost eight thirty. There'd been no sign of any elephants. He was beginning to think seriously about calling the whole thing off.

"I see tracks! Stop!" Mason shouted, pointing ahead.

Kaseke slammed on the brake and the Nissan skidded to a sudden stop. To avoid a rear-end collision, Stanley was forced to swerved right and the Toyota left the road, climbed an embankment, and came to rest with its front end buried in a large thorn bush. Shaken, he and his passengers climbed out.

Mason was crouched on the trail, examining the sandy top layer of dirt. "They are going that way," he said pointing south away from the river."

"*Teerera!* Everyone listen up!" Kaseke ordered. "If you don't have a weapon, get one now. Take two clips of ammo. Load one in your weapon and put the spare in your pocket. When you're ready, line up in front of my truck."

Kaseke picked up his M4A1 and stroked the barrel lovingly. He was proud of his top-of-the-line, modern, automatic weapon. He fumbled around the ammo boxes for the one containing the magazines for his rifle.

"Stanley, where's the ammunition for my gun?" he demanded.

Kaseke's assistant rushed forward and hurriedly searched through the ammo boxes. "I put two boxes in here, Sir," he insisted.

"Well, where are they?" Kaseke shouted, his eyes narrowing.

"Sir, I don't know," Stanley replied his head bowed.

"*Eh, waka pusa iwe*, you stupid idiot. Why do you lie? You didn't load it, did you?" he bellowed, the sinews in his neck taut with rage.

Kaseke dropped the M4A1 onto the ground and wrested Stanley's weapon away from him, thrusting it into the hands of a man behind him. Then he balled his huge fist and punched his chief assistant square in the face. The blow sent Stanley reeling backwards. He fell to the ground with blood streaming from his mouth. Kaseke rubbed his bruised knuckles and, as his team looked on in dismay, he savagely kicked his foreman repeatedly in the face, head, and chest, before walking away. Stanley lay face down in the dirt, battered, bloody, and groaning in pain. His injuries included a broken jaw, facial cuts and contusions, missing teeth, and several cracked ribs.

Kaseke pointed to the rifle on the ground. "Mason, lock it up in the cab," he commanded in a gruff voice. Then he turned to the remaining men who were standing in line, nervously shifting their feet, and barked, "*Endai,* let's go. Follow me," and he took off up the road. Mason caught up with them and darted in front of the group to resume tracking the elephant spoor.

The men marched along the game trail, their boots creating audible thumps as they kicked up tiny plumes of dust. Up ahead, they heard elephant rumbles and the sounds of breaking branches, as the huge animals foraged in the trees. When Mason found the spoor turning south, Kaseke raised his hand to signal a halt.

"Now we must be quiet! Don't stamp your feet," he whispered hoarsely. Elephants are too clever and they can feel movements on the ground. We must go slow now. Don't forget what I told you. I take the first shots. When the elephants come together, the big ones on the outside and the small ones on the inside, that's when we shoot the big ones. After they are down, we can kill the babies."

When they left the trail and followed the spoor into the bush, the sounds of the elephants became louder.

*   *   *

Ten minutes earlier, Jessica thought she'd detected the faint sounds of men's voices, but they'd faded away and she'd heard nothing more. From her perch atop the high granite outcropping, she enjoyed watching the activities of Chembere's family. Surprisingly, their visitor, Fundisi, had not yet moved on. She knew bulls didn't usually hang out with groups of cows and calves, unless there were available females in estrus. The bull had been wandering among the adult females, but none had interested him. In that case, she wondered, why hadn't Chembere's family already sent him packing?

Jessica's musings were suddenly cut short by the ear-splitting crackle of automatic rifle fire. Her heart sank as she witnessed the legs of an adolescent female elephant buckle, as she slumped onto the ground. From around her, Jessica heard the returned gunfire. The shots were accompanied by explosive thumps and cracks, as bullets splintered tree limbs. Rounds ricocheting off nearby rocks delivered a piercing whine. Terrified, she clung to her granite outcrop until the shooting ceased and she heard Kaminjolo's booming voice, amplified through a megaphone.

"Drop your weapons immediately and show yourselves! Put your hands in the air! This is Hector Kaminjolo, Chief Ranger, Zambezi East, for the Zimbabwe Parks and Management Authority."

*   *   *

The returning gunfire took Kaseke totally by surprise. He and his men took immediate cover behind nearby rocks and trees. He was relieved to find none of his people had been shot, but since their opposing force was nowhere in sight, he could not tell how large a force he was up against.

*   *   *

After the shooting, Jessica saw the cows and calves milling around in distress. A short distance away, Fundisi stood with his ears spread wide and his trunk raised, sniffing the wind. He wheeled around to face the direction from which the first shots had come, and let out a deafening trumpet. Lowering his head, he charged through the line of trees, his tail lifted high like a battle flag.

179

*   *   *

The huge bull was almost upon Kaseke and his men, and the poacher suddenly found himself in an impossible situation. If he fired at the charging bull, he would alert the rangers and give away his position. He signaled urgently to his men to withdraw and they raced back to their trucks.

*   *   *

From her vantage point, Jessica could see the frightened elephants milling around their fallen family member, Chiripi-Piri. Although Chiripi's oldest daughter had been seriously wounded, she seemed to have survived. Her mother and grandmother were attempting to hoist her back onto her feet. However, at age fifteen – old enough to bear calves of her own – she was too heavy for them to lift, and after repeated attempts, they abandoned the effort. Nevertheless the family remained circled around her.

Jessica's two-way radio vibrated.

"This is Piet. Are they gone? Over."

"Piet, I saw them running back toward the river. That's all I can tell you. You know those SOBs shot Chembere's oldest granddaughter. She's the young female I told you might be carrying a calf. Over."

"Is she dead or wounded? Over."

"Can't tell for sure. Two cows have been trying to get her up, but they haven't succeeded. Over."

*   *   *

When Kaseke and his band of poachers returned to their vehicles, they discovered Stanley and the Toyota were gone.

"*Hazvigoni kutendeka*. I don't believe it!" Kaseke raged, his eyes fiery bright. Gesticulating wildly with his AK-47, he roared, "When I catch that bastard, I will plug a thousand rounds into his stupid, fucking face!" As if to prove a point, he triggered a burst of gunfire, skywards. It left his henchmen, who were busy loading their weapons into the Nissan, feeling unnerved. They had never before seen their boss so enraged. In silence, Mason climbed aboard next to Kaseke, while five others squeezed into the back seat.

One of the four remaining men called out, "We will take the boats back to Fataran," and they took off, racing towards the river.

*   *   *

After it seemed the poachers were gone, Jessica climbed down from her lookout and joined van Rooyen, Kaminjolo, Blair, and the others. Before they left to return to their vehicles, she took Kaminjolo aside and pointed to the group of elephants clustered around Chiripi-Piri.

"Hector, is there anything we can do to help her?"

"Not too much, Jessica. Very sorry. We can't get close to her because of the others. I'll send one of my rangers to check on her tomorrow. If the rest of the herd is gone, and she's still alive, he can stop her suffering."

Saddened, Jessica nonetheless realized Hector was correct. They could do little for her. In a perfect world, there would be special, heavy-duty equipment to lift Chiripi-Piri, who weighed close to four thousand pounds, and state-of-the-art veterinary care to save her. Neither was available in the here and now.

Before they left to return to their vehicles, she took one last look back at the elephants clustered around Chiripi-Piri and prayed silently that, somehow, she and her unborn baby would survive.

Kaminjolo's group walked silently through the tall grass back to their vehicles. They were almost halfway back to the road when they heard an engine cough into life and the sound of wheels spinning in the gravel. The vehicle sounded as if it was departing to the east. Moments later the growl of its motor faded away.

As they crossed the road, van Rooyen looked down at the new tire tracks. The treads wouldn't be much help in identifying the poacher's vehicle, he thought. They could belong to any number of popular truck tires; no help at all.

"Something bad happened here," Ananias said pointing to several dark red stains in the sand, a few yards away. "Looks like blood; quite recent."

"Poor sod," Skip Brankhorst commented, "I wonder whose blood it is, and what those buggers did to him?"

"I doubt we'll ever know," van Rooyen commented.

Before they climbed into their vehicles, Kaminjolo stepped up onto his running-board and addressed the group.

"Everybody! Thanks for your help. We didn't get the poachers, but I believe we saved all but maybe one of the elephants."

"We have to give credit to Fundisi," Jessica added. "If he hadn't charged and scared the pants off them, we could have been shot along with the elephants." Everyone murmured in agreement. As he and Jessica moved to drive away, van Rooyen called out his window.

"Thanks everyone. We'll see some of you back in Kariba. And Blair, thanks again mate. We'll give you a ring."

He turned to Jessica, "I've got to tell you, my girl, it worried the hell out of me—you being exposed to that field of fire. But damn, I'm impressed. You were just as cool as a cucumber."

Chapter 22

Friday, October 3, 2008

At 12:30 p.m. in the Lusaka offices of Tembo Travel and Tourism, George Tembo prepared for his 1:30 p.m. appointment with Chinese diplomat and ivory buyer, Shubo Gu. He viewed this meeting at the embassy with some trepidation, still unsure he would be able to fulfill his contract to provide Gu with two thousand, five hundred kilos of ivory by year's end.

Presently stored in Tembo's Lusaka warehouse were only the 2,040 kilos Kaseke had delivered last July. Another shipment of 260 kilos should have arrived last Tuesday, but its conveyance, a chartered, DC-3 aircraft, had been beset with mechanical difficulties and was not expected until Friday, November 6.

More than a week ago, Tembo had tipped Kaseke off about a herd of elephants moving east along the southern bank of the Zambezi. The man assured him that he and his people would hunt them down and include the additional ivory in his next shipment. Frustratingly, he hadn't received word from Kaseke since then, and had been unable to reach him on the phone. Was he out hunting, or just ignoring the calls? Tembo bristled with annoyance.

Tembo arrived at the Chinese embassy fifteen minutes early for his meeting with Gu. The trafficker knew Chinese businessmen valued promptness. In an elaborately decorated reception area, an oriental woman wearing a green, collarless suit and a silk blouse with the traditional, chi pao-style collar, greeted him.

"Welcome to the Embassy." She said looking up at him with a somber expression. "Do you have an appointment?"

"Yes, I do. With Mr. Gu," Tembo replied curtly.

"Your name?"

"George Tembo."

She scanned the appointment register.

"Yes, Mr. Tembo. He's expecting you. Please take a seat and I'll tell him you are here."

Tembo chose not to sit. He paced the waiting room inspecting several large, gold-framed paintings of serpents and dragons in shimmering hues of pink, turquoise, gray, ruby and indigo.

"Mr. Tembo, I'm glad to see you."

Alerted, he turned around to find Gu standing beside his receptionist's desk. He was several inches taller than the average Chinese male, and as thin as a bamboo pole. His face was bland, unreadable, and he had a pair of heavy, black-framed glasses perched on the end of his nose. His shock of white hair aged him beyond his fifty-four years.

Tembo approached and shook Gu's outstretched hand. He grasped the man's cold, bony fingers several seconds longer than necessary. Then he leaned forward, nodded, and gave a quick bow, a gesture of traditional Chinese courtesy. Any Westerner might have considered Gu's limp handshake a sign of weakness, but Tembo knew a timid handshake, to the Chinese, was a mark of special respect.

"We go to my office, please," he said, leading Tembo from the reception area.

Tembo had never before been invited into Gu's private domain. Their previous meetings had all taken place in one of the Embassy's many conference rooms. The unmistakable stale odor of tobacco permeating the room, did not surprise him. Smoking's health hazards had not yet been universally accepted by the Chinese.

An oversized, elaborately carved, teak desk dominated his office. The seat of its matching high-backed armchair was upholstered in silk. Along the length of one wall stood a tall bookcase, its shelves crammed with loose-leaf binders and books. Gu's desk and both visitors' chairs were piled high with papers and file folders. Gu cleared off one of the visitors' chairs by dumping the stack of documents on the floor, and offered Tembo the seat.

"Must forgive my untidy office, Mr. Tembo, but I am always too busy," Gu apologized, holding out a gold cigarette case. Tembo accepted a cigarette, placed it between his lips, and took a deep drag as Gu offered him a flame from a sterling silver table lighter.

"Yes, Mr. Gu, I can tell you've been working very, very hard," Tembo said somewhat sardonically as he exhaled a small cloud of smoke.

"Papers, papers, more papers," Gu exclaimed, dropping his cigarette into an ashtray and throwing up his hands. "Many, many government rules, papers to read, and forms to fill out. Never stops," he added as he rearranged the piles on his desk to clear a space for his visitor. "Anyway, we should forget about these things. How are you?" he said, peering over his eyeglasses. "And how is the elephant hunting business?"

"Not as good as we expected," Tembo replied with a frown. "In Zimbabwe, where I get most of my ivory, commercial hunters are coming in from Europe and America and taking the biggest bulls with the heaviest tusks," he complained. "President Mugabe wants the foreign exchange he gets from selling all those hunting permits. But don't worry; I'm sure we can get you the remaining 460 kilos by the end of December," he added hurriedly his face brightening. "Kaseke already has a shipment of 260 kilos in his warehouse, right now, which he will airlift to me soon. Today he's out hunting for another herd that could bring him another 200 kilos."

"How is he sending the shipment?"

"It will arrive on a chartered, DC-3 aircraft from Mozambique."

"Big plane! Where do you land that thing? Lusaka International?" Gu's eyebrows arched upwards.

"No. No," Tembo explained. "Too many problems if he lands at the airport. We'll use an old grass air strip close to the T-2, between Lusaka and Chirundu."

Gu quizzed him on the plan's practicality. "Far from Lusaka?"

"No. It's only twenty eight miles. I measured the distance in my car."

"Many people near the air strip?"

"No. Nothing close. The runway's half a mile from the main road."

"How do you get to the plane?" Gu wanted to know.

"From the T-2 we drive on a dirt road through the bush."

"What is on the east side of the strip?"

"Long rows of gum trees."

"And on the other side?"

"Just farm land."

"There are farm buildings?"

"None close. I checked with Google Maps," Tembo said. "The farm buildings and the farmhouse are at least five miles away."

"Did you look at the runway?"

"I drove my car up and down the strip a couple of times. It was okay. Also, Manuel Chipenga, the DC-3's owner and pilot, has landed there before."

"Well Mr. Tembo, you have things under control. When will I hear from you again?"

"Mr. Gu, I will be at the air strip on the 6th of November waiting for the plane. That's five weeks from now. Mr. Kaseke will phone me as soon as the plane takes off and give me an ETA. After we unload the shipment into my truck, we'll and take it to my warehouse on Mumbwa Road. Afterwards, I'll phone you to arrange delivery."

"Okay Mr. Tembo, it is all good," the Chinese diplomat said, stubbing out his cigarette in the ashtray and rising to his feet. "Thank you for coming. Anything else we must talk about?"

"No, I can't think of anything else, Mr. Gu," Tembo said.

He left Gu's office and walked down the corridor to the reception area, where a young Chinese couple was seated. He waved to the unsmiling receptionist and left.

*   *   *

Gu stepped out his door, and his eyes followed Tembo as he disappeared into the reception area. While his untidy office had indeed been an embarrassment to him, Gu had been truthful about his being overworked in recent days. He had chosen not to reveal his frantic preparations for the four upcoming CITES-sponsored ivory sales, since Tembo played no part in these transactions. The sales, scheduled for later this month and in early November, were open only to registered Chinese and Japanese buyers.

The application to register as an authorized ivory buyer called for him to meet stringent environmental trade standards. Compiling and, in most cases, fabricating his personal trading credentials took weeks of research and study—a difficult task, but one which stood to bring him huge profits.

In less than a month, more than 101 metric tonnes of ivory would be up for bid at auctions in Botswana, Namibia, South Africa and Zimbabwe. Just yesterday he learned CITES had approved his preferred buyer status. Today, he would be making final arrangements to attend all four ivory auctions.

CITES announced the sales back in 2007, assuming all four countries were managing their elephant populations well. When it came to Zimbabwe, however, Gu knew otherwise, through Tembo and his other Zimbabwe contacts. Nonetheless, it was not in his best interests to disseminate this information.

That Tembo was aware of the forthcoming sales, Gu was certain. He doubted, however, that Tembo realized he planned to attend them all to purchase stocks of ivory. The Zambian's reaction to his plan would likely be unpredictable, Gu thought. On the one hand, his duplicity might raise Tembo's ire, but on the other, Tembo might be thankful his buyer had an alternate ivory source and therefore would not hold him to their contract. Therefore, he'd just let the chips fall where they may, Gu decided.

Gu looked forward to attending the forthcoming auctions. With financing supplied by several large Chinese art syndicates, he stood to make huge profits from his purchases. His boss, Zambia's Chinese ambassador, knew all about Gu's ivory business, and turned a blind eye to these activities. Of greater importance to the ambassador was the availability of imported ivory so crucial to China's preservation of its traditional artisanship of ivory carving. Since prehistoric times, it had been considered one of the most highly revered arts in the Chinese culture.

The international ivory ban of 1989 had forced the Chinese to seek alternative materials. The carvings fashioned from the teeth of Arctic, toothed whales and walruses, however, were not as highly prized as those of elephant ivory. Within a decade of the CITES-imposed ban, the demand burgeoned to the extent that the poaching of African elephants was once again rife, and illegal shipments of ivory were once more reaching the shores of China and Japan.

As a boy, Shubo Gu had been befriended by an elderly ivory carver, who had taught him the intrinsic value of ivory – a unique, all-natural milk white material that had the smoothest of textures, and an incomparable sheen. Gu also learned that age and the weathering of ivory added significantly to its value.

Gu had never been a career diplomat, but his superior knowledge of the Chinese culture led to his recruitment as cultural attaché for the Embassy in Lusaka. From here, he well positioned to mastermind the funneling of ivory from Africa into China.

Chapter 23

Friday, October 3, 2008

After consorting with Chitatu for three days, Nkosikaas's first born son, Ngomo, left matriarch Chembere's family and set off in search of other receptive females. He followed the Kariba lakeshore, heading for the dam wall. At midday, he plodded down to the water's edge where a small herd of impala drank. When he approached, the buck scattered, affording him clear passage.

Wind-blown waves lapped the shoreline, and the massive beast with the broken tipped right trunk, stepped into the water up to his knees. He dropped his trunk into the lake and began to drink, repeatedly drawing up liquid and emptying it down his throat. Then he cooled himself by spraying trunkfuls of water over his head, back, and sides. Later he moved on.

That evening he came upon a campground in the Charara Safari Area where teenagers had gathered. At a campsite approximately 100 yards from the lakeshore, Ian Chappel was celebrating his eighteenth birthday with a group of teenaged friends—nine boys and seven girls. The partygoers lounged in deck chairs around a fire pit. Their battery-powered boom box, sat on a tree stump a short distance away, giving vent to the loud pulsing beat of an Aerosmith hit song. The music boomed across the water and reverberated through the surrounding bush. Overhead, a million stars sparkled in the cloudless sky, and a bright, waning moon cast a wide beam across the water. The shaft of light appeared to quiver in time to the beat of the tune.

Several hours earlier, the roaring blaze had shot flames six feet in the air. Now just a few glowing chunks of wood in a bed of dying embers were all that remained of the bonfire. Dozens of empty beer and cheap wine bottles were strewn over on the flattened grass.

"Hey look. We've got a gate crasher," one of the teens shouted—a blonde, mop-haired school friend of Ian's named Carl Meyer, who spoke with a noticeable German accent. His black tee shirt had an image of his favorite rock band, Metallica, splashed across his chest. Carl's father, Otto Meyer, was the German Ambassador in Harare.

Carl stumbled as he leapt up to point at Ngomo, whose white tusks gleamed in the moonlight. The bull was less than thirty yards away, reaching into a tree for seedpods. Alerted by Carl's remark, Ian and another teen, Neil de Klerk, staggered to their feet.

"Let's give that 'bugga' a warm welcome," Ian slurred, waving around a bottle of Lion Lager. Swaying drunkenly, he stooped to pick up an empty and hurled it at the elephant.

The glass bottle struck Ngomo on the shoulder, startling him. He turned his great head towards the teenagers and everyone nervously wobbled to their feet. Neil and other boys threw more bottles.

"Stop it," shouted Melanie Cox, a seventeen-year-old brunette, wearing shorts and a tank top. "Don't piss him off anymore. We could get killed."

"No, we won't," Carl declared, marching over to the campfire and picking out a hefty tree branch with a fiery tip. "He'll leave after I send him this," and the youth tossed the burning limb at Ngomo. Cartwheeling over the elephant's back, the log came to rest across his broad shoulders. He experienced a sudden, intense pain as the ember scorched his hide. He swung around and the branch slid onto the ground. The removal of the burning wood did little to ease Ngomo's agony. He tossed his head about, his ears making cracking sounds like canvas sails buffeted by the wind. He let out a shrill trumpet.

Alarmed, Melanie and three other young women screamed and ran towards the vehicles parked along a hunting trail, a hundred yards away. The remaining women followed. A young blonde tripped and fell, her companions turning back to help her up. The girls waited near the cars for the boys to join them.

The vehicles were parked in single file along a narrow, one-way, rutted dirt track. In front was Ian's double-cab pickup. Melanie, his girlfriend, had its keys in her pocket. She jumped behind the wheel and hooted the horn.

"Ian, let's go!" she yelled.

The young men made no move to leave. Ian pulled a firecracker from his pocket, lit the fuse and threw it at the elephant. It ignited with a thunderous explosion just a few feet from Ngomo. While causing him no injury, the blast unleashed in him an overwhelming sense of anger and indignation. As the smoke cleared, Ngomo spread his ears, lifted his trunk, and with an ear-piercing bellow, charged out of the trees towards them. With only the moon to light their way, the seven young men ran for their cars. Behind them, the bull thundered in close pursuit.

Terror-stricken, they piled into their vehicles. Melanie and Ian moved off quickly. Carl, driver of the second vehicle, a new BMW, hunted feverishly for the ignition keys. Neil's Toyota Corolla was parked behind him.

Ngomo reached the Toyota first and sidled up next to the passenger door and began rocking the car dangerously; tipping it from side to side. Panicked, Neil and his passengers leapt out the doors on the driver's side and fled down the road. Ngomo flattened the Toyota in less than two minutes. Rearing up on his hind legs, he slammed his forefeet onto the roof, then hoisted up the car's front end and flipped it over.

In the BMW, meanwhile, Carl frantically searched around the driver's seat and on the floorboards for the missing keys. His passengers, hearing the deafening sounds of destruction behind them, urged him to give up the search. Seconds later, they abandoned the vehicle in a blind panic, scurrying off into the darkness. As Carl glanced over his shoulder, his heart sank into the deepest of pits when he saw in the dim light, the beast demolishing his Papa's beloved BMW.

Melanie and Ian had driven at least a mile before they realized they were not being followed. They stopped and after the dust settled, Ian called out to the passengers in the rear seat. "Are there any headlights behind us?"

"No," they chorused.

Melanie slammed the pickup into reverse and began backing up along the narrow track. They found the other party guests, fifteen minutes later, stumbling up the road in the dark. With six teens in the twin cabs and another eight riding in the truck bed, they headed straight for the Kariba Police Station.

When they arrived, Ian, Carl, and Neil went inside to speak to the member-in-charge. Corporal Gwezere of the Zimbabwe National Police patiently took their statements. After hearing their complaint, he smiled at them benevolently, and shook his head.

"*Eh eh*, I'm too sorry, but I can't help you," he said. "You must go and report it to the Charara game warden."

At half-past-one, the three boys returned to the car to find the girls clamoring for attention. "Ian, you're going to have to take us home. Our folks are going to kill us," Melanie said.

Ian sighed. "Okay I'll take you home. But Neil and Carl, you need to come with me to speak to the game warden. And the rest of you guys, I suppose you want me to drop you off, too? "

"Ja," they chorused.

Neil cut in, clearly annoyed. "You women think you're the only ones who're in trouble. What about me and Carl? What are we supposed to tell our folks about the cars?" Carl shuddered at the thought. He could well imagine what his father was going to say about his brand new BMW.

"Well Carl, you and Ian are to blame," Melanie replied sharply. "You're the ones who started all the damn trouble!"

"I'll take you all home," Ian sighed. "It's nearly two in the morning. We're all tired, and we're not going to be able to speak to the warden until tomorrow."

Not another word was spoken as he drove to the Caribbea Bay Resort, where Carl and his parents were holidaying. Afterwards Ian drove around Kariba's residential areas, dropping off his other friends, before returning home.

Chapter 24

Saturday, October 4, 2008

The next morning, Kaminjolo was eating a breakfast of bacon and eggs at his home in Kariba's Boulder Bluff housing area, when the telephone rang. His wife, Elizabeth, rose to answer it.

"Call's for you."

"Who is it?" he asked, taking the handset from her and holding his palm over the mouthpiece.

"*VaZanunga*." she replied and Kaminjolo rolled his eyes. What urgent problem did his boss need to talk about on a Saturday morning?

"Good morning, Sir."

"Kaminjolo!" his boss said, curtly. "I ordered you to shoot all your rogue elephants. You obviously did not! At six o'clock this morning, I got a rude phone call from Mr. Otto Meyer, the German Ambassador. He is very angry—complaining an elephant in the Charara destroyed his brand new BMW. He's staying at the Caribbea Bay in Kariba and he went out to look at the car today. He told me it's totally wrecked—squashed flat."

"General Zanunga, *ndakutadzira*, I'm sorry you were inconvenienced, Sir. I will open an investigation right away."

"I don't care about your stupid investigations, Kaminjolo, I just want the damn animal shot. Don't forget my office has to do the paperwork to submit the ivory into the national storehouse, so after you destroy the beast, make sure you deliver the tusks to me."

"Yes Sir! I need a description of the animal. I don't want to shoot the wrong one."

"What does it matter, Hector. Just make sure I get the ivory." The line went dead.

Kaminjolo's face contorted in anger.

"What's going on?" His wife said with a look of concern.

"It's happening again," he growled in frustration, slamming his fist on the table. "An elephant evidently demolished the German Ambassador's BMW last night. I'll have to investigate it, but I'm thinking it's just another "Tusker" incident. Remember last New Year's Eve, when some kids had a party at a Charara Camp and harassed an elephant that retaliated by stomping on some cars?"

"Yes I remember it well," she sighed.

"Zanunga's ordered me to shoot the elephant. He says, 'any elephant.' He doesn't care if the wrong one gets shot. I hated doing it, the last time, and I refuse to do it again. He says he doesn't care about my 'stupid investigations,' as he calls them. I don't think Mr. Zanunga even cares about the teenagers, the car, or even the German ambassador. I believe he just wants the ivory. Well, I'll just parcel him up the tusks we retrieved yesterday from the young, female elephant the poachers shot."

"You are doing the right thing," Elizabeth assured her husband. Do you think *VaZanunga* just wants the ivory, so he can put the money in his own pocket?"

"It's possible. This will be the third bull, in a little more than a year, that he's ordered be shot."

"Then he must be just like our president who steals money from all the Zimbabwean people."

Kaminjolo nodded silently as he calmed himself while sipping his cup of tea.

"Everywhere, things are bad right now," Elizabeth commiserated. "I was lucky to get these eggs I cooked for you, this morning. I got them from my friend, Lily, whose mother keeps chickens. All the shelves in the shops are empty. This was also the last of our bacon from the deep freeze. There's no money anywhere, and people are waiting in long lines outside the banks. Then when they get inside, the teller gives them only enough cash to buy a loaf of bread."

"I've seen those lines going round and round the block," Kaminjolo said. "I've been wondering how working people have time to spend in these queues. How did you pay your friend for the eggs, by the way?"

"I gave her some tomatoes from our vegetable garden."

Like her husband, Elizabeth Kaminjolo was a respected member of

192

the community. She taught school at one of two local government primary schools. Because the Kaminjolos had no children of their own, they devoted much of their time to helping out at the local orphanage.

"I hope our Mr. Tsvangirai and Mr. Mugabe are able to settle their differences, so Zimbabwe can go back to the way it used to be," Elizabeth said. "One of the teachers at my school told me yesterday, she thought life was so much easier eight years ago. In those days, we had everything we needed, and she could even afford to buy her kids new school uniforms every year. But now everyone is struggling. The teachers in Harare, she said, have not gone to work since the schools opened, because the government doesn't pay them enough to live on. She told me her Harare friend was thinking about leaving for South Africa."

"That's what a lot of people are doing," Kaminjolo agreed. He rose and kissed Elizabeth, thanking her for the eggs and bacon. "Hopefully this investigation won't take too long because I want to go down to the orphanage this afternoon and kick around a soccer ball with some of the boys."

"That would be nice," Elizabeth said. "I might come with you. I promised to teach the little girl, in the wheelchair, how to knit."

Minutes later, Kaminjolo was driving away from his home in the suburb of Boulder Bluff, perched on the hills overlooking the lake. This morning the calm, blue water stretched over to the west as far as the horizon. In less than fifteen minutes, he arrived at his office. He greeted his receptionist who worked Saturdays, until noon.

"Good morning, Violet. Have you seen Amos Manjengwa?"

"Yes Sir. I believe he's outside in the motor pool, filling up his pickup."

"Thank you. I'll drive round and find him."

The large, fenced-in area at the rear of the building was where Zim Parks stored its vehicles, trailers, boats, rolls of fencing, and other equipment. Upon entering, he spotted the game warden in his khaki uniform, refueling his brand new, white Toyota pickup. The petrol and diesel pumps stood on a concrete island in the center of the motor pool. Their underground storage tanks were generally topped up by NOCZIM, the National Oil Company of Zimbabwe, whenever fuel became available. Since 2000, supplies of diesel, petrol, and kerosene had been unpredictable, due to the country's lack of foreign exchange and its poor credit history.

"Good morning Amos," Kaminjolo said, as he climbed from the Land Rover. "How much petrol do we have?"

"*Mangwanani, VaKaminjolo.* Violet told me that NOCZIM filled up the tanks last week. She said Director General Zanunga had arranged for a special fuel delivery for local government officials."

Although Kaminjolo made no comment, he wondered whether this was another of the President's ploys to curry favor with his supporters. Why had Zanunga not informed him, the district's chief ranger, but instead had told his receptionist? Was Violet a ZANU-PF stooge? He pushed this unpleasant thought aside for the moment, reminding himself to investigate the matter later.

"And how are you liking your new Toyota pickup?" he asked Amos, a Charara Safari Area ranger. "Our sector was lucky to get just one of them. In fact, our field stations ended up with hardly any. Mostly, they went to important people in the Harare office."

"This is a good truck, *VaKaminjolo*. The engine is powerful, and after the rains come I'll be happy to be driving this," he said, pointing to the tall, black, elevated air intake pipe, which allowed the vehicle to push though deep water in rivers and streams. "Only one problem," Amos commented, "the white paint job. It makes it hard to creep up on animals or poachers in the bush without them seeing me, first."

"You're right, Amos. If we ever get more money in our budget, I'll tell the garage to paint it camouflage for you."

"*Ndatenda chaizvo*, thank you *VaKaminjolo*," the beaming ranger said, offering the traditional bow and silent handclap of gratitude.

"Amos, I spoke with Mr. Zanunga this morning. He said he got a telephone call from the German Ambassador about his new BMW. An elephant smashed it last night at the Charara camp. Zanunga told me to shoot this bull, but we don't know which bull did it. Have you seen any bulls hanging around in Charara, lately?"

"No Sir! All week I worked on fixing a bridge on the southeast side, where the tourist buses go. No elephants around there."

"Okay Amos. I'll talk to some people who may remember the bull."

Kaminjolo drove to the Caribbea Bay Resort, in search of the German ambassador's son. The hotel overlooked the lake, and its sprawling, Sardinian-style, multi-level structure was painted the color of earthen rose. With the property's evergreen foliage, vines, lush lawns, and colorful flower gardens stepping down to the shore, it looked like some of the Mediterranean resorts he'd seen featured in travel magazines.

He walked up to the reception desk and smiled at the young black woman behind the counter. Fashionably dressed in a maroon, business suit with a ruffled, beige blouse, she wore eye glasses of the latest style, with slim, decorative, gold frames.

"Good morning, Mr. Kaminjolo, how can I help you?"

"I need to speak to one of your guests – a young man called Carl Meyer. I understand he is staying here with his parents, Ambassador and Mrs. Meyer."

"The Meyers are here. Their rental car is parked right outside. The company dropped it off only an hour ago. I heard they had some trouble with their own vehicle. Anyway, they're in Suite 20A. Take the staircase behind you to the second floor, and their room is at the end of the corridor."

Kaminjolo wondered if it was his uniform, compelling her to divulge a guest's private details about his car troubles.

"I'd prefer speaking to the son alone; not in the presence of his father," he said, leaning forward and whispering. "A personal matter. Would you arrange for him to meet me in the guest lounge?"

She gave him a conspiratorial wink. "Of course. I'll phone and tell him he has a special visitor. He might think it's the pretty girl, who visited him, yesterday."

Kaminjolo smiled without comment. She picked up a telephone and dialed Room 120A.

"Hello. This is Miss Zindoga from the reception desk. May I speak to Mr. Carl Meyer? Thank you, Mrs. Meyer. She's going to put him on," she murmured to Kaminjolo, her hand covering the mouthpiece.

"Let me speak to him, when he comes on," Kaminjolo said.

"Okay," she mouthed, and moments later handed him the receiver.

"Mr. Meyer. Good morning, this is Chief Ranger Kaminjolo. I am investigating the unfortunate damage to your father's BMW, last night. Can you come downstairs and meet me in the guest lounge. I need to get some information from you, so we can identify the elephant involved." After a brief pause, he continued, "Good. I'll see you in a few minutes." He then returned the handset to the receptionist. "Thank you, Miss Zindoga, I'll wait for him in there," he said, pointing to the double doors leading into the lounge.

Easy chairs, upholstered in a burgundy and beige striped fabric, were clustered in groups of four or six around low, mahogany tables. He selected a seat adjacent to windows, overlooking the lake, and sat down and gazed out across the water towards the shores of the Matusadona National Park.

When Carl Meyer arrived, Kaminjolo patted the chair next to him, inviting the young man to take a seat. Carl was dressed in a pair of light blue shorts and navy tee shirt, embellished with a slogan in old German lettering. On his feet were a pair of brown, leather sandals.

"Good morning Carl," he said, "I appreciate your coming down." He handed him his business card.

"That's okay, Mr. Kaminjolo," Carl said, noting the name on the card."

Speaking in a heavy German accent, he responded warily to the ranger's questions, giving his account of the incident. He suggested the bull elephant had charged the group, without provocation, and that Ian had tossed a stick at the animal to scare it off.

"Carl, did you notice anything special about this elephant that would help you recognize it again? Such as cuts on the edges of its ears or a broken tusk?"

"It looked like any elephant. I didn't have time to see anything, because I was running away," he replied in a mildly belligerent tone."

"Who were the other witnesses? Do you remember their names?"

"No. They were friends of Ian's. I only know Ian, because he goes to my school in Harare."

"Do you know Ian's surname?"

"*Ja, doch!* Of course," he snapped in German.

"What is it?" Kaminjolo asked, realizing he'd likely have to drag each snippet of information out of the youth.

"It's Chappel. I think he spells it with two Ps."

"Where does Ian Chappel live?"

"Here in Kariba."

"Where in Kariba, Carl? Do you know his address?" Kaminjolo was getting highly irritated.

"No, Sir. He drove over here and then I followed him when he drove around to pick up the girls. We met another guy at one of the girls' houses and he followed us in his car."

"A Toyota?"

"Yes, I think so. A black car."

"The girls' houses; can you direct me to any of them?"

"No, but Ian can."

"Other than what you've told me, is there anything else you can think of?"

"No Sir."

"Well you have my card. If you remember anything else, phone me. Thank you for your time, Carl."

The young man rose, shrugged his shoulders, and without a word, headed out the double doors. Kaminjolo returned to the reception desk, where he thumbed through the local telephone directory and found an entry for William Chappel, 1945 Hillcrest Street. He scribbled down the address on a small note pad and replaced it in his breast pocket.

The town of Kariba, home to approximately thirty thousand, rambled across some twelve and a half miles of hilly, lake shoreline. With no distinguishable business district, its banks, shops and service centers were scattered over an unconsolidated, two level jumble of neighborhoods and districts. Hotels and other tourist-related establishments occupied sites, which offered the best lakeside vistas.

Kaminjolo left the hotel and drove up the meandering road leading to

Kariba Heights, one of the town's more affluent suburbs. He pulled up at 1945 Hillcrest Street. Parked in the driveway was a white, Nissan twin cab pickup. He approached the front door and knocked. A tall, dark haired, young man cracked open the portal.

"Are you Ian Chappel?" Kaminjolo asked.

"Yes, why?" The youth replied with an air of arrogance.

Handing the young man his business card, he introduced himself. "I'm Chief Ranger Kaminjolo and I'd like to speak to you about the bull elephant that damaged some cars, last night, at the Charara Camp Ground. Were you there?"

"Yes I was. So what?" the youth replied in an impertinent tone.

"May I come in? Or would you prefer to step outside for a few minutes."

With an audible sigh, Ian pushed open the door and walked out, squinting in the bright sunlight. He pulled the door shut behind him. At well over six feet, he towered over Kaminjolo.

"What happened last night, leading up to the elephant trampling the cars?" Kaminjolo asked.

Ian's story was similar to Carl's, except he claimed it was Carl, who had tossed the burning branch on the elephant's back. "He wanted to scare it away. I think that was what made it charge."

Hardly surprising, Kaminjolo thought, as he pulled out his notebook. "Can you give me the names of the other guests at the party?"

"I don't know all their names," Ian said, shifting his feet, nervously. "They were mostly friends of friends."

"You must know your girlfriend's name," Kaminjolo replied, raising his eyebrows. "Carl told me she was there."

"Oh, *ja*. Melanie Cox."

He wrote the name in his notebook. "And her address?"

"She lives two houses down the street," Ian said, pointing to his right.

"Then her address must be 1941 or 1949 Hillcrest Street. Which is it?"

"It's 1941."

"Okay," he said, jotting down the number in his notebook. "One more thing. Did you notice any particular physical characteristics, which might help you recognize this elephant again? Things like a tear on the edge of its ear or a broken tusk."

"Nothing. Just that it was *mukuru, mukuru*; the biggest, bloody elephant I'd ever seen in my life!" he said dramatically, spreading his arms wide.

"Okay Ian, thanks for the information. If I have any more questions, I'll give you a ring," Kaminjolo said, pocketing the notebook and returning to his vehicle.

His next stop was Melanie Cox's house up the street. During his interview with her, he heard precisely what he'd expected to hear—that the elephant had, indeed, been harassed and mistreated prior to taking out its frustrations on the two vehicles. She also told him the bull was missing the tip to his right tusk. This piece of key evidence confirmed it was none other than 38-year-old, Ngomo.

Since poachers had recently slaughtered Ngomo's maternal family group, Kaminjolo knew the bull's genes were vital to the preservation of a healthy genetic diversity—a fact that Jessica's records confirmed. There was no way, therefore, he could justify killing Ngomo. Now the question was could he defy his boss's orders? He'd speak to van Rooyen. If they fitted Ngomo with a GPS collar, his rangers could watch him and keep him away from the lakeside picnic areas.

*   *   *

Earlier Saturday morning, while Hector and Elizabeth Kaminjolo were eating breakfast, van Rooyen and Jessica were only a few miles away. They had been driving from her Kariba Heights home to Mahombekombe, one of Kariba's two high-density suburbs situated along the lakeshore. Mahombekombe was home to thousands of local fishermen and tourist industry workers, most of whom were now jobless. Van Rooyen had volunteered to assist a local, non-profit distribute food here to Kariba's poorest and he'd invited Jessica along. The call for help came from Mark Lindsay, an old school friend of van Rooyen's, and a founder member of the Wildlife Protection League.

As he steered the Land Rover away from her house, Jessica studied his strong facial profile. In recent weeks, she had developed deep feelings of affection and respect for him. His volunteering to help the hungry, seemed to be quite typical of the altruistic and big-hearted man she'd come to know.

Mahombekombe's narrow streets crept up the slopes of Sugar Loaf Hill, lined with a conglomeration of small brick houses, lean-tos, shacks, and mud huts. The bus terminal, which served the area, had once been a hub of activity, with coaches constantly rolling through to pick up and disgorge passengers. Nowadays, however, with the country's economy in tatters and diesel fuel in short supply, fewer than three buses a day stopped here on their way north to Lusaka or south to Harare.

Van Rooyen parked the Land Rover behind the terminal's ticket office. Up ahead was a large truck. Behind the lorry's rear, open doors, stood a white man gesturing animatedly as he shouted instructions to workers unloading sacks of grain. As Jessica and van Rooyen walked towards him, he turned and waved.

"Howzit Mark," van Rooyen said, shaking his hand.

"Damn good of you to come, Piet," Lindsay replied. "And who's this attractive young lady?"

"Mark, let me introduce Jessica Brennan," van Rooyen said. "Jessica's been here in Zim for almost five years now, studying elephants for the Global Defense Force for Wildlife. I twisted her arm into agreeing to come and help us today."

Jessica saw an attractive man with a slightly receding head of sun-bleached hair and piercing blue eyes. Like Piet, he wore ankle-high, veldskoens, with beige, calf-length socks. His short-sleeved, checkered shirt revealed suntanned, well-muscled forearms and his abbreviated shorts displayed a pair of bronzed, muscular thighs.

"Pleased to meet you, Jessica," he said, with a wide smile, shaking her hand and giving it a flirtatious squeeze. "I'm surprised, hey, I haven't run into you before now," he added, giving her a devilish wink.

"I'm glad to meet you, Mark." Jessica replied, with an uncertain smile. While flattered, she was taken aback by his obvious come-on.

"So you're from America." Lindsay quipped. "Welcome to good old Zimbabwe."

"Mark, how can we best help?" Van Rooyen cut in hurriedly. Jessica could tell from his frown that he evidently did not approve of his friend's playful, but mildly provocative, interchange with her. Nonetheless, Piet's reaction pleased her and her cheeks warmed.

Lindsay pointed up the hill to a shaded area under some trees, where families had begun to assemble. He said, as he slapped the side of the five-ton truck, "This load has enough mealie-meal, beans, and fish to feed at least two thousand people for a month."

"How many families are we expecting?" van Rooyen asked. Up the hill, he could see a constant stream of men, women, and children joining the throng under the trees.

"We've got at least five hundred families," Lindsay said, explaining that each head-of-household had a coupon book. "On the front cover is the family's name and the number of household members," he said, adding they had set up seven stations, according to family size, where families would pick up their rations.

"I'll need one of you, positioned up front, to check coupon books and direct them to the correct station. That sounds like a good job for you, Jessica."

"Sounds simple enough," she said, thinking any kindergartner could probably handle such a task..

"Piet, would you assist at the stations? I'll be handling stations five, six, and seven. You take one through four," he said, explaining each station had scales and measuring containers for aid workers to calibrate correct amounts. "Just keep an eye on them to make sure they don't short-change anyone, or hand out extra to their *shamwaris*. Each family brings their own bags, buckets, baskets or what-not," Lindsay said, adding, "We have extra bags to give out, if necessary. Mainly, it's a case of keeping an eye on those stations and alerting me to any problems."

"Not a problem," van Rooyen responded.

"Oh! One other thing, I almost forgot. The station bosses are supposed to sign off on the food disbursements in everyone's coupon book and enter the exact amount of each product they receive. So, I need you to check their books on their way out."

"What's to stop people from taking off from their stations, while I'm tied up at another?" van Rooyen asked.

Jessica, overhearing the conversation, back-and-forth, wondered if Mark had ever been in charge of one of these food distribution affairs before.

"Mark, I have a suggestion," she ventured timidly. "If you could find someone else to replace me at the front end, I could set up a final check point to examine the books, before the folks leave. We just need to set up tape barricades to direct people from the seven stations to the exit." She looked over at van Rooyen who, out of Lindsay's sight, was smiling and giving her a thumbs-up.

"I suppose it would work," Lindsay said. "I don't have any tape, but we could use some of this *tambo*," he said pointing to a ball of sisal twine sitting at the rear of the truck bed.

Thirty minutes later, after Jessica and van Rooyen had set up the queuing system, all was ready, and the Mahombekombe residents began descending the hill in single file—men, women and children of all ages. Some of the women had babies strapped to their backs, carried empty buckets balanced on their heads, and were followed by older children clutching extra baskets and empty hessian sacks. The elderly and infirm limped along, assisted by relatives or propped up with crooked walking sticks. But the ones, who tugged hardest at Jessica's heart, were the hundreds of orphaned children, who followed behind, clutching their siblings' hands.

She knew the prevalence of HIV and AIDS in Southern Africa accounted for the largest proportion of destitute orphans. She'd learned young orphan girls were especially vulnerable to contracting this and other sexually transmitted diseases, because they often had to resort to a life of prostitution to help support their younger brothers and sisters. Recently she'd seen the results of a study based on a sample of nearly four thousand households in Kariba's high-density suburbs, which revealed that more than half the family units in these townships were led by orphans. Sadder still was the fact that almost a third of all school-aged, orphans received no education because they couldn't pay for school fees or the required uniforms.

Hour by hour, streams of people passed through the aid stations. By late afternoon, food stocks were almost depleted and one of the last to arrive was a skeletal, frail, and grizzled old man. He limped towards Jessica with a food sack slung over his bony shoulder. He handed her his coupon book, which identified him as Tsiga Chitata, aged 79.

Jessica greeted him with a smile. "Good evening, Mr. Chitata. I hope you got everything you needed." She verified the proper signatures, written beside the weights of foodstuffs he had received, and returned the book to him.

He raised his deeply wrinkled face and looked at her with tired eyes. His smile revealed wide gaps between his stained front teeth.

"*Medem*, I am finished," he croaked. "Long ago, I was a very important man and I stayed with governors and rich businessmen in their big houses, and they gave me everything I needed. Now, I get my food out of rubbish bins or from nice people like you."

Jessica looked at the barefoot, old man in his soiled and tattered shirt and trousers and wondered if she could give any credence to his elaborate claims.

"Who were these important people?" she asked gently.

"Well, I dined with our Prime Minister Mr. Garfield Todd, in 1955; Sir Humphrey Gibbs in his place at Government House in Harare, in 1959; and later with Prime Minister Mr. Ian Smith, in 1965."

While Jessica didn't claim to be an expert in the history of Zimbabwe, formerly known as Southern Rhodesia and Rhodesia, some of the names he mentioned had a familiar ring; particularly that of Ian Smith, who had turned over the reins of power to Robert Mugabe in 1980. She'd heard Smith had passed away less than a year ago.

"Forgive me for not recognizing all those names. You see, I'm from the United States of America," she said.

"A great country," the old man said. "I remember seeing your Senator Barry Goldwater, when he came to Victoria Falls, in 1967."

Aghast, Jessica wondered about this feeble, old man, who was claiming to have hobnobbed with so many prominent political leaders?

"How did you come to meet all these famous people?"

"I have been a witch doctor for fifty years. If you want to come to my place, I can show you my Certificate of Practice from the Zimbabwe National African Traditional Healers' Association and the badges I received in South Africa, Zambia, the Democratic Republic of Congo and Mozambique."

"You are certainly well traveled in the region," Jessica said, still uncertain whether she could accept this colorful character's far-fetched claims.

"I worked with the mines, all over, treating ailments and providing charms to cure cancer, barrenness, and many other conditions."

"Do you have a wife and children?"

"No, *Medem*," he gulped, shaking his head excitedly. "I have never loved a woman, because if I ever touched the breast of a woman, my charms would go away."

"Really? What brought you to Kariba?"

"I came to Kariba in 2002, because people told me there was lots of business here. But it was good for only one year."

"What happened then?"

"I ran out of my charm and most of my special medicines. The people I helped have abandoned me. Too many people here have turned to apostolic faith healing. There is no longer a market for me. So I just live up there in my house," he said, pointing up the hill.

"If there's no business left in Kariba, can you go and work somewhere else?"

"I am too old now, *Medem*, to go to other places. I am just waiting to die," he said, looking up at her with his dark, rheumy, bloodshot eyes.

Before she was able to express her feelings of compassion to the old man, she felt a hand on her shoulder. She turned around to see van Rooyen smiling down at her.

"Oh Piet, I want you to meet Mr. Chitata. He's been sharing his life story with me and it's quite fascinating," she said, hoping she didn't sound too patronizing.

"*Manheru VaChitata. Makadini*, good evening, Mr. Chitata. How are you?" van Rooyen said.

"*Tiripo kana, makadiniwo*, I'm fine, and you?" the old man replied.

"*Zvakanaka, ndatenda chaizvo*, I'm well, thank you."

"Piet, Mr. Chitata has been a traditional healer for fifty years," Jessica said. "His house isn't far. I'd like to help him carry his food home. Want to come?" Jessica asked.

"Certainly," van Rooyen replied, turning to the old man. "*Mudhara*, may I carry your food bag?" he said, taking the sack from him.

Jessica and van Rooyen, hand-in-hand, followed the old man as he limped slowly up the hillside towards Mahombekombe, a settlement crammed with small dwellings of every kind and quality. Before they reached the entrance to the community, with its single bank and small supermarket, the old man led them off into the bush towards a rocky outcrop next to a collection of smelly, refuse bins. On the far side of the rocks Jessica spied a low shelter, fashioned out of discarded pallets, and covered in plastic sheeting, grass, and sections of an old Formica counter top. The hovel was no more than six feet long, five feet wide and less than four feet in height.

"Wait here," the old man told them, and he crawled into his makeshift shack. He entered through a small opening, furthest away from the smelly garbage cans, and returned with an old cigar box. He handed it to Jessica.

She opened it, unfolding a worn, faded, and stained document. "Look Piet, these are his credentials he wanted to show me," she said, and scanned the document.

It was a license, 'Issued to the undersigned, Tsiga Chitata,' by the Zimbabwe National Traditional Healers Association, permitting him to administer traditional cures and treatments. It looked authentic and she passed it to van Rooyen. While she examined the identification badges, issued by the governments of South Africa, Zambia, Democratic Republic of Congo and Mozambique, the old man stood beside her, beaming with pride.

"These things show you are an important man," van Rooyen said, and returned them to Jessica, who carefully replaced each item to the cigar box.

"Thank you, Mr. Chitata," she said, handing it back to him. "But before we go, I have a question for you," Jessica said with a frown. "Did you hear about President Mugabe's Operation Murambatsvina, two years ago, when he ordered bulldozers to tear down people's business stalls and houses in Harare? Do you have any worries that someone will come and tear your house down?"

"Yes, I heard about his 'drive out the rubbish' business," the old man hissed angrily. "It was bad, very bad. But I'm sure the Kariba Town Council will not tell me to go away or send a bulldozer to scrape away my house, because they are afraid of my magical powers. They know what I used to be able to do."

Jessica smiled, as she and van Rooyen stepped forward to shake the old witchdoctor's wizened hand. Van Rooyen handed him back his food sack.

"Well, we have to go now," Jessica said. "It was a great pleasure speaking with you, Mr. Chitata. I hope we will see you again."

They turned to walk back down the hill and Jessica looked over her shoulder to see the old man crawling back into his hovel, while dragging the food bag and clutching his cigar box with its precious contents.

"It's pitiful the way that old man has to live," Jessica said "I've never met a witchdoctor before," she added. "I've always imagined them dressed in skins and feathers to heal believers with medicinal plants and potions. I've also read they have supernatural and magical powers and can use their spells both to heal the good and destroy the wicked."

Van Rooyen chuckled. "Jessica, have you considered that he actually might be extremely dangerous?"

"Oh, for heaven's sake, Piet, he's just a little, frail old man."

"Jessica, why do you think he lives outside the boundaries of Mahombekombe, next to the rubbish bins?

"Now you mention it, he did tell us the Kariba Town Council would never evict him, because they feared him."

"There, you see it. That's your answer," he said, putting his arm around her and hugging her.

"But Piet, he's still just a pitiful old man. How can anyone not feel sorry for him?"

"Because it's possible he could compel his believers to commit horrendous crimes. Keep that in mind!"

When the pair reached their Land Rover, Lindsay was leaning against the vehicle, waiting for them.

"Hey, thank you both for your help," he said. "We did an amazing job. In less than eight hours, we doled out thousands of pounds of food to almost two thousand people. Quite a feat! Jessica, I must say it was thanks to your queuing system that we were able to do it so quickly and efficiently."

She smiled. Perhaps this guy wasn't that bad after all. "I enjoyed being a part of the effort and I'm glad I could contribute. Thanks for giving me the opportunity, Mark. Maybe we can do it again sometime."

"Perhaps we will," he replied.

Then he turned to van Rooyen. "Great to see you again my man," and as they slapped each other on the back, he chuckled, "By the way, you've got a fine woman there. Better take good care of her, or I'll claim her for myself."

"Not a chance," van Rooyen said laughing out loud as his friend strode away.

Chapter 25

Tuesday, October 7, 2008

On Tuesday evening, while van Rooyen and Jessica relaxed on deck chairs beside the pool, he spoke of his concerns for his friends, Angus McLaren and Dave Packer.

"I need to find out what's going on in Karoi," he told her, his voice throaty with worry. "I'm thinking of driving down tomorrow to check up on them and take Angus all those cardboard boxes we've collected."

"I'm coming with you," Jessica said.

"No you're not! Far too risky."

"Nonsense, Piet! Total garbage! You're not going without me. Last month at the shooting range, you told me I'm a darn good shot. Give me a gun and I can defend myself," she insisted, her green eyes flashing with indignation.

Reconsidering for a minute or two, his chin and cheek cupped in his left hand, he capitulated. "Well, okay." Somehow those eyes always had the power to melt him? After just an hour's instruction, she'd more than proved she could handle a firearm.

The next day he and Jessica left Kariba, driving south towards Karoi, a small town fifty-five miles away, boasting a population of fifty thousand. While motoring down the busy, two-lane A-1, van Rooyen pointed to the untilled, barren fields, stretching for miles along both sides of the road.

"Jessica, look around. Not too many years ago these lands produced huge amounts of maize, cotton, tobacco, peanuts, and other crops. Check them out now," he exclaimed, his voice rising in anger. "No wonder this country exports nothing today, earns no foreign currency, and is forced to rely on donated food imports to feed its people."

"Such a tragedy," Jessica agreed.

In an hour and a half, they had reached Karoi. They turned left off the A-1.

"You might call this my home town," van Rooyen commented while steering through the small town's business district.

"Karoi's really been crushed by the failed economy," Jessica said, as they drove by scores of empty storefronts with 'closed' notices pasted on their front doors.

Deserted sidewalks lined the shopping areas. Outside the bank, however, crowds of people stood in long queues stretching for several blocks.

"On the radio this morning, they reported banks had run out of paper currency, because they'd raised their daily withdrawal limit to twenty thousand Zimbabwe dollars," van Rooyen said.

"That explains the crowd," Jessica said. "According to the paper's latest exchange rate, that same amount is now worth only thirty five U.S. dollars. Would you believe that? Thank heavens my funding comes in good ol' American greenbacks."

"Hell's bells," van Rooyen teased, "I'm sitting right next to a trillionaire!"

After they departed the business district, they turned down a highway leading to the farming areas. Ten minutes later, van Rooyen pointed to a weather-beaten sign on the left-hand-side, which read "Kigelia Farm."

"Here's the turnoff to my old place." His expression was grim.

Jessica said nothing, but reached out a comforting hand. He looked at her, noting her downcast eyes and her lips pursed in an expression of compassion, and felt encouraged. Today, with Jessica at his side, the painful memories this marker always invoked, seemed far less intense.

They drove another mile and reached the turnoff, taking them to Angus's Glengarry Farm. Only six weeks ago, van Rooyen had driven this same route. For several miles it bisected planted fields. Rooted in the rich red-brown soil, atop long furrows, he'd seen row upon row of healthy maize and tobacco seedlings, stretching to the distant tree line. Today, the tender young plants lay parched and trampled, and scores of wooden markers had been pounded into the dirt to divide the acreage into smaller lots. A dozen or more rickety lean-tos and thatched huts had sprouted up in the subdivided plots. Gone were the giant, steel irrigation gantries arching over the fields to spritz the growing crops. Missing also were the fat, Hereford and Black Angus cattle that had grazed near the dam. Van Rooyen stopped the Land Rover briefly to take in the totality of the scene.

"So much damage," he sighed. With a voice thickened with emotion, he haltingly described to Jessica how everything had looked, less than two months ago.

They arrived at the homestead at ten thirty. He breathed a sigh of relief when he pulled up to the padlocked gate and discovered the tall, chain-link, security fence surrounding the house was still intact. Horses in the stables—a bay, chestnut, and gray—poked their heads over the stable doors and van Rooyen suspected something was wrong. At this time of the day, *lo mahachi* should have been out grazing and frolicking in the paddock.

"Visitors usually hoot the horn until Angus's guard opens the gate," he said, adding "Last time, Angus's two large dogs alerted their master to my arrival. It was later that evening that those bloody bastards shot Zimbo, his black Lab," he growled, through gritted teeth. "Patsy now has the ridgeback with her to Harare. Today I'm sensing something's definitely wrong, so I won't announce our arrival and attract a crowd of squatters."

Van Rooyen reached behind the seat for the shotgun, handing it to Jessica.

"Here, be careful; it's loaded. I'm going to walk around the back of the house. Angus may be there, on the verandah."

Jessica took the gun and van Rooyen retrieved his FN rifle. Slowly, he opened the driver's door, but before he had time to set a foot on the ground, they heard the kitchen door's hinges creak. Primed, van Rooyen took aim at the doorway, hissing at Jessica to duck down.

Before dropping out of sight, Jessica spied someone stepping through the doorway.

"Piet, it's a white guy," she whispered.

Van Rooyen looked up and recognized his friend. His taut nerves relaxed and his lungs expelled a sigh of relief.

"Hey, Piet, it's good to see you," Angus called out as he approached the gate, jingling a bunch of keys. "Now put that bloody rifle down and bring your truck inside," he chortled, as he unlocked the padlocks and swung open the double gates.

"Sorry man. I wasn't sure who was coming out," van Rooyen grinned and slid the weapon behind the seat. If his friend ever kidded him, one day, about being over cautious, he'd just remind him he'd had a lady to protect. "We brought you some boxes," and pointed to the bundles of flattened cartons in the bed of the Land Rover.

"Can't thank you enough, Piet. I really need them. Here, hand me a stack and come on in."

They carried the cartons into the kitchen and van Rooyen introduced Jessica. Angus led them out to the verandah.

"What a magnificent view," Jessica said, as she looked out across the wide expanse of lawn and, in the background, the hills covered in Msasa trees. Their brilliant, early September, hues of red, copper, and gold had now morphed into a solid green.

"Can I get you anything to drink?" Angus asked.

"Something soft will be fine," van Rooyen replied. "You got orange juice?"

"Plenty. Not cold though, I'm afraid. ZESA's been off for more than twenty four hours, so no fridge. I didn't bother to restart the generator. You noticed, I suppose, that our new neighbors trampled the crops, and then made off with my irrigation system," Angus said, with more than a hint of sarcasm. "What about a drink for you, Jessica?"

"OJ's fine for me too," she smiled.

Angus left for the kitchen, returning with three tall glasses of Mazoe orange juice. After passing them around, he raised his glass, clicked it against those of his guests, and offered a toast.

"Cheers to Robert Mugabe, and may he rot in hell."

"Cheers," they chorused.

"I hope you didn't wait at the gate too long," Angus said. "Those bloody buggers showed up again this morning with three lorries and carted off my workers, their families, and even the household help. I'm assuming they took them to local ZANU-PF political re-education classes."

"That explains why the horses were still in their stables," van Rooyen said. How long has this been going on?"

"It's been happening ever since Morgan Tsvangirai garnered more votes in last March's election. Afterwards Mugabe's hangers-on began setting up torture camps to re-educate people they suspected of voting for the opposition – a brutal strategy designed so he can cheat his way to retaining power. My old gate guard, Tobiwa, is now pushing eighty. I hope they don't hurt him."

"I'd be worrying about Tobiwa too," van Rooyen said. "He's one of the best. Did I tell you that the last time I was here, he remembered me immediately. I was amazed; it had been years since he'd laid eyes on me."

"That old man – he doesn't forget much. He often sets me straight on a lot of stuff. By the way, about the horses, Patsy called the ZNSPCA and has asked them to come out and pick them up. I'm expecting their trailer later today or tomorrow. We know of some of the most horrific things those bloody fools have done to farm animals, after their owners were forced to abandon them. It would take me hours to tell you even a fraction of what we've learned. Anyway, it's fortunate Patsy has been able to arrange stabling for ours with a friend near Harare." Angus said. Van Rooyen detected a tremor in his friend's voice.

"Meryl Harrison of the Zimbabwe SPCA has rescued thousands of abused and traumatized pets and livestock from seized farms." Jessica said. "I've read about many of her rescues, which I can only describe as incredibly courageous feats so I'm totally in awe of her bravery."

"I agree. She's one fearless woman," Angus said.

Jessica's impassioned opinion of Harrison's work, van Rooyen found moving.

"Now, with regard to the workers," Jessica volunteered, "I read a report, recently published by the U.S.-based Human Rights Watch. They claim to have documented, so far this year, at least thirty six politically motivated murders and two thousand other killings, kidnappings, beatings and torture perpetrated by Mugabe's ruling party."

"Although I can't verify the accuracy of those figures, they sound low," Angus said. "I can, however, give you a pretty good idea of the true horrors our blokes have faced at these re-education camps."

"Carry on," van Rooyen urged him.

Angus went on to describe what his tractor driver, Mishek, had told him, the last time ZANU-PF thugs forced him, at gunpoint, to take a trailer-full of farm workers, their wives, and children, to such a camp.

"Well, at first Mishek was so distraught he couldn't speak about it. We had just returned from the mission hospital, where I'd taken him and six others for treatment for some pretty serious injuries," Angus said. "I finally got him talking and he told me that when they arrived at the camp, they were ordered off the trailer by a cadre of Green Bombers and men with shaved heads. He said the camp, was on Kigelia—your old farm, Piet."

Van Rooyen's heart dropped like a stone. It aggrieved him to know the land, on which he'd grown up, married, raised crops and reared his children, had again become a place of evil and tragedy.

Angus continued. "There were farm workers from every corner of the district, already assembled at the camp, Mishek told me. Perhaps as many as two hundred, all lined up in columns and being forced to chant political slogans. When he and our workers and their families arrived, he said, organizers shoved them into the throng to dance and sing songs. For hours, they had to praise Mugabe and ZANU-PF and denounce the MDC."

"And if they refused," Jessica asked.

"There was no refusing, Jessica." Angus replied. "And those who didn't sing loud enough, or dance fast enough, were yanked aside by camp officials, and whipped. Mishek said it was hot as hell, and no one got anything to drink. Meanwhile their tormentors swigged on bottles of Coca Cola. People collapsed; mostly pregnant women and the elderly, including Tobiwa. To save them from being trampled by the dancers, relatives and friends dragged the fallen away and to lie in the shade under the trees. These good deeds, he said, earned their benefactors severe thrashings."

"What was the long term effect on your workers," van Rooyen enquired.

"Among the unwilling dancers was my gardener, Jeremiah Nkala, his wife, and infant daughter. Tobiwa said she had the baby on her back when she went down. A green bomber screamed at her to get up, and when she didn't move fast enough, he kicked her and the little one with his jackboot. Jeremiah stepped up to try to help his wife and daughter, but the Bombers tackled him, determined to teach everyone a lesson. He suffered a broken jaw and nose, severe facial lacerations, a fractured arm, and bruising over much of his body. When I got him to the hospital the next day, his face was just an oozing, bloody pulp," Angus moaned.

Van Rooyen buried his chin in his chest. How agonizing for Angus to learn, firsthand, of the tortures inflicted upon his workers—those men and women, who had served him well for many years, and whom he felt honor-bound to protect.

"What about Jeremiah's wife and little girl?" Jessica asked, her lips trembling.

"They were knocked around pretty badly. There's more, I'll tell you later," Angus replied. "But in the meantime, after the chanting and singing was over, the Bombers forced the remaining able-bodied, people to run laps. Armed men, posted around the perimeter, threatened to shoot anyone who tried to escape. Afterwards, they ordered everyone, now hungry, thirsty, and totally buggered, to sit in a circle facing a ZANU-PF instructor, who gave them the name of the individual, they had to vote for in the next election. He warned them of the grave consequences they'd face, if they failed to comply."

"Piet, Jessica," Angus was running his hands through his hair, "I confess I had a hard time, at first, believing everything Mishek told me. Could the Bombers, just kids themselves, treat their own people like that? But I swear it was nothing compared with what came next! Following the indoctrination, the instructor summoned a foreman from one of the farms to step forward. Terrified, the man in question did not stand up. So the Bombers jumped in and started attacking his people for no good reason. Sufficiently intimidated, the man in question, finally identified himself. Those in charge of the camp then ordered his kids to punch, kick, and beat their father."

"Good God!" Van Rooyen exclaimed in horror. He knew that according to the Shona culture and tradition, parental respect was sacrosanct. Now here was a man being publicly attacked and humiliated by his own children.

"That's not all, Piet. Afterwards the workers this bloke supervised were called up and given the same order. By the end of the day, foremen from every farm in the district were subjected to the same treatment. Can you imagine the affect it had on these guys?"

"It had to be more than dreadful," van Rooyen responded.

"I can tell you my guy, Titus Chichumbiri, never recovered. His cheerful personality vanished overnight. He became sullen, depressed, and quick-tempered, and from then on was totally incapable of managing and inspiring his workers. Not long afterwards, he got sick, quit his job, and left the area. This incident also had a terrible effect on the women," Angus added, as he described how Mishek, with had tears streaming down his face as he related the activities of the night, when the women were hustled away into the bush.

"Mishek also told me he and the other men had to hear their wives, girlfriends, and daughters screaming in fear and agony, as they were raped repeatedly. He was bawling, as he described how he couldn't stop them from dragging off his Winnie and Jeremiah Nkala's wife, Sally. He told how one man fought back when his daughter was ripped from his arms—she was only fourteen—and how they thrashed him with a knobkerrie, tied him up, and made him watch as they used her. They nearly killed the poor girl, he said, and from then on no one dared protest for fear of making things worse for their loved ones."

Van Rooyen and Jessica were stunned. Tears filled Jessica's eyes.

"I'll tell you for damn sure, Piet, I'm scared to death they might be getting more of the same right now, perhaps something far worse," Angus said, burying his face in his hands.

For several minutes all three sat in silence. For van Rooyen, these accounts had struck way too close to the bone. He needed to switch gears.

"Angus, I've had a look at some of the damage they did to your tobacco and maize lands. Hell, there's no sense to it at all! Essentially, they now have the land, so why did they destroy the crops? In the end, everything they reaped, they could have sold for a lot of money."

Angus had a quick answer. "The trouble is, Piet, your way would require them to actually put out some effort. The truth is most of them know bugger-all about farming. They don't want the land, per se; they just want the money ZANI-PF is promising to pay them for kicking the farmers off. Now bear in mind, things might have been different if they'd been given free seed and fertilizer, as well as assistance in working their new plots. But considering what's taken place so far, that's bloody unlikely. Even if a miracle happens, how are they going to water their crops? They've already ripped the irrigation system apart. I'll bet the bloody idiots have sold the pipes and fittings for practically nothing and have already squandered the proceeds on beer. Something else the squatters haven't figured out yet is that some ZANU-PF big-wig will show up and send them packing. He'll move into this house and, from then on, the farm will become his weekend retreat."

"What a terrible waste," Jessica said, slowly shaking her head from side to side.

"Angus, can we do anything to help?" van Rooyen asked.

"As I told you on the phone, Piet, I'm packing up. I took Patsy off the farm in a damn hurry, so she left with hardly anything. I've packed up more of her things and some of mine in a couple of old suitcases. If you'd be willing to take this stuff to her in Harare, we could load them and some other valuables in your Land Rover," Angus said.

"No problem at all." van Rooyen replied. "As soon as we leave here, we'll head straight for Harare and drop it all off with her.

*   *   *

On the following Friday, Jessica spent most of the morning in her office, updating her study records and drafting the monthly report she mailed off to her sponsor in Washington, D.C. After lunch, as a welcome respite from the morning's hum-drum, paperwork routine, she decided to drive over to the nearby wildlife rehabilitation center and check on the orphan calf, Narini-Ina. In recent months, she and the center's director, Precious Chitora, had become close friends. Jessica found her visits to the center, just a fifteen minute drive away, interesting and enjoyable. Hopefully, she'd be able to relay to Piet a favorable report on the calf he'd saved from near death a little more than nine weeks ago. She knew the baby elephant occupied a special place in his heart.

Today, Precious took her back to a two-acre paddock behind the main building, where they found three-month-old, Narini-Ina, squealing with excitement. She was engaged in a boisterous game of chase with her unusual companion, a patient, fifteen-year-old, bay mare. Although, the little elephant stood almost thirty-six inches tall at the shoulder, she could still wriggle under the old mare's belly. She was growing fast, however, and wouldn't fit for too much longer, Jessica thought.

"I moved her out of the stall a week ago," Precious said. "She's doing well and weighs nearly three hundred pounds now. She's gained at least forty, since she arrived here. I had no other young elephants, so I paired her up with this mare to give her some company. She's an ex-racehorse now a brood mare, named Angerona, who was abandoned six months ago when her owners had to leave their farm."

"They seem to be getting along well," Jessica chuckled, as she watched the pair cavorting about. Having caught up with the mare, the calf made repeated, clumsy attempts to grab the end of her swishing tail with her trunk.

"They certainly are," the large, good natured woman agreed with a giggle. "I believe she'll be ready for release into the bush, just as soon as you and Piet can find a lactating female, preferably one that's recently lost a her calf."

"We're keeping an eye out," Jessica assured her.

She'd found Precious not only an expert on the area's wildlife, but also a storehouse of knowledge in local history. Today Precious had promised to tell her the story of Rupert Fothergill's Operation Noah rescue of a herd of buffalo, involving a mongrel named Crackers.

"The story takes place in 1959 after the completion of the Kariba dam wall," Precious began. "Animals had moved to higher ground as the lake filled. But many had been trapped on new islands. One day my grandfather and Mr. Fothergill went out in a boat with three game scouts, looking for these stranded animals," she said. "They had small dog called Crackers with them."

"Couldn't the animals swim for safety?"

"Not all of them. Some of the islands were too far away from the mainland. Although others were closer, not all animals are good swimmers, and some fear the water," she replied. "Anyway, when Grandfather and Mr. Fothergill stopped at one of the bigger islands, they found this herd of buffalo. Grandfather said the lake was rising at a rate of three feet a day. Consequently, if they weren't moved soon, they could drown. The buffalo had bunched together at the far end of the island. They are strong swimmers and since they didn't have too far to swim, Mr. Fothergill told the team to drive them into the lake. However, he warned everyone to beware because buffalos are bad tempered and can be dangerous. He suggested they chase the big bull into the water, so the rest of the herd would follow."

Continuing with the tale, Precious described how everyone set off on foot towards the herd with the little dog leading the way. She said her grandfather and Mr. Fothergill carried rifles, while the scouts had sticks and empty cans, which they beat loudly to drive the herd forward.

Jessica listened on, entranced. She found Precious's animated style of storytelling, exciting and suspenseful.

"Grandfather knew the people and the noise were making the bull nervous and upset. When they got closer, he put his great, big head down and began pawing the ground, kicking up clouds of dust."

To illustrate, Precious lowered her head and shuffled her feet in the dirt. Jessica could tell she thoroughly enjoyed acting the part.

"He was closer now," she continued with a wide smile, "and my grandfather noticed a bad scar on the bull's shoulder, which he believed had come from a hunter's bullet. When the bull smelled the people, he snorted in anger, bellowed loudly, and charged the rescue team."

"What happened next?" Jessica squealed.

With her lashes lowered and speaking in a low timbre, Precious continued. "My grandfather said everybody was scared and looked around for trees to climb. Both he and Mr. Fothergill gripped their rifles and disengaged the safety catches. They knew they had no choice but to shoot, if any team member was in danger. My grandfather was raising the barrel to line up the sights, when suddenly something burst out of the tall grass and tackled the bull, grabbing on to its big, black nose.

"What was it?" Jessica trembled in anticipation.

"It was Crackers!" Precious screamed, doubling up with laughter.

"The dog? Why what happened?"

"Yes, the dog! He attacked the bull, and when Crackers found himself dangling over the lake, he let go of the bull's nose and dropped into the water. Fortunately, he managed to escape the pounding hooves of the rest of the herd, following the bull into the lake. Afterwards, Crackers climbed out, and everyone cheered him."

"In the meantime," Precious continued, "the old bull and his herd were paddling like crazy to the mainland and my grandfather and his scouts jumped in their boat and kept them swimming safely back to land."

"Such a brave little dog," Jessica exclaimed. "What happened to him afterwards?"

"Grandfather told me Crackers went with them on many future rescues and his picture appeared on the front page of the *Rhodesia Herald*. Eventually they took him to the Marangora Wildlife Station not far from here. There, they have a framed newspaper article about him with his picture that says his life ended just as he had lived it – in service to mankind. He eventually died from a snake bite, but only after alerting the station's staff to the presence of the poisonous cobra."

"Oh Precious! Crackers was certainly a hero. What an incredibly touching tale. Thank you for sharing it with me. What happened, by the way, about the wildlife rescue?"

"Operation Noah officially ended in June 1963 and Grandfather's and Mr. Fothergill's teams received credit for saving nearly five thousand animals from drowning or starvation."

"Well, I've taken up enough of your time, so I'd better be going. Precious, I do enjoy my visits here and I'll let Piet know, the next time I run into him, how well Narini-Ina is doing. I know he'll be pleased. By the way, I love your wonderful stories. I'd keep coming just to hear more of them."

"Jessica I was glad to have you," Precious said, giving her a hug. "Drive carefully and I'll see you next time."

As Jessica drove away, Precious waved her a cheerful goodbye.

*   *   *

That evening after supper, Jessica was relaxing on the sofa, reading a Wilbur Smith novel, when the telephone rang. She leant over and picked up the receiver.

"Jessica, this is Piet." Her heart raced at the sound of his voice.

"Hi," was her brusque reply, intentionally designed to disguise her true feelings.

"I wanted to tell you I just heard from Patsy. She said Angus and his neighbor, Dave Packer, were both arrested this morning on charges they failed to evacuate a farm listed for acquisition."

"Oh no! That's dreadful news." A flutter of anxiety rippled inside her. "What can we do?"

"Not much right this moment, but I'm thinking I should drive into Harare tomorrow first thing, to see Patsy and go with her to see Angus at the jail. Want to come?"

She knew, of course, she wanted to be with him. "Sure! What time are you leaving?"

"I'll pick you up at six, sharp. Bring an overnight bag with something to wear to the horse races on Sunday."

"The horse races!" she cried out, leaping off the sofa in excitement. "Ooh! That'll be fun! I'll be ready and waiting."

"See you tomorrow," he said. And, after a measurable pause, he added softly, "Jessica, I love you," and hung up.

Chapter 26

Saturday, October 11, 2008

Last night, after he'd hung up the phone, van Rooyen had groaned, burying his head in his hands. Damn! Had he made a total fool of himself? What was he thinking? More important, what was she thinking?

Today he and Jessica were driving into Harare. Shortly before 11:00 a.m., they had arrived and were turning onto Churchill Avenue. During the drive, so far, not a word had been exchanged between them about his declaration of love the night before.

"What are these beautiful, old trees called?" Jessica asked.

"In Africa, they're mostly called Flamboyants, but in Central America they're known as Royal Poincianas. You probably saw them last spring, when they were in full bloom and all covered in scarlet flowers," van Rooyen reminded her.

"These are those trees? Yes, of course. They were magnificent."

They drove past the University and turned onto Borrowdale Road, heading north.

"The racecourse is up ahead on the right," van Rooyen said. "Just a few miles further is St. Michael's Lane. Patsy said her aunt's house is on the left, across the road from the primary school."

"I'm so looking forward to going to the races. I just wish I had a fancy hat."

"Don't worry. It'll be nothing like the Kentucky Derby, Jessica, you won't need a hat," van Rooyen assured her with a grin. "In the 1960s, I'm told if you wanted to dress up, the races at Borrowdale were definitely the place to go. My Grandmother loved going to Borrowdale Park. In those days people also dressed-up when they travelled by air. Nowadays, no one wears their best togs to catch a plane."

"You're right, Piet. Times have changed," Jessica sighed. "Today people don't get dressed up, even for church, unless it's for a wedding or a funeral."

Twenty minutes later, they turned into a driveway and parked behind Patsy's small Nissan hatchback. They knocked and she met them at the door. Her face was drawn, and her hair pulled back into a pony tail.

"Hello Piet. And you must be Jessica." They shook hands. "So glad you're both here. My aunt's off at her regular, weekly, bridge game, so we're here alone."

"Any news of Angus or Dave?" van Rooyen asked.

"Not a thing. I'm just relieved Angus managed to phone yesterday to let me know where they were taking him."

Patsy had a forlorn look on her face, so Jessica wrapped her arms around her, and gave her a quick hug. "I'm so sorry you have to go through all this," she said.

Afterwards Patsy stepped back, giving Jessica a grateful smile.

"How's Joyce holding up?" van Rooyen said.

"I haven't seen her in several days. She's with her daughter in Marondera. Let me make a pot of tea," Patsy looked back as she strode to the kitchen.

Van Rooyen caught Jessica's eye. He shook his head, and pointed to his wristwatch.

"Patsy," Jessica said, "please don't worry about tea. Perhaps we should leave now. We've got no idea when the jail's visiting hours will be over," Jessica said.

"You're right," Patsy replied. Then the telephone rang. "Hold on a sec,' let me get this," she called out, as she ran for the phone.

Five minutes later, she returned with a canvas bag, filled with water bottles, sandwiches wrapped in wax paper, and an assortment of fresh fruit – bananas, oranges, guavas and mangoes.

"Okay, let's go," she said. "That was Jocelyn, by the way; Joyce's daughter in Marondera. She says Joyce isn't well, so they won't be driving in today. She doesn't want to worry her father, so she asked me to tell him car trouble delayed them and that they'll drive in on Monday."

"Nothing serious, I hope," van Rooyen looked concerned, while they walked out to Patsy's Nissan hatchback.

"She didn't say," Patsy replied, getting in behind the wheel.

Jessica climbed in the back.

"Is this for Angus?" van Rooyen asked, as he took the bag of foodstuffs from Patsy and stowed it behind the driver's seat.

"I'm told the food there is inedible, so I thought I'd bring them something."

*   *   *

In less than thirty minutes, they reached the remand prison located in a large colonial-era complex, behind the Harare Central Police Station on Kenneth Kaunda Avenue. Locals referred to the building as 'Law and Order.'

The jail consisted of four long buildings, enclosing an open, exercise yard. Tall guard towers stood at each corner of the somber, concrete walled structure manned by armed guards, whose gun barrels protruded through turrets on all sides. A tall, heavy-duty security fence, topped with razor wire, surrounding the entire prison compound to serve as an effective escape deterrent.

Patsy parked the Nissan in the visitors' parking area. As van Rooyen observed his surroundings, he was immediately struck by the gloominess of the place.

Outside the gate, a crowd had gathered. The men wearing business suits and toting briefcases he assumed were attorneys. Others were likely the inmates' friends and family members, their attire indicative of their varied levels of poverty or prosperity. Most carried boxes and paper bags – probably containing gifts of food for their loved ones.

Van Rooyen, Jessica, and Patsy joined the queue behind thirty others. In front of them was a black man in sharply pressed trousers, his brown leather shoes, polished to a high gloss. His hair was neatly cropped, and he appeared to be in his mid-twenties.

"How long are the visiting hours?" van Rooyen enquired.

"From one o'clock until three. However the guards take too long to process everyone, so sometimes we may not get in until after two," he said, folding and tucking his newspaper under his arm.

"That much time?"

"Yes," he replied with a sigh. "I often wait in this line for hours to visit my brother. More than once it took too long and they turned me away."

"Terrible," van Rooyen said, shaking his head in sympathy. "If you don't mind me asking, how long has your brother been here?"

"Over eight months. He's a member of the MDC, arrested by ZAPU-PF strongmen, before the elections."

"What crime did they charge him with?"

"Resisting the government."

"What?" van Rooyen exclaimed in astonishment. "How was he resisting the government?" His tone dripped with sarcasm.

"He was Morgan Tsvangirai's aide and speech writer."

Van Rooyen felt a surge of indignation; yet another case of ZANU-PF's illegitimate control over the opposition party. "Your brother must be a talented man. I'm very sorry for his difficulties," he said.

Van Rooyen stepped closer and whispered into the man's ear, "In my opinion, your brother's imprisonment isn't legal, or fair. I admire Mr. Tsvangirai's stance against President Mugabe and his party's heinous policies. I'm Piet van Rooyen, by the way," he added. "I used to farm in Karoi, but they kicked me off my place in April 2001. I'm here to visit my former neighbor, who was arrested yesterday for not turning his farm over to Mugabe's *shamwari*, Comrade Disaster, AKA Ishmael Gondo."

The man took his proffered hand and murmured, "That Ishmael Gondo is an evil one." Continuing in a normal conversational tone, he added, "Mr. van Rooyen, my name is Luke Watakama and I'm pleased to meet you. My brother is Matthew. Our mother is a devout Christian," he added with a laugh. "She insisted we all have biblical names. Our sisters she named Mary and Sarah."

Van Rooyen introduced his new acquaintance to Patsy and Jessica.

"Are the conditions in the prison as bad as they say?" Patsy asked quietly.

"I've not seen them for myself, Mrs. McLaren. The visitor's area is separate from the cells, but," he whispered, "I trust Matthew when he tells me it's very, very bad in there. Your husband must find a good lawyer, so he can get out fast. Matthew says that two prisoners die in there every day."

Patsy's face looked anguished. "Mr. Watakama, can you recommend a good lawyer for my husband?"

"I know of some excellent lawyers," he replied. "The best, in my opinion, is a lady who gained the release of a number of American and British journalists—Susan Makova. Another is Edison Chamboko. He defended that farmer, last year, charged with murder when he shot the person who slashed the Achilles tendons on the back legs of several of his champion bulls. Mr. Chamboko got him off on self-defense."

"Thank you very much Mr. Watakama. I appreciate your help," Patsy said as she scribbled the names on a scrap of paper.

Van Rooyen, Jessica, and Patsy finally reached the guard post at the visitor's entrance at 1:15 p.m.

"Driver's licenses or other official identification," barked the scowling guard, sitting behind a steel mesh-covered window.

Van Rooyen collected everyone's IDs, and passed them through a slot in the window. Stepping back, he motioned Patsy to the front.

The guard stared long and hard at Patsy, agonizingly slowly lowering his eyes to study the picture on her driver's license. He repeated this procedure several times and three full minutes later, he slid her ID back under the grate.

"Any weapons on your person?" he growled.

"No."

"Step aside," he ordered. "Wait over there, by the door. Next."

Jessica stepped forward and the guard's infuriatingly slow process of matching the visitor to his or her identification began anew. Only after van Rooyen was vetted, did the door on the right finally open and a female guard appear. She ordered Patsy and Jessica to enter and slammed it shut after them. Later, a male guard admitted van Rooyen.

By the time all three of them had been frisked, their pockets emptied, shoes, handbags and Patsy's food sack searched for contraband, van Rooyen's watch read almost 2:00 p.m. Patsy was tapping her foot impatiently. He patted her on the shoulder and gave her a comforting smile.

Fifteen minutes later, guards ushered them into a large hall furnished with tables and chairs, where inmates requiring minimum security could sit and mingle freely with visitors. Higher risk prisoners sat behind steel bars running around three sides of the room. Van Rooyen noticed prison guards, armed with batons, positioned at the entrance and every twenty feet behind the barricade.

He spotted Angus, behind the barrier on the left side of the room and ushered the two women to a bench facing him, where they seated themselves. Prominently displayed along the barrier were signs in English, Afrikaans, Portuguese, Shona, Ndebele, Manyika, Chinyanja, and Tonga, forbidding physical contact with prisoners through the bars.

Van Rooyen was appalled at his friend's appearance. Angus had visible bruises, a black eye, a gash across his forehead, and a nasty abrasion on his right cheek.

"What have they done to you, Sweety?" Patsy whimpered, her eyes filling with tears.

"I'm okay, Babe. Truly I am. I swear it looks much worse than it is," Angus reassured his wife and friends with a forced smile. "I'm just bloody happy you're all here. Thanks for coming."

"Angus, tell us what happened," van Rooyen said.

Angus took his mind back to dawn on Thursday.

*   *   *

He had awoken to the loud, thwop-thwop sound of an approaching helicopter. When it landed, he leapt from his bed and peered out his window into the early morning gloom. The chopper stood in an open field, its spinning propeller slowly losing momentum. He pulled on a pair of khaki shorts, shirt, and socks and stepped into some work boots. He heard the sound of arriving vehicles.

From his kitchen window, he spied a gray, police van pull up outside the security gate. Following it were two sleek, black sedans. Three policemen alighted from the van, and four men in business suits stepped from the cars. They huddled together, deep in conversation, taking sideways glances at the homestead, behind the tall security fence. Angus noticed three of the men in business attire held automatic pistols. CIO agents, he figured, and his breath quickened in fear.

He returned to the bedroom and peered through the window at the helicopter, bearing a Zimbabwean emblem. He'd never seen a chopper like this one before. In the emerging daylight the military gunship appeared formidable. Its fuselage bristled with machine guns, rockets, and missile launchers, mounted on spars extending from either side. A sizeable aircraft, Angus thought. Bigger than the American Huey helicopter featured so often in Vietnam War movies. Its three crewmen, dressed in military flight suits, had disembarked and stood around it.

Angus shifted his mind into high gear, recalling the myriad plans he had formulated in his mind these past few weeks. They included strategies broadly divided into the categories of fight, flight, or surrender. The scenarios he'd envisaged, however, were based on the return of Comrade Disaster and his riffraff gang—not on a military-style raid, mounted by army, police and top-secret intelligence personnel, armed with sophisticated weaponry. He realized his situation had worsened way beyond even his most dire predictions.

Any plan he devised, which involving putting up a fight, was obviously no longer viable. How could he defend himself against machine guns, rockets and heat-seeking missiles, with just his small collection of hunting rifles? Flight also appeared to be a non-option. With the helicopter's eyes in the sky, a successful escape seemed improbable, if not impossible. Surrender looked to be his only viable alternative. Nevertheless, he wanted to keep his options open for now.

Back outside the kitchen window, nothing much was going on. The police officers and their civilian counterparts were still standing around idly, talking, and laughing. Not a farm worker was in sight. Isaiah, the house servant, and gate guard, Tobiwa, were also nowhere to be seen. He was relieved the men and their families were steering clear. He took advantage of the current inaction to make himself a cup of tea and a light breakfast. At least he'd face whatever was in store with a full stomach.

When he next looked outside, the pilots had joined the others. The group's hilarity was punctuated with much exaggerated posing and gesturing. They were obviously enjoying themselves. Until he'd run across the likes of Comrade Disaster, Angus had enjoyed an easy camaraderie with the Shona people. He'd grown up with them, and had always loved them for their gentle natures, their social courtesies, their keen sense of humor, and their love of art and music. What had happened over the past eight years to change all that?

A policeman climbed into the van and reappeared with a pair of bolt cutters. The group fell silent as he approached the security gate and cut the padlocks. When he flung open the gates, Angus knew the game was up. Now he was in life-preservation mode, so he exited the kitchen door and held up his hands in submission. In their hurry to enter the house, the CIO agents almost knocked him to the ground. A police officer fastened the handcuffs around his wrists.

"Where are you taking me?" Angus asked, as two officers frog-marched him to the van.

They did not reply. While an officer fumbled with the keys to the van's back door, a man in an expensively tailored, dark gray suit approached. He appeared to be unarmed, so Angus figured he was not a member of the CIO.

"Good morning Mr. McLaren. I have been looking forward to meeting you," he said in carefully enunciated English. "I would shake your hand, but I see that would be a little difficult at the moment," he added with a smirk. "Anyway, I am Mr. Ishmael Gondo, the new owner of your farm and also Mr. Packer's farm, next door."

"No way in hell, do you have any right to this bloody farm," Angus hissed between bared teeth. "Get the hell off my property right now."

"Mr. McLaren, I'm afraid there's nothing you can do. You are going to prison for crimes against the nation of Zimbabwe."

"What crimes? I've committed no bloody crimes."

The man walked away without responding. The police van's rear door was open and the second police officer stepped forward to help his colleague lift and heave Angus into the back of the van. They slammed the door leaving Angus in total darkness, lying prostrate on the hard floor of the windowless vehicle. A strong odor of human waste permeated its interior.

Alone in the blackness, time dragged on. Outside were voices speaking in Shona. The ridges in the metal floor pressed uncomfortably on his hips so he turned over and wriggled himself into a sitting position. With the day's rising heat, the van became stifling. Beads of sweat formed rivulets down his face. Unable to wipe them away, their saltiness stung his eyes.

Later, he heard a second helicopter approach and land nearby. As the whirring of its rotary wing slowed to a stop, he could hear voices; people shouting. Minutes later, his captors opened the rear door and flung someone else inside. With his eyes adjusting to the sudden brightness, Angus had only seconds to see who it was, before the door slammed shut. It was Dave Packer, his neighbor, who lay at his feet groaning, obviously in great pain.

"Dave, hey man. Are you okay? What did those sods do to you?'

"Angus, thank God," his friend replied in a raspy voice. "They roughed me up quite a bit. I think my right shoulder's dislocated and my left arm may be broken, but otherwise I'm okay. Just mad as hell."

Fifteen minutes later, the van's motor roared into life and he and Dave were on their way to who knows where. Dave cried out in pain as they bumped over the rutted, farm roads. A short time later, the van turned onto a tarred road and they heard the sounds of trucks and cars whipping past.

"I think we're on the A-1 to Harare," Angus said.

Approximately an hour later, the vehicle pulled off the highway and parked outside a roadside store, Angus assumed, from the cacophony of voices outside. The driver and his fellow officers got out and reboarded ten minutes later. Before they drove away, Angus heard the popping sound of soda cans being opened. The sounds of their captors' slurping their drinks only worsened Angus's ferocious craving for water.

The van had been cooking in the sun for hours. With no ventilation in the rear, closed cargo space, the heat was intolerable. Angus's and Dave's clothing was drenched with sweat, and they were both dehydrated. Angus's mouth felt dry and his skin was on fire. He caught himself drowsing periodically.

Finally, the van came to a stop, the rear doors flung open, and Angus realized they had arrived at the Harare Remand Prison. Dave screamed with pain, as the guards dragged him from the van and hauled him into the building. Angus staggered in after them, and police hustled him into an interrogation room. Where did they take his friend? He knew Dave needed immediate medical attention and hoped they had taken him straight to the prison infirmary. For more than an hour he waited, still handcuffed, until two gun-toting, CIO agents and several guards appeared.

An agent pulled up a chair and sat across from Angus. He ordered a guard to remove his restraints. He had a pad of paper and a pencil in front of him on which he scribbled a few notes. Then he looked up, glared at Angus, and the interrogation commenced.

"I need something to drink," Angus croaked. He could barely speak; his mouth was dry and his tongue felt as though it had swollen to twice its size.

"Get the prisoner some water," the agent barked at a prison guard.

The guard returned with a Coca Cola bottle filled with a clear liquid. Brown flecks swam around in the liquid. Too thirsty to care, Angus guzzled it down. He prayed the flecks were nothing more sinister than small drops of cola residue.

"Ready?" the agent growled.

"Yes," Angus nodded.

"We found petrol cans on your farm. When did you start petrol-bombing police stations?

"That's ridiculous!" Angus shot back. "We used them for fueling lawn mowers and other equipment. I can assure you I have never petrol-bombed any bloody police stations."

"Even so, Mr. McLaren, we also have proof you have been working with the MDC. You know very well that Tsvangirai's stupid organization is nothing more than a puppet opposition party, whose aim is to hand the country back to the whites."

"What possible proof do you have to support such a ludicrous claim?" Angus demanded angrily, his fist hitting the table.

The agent rose to his feet and looked down at Angus with narrowed eyes. "We searched your house, Mr. McLaren, and we found a large weapons cache. We have evidence you have been training MDC terrorists, and you will be brought up on charges of treason, a very serious crime. If convicted, you will be put to death," he said, slapping the tabletop with an air of finality.

"Good God! You call my six, low caliber, hunting rifles a large weapons cache?" Angus retorted. "You buggers must be totally out of your minds." He sat back in his chair and began to laugh uproariously.

"So you think it is funny?" the agent said, with narrowed lips. He pointed to a prison guard and said, "Restrain him and soften him up. We'll continue the questioning tomorrow." The CIO agents walked out of the room and soon afterwards, the beating began.

*　　　　　*　　　　　*

Angus summed up his experience of the arrest and interrogation as well as he could. He circumvented the goriest parts, to save Patsy from becoming totally unglued. Even so, after he was done, Patsy let out a strangled cry. Jessica put her arm around Angus's wife to comfort her, while she buried her face and sobbed on Jessica's shoulder.

"Angus, she's freaked out," van Rooyen whispered. "Someone told her that two people a day get killed in here."

Angus looked at Patsy and said, "It's not so bad."

"Really?" she replied.

Angus fixed her with a wry smile, "The food's edible on Tuesdays and I have a dry place to sleep when it's not raining. Besides, no one comes in here and tries to steal my stuff."

"That's because you don't have any stuff."

Angus shrugged.

"What about the murders?" Patsy asked.

"What murders?"

She wagged a finger at him. "Don't play dumb with me, a man outside told me two prisoners die in here every day."

"Every day?" Angus laughed.

"Don't make jokes, this is serious."

Angus sighed. "Listen Babe, only the long-term inmates die in here. I don't plan on staying here too long."

Patsy's mood brightened a little and she fumbled in her pants' pockets for the scrap of paper bearing the names of the attorneys.

"Angus, here are the names of two lawyers. I'm told they're the best in Zimbabwe. They are Susan Makova and Edison Chamboko. If you want, I'll contact the woman first. I'm familiar with her name. She's often been mentioned in the paper, in connection with some incredibly tough cases."

"If you think she's good, contact her first thing, Monday morning," Angus said.

"Seriously, Angus, how are things, really, in here?" Jessica asked.

"Well, I've been in this rat and lice-infested hell hole for less than twenty-four hours, so I can't give you a complete overview."

"What are the accommodations like?"

"Cramped. My cell measures about 20 feet by 12 feet. Sounds big, until I tell you there are more than thirty of us crammed in it. I'm told we're fortunate; some cells have more than fifty inmates."

"How do they fit thirty beds in there?"

"No beds. We sleep on filthy mats and we're lucky if we're issued with a thin, blanket that's foul-smelling and full of lice, fleas and other bugs. Cold is not so much of a problem at this time of year, but I imagine it's total hell in the winter. The heat and the stink are mostly what we have to contend with, now."

"What about ablutions?" van Rooyen asked.

"Oh shit!" Angus laughed. "The sanitation is deplorable – practically nonexistent." He gave them a humorous run down on the prison's hygiene system.

"There are three buckets per cell," he chuckled. "One for the toilet, and the others for washing and drinking. They are never emptied or refilled often enough. I'm told each of us is supposed to get half a toilet roll and a small bar of blue soap, once a month, but I haven't seen mine yet. When it comes to the buckets, people tend to forget which is which, and whenever there's a fight, the crap bucket invariably gets kicked over. I asked one bloke, who's been in here for two years waiting for his trial, how often the cells were cleaned, or hosed down. He told me never."

The women's eyes widened, and their mouths gaped.

Van Rooyen already knew that the source of the prison's drinking water was suspect. The independent press had reported that the city had a history of water shortages. They said it was due to the lack of maintenance and repair of the city's reservoirs, pumping stations, and underground distribution system—all of which dated back to the 1940s. A little over a year ago, the dumping of untreated sewage into Lake Chivero, the city's main water supply, had caused a huge upsurge in cases of cholera, diarrhea, and dysentery. He hoped his friend's release would happen soon—before he contracted any of these diseases.

"Sweety, I brought you and Dave a few things," Patsy said, holding up the food bag.

"Appreciate that, Babe. See that man over there?" Angus pointed to a prison guard behind the barricade to his left. "That's Officer Ncube. He seems to be the only half-decent bloke I've come across in here. When you leave, give the bag to the guard, and tell him it's for me, in Cell 95; ask him to give it to Officer Ncube." Angus blew his wife a kiss, and thanked her for the goodies.

"What's the food really like, here?" van Rooyen asked.

"Seriously, not much to write home about," he replied. "We eat once a day—*sadza* and stringy, watery, cabbage in a plastic bowl. By the way, Piet," he added, "I haven't seen Dave since we got here. I've asked about him numerous times. They just tell me he's in another cell, and won't give me the number."

"That doesn't sound good," van Rooyen said.

At three fifteen, the visitors left the prison. During their drive back to the house on St. Michael's Lane, Patsy informed Piet and Jessica that her aunt had readied two spare bedrooms for them to stay over, both tonight and tomorrow night.

"How very sweet and considerate of her," Jessica said, patting Patsy on the shoulder. "We'd love to stay tonight, but we have other plans for Sunday night."

Van Rooyen turned to her in the rear seat, his face a picture of confusion. "What are you talking about?" he mouthed.

"Tell you later," she mouthed in reply.

Before they retreated to their separate rooms for the night, Jessica told him quietly that she had made them a reservation at Meikles Hotel for the following night.

*   *   *

The thoroughbreds in the first race at Borrowdale Park were already circling the parade ring when van Rooyen and Jessica arrived the next day. Van Rooyen had purchased badges for their admission into the Members' Enclosure and they studied the race card to identify each of the horses.

While they observed the runners parading before the race, it wasn't just the horses capturing van Rooyen's interest. He was admiring Jessica. Her sharply pressed, peach linen pantsuit showed off her long, slender legs and her auburn hair falling about her shoulders, framed her face in soft curls. Occasionally she gave him a sidelong glance with her dazzling, emerald eyes and it made him feel weak at the knees.

It was a small field; only six runners in the first race—a one thousand meter, maiden juvenile plate for two-year-old fillies. Four of them were competing for the first time.

"Do you see the pretty chestnut filly over there?" Jessica said, pointing to horse number three. "Her name's Tambourine. I'll think I'll put a place bet on her."

"My goodness, aren't we taking a weighty gamble" van Rooyen teased.

"I think I'll put a wager on number six, Razzmatazz, to win."

They placed their bets at the tote window and walked down to the railing to watch the field canter down to the starting gate. The jockey riding Tambourine wore white colors with red braces, striped sleeves and a red cap.

"She's definitely the winner," Jessica said, looking up at van Rooyen and flashing him a wide smile.

"Don't know about that," he countered. "Razzmatazz is more experienced. She's already had two outings and placed both times."

It was a bright, sunny, October afternoon with a just a few puffy white clouds sailing in a brilliant blue sky. A light breeze cooled the day's warm seasonal temperature, the high eighties Fahrenheit.

"It's a gorgeous day, Piet," Jessica commented, as she leaned over the railing to watch the horses milling around the distant starting gate.

Standing downwind, van Rooyen caught a whiff of her perfume. The alluring fragrance, along with the sight of her auburn tresses rippling in the breeze, consumed him with an aching desire to reach for her. However, in this public place, it would have been wildly inappropriate, so he cleared any such thoughts from his mind.

"It is a beautiful day," he agreed, placing his arm around her waist and drawing her towards him. She glanced up at him and smiled.

"The field's under starter's orders." The commentator's voice boomed through the public address system.

Van Rooyen glimpsed Jessica shivering with excitement. Down at the end of the straightaway, the horses were being loaded into the starting gate.

Moments later, a bell clanged and the commentator bellowed, "They're off!"

In a contest lasting fewer than sixty seconds, the field of six raced to the finishing post as their riders frantically jockeyed for position. The commentator bawled out the names of the front runners, and the crowd erupted, urging on their favorites. With pounding hooves, the thoroughbreds galloped fearlessly to earn the right to appear in the coveted winner's enclosure. After the horses passed the post, with its flashing photo finish camera, the sounds of their hooves faded and they slowed to a stop.

"And the winner is ...Tambourine, by ... half a length," the commentator's voice bellowed, "with Mamma Mia coming in second, and Polar Cat third."

Van Rooyen hugged a beaming Jessica. "Congratulations," he said grinning. "Your horse won and poor old Razzmatazz came in stone last. Beginners luck, of course. Anyway, let's go and claim your winnings."

"No way was it beginner's luck," she said faking a pout. "Just call me a good judge of horseflesh."

"Talking about champion horse flesh, did you know that a horse bred right here in Zimbabwe won a race in America, at Kentucky's famous Churchill Downs?" he said.

"Are you serious?" she said, with sly smile, which told van Rooyen she didn't believe a word of it.

"Positive," he said, wearing a deadpan expression. "It was a filly called Ipi Tombe. As a two-year-old, she won her first race here so decisively her owners decided to enter her in races in South Africa. She won more races down there, including South Africa's premier race, the Durban July, in 2002. Afterwards, she competed against international champions in Dubai, Saudi Arabia, and won another three races there."

Continuing Ipi Tombe's saga, van Rooyen said she was sold to new owners, who took her across the Atlantic and in June 2003, she won the Locust Grove Handicap at Churchill Downs. This win was supposed to mark the beginning of a series of appearances in major U.S. turf races over the late summer and autumn. However less than a month later, she suffered a leg injury, which cut short her fourteen-race career.

"Altogether, she won twelve races, placed second, twice, and earned the equivalent of more than one-and-a-half million U.S. dollars in prize money. Not bad for a Zimbabwe horse, don't you think?"

"Piet, you must have been a huge Ipi Tombe fan, to have memorized all that."

He grinned sheepishly and pulled from his trouser pocket a folded piece of newsprint. He opened it up to display the horse's picture with a summary of her racing history.

"What a cheat!" she gasped, stepping back open-mouthed. Then, doubled over with laughter, she said, "Honestly, you had me believing you remembered every bit of that!"

"Not quite. Ipi Tombe had an enormous following here and the news media even kept track of her exploits long after she left the country. Her name in the Xhosa language means 'Where's the Girl.'"

"Well, I must agree she certainly had an amazing record."

"She did."

After Jessica presented her tote ticket at the claim window, she received $1.35 in winnings for her one-dollar bet.

"I won't get rich quick, this way," she giggled. "But I'll treat you to a beer, anyway."

The afternoon progressed and van Rooyen's luck improved. He selected the winners of the next two races, putting him ahead. Jessica tied up the competition, however, when she chose the winner of the last race, a beautiful gray named National Anthem.

"Well I think we enjoyed ourselves and didn't break the bank," van Rooyen said, while they walked hand-in-hand to the parking lot after Jessica had picked up her winnings.

"Piet, I haven't had this much fun in years. Thanks for suggesting this outing. I hope we can come back again soon."

"Of course we can." He replied as he guided her to the Land Rover.

It was almost dark when they drove up to the front entrance of Meikles Hotel. Van Rooyen let Jessica out with their two overnight bags and went to park the car. Jessica registered at the reception desk and had the room key when Van Rooyen returned.

*　　　　*　　　　*

Upstairs in their room after dinner, van Rooyen took Jessica in his arms, and gently laid her down. They kissed and his hands caressed her back, stroked her sides, and then moved inexorably to her breasts. Her heart was hammering and her breathing quickened.

He loosened her blouse and when he cupped her left breast in the palm of his hand, it rose under his touch and the nipple hardened. She moaned aloud from the pleasure of it. With heat blossoming on her cheeks, she undressed, climbed into the bed, and stretched out between the sheets. Moments later van Rooyen joined her

He smothered her face with kisses then his lips covered hers. The kiss began slowly and softly, but took on an urgency and passion. When their lips finally parted, he buried his face in the softness of her neck and smelled her scent.

"Damn!" he moaned. "You feel so good," and he groaned between more kisses.

For weeks, Jessica had longed for this closeness and connection with Piet. The fear of rejection that Paul had left her with no longer imprisoned her and her heart pounded.

"I've been wanting you for so long!" she breathed.

He ran his fingers through her hair and kissed her with all the longing, all the love he felt for this woman. He'd dreamed of this moment for months. Was Sandie's ghost, however, still lurking in the background, holding him back? He pushed the question back to the furthest reaches of his mind. Every nerve in his taut body was alive and ready. When he entered her, they both let out a cries of pleasure.

Afterwards, propped up on an elbow looking down at her, he said simply, "I love you."

Overcome with emotion, tears of happiness filled her eyes. His lovemaking had been tender, passionate, and exciting – the best she'd ever known. And for the second time he'd used those three little words. She felt she no longer had any reason to doubt him.

*   *   *

The next morning Van Rooyen awoke with the sun streaming through the window. The early light created a soft glow around Jessica's head resting on the pillow. He hated to wake her. She looked so angelic, so peaceful. He reached over to retrieve his wristwatch from the nightstand. It was a quarter past six. He pushed back the covers, revealing the gentle hollows and curves of her body and he looked down at her entranced. He tingled in the happy realization that their lovemaking had forged a firm bond between them.

He dressed and plugged in the small electric kettle in the bathroom to boil water for their morning cup of tea. When he returned, he covered her with the sheet to preserve her modesty, bent over, and planted a gentle kiss on her mouth.

"Good morning, my love. The kettle's boiling."

Her eyes opened. With a smile, she reached up and clasped him around the neck, pulling him down towards her. They shared long, intimate kisses.

"I love you with all of my being, Piet van Rooyen," she said as she released him and clambered out of the bed. Wrapped in a sheet, she headed for the bathroom.

They ate a continental breakfast in the hotel lobby before returning to Patsy's aunt's house in Borrowdale.

"Coming here to the races was so much fun and last night was unbelievable. I've never known such happiness," Jessica said, hugging his arm as they drove past Borrowdale Park.

Chapter 27

Monday, October 13, 2008

Van Rooyen was happy he and Jessica were accompanying Patsy to the lawyer's offices. He thought she definitely needed the moral support

"Thanks for coming with me," Patsy said, on the drive over to the law offices of Makova and Makova, Legal Practitioners, on Nelson Mandela Avenue.

When they arrived, they discovered the lift was out of service, so they climbed several, darkened flights of stairs to reach the attorneys' offices. He shook his head in annoyance. "Par for the course," he thought to himself, realizing it was undoubtedly just another citywide, power cut. Upstairs on the third floor, the door to the lawyers' offices opened into a large waiting room, lined with tubular steel chairs, with padded seats and backs upholstered in a turquoise fabric. He thought it looked rather cut-rate for a lawyer's office.

A young receptionist sat at a large, semicircular, dark mahogany desk. She looked up and smiled.

"Are you here to see Sephas or Susan?" she enquired.

"Susan Makova," said Patsy, stepping forward as van Rooyen and Jessica seated themselves against the far wall.

"Susan. Right. Fill out your particulars on this form, please," the receptionist said, pushing a pad across the desk towards Patsy.

Twenty minutes later, Susan Makova appeared from an inner office. Van Rooyen looked up and saw a tall, striking, black woman with hair pulled back into a bun at the nape of her neck. She wore a tailored, red and green, business suit and a pair of glasses with heavy, black frames rested on her nose. Impressed, van Rooyen rose to his feet.

"Good morning," Susan said, with a welcoming smile. Then nodding in his direction, and added, "Please sit." He sank back down on the chair.

"Which of you ladies is Mrs. Patsy Mclaren?" Susan asked, peering over her lenses.

"I am," Patsy replied, getting to her feet.

Susan Makova stepped forward, shook her hand, and said in a soft voice, "I'm Susan Makova. Please follow me to my office, so we can talk."

"I'd like my friends to come too, if that's all right?" Patsy turned, pointing to van Rooyen and Jessica.

"Of course. Everyone, follow me."

She turned on her heel, removed her glasses, and while twirling them by an earpiece, she led them past the receptionist's desk into a rear corridor. She then ushered them into her office and closed the door.

Van Rooyen saw it was a large office. On one wall, a picture window offered a panoramic view of the National Sports Center. Tall, ceiling-high bookcases, crammed with leather bound, legal journals and binders stuffed with government gazettes lined two other walls. Compared to the waiting room, this place seemed far more lawyer-like, he thought.

Patsy spoke first.

"*MaMakova*, please let me introduce my friends, Piet van Rooyen and Jessica Brennan. Piet was our neighbor for many years."

"I'm pleased to meet you both," she said, shaking his and Jessica's hands. "Please call me Susan. I'm in partnership with my husband, Sephas Makova, and because we have the same initials, it's less confusing if we just use first-names."

"Okay, we understand," Patsy responded. Van Rooyen thought it made perfect sense.

There were only two visitor's chairs facing the attorney's desk, so Susan pulled up a third from the back of the room.

Van Rooyen stepped in, taking the chair from her. "Allow me."

She gave him a dazzling smile that revealed a row of brilliant, white teeth between her attractive, full, bronze lips.

With everyone seated, Susan scrutinized Patsy over the top of her lenses.

"Patsy, how can I help you?"

Taking a deep breath, Patsy began to speak, haltingly at first. Van Rooyen paid rapt attention, as she detailed the seizure of Glengarry Farm and the arrests of her husband and neighboring farmer. As she recounted the scary events, her lawyer penciled notes onto a lined pad.

Van Rooyen butted in, with, "I can verify much of what Patsy says, because I was there the day those buggers first showed up."

After Patsy was done thirty minutes later, Susan continued writing until she had filled up at least six pages of notes. Then she looked up.

"To make sure I got all the facts straight, I want to repeat back to you what you told me. Interrupt only to clarify a point, or to correct something. Okay?"

Patsy nodded, turning to van Rooyen with a questioning look. He nodded in affirmation.

Susan summarized in detail all she had heard, regarding the events that took place at Glengarry Farm on the night of Saturday, August 23rd. Part way through, she paused.

"By the way," she said, smiling at Patsy, "I can confirm that Ishmael Gondo, the Deputy Minister for National Housing and Social Amenities, is in fact a card-carrying member of ZANU-PF, *and* a very close friend of President Mugabe's."

Van Rooyen saw Patsy's smile and quick sigh of relief. He knew she was feeling gratified that someone was actually taking Angus's situation seriously.

Afterwards, Susan Makova set down her pencil and looked across the desk towards her client and her two companions.

"According to court dockets, which I checked this morning, Mrs. McLaren, your husband is charged with five counts of treason," she said. Then she proceeded to itemize each one: illegally occupying a farm listed by the government for acquisition; petrol-bombing police stations; supporting a puppet opposition party, whose aim is to turn the country back to white colonists; actively training MDC terrorists, and lastly, maintaining a large weapons cache.

Van Rooyen recognized them all as trumped up charges, but they certainly sounded serious, and he saw tears forming in Patsy's eyes. He patted her arm to comfort her.

Despite his initial fears, he was thankful that Susan was able to offer words of assurance.

"Don't worry, it's not as bad as it seems. And we have a viable defense," she said, exuding an air of confidence.

She explained that firstly, authorities had never listed Glengarry Farm for acquisition in the government gazette, and that secondly they could prove there was not enough petrol stored on the farm to do anything more than fuel the farm machinery. The government's third charge, she said, also failed to hold water since the MDC was an officially registered political party in Zimbabwe, and lastly, the prosecutors would likely be unable to produce any evidence that Mr. McLaren owned any weapons, beyond his six low-caliber, officially licensed, hunting rifles.

"After all, your husband was a farmer who clearly had no knowledge of or any involvement in terrorist training," she concluded.

Van Rooyen breathed a huge sigh of relief, and beside him, Patsy unclenched her hands and relaxed, back in her chair.

"If that covers it, I'll draw up the papers and file them tomorrow with the Harare Magistrate's Court. Hopefully we'll get an early court date," Susan Makova said.

Patsy's eyes were moist. "You captured every detail with great accuracy. I can't thank you enough, Susan. The sooner we can get my husband and Mr. Packer out of that hell hole, the better."

Van Rooyen leaned forward to speak, his brow creased in concern, "Susan, we're worried about Dave Packer. Would it be possible for you to investigate his whereabouts? They arrested him along with Mr. McLaren. But Angus told us yesterday that he'd not seen him since they got to the prison on the ninth of October."

"I can certainly launch an enquiry into his disappearance, on behalf of Mrs. McLaren, but I'll need his family to engage my services, before I can actually represent him in court," she said.

"I'll be speaking to his wife, Joyce, tomorrow," Patsy interjected. "She's staying with their daughter, Jocelyn, in Marondera. As soon as you're able to locate him, I'll give her your contact information."

The lawyer rose to her feet. "Unless you need me to do anything else for you, Mrs. McLaren, let's conclude this meeting and I'll be back in touch with you as soon as a court date is set, or sooner if I get any information about Mr. Packer."

Patsy reached over to grasp the attorney's outstretched hand. "Thank you so very much, Susan," she said.

*   *   *

During their drive back to Kariba later that day, van Rooyen and Jessica discussed the morning's meeting.

"I think it went well," van Rooyen said, as he steered around a deep pothole in the A-1's left lane. "I'm confident if anyone can get Angus and Dave out, Susan Makova can."

Jessica agreed. "I'm truly amazed at how easily she boiled down Patsy's rather rambling account into such a concise list of objective and verifiable statements."

235

"Yes, she did an excellent job! Remember she's a trial lawyer after all, and that's what they're paid to do."

"Piet, after Angus and Dave are released, what's going to happen? Neither of them have farms they can go back to."

"Yup. I've been thinking about that. Maybe I could hire Angus to manage the fish and bait shop. The problem is that I really don't want to fire Moses. He's worked for me for five years. He's reliable and has done an excellent job. Besides, we only keep it open on weekends."

"Could Angus help you with the league's anti-poaching patrols? You've been under a lot of pressure recently."

"I can certainly put the matter before the League's Board of Governors. Angus is an expert tracker, and a master at bush craft. He picked up those skills while he was serving with the R.L.I. during the bush war. Great suggestion!" he said, beaming at Jessica. He reached over and squeezed her hand. "Perhaps I could even recruit Dave Packer as well. I'll make some phone calls this evening."

Van Rooyen's mind spun in exhilaration. With Angus and Dave to lead additional anti-poaching patrols, the League might finally have the resources it needed to put a significant dent into the poaching of the valley's wildlife. Much as he admired his friend, Hector, recognizing his concern and respect for the country's environment, he knew Kaminjolo was literally bound hand and foot by his nefarious superior, Nelson Zanunga—a ruthless man, known to be a staunch Mugabe supporter, at least for as long as it suited his purposes.

It was early evening when they pulled into Jessica's driveway. Van Rooyen carried in her small suitcase.

"Thank you, my love. Just leave it outside the bedroom door," she said. "Go sit out on the back porch. I'll bring us each a glass of wine, so we can relax for a few minutes, before I fix supper."

Van Rooyen stretched out in the deck chair, and looked across the lake as the last crimson vestiges of the sun dipped below the watery horizon. He could hear Jessica, indoors, opening cupboards and clinking glasses. His eyes followed the flight of a giant, brown moth, as it executed a jerky orbit around an outdoor light near the kitchen door. Moments later, Jessica appeared carrying a small tray with two glasses of wine.

"Oh darn," she said, as the moth fluttered past her into the kitchen. "I'll have to catch that guy later."

After she had placed the glasses onto a small table, van Rooyen rose to his feet, took her in his arms, and kissed her hungrily.

"I've missed having you all to myself, today," he said, holding her close.

"Me too," she murmured, pulling his head down so her lips met his for another lingering kiss. A few minutes later, the telephone rang and she breathlessly, extricated herself from his embrace and retreated inside.

"It's Patsy," she called out, motioning to van Rooyen to come inside and take the call.

"Hello, my girl," he said cheerfully. "How's everything?" At first, the tearful cry at the other end of the line was almost unintelligible. His eyes followed Jessica as she walked out of the kitchen into the pantry. Then he heard the words, "Terrible news."

"What terrible news?" His stomach lurched. Patsy's disconsolate voice returned. He could tell she was fighting to regain her composure.

"It's about Dave," she said tearfully. "Susan Makova says he apparently died at the prison three days ago; the day after he and Angus were brought in."

"Died? How? Why was no one informed," van Rooyen replied, his voice hoarse.

"She told me the official cause of death is suicide. According to the police, he was found hanging in his cell," Patsy whimpered.

"Rubbish!" Van Rooyen exploded. "I don't believe it! Not for one bloody minute! Not in a million years would Dave ever knock himself off." His mind whirled in disbelief and shock.

"That's what I told her, too," Patsy wailed. "And after speaking with Angus, Susan said she too has serious doubts."

Van Rooyen's heart sank. "You know, Patsy, the worst of it is, we may never ever get to the real truth."

"Perhaps we will, Piet. Susan assured me she has reliable sources within the prison, who can find out what really happened. But, in the meantime, if you happen to hear from Joyce, please don't breathe a word about this until we get the whole story. I phoned Jocelyn after you left, and she mentioned Joyce is being treated for some serious heart problems. I'd never forgive myself if we gave her this news prematurely, and the shock brought on a fatal attack. Especially, if the story later turned out to be untrue."

"I'll keep a lid on it," van Rooyen assured her. "But make sure you keep me posted."

"I will. By the way, I want to thank you and Jessica, for all your help and support."

"Only a pleasure, my girl. Incidentally, did Susan mention anything about Angus's possible release?"

"She said there's a hearing scheduled for 9:00 a.m. in the Magistrate's court on Tuesday, 28 October—two weeks from tomorrow."

"Wonderful Patsy! By the way, I've been thinking about the possibility of the two of you coming here to Kariba, after Angus is released. I could really use the help in my anti-poaching work, and I know Angus would be a great asset. Would you mention it to him, when you see him next to see what he says?"

"Of course I will, Piet. I'll be seeing him tomorrow. Thanks for thinking of us. Perhaps I'll even come away with better news about Dave. Talk to you soon. Bye." She hung up.

Twenty minutes later, over a bowl of steaming, tomato soup and a ham sandwich, van Rooyen recounted the conversation.

Afterwards Jessica said, "I really hope it was an erroneous report and that Dave is okay. I've never met him and Joyce, but from all you've told me about them, I feel as if I know them well."

"You'd like Dave. Unlike Angus, who harkens back to his rather staid, Scottish roots, Dave's lighthearted and a real comic—funny as hell."

The next morning, after conferring with the league's four other governing board members, van Rooyen received the official go-ahead to add Angus to the payroll to expand their anti-poaching efforts. He hadn't mentioned Dave. First, he needed more reliable information about his condition.

That evening he phoned Patsy to break the good news.

"Hello Patsy. It's Piet. Do you have a moment?"

"Oh Piet! I'm so glad you phoned. I was just getting ready to phone you myself. I have encouraging news. I spoke to Susan Makova, this morning, and she said she's optimistic that Angus's case will be thrown out of court, so they'll have to release him immediately."

"Hey, that's good news, Patsy. By the way, what did Angus say about moving up to Kariba and helping us to save Zimbabwe's wildlife?"

"Oh Piet! Seriously, it would be hard to describe how happy he was. When I told him what you said—I swear, my man is not one to easily show his emotions, but I'd be lying if I told you he didn't have a few real tears in his eyes. By the way, he must be deadly serious because he's already given me instructions to start packing."

"If you need help in moving your stuff, just phone, and Jessica and I will be there to help."

"Thanks so much."

"Did Susan Makova find out anything more about Dave?"

"She did, and I'm afraid it's not the news we were hoping for." Patsy's voice cracked with emotion. "The suicide story, of course, was a l… lie. Susan's source told her that the day after Dave was brought in, CIO agents interrogated him and ordered prison guards to beat the truth out of him." After a pause, her voice broke. "He died of his injuries less than twenty-four hours later."

Van Rooyen's anger surged. He fought to control it.

"Is anyone going to be held accountable for his murder?" he thundered.

"Piet, Susan Makova assured me she's turned over every shred of information she has, including the name of the witness, to the chief police prosecutor. But, she told me she holds out little hope that charges will ever be brought against those agents and guards."

He heard her break down and sob. "Piet, how could this happen?"

Although he was battling his own feelings of fury and outrage, van Rooyen realized he needed to calm her down.

"Patsy, believe me I'm as outraged as you are. But the sorry, bloody, shame of it all is that there's not a bloody thing we, or any civil-minded person, can do about it. Even if Angus had called the police when those sods first arrived to take your farm, the cops would have done bugger-all, absolutely nothing, to help him. Simply put, the police in Zimbabwe have no authority whatsoever, to uphold any damn law, because those bloody farm invaders had President Mugabe's personal permission to steal your bloody farm. Excuse my language!"

Through the receiver, he could hear Patsy weeping.

"You're right, of course, Piet." Her voice was trembling. "I know it, we all know it. This is what happens to everyday people in a country that doesn't enforce its laws."

Van Rooyen had no other answer to her question: How could this happen? He only had other questions of his own. How was it he survived, when his wife and children had to die? Now, he needed to add Dave to that equation.

Chapter 28
Saturday October 25, 2008

The next morning, an announcer was delivering the news over Radio Free Zimbabwe, as Jessica and van Rooyen were drinking their coffee on her back patio, overlooking the lake.

"A Movement for Democratic Change spokesman said Prime Minister designate Morgan Tsvangirai will attend a last ditch, regional meeting, on Monday, to try and remove a deadlock on filling top cabinet positions in the new government of national unity. He said he is attending the talks, even though many conditions agreed to in the power sharing agreement, signed on September 15, have been broken by President Robert Mugabe's ZANU-PF."

"Will they ever come to any reasonable agreement?" Jessica asked, as the newsreader droned on.

"If they do, it'll be a miracle," van Rooyen commented. "Mugabe's not going to step down voluntarily."

In the background, the news program continued.

"Diamond smuggling is costing Zimbabwe more than one point, two billion U.S. dollars, a month, the country's central bank chief, Governor Gideon Gono, said this morning. He blamed the smuggling on more than five thousand foreign syndicates and some senior government officials, who were illegally dealing in the precious stones. He said the squandered wealth was more than enough to solve the economic challenges Zimbabwe is currently facing. Gono said it would take a

fraction of that, just one hundred million U.S. dollars, a month, to resuscitate its economy and overcome current shortages of fuel, food, and electricity."

Van Rooyen reached out to silence the radio.

"So while senior ZANU-PF government officials fiddle," he said," Zimbabwe burns, and while our political leaders haggle over cabinet posts, ordinary Zimbabweans either flee across the borders for food, or resort to desperate means at home to find a few morsels to eat."

As he sipped his tea, he contemplated the country's sorry situation. Shops were now refusing to accept local money, only trading in U.S. dollars, British pounds, or South African rand, which were beyond the reach of the poor. Therefore, they can't buy meat, so they fish in small dams, and when the fish run out, they eat rats. Meanwhile, others follow the railway lines and the roads used by the grain trucks, to scoop up any seed or grain that falls off. There is little else they can do."

Jessica broke in. "People are really suffering. I wish me ... " The sound of the telephone ringing indoors cut her off. She leapt up to answer it and went inside.

"Piet," she called out, "It's Patsy, for you."

He went in and took the receiver.

"Hello Piet," Patsy said. "I'm so sorry to again be the bearer of bad news. I got a call from Jocelyn at midnight. Last night. Joyce died of a massive heart attack, late Thursday night at the Marondera Hospital."

Grief clutched at van Rooyen's heart. "Damn! I'm so sorry. How tragic that Jocelyn has lost both her Mum and Dad in less than two weeks. She knew about Dave, didn't she?"

"Yes, I broke the news to her last week. She withheld it from Joyce though, thinking her health was too fragile. Now she's wrestling over that decision, wondering if she made a huge mistake, thinking now that her Mum had the right to know the truth, before she died."

"How's she holding up?"

"She's holding up. However, the full impact is going to hit her later. Right now she's frantically trying to locate her father's remains and make arrangements for a joint funeral."

"Do you know when it will be?"

"Because she wants both you and Angus to be pall bearers for her dad, she's tentatively making plans for next Wednesday, after Angus's release."

"Does Angus know about Joyce's death?"

"Not yet. But I'm seeing him later this morning, so I'll break it to him then."

"Patsy, please accept my sincere condolences and pass them on to Angus, too. I know how close you both were to Dave and Joyce. "

"So were you and Sandie," she reminded him.

The orb of time spun in reverse and van Rooyen found himself back in the 1990s, when he and Sandie, Dave and Joyce, and Angus and Patsy lived and worked on their neighboring farms. It was here they prepared the land, produced their crops, reared their children, and socialized with other local farmers at the Karoi Club. Had Sandie survived, he knew Dave's death and Joyce's passing would have devastated her. But this was another day, and he knew that Sandie, Brian, and Bernice must have already welcomed Dave and Joyce joyfully into the house of the Lord.

As he hung up the phone, he brushed the moisture from his eyes, stepped back outside, and sat beside Jessica, wrapping his arm around her.

"Joyce passed away Thursday night," he said. "Jocelyn is arranging a joint funeral for her parents on Wednesday, in Marondera. We'll drive into Harare on Monday, go to the hearing on Tuesday, then drive up to Marondera for the funeral with Angus and Patsy. Sound okay?"

Jessica turned and wrapped her arms tightly around him. "Of course it's fine with me. Piet, I'm so sorry, I know you were close to them for many years."

As they embraced, their shadows on the patio morphed into one.

*   *   *

Jessica spent the next day, Sunday, helping van Rooyen ready his houseboat, in preparation for Angus's and Patsy's arrival on Wednesday.

"I want them to have the master bedroom," he said.

"That'd be nice Piet."

She wondered what living arrangements he might have in mind for himself. Even though, for the last month, they had spent most nights together at her house, neither of them had spoken about his moving in permanently. She had no doubts about her feelings for him, and he had professed his love for her. Although they'd become intimate two weeks ago, he'd not yet broached the subject of marriage. They were not engaged, therefore, and many unanswered questions remained. Had his loss of Sandie and the children reached any point of closure? Was he ready to move on, love another, and begin anew? To confuse matters, she was sure the deaths of his close friends, Dave and Joyce, had to be tearing open many of his old wounds.

She also had questions of her own. If they were to marry, would they begin their new lives together in the United States, or here in Zimbabwe? If they stayed here, could she accept a life half a world away from her parents and younger brother? On the other hand, if they settled in America, could Piet adjust to life there? It all seemed incredibly complicated, so for now, she forced herself to focus solely on the job in hand. By late afternoon, the houseboat was in ship-shape condition.

Early Monday afternoon, van Rooyen and Jessica left Kariba in her Toyota Land Cruiser, bound for Harare. The Toyota had more cargo and passenger space than the van Rooyen's Land Rover and they expected to return with a full load of Angus and Patsy's personal effects. With Jessica at the wheel, they sped south along the A-1.

*   *   *

Patsy, meanwhile, was driving home after leaving Angus at the Harare Remand Prison for what she hoped was the last time. She'd found him upbeat, assured by Susan Makova that after tomorrow's hearing at the Magistrate's Court, he'd be a free man. Her delivery of the news of Joyce Packer's death had hit him hard, however.

Susan had also informed him that prison authorities had located Dave Packer's body. They had evidently declined to schedule an autopsy and had ordered the remains be returned to the family. While overjoyed about Angus's release the next day, Patsy dreaded the forthcoming joint funeral services, but was happy their daughter and son-in-law, Libby and Nick Coetzee, would be there with them, along with Piet and Jessica.

When she arrived home, her Aunt Rosemary had not yet cleared away the afternoon tea tray.

"Patsy, I'm so glad you're back. I was worried. The radio has been reporting riots in town and I was so afraid you might get caught up in it."

"I did see some disturbances going on along Second Street. What were they about?"

"Wait just a sec. I'll tell you all about it, but first let me put some water on to boil, and then we can have tea."

Patsy adored her aunt, Rosemary Campbell, her late father's only surviving sibling—a tiny white-haired woman, with an indomitable spirit. A retired librarian, Aunt Rosemary was an avid historian and genealogical researcher—always willing to talk to anyone about his or her ancestry. She had never married.

While waiting for the tea, Patsy stepped out onto the lawn at the back of the house and Angus's Rhodesian ridgeback, Skellum, bounded up to greet her.

"Hey boy, how are you doing?" she said, bending down to stroke his sleek, rich brown, coat with its unique ridge of hair running along his back. He wagged his rear end joyously, and raced off, running circles around the garden. Patsy wished she had just a fraction of the dog's energy.

She glanced at the row of packed, cardboard boxes lined up along the verandah, waiting for transport to Kariba. They contained all their belongings—a fraction of what she and Angus had been forced to abandon when they were evicted off Glengarry. Tears pricked at the corners of her eyes and she struggled to contain them, as memories flooded back of the many happy years she and Angus had spent on the farm. Hearing her aunt's call, she hastily wiped her eyes and went inside.

While sitting together, drinking tea and devouring Aunt Rosemary's famous, strawberry cream scones, her aunt spoke of the news she'd heard on the radio about today's demonstrations.

"They said the demonstrators were mostly student activists and members of women's groups, who were angry because the stores were no longer accepting Zimbabwe dollars. I imagine a lot of people are going hungry."

"That's awful. We can't really blame them, can we?" Patsy said, feeling guilt-ridden as she sank her teeth into one of her aunt's delicious scones.

"They reported the police were out in force this afternoon, and that about a hundred and forty-seven demonstrators were arrested, while maybe fifty others had to be taken to hospital because of police beatings,"

"That's terrible!" Patsy said, looking at her watch. She was surprised to see it was already 5:45 p.m. "I'm worried about Piet and Jessica," she said. "It's way past five. They should have been here by now."

"They do seem to be running rather late. Oh, I forgot to ask you, was Angus in good spirits, today?

"He was, Aunt Rosemary, at least in terms of his impending release tomorrow. But he's distraught over Dave's and Joyce's deaths. They were such good friends and wonderful people. Honest to God, we never expected to lose them so soon."

"Had Joyce ever had heart problems before?"

"None that we know of. It came as a total shock to everyone."

"It's amazing what stress can do. Excuse me, Patsy, while I check on our supper." Aunt Rosemary left for the kitchen.

Patsy slumped back in the chair, looking at her watch again. It was now close to six and getting dark. She was now most concerned and began mentally compiling a list of possible ways she could locate Piet and Jessica. She could call the police, to see if they'd been in a car accident or just start driving towards Kariba, in case they'd broken down. Then she remembered van Rooyen had a radiophone. Therefore, he'd have telephoned her if they had encountered a real emergency.

Moments later, she heard the crunching of wheels on the gravel driveway.

"I think that's them," she called out, racing for the front door. "It is!"

*   *   *

Over supper, van Rooyen and Jessica described to Patsy and her aunt their being caught up in the demonstrations on Second Street.

"We'd just crossed Lomagundi Road when we became totally entangled in a crowd of demonstrators," van Rooyen said.

"I heard all about it on the radio," Aunt Rosemary said, passing along a bowl of mashed potatoes.

"Jessica was driving," he continued, "and we tried to double back to Lomagundi Road, so we could avoid the area, but the demonstrators forcibly stopped us from backing up, and we were totally stuck."

"At one point it was quite frightening," Jessica added, "especially when they smashed a rock into our rear window. It didn't break, thanks to shatter-proof glass. Then we were stuck there for a while, but when I put the Land Cruiser in neutral, they started pushing us down the road. People climbed all over the hood and onto the roof, and they were laughing and cheering, like they were having loads of fun."

"Well it at least saved you some petrol," Patsy laughed.

"Then other students showed up with printed flyers and started taping them all over the sides and the back of our vehicle," van Rooyen said. "I was just glad they didn't totally cover the windscreen."

"They were still pushing us along, laughing like crazy, as we moved down Second Street," Jessica continued. "At that point, we'd decided our best alternative was to just go with the flow, so for at least an hour we served as their moving billboard."

"The real trouble started," van Rooyen said, "when the crowd ran across some police vehicles. Fortunately, they left us alone, but we saw some of those cops beating the students mercilessly – even the young women."

"It was just awful," Jessica said, "talk about police brutality."

"The demonstration finally broke up when we got down to Speke Avenue, almost two hours later, around five o'clock," van Rooyen said. "When we were finally able to depart under our own steam, our first stop was at a service station to scrape and wash all that crap off the vehicle."

"Quite an adventure," Aunt Rosemary commented. "You were lucky you got away with just a broken rear window. It could have been far worse."

"You're right! We were lucky. Damn lucky!" van Rooyen agreed.

*   *   *

The next morning, van Rooyen and Jessica accompanied Patsy to the Harare Municipal Court for Angus's 9:00 a.m. hearing. Attorney Susan

Makova was there already, waiting in the parking lot beside her 2007, iridium silver, Mercedes Benz.

"Good morning," she said cheerfully, shaking hands all around.

They returned the greeting.

"I'm not expecting any surprises, this morning," she said. "The hearing should be over quite soon."

After they passed through inspection, Susan led them down a wide corridor to one of several courtrooms. It was thirty minutes prior to the beginning of the day's judicial proceedings and the courtroom was deserted.

"Take a seat," she told them "I'll be back in a minute."

Jessica's eyes roamed the courtroom. It had a layout similar to most American courtrooms, with the clerk's table on the left, the judge's bench in the center, and a witness box on the right. Tables for the defense and prosecuting attorneys faced the bench and behind them, six rows of spectator seating, with aisles on either side. Two doors on the rear wall behind the judge's bench were marked 'Clerk of the Court' and 'Judge's Chambers.'

Soon the public filtered in and a man and woman entered and seated themselves at the clerk's table. After Susan Makova returned, a police officer brought Angus in, wearing handcuffs. The officer removed his handcuffs and he and Susan took their seats at the defense table. Angus turned to look back at Patsy, van Rooyen and Jessica and winked. Minutes later, the prosecutor, a short, rotund man, took his place at the prosecutor's table.

At precisely nine o'clock, the bailiff stood, rapped the gavel and announced, "All rise and give your attention! The Honorable Magistrate, Judge Miriam Charamba is presiding." Jessica watched the gray-haired justice enter from the judge's chambers and seat herself.

"This Court is now in session," the bailiff announced.

"Thank you Bailiff," Judge Charamba said. "Everyone be seated. This is the case of Zimbabwe versus Mr. Angus McLaren. Are you ready, Counsel?"

Susan Makova rose to her feet. "Yes, Your Honor," she said, and sat down.

"Are you prepared, Mr. Prosecutor?"

The prosecutor rose to his feet. "Yes, Your Honor, we are ready."

"Then proceed," Judge Charamba ordered, adding, "I understand both sides have settled on a plea agreement in this case. Is that correct?"

Wide-eyed in surprise, Patsy nudged van Rooyen, "Did I miss something, Piet? I don't remember Susan saying anything about a plea agreement," she whispered.

"Interesting. Let's wait and see what happens," he murmured.

"This is true, Your Honor," the prosecutor said. "I'm advised that Mr. McLaren has agreed to plead guilty to one count of trespassing on the property of Mr. Ishmael Gondo, the Deputy Minister for National Housing and Social Amenities. The State has agreed to drop all other charges, in return for time served."

"Oh no!" Patsy murmured, "Does this preclude us from ever legally reclaiming the farm in the future?"

"Not at all, Patsy," van Rooyen said in a whisper, leaning towards her. "Until Angus signs over the land deed, the farm's ownership will remain registered in your names."

Susan Makova rose to her feet and said, "My client has indeed agreed to plead guilty to trespassing on his former property and we ask that the court release Mr. McLaren, forthwith."

Anxiously, Patsy, van Rooyen, and Jessica waited for the judge's response.

"The court is satisfied that justice has been served and Mr. McLaren is free to go. This hearing is adjourned," the judge declared, striking the bench with her gavel.

"All rise," announced the Bailiff in a solemn voice as Judge Charamba got to her feet and exited the courtroom.

Almost immediately, the courtroom came to life with a buzz of conversation. Angus was shaking Susan Makova's hand and Patsy darted forward to join them. She embraced her husband, then turned to his attorney and hugged her enthusiastically.

"Susan, this is wonderful! We're so happy! Thank you! Thank you," she gushed, with tears of joy spilling down her cheeks.

Van Rooyen and Jessica joined the group surrounding Susan Makova. "Congratulations, Susan. Congratulations!" Van Rooyen was beaming. "How did you manage to pull that off at the last minute?"

"It wasn't too difficult," she said. "The prosecution was clutching at straws. They hadn't lined up the witnesses they needed to make the charges stick, because there weren't any."

At a little after ten o'clock, both couples left for Aunt Rosemary's home in Borrowdale. After they dropped the McLarens off, Piet and Jessica went in search for a garage to replace the smashed rear window.

*   *   *

The next day, van Rooyen, Jessica, Patsy, Angus and Aunt Rosemary were finishing their lunch, when Patsy's and Angus's daughter, Libby, and her husband, Nick Coetzee, arrived.

"Hello Mum, Dad, Aunt Rosemary," Libby said, as she poked her head around the door.

"Oh my sweet, baby girl," Patsy cried, as she shot up from the table, rushed towards her daughter, wrapping her arms around her. "We weren't expecting you for at least another hour."

"We left a little early," Nick said, grinning. "You never know these days if a car crash or some police road block is going to create problems on the A-1."

"Good planning, Nick," van Rooyen said, giving him a thumbs up.

"Howzit, Piet. Good to see you," Nick said cheerfully, as he approached to shake his hand.

"Nick, let me introduce you to a good friend, Jessica Brennan, a real wildlife professional."

Jessica's smile was forced. Why had Piet introduced her in such a perfunctory manner? Was she only 'a good friend?' His words felt like knife stabs. True—they weren't engaged, there'd been no talk of marriage, but at least he could have called her his girlfriend.

"Oh hello, Jessica," Nick said, shaking her hand, "I'm pleased to meet you, at last. Mum's always singing your praises. Hey Sweetie," he called over to his wife, "I don't think you've met Jessica. She's Piet's girlfriend, who Mum's always talking about."

"Hi Jessica, I'm so happy to meet you," Libby said, giving her a hug.

Well at least Nick got it right, Jessica thought. Or had he?

Nick approached Angus, seated next to van Rooyen, and patted his father-in-law, affectionately, on the shoulder. "How are you doing, Dad? After what you've been through, I hope you're not too worse for wear."

"I'm just fine, Nick—bloody happy to be out of that stinking rat hole. I owe my freedom to the lawyer, Mum lined up for me—Susan Makova. She's a wonder woman. Let me tell you, man, if you ever run into any legal problems, get that lady to help you."

Van Rooyen looked at his watch. It was approaching one o'clock.

"The funeral starts at three thirty, if we want to get there in good time, we should probably get going soon," he said. "We should all fit into two cars. Jessica and I can take three. Who else wants to drive?"

Libby spoke up. "Mum and Dad, why don't you ride with Piet? We'll take Aunt Rosemary?"

"Sounds good to me," Patsy said, and twenty minutes later the Land Cruiser and Nick's small red Mazda pulled out of the driveway, headed for Marondera, fifty miles to the southeast.

Close to one hundred mourners attended the service and there were few dry eyes among them. Jessica assumed they were mostly the Packers' farming friends from the Karoi, Chinhoyi, Banket, and Darwendale areas. She found the combined graveside service very touching.

Afterwards, almost everyone gathered for a short wake on the lawn in front of Jocelyn's and her husband's house in Marondera. Instead of tagging behind Piet, as he walked around conversing with his friends among the mourners, Jessica remained in the background, assisting Jocelyn in serving the tea and carrying platters of deserts and cookies around to the guests.

She was relieved the solemnity of the occasion did not necessitate her keep a smile on her face because, inside, she felt cheerless. She had not yet recovered from the hurt of Piet's introducing her as his good friend. Was she being overly sensitive? Jessica cursed herself. Why was it that in almost every aspect of life, she brimmed with self-confidence, except when it came to matters of the heart?

Later, during the hour's drive back to Harare, she maintained a solemn silence. Infuriatingly, Piet didn't even seem to notice. Instead he chatted, non-stop, with Angus and Patsy, sharing all the latest news and gossip they'd heard that afternoon— news about whose farms had, or hadn't, been seized and where all the dispossessed farmers had gone, or planned to go; places like South Africa, Mozambique, Zambia, the U.K., Australia, America, or elsewhere.

As they neared Harare, there was a lull in the conversation, and van Rooyen reached out for her hand. Still hurt and angry, she jerked it away, staring straight ahead. He looked at her with a puzzled expression.

That evening Van Rooyen took Jessica aside, coaxing her outside into Aunt Rosemary's garden. When he took her in his arms, she stiffened.

"What's the matter?" he said. "You've been avoiding me. What's going on?"

Jessica looked away. She didn't want him to see the tears welling up. She brushed them away and looked up at him, her green eyes flashing. "Am I just your good friend?" she challenged. "It hurt a lot when you introduced me to Nick and Libby that way. I thought I meant more to you than that."

"You do, Jessica. Oh, my girl. You're my whole world, my everything. Please forgive me for being such a silly bugger. I swear, I never meant to hurt you," and he opened up his arms and pulled her towards him. She allowed him to hold her briefly, but stepped back. His apology was still not enough to heal the wound. All her old doubts, fears, and insecurities, had come flooding back.

After breakfast, Thursday morning, van Rooyen and Angus loaded all the boxes into their two vehicles. Angus and Patsy kissed Aunt Rosemary goodbye, and tailing Van Rooyen and Jessica in the Land Cruiser, they set off for their new home in Kariba.

Chapter 29

Friday, October 31, 2008

For several days, Muchengeti and her family had foraged close to the Zambezi in the Sapi Safari Area, east of Mana Pools. The matriarch's 14-year-old granddaughter, Chikoma, had been in labor for the past forty-eight hours, struggling to give birth to her first calf. While the family awaited the imminent delivery of its newest member, Muchengeti was unwilling to lead the herd away from the river to new grazing grounds. It was the tail end of the dry season, and the interior's parched veld had received no rain in almost five months.

The cause of Chikoma's long and difficult labor was unknown. That evening, however, the mother-to-be finally gave a monumental push, expelling a slimy, white, membrane-covered bundle onto the ground. As the new mother swayed on shaky legs, the infant's grandmother, Umsizi, stepped forward to tear open the fetal sack, revealing a tiny, wet, obviously premature, male calf. Experience told Muchengeti that something was seriously wrong with this undersized baby, so she joined Chikoma and Umsizi in trying to raise the slippery newborn onto his feet. Each time, however, he slipped motionless to the ground.

Chikoma stood transfixed over her lifeless, newborn calf. She alternately nudged him with her foot and stroked him gently with her trunk, seemingly puzzled by his stillness. Realizing no life existed in the calf, the other adult females drew his mother away and began to cover her dead infant with a pile of dried grass, leaves, and small branches. Eventually Muchengeti let out a deep rumble, signaling her family to move on, and the small herd ambled down towards the river.

At first, the young mother doggedly refused to leave her dead calf, but when her last family member disappeared from sight, Chikoma reluctantly abandoned the brush-covered remains and followed them. When she caught up with her family, they saw the stringy piece of blood-tinged, membrane hanging beneath her tail—the only remaining evidence of her firstborn's brief existence. Muchengeti let out a low, mournful trumpet.

The next morning, a flock of vultures following the odor of death, swooped down and with loud, squawking cries, fought among themselves as they uncovered the calf's body. Mana Pools Ranger John Chitsaru was driving nearby with Albert, his game scout, when the presence of the carrion birds sparked his curiosity. Park personnel had recently been encountering large numbers of dead antelope and other game species, the victims of snares. He and Albert, stopped to investigate, and once they'd scared off the large, bald-headed birds, they came across the carcass of a newborn elephant calf. Later that day, Chitsaru mentioned their find, in passing, to his boss, Hector Kaminjolo.

*   *   *

That afternoon, Precious Chitora phoned Jessica to let her know National Parks had discovered the remains of a newborn elephant in the Sapi Safari Area, east of Mana Pools National Park.

"Jessica, I've got some news. Hector Kaminjolo is here with me. He says one of his rangers may have discovered a possible foster mother for our orphan calf."

"Wonderful!" Jessica's skin prickled in anticipation. "Does Hector know who she is and where we can find her?"

"I'm putting him on the phone. He can fill you in, himself."

Kaminjolo came on the line to tell Jessica his Mana Pools ranger had found the remains of a newborn calf, and had determined its mother was a young cow in Muchengeti's herd. He went on to say he believed, according to the ranger's description of the mother and Jessica's identification charts, that it was Umsizi's daughter, Chikoma.

"Wow! I'm surprised. I didn't even know she was pregnant."

"John Chitsaru says she may have aborted her fetus prematurely," Kaminjolo said. "He told me he found its fresh carcass, yesterday, less than a mile from the Zambezi, west of the Chewore River. He found Muchengeti's herd, this morning. They were in the area and he's sure Chikoma's the mother. She has some afterbirth still attached to her."

"Sounds hopeful. Do you think she will be able to nurse the calf?"

"Don't know for sure, but we'd better get them together soon, before her milk dries up," Kaminjolo said.

"Would Monday be too late?"

"I don't think so, but let me put Precious back on the phone so you two can talk about it. She told me she'd like you to be involved."

"Hello again, Jessica. Monday's a good day for me. We'll have to take two vehicles, because I will need several of my guys to help take Narini-Ina off the lorry."

"No problem, Precious. I could ask Piet to fly up the valley first thing Monday morning, to pinpoint Muchengeti's location. Once he finds her, he could radio us her exact position. Save us a lot of time if we didn't have to hunt her down."

"Good! If Piet can do that, it would be wonderful," Precious replied.

"I'll get back to you by midday tomorrow, at the latest," Jessica said, and hung up.

Sunday evening, while dining with Piet, Angus, and Patsy over at the houseboat, Jessica put the question to van Rooyen.

"No problem," he replied. "I've been talking to Angus about flying him up the valley anyway, to give him a sense of the range we cover. We'll take off bright and early."

*   *   *

The sun had barely risen over the escarpment the next morning, when Van Rooyen took off from Kariba at 5:30 a.m. On board was Angus McLaren in the front passenger seat, and game tracker, Ananias, in the rear. It had been five days since Angus and Patsy had taken up residence in van Rooyen's houseboat, anchored in a quiet inlet south of the dam wall.

"Here, Angus, Ananias," van Rooyen shouted above the loud drone of the engine. "Put on these headsets. I just got them. Plug the wire into that socket on the side of the armrest and 'voila!' Now we'll be able to talk without having to shout."

They plugged in their headsets.

"Are they working?" Van Rooyen asked.

"Working well," relied Angus.

"It's good," Ananias agreed.

They climbed to two thousand feet, and below them, the Zambezi snaked north. The sky was clear, except for some white cirrus scattered over the distant Zambian hills to the north. In sight, twenty-five minutes later, were the Chirundu Bridges. Here, they followed the river as it turned eastwards.

Facing the blinding sun, van Rooyen pulled the visor down and donned a pair of sunglasses. Angus followed suit.

"Our plan this morning," van Rooyen said, "is to locate one of Jessica's elephant matriarchal groups, led by an old girl with a broken left tusk, called Muchengeti. There's a young female in the group, Chikoma, who gave birth to a stillborn calf two days ago. Jessica and Precious Chitora want to release the orphan calf with this herd, in hopes Chikoma will foster her."

"What calf?" Angus wanted to know.

Van Rooyen and Ananias described the August massacre of Nkosikaas's herd and explained how they had rescued the calf and taken her to Precious Chitora's wildlife rehabilitation farm in Kariba.

"I'll take you to meet Precious very soon. She's a great lady," he told Angus. "It was a miracle that calf survived and she's quite special to me."

With the gorge now behind them, the valley opened up into a wide flood plain, where the river slowed, splitting into separate channels, forming the familiar multitude of small ponds and pools.

"Up ahead is Mana Pools and the National Park," van Rooyen said. "Soon we'll see the Kafue River, which flows into the Zambezi from those northern hills, over there," he added, pointing to the left.

"Crikey, look how dry it is out there, right now," Angus commented.

"We'll come back in a week or so, after the rains start. The difference will amaze you," van Rooyen said, as he reduced power and the aircraft began to sink. He leveled out at one thousand feet and they continued flying east.

"That's the Sapi," he said, pointing ahead to a dry riverbed. "The elephants should be around here, somewhere."

They had flown less than two miles further when Angus pointed down.

"There, Piet. I see a herd of elephants just south of that tree line."

"How many?"

"Eleven. No twelve."

Van Rooyen circled to get a better look.

"That big old girl over there," he said, "definitely looks like Muchengeti. Her left tusk's just a stump," van Rooyen said. "I'll radio their position to Jessica and then we're free to go on our way." He turned the Cessna east towards Mozambique. While pulling back on the yoke, he pushed in the throttle and they gained altitude.

"I wish I could be a fly on the wall at the CITES ivory auction in Harare, today," van Rooyen commented, as he leveled out at four thousand feet.

"Fill me in. What's a CITES ivory auction?" Angus asked.

For the next twenty minutes, van Rooyen gave Angus a broad overview of the worldwide body's effort to save endangered species and control international trade of rare and protected animals. He spoke of the 1989, ivory ban to curb the poaching of ivory, which had decimated Africa's elephant populations.

"If trade in ivory was banned in 1989, why are these auctions taking place?" Angus asked.

"Good question," van Rooyen replied. "It turns out Namibia, Botswana, South Africa and Zimbabwe were highly pissed off when the ban stopped sales of ivory. So they appealed, insisting they needed the proceeds from the sales to finance their social and rural development schemes, as well as their elephant conservation programs."

"So what happened?"

"At a CITES meeting in June 1997, they joined forces to justify their need to flog their accumulated stocks. So CITES approved their exporting existing stockpiles to approved buyers from China and Japan, provided the ivory came only from natural deaths or controlled culling of problem animals."

"And since then?"

"Well, last year, at their meeting in the Hague, CITES caved and gave the four, Botswana, Namibia, South Africa and Zimbabwe permission to auction off as much as 108 tonnes of ivory to Chinese and Japanese buyers. Again, the condition was that the ivory came from legal sources."

"But how do they know that the ivory really comes from legal sources, and not from poaching?" Angus asked pointedly. "Poachers will find a market somewhere for their ivory. What's to say they aren't selling it to Zimbabwe Parks & Wildlife, so it becomes part of this country's official ivory stocks?"

"Hell Angus, you're amazing. You could ferret out any number of loopholes! I'm glad you're on our side! Back to your question. CITES undoubtedly sees a real problem here. Now they're saying that, after this year's auctions, there's going to be a nine-year moratorium to give researchers time to study the link between these one-off sales and the illegal trade."

"They'd better damn well come up with an answer before those bloody idiots kill off the lot," Angus said, his face flushed with anger.

"DNA could be the answer," van Rooyen said. "Researchers have created a genetic map of Africa's elephants, pinpointing the exact region where the ivory originates. In fact it's identified Zambia as having been a major source of Africa's poached ivory, in recent times."

At 6:45 a.m. van Rooyen radioed the herd's position to Jessica. Far ahead, on the horizon he noticed a tall, dark, forbidding bank of nimbus. Perhaps the annual rains were actually on their way.

While flying across the Chewore and Dande safari areas, van Rooyen and Angus saw hundreds of dead and dying animals littering the veld. Almost all appeared to be victims of snares. Once they got home that night, van Rooyen phoned Kaminjolo and described what they had seen.

"Hector, it's bad," he said. "We saw hundreds of animals caught in snares. Some still alive. There was even a young giraffe, strangled, hanging in a tall bush willow tree.

"It is a big problem, I know, Piet. Because many people are hungry these days, they are turning to bush meat. The bad thing is, I don't have enough rangers to send out and stop them," Kaminjolo replied, his voice ragged with genuine regret.

"Hector, I know you have your limitations. But the League has manpower and resources to help, thanks to the generosity of so many of Zimbabwe's hunters and environmentalists."

"You know I am always thankful for your help, Piet."

"I know and appreciate that, Hector, and there's good news—the League's taken on another body to help out with anti-poaching patrols, so we'll be able to do more. You may have already met our new chap, Angus McLaren. He was at the last Harare Rifle Club meeting."

"There were lots of people there. I don't remember him, Piet."

"It's not important. Next time I come to your office, I'll bring him over and introduce you. In the meantime, we are taking a ground team out tomorrow as far east as Kanyemba. Our mission will be to retrieve every bloody snare we can find, and cut loose all the surviving game. We'll treat all the injuries we can, destroy the animals we can't save, and leave their carcasses for the scavengers."

"*Mazwita shamwari*, thank you my friend," Kaminjolo said.

*   *   *

Precious and Jessica had left Kariba that morning at eight thirty. Precious led the way in her powerful Nissan twin cab, pulling a horse trailer with 'Chitora Wildlife Rescue & Rehabilitation' printed in colorful block letters on its sides and rear. Her chief animal keeper, Titus Chigaru, was at the wheel, and accompanying them were three other men seated in the rear. Inside the trailer, standing on a bed of wood shavings, was Narini Ina, on her way to be united with her foster mother. Jessica and Patrick followed in the Toyota.

They traveled at a steady, thirty-five miles per hour, reaching Makuti at nine thirty, where they turned onto the A-1. At Marongora, ten miles further north, they left the tarmac and entered the Mana Pools National Park through the Nyakasikana Gate. At a little past eleven o'clock they reached the turnoff to the park's headquarters on the Zambezi, and continued east towards the Sapi River.

Van Rooyen had reported the herd was between here and the river, so they drove on for several miles before stopping. Alighting from the vehicles, they looked around. Storm clouds gathered to the east and in the distance, they saw lightning flashes and streaks of precipitation falling to earth.

Silently, everyone kept their ears attuned to the surrounding bush sounds. They heard insects buzzing, birds chirping, and the occasional grunt from hippos in the river. Aloft, they heard the high-pitched scream of a fish eagle, as it soared overhead, and the soft roll of distant thunder. But where were the sounds of elephants they'd hoped to hear? The deep rumbles, a calf's squeal, an adult's trumpet, thuds from approaching footfalls, or the cracking and tearing of tree limbs as they fed. The only sounds of a nearby member of the genus, *Loxodonta africana,* were the snuffles, thuds and creaks, emanating from the horse trailer as the calf moved about exploring her confined space.

"Before we go any further," Jessica said, "Perhaps someone should shimmy up this tree and take a look around through the binoculars."

"Good idea," Precious agreed. "Titus, who's our best tree climber?"

Immediately, Patrick stepped forward. "I can do it," he said. Jessica handed him the field glasses.

Close to the road was a large *Albida Acacia* tree with low-hanging branches. Patrick nimbly shinned up it to a height of twenty feet, and peered out through the binoculars, panning eastwards across the dry veld.

"I see elephants," he said, pointing east. "Over there. They are coming this way."

"Keep an eye on them, Patrick, while we get the calf out of the trailer," Precious said.

The time was half-past twelve, when Titus unlatched the trailer's rear door and lowered it to the ground. Walking up the ramp, followed by his three assistants, he removed the chain tether from the calf's rear leg and the men guided her down the ramp onto terra firma. The distant rolls of thunder and flashes of lightning sounded closer.

"They're still coming," Patrick reported from his perch in the tree.

Precious pointed to a small, rock-covered kopje fifty yards to their south.

"Jessica, Titus, we should get the vehicles out of the way. Let's park them behind that *gomo* over there," After they'd moved the vehicles, Jessica jumped down from the Land Cruiser.

The calf, now unrestrained, stood in an open area. She looked around and trotted in a wide circle, obviously confused.

"Patrick, how far is the herd from us now," Precious called out.

"Not far now, *MaChitora*. Two hundred yards," he replied.

"Well, Patrick, come down now. Let's get out of the way and wait near the vehicles," she said.

Patrick descended the tree and joined the others behind the *gomo*. Everyone waited expectantly for the arrival of Muchengeti and her family.

"We have a few minutes, Jessica. Let me tell you about a man who came to see me a few days ago," Precious said. "He said his name was Stanley Matombo. He showed me his driver's license to prove it."

"What was that all about?"

"He said he had knowledge of poaching operations taking place at Fataran Farm, and …"

"Really?" Jessica gaped, wide-eyed, cutting her off in mid-sentence. "Sorry for butting in, but I know that place. I've had suspicions about it for some time – ever since Patrick told me his cousin had seen guards at the gate armed with machine guns, when he went there looking for work."

"When was that?" Precious asked.

"Around the middle of August. Later, I told Piet about it, but he didn't give my suspicions too much credence. To be honest, I've not been able to put it out of my mind."

Fat raindrops hit the ground, sending small puffs of dust into the air. As the women ran for their vehicles, Jessica drew in deep breaths, savoring the earthy, sweet-smelling scent of a first rain. They could see the calf, facing east, raising her floppy little trunk. Jessica wondered if she was uneasy about the advancing weather or if she'd caught a whiff of the approaching herd. She prayed it was the latter.

"Jessica, I don't like the looks of this storm," Precious shouted out her window. "Pulling the trailer on muddy, slippery roads is a big problem. If you can stay for a while to see the calf get together with the herd, we'll leave now."

"No problem," Jessica shouted back. "Patrick and I will stick around a while."

Shortly afterwards, the twin cab with Precious, Titus, and the three assistants, pulled out from behind the *gomo* and headed west, the empty trailer bouncing behind them along the rutted, dirt trail.

"Muchengeti should be getting here soon," Patrick assured Jessica. He was now in the passenger seat.

The first raindrops had created a dark, polka-dot pattern on the calf's back. She tried to catch the water globules, failing more often than she succeeded. She had yet to gain total control over her immature trunk.

Expecting Muchengeti and her family to appear at any moment, Jessica and Patrick waited in the vehicle, keeping their eyes fixed on the calf in the clearing. Through the windshield, they saw forks of lightning flash across the massing clouds. A lightening bolt's sudden, resounding crack startled Jessica;

its brilliant flash followed, seconds later, by an ear-splitting crash of thunder. The rain was now falling in torrents, hammering on the roof of the vehicle.

"This is terrible," Jessica shouted over the din.

"In Africa, we see these storms often," Patrick assured her. Evidently, he was not as scared as she was.

Meanwhile, the calf had disappeared from view. Solid sheets of rain obscured everything and as the storm's intensity increased, thunder rolled and the wind tore through the bush, flattening shrubs and doubling-over smaller trees. Brilliant white bolts of lightning forked down from the dark, swirling clouds, striking rocks and trees with explosive cracks. Although, back home in Georgia, hurricanes, and tornados were an occasional threat, Jessica had never experienced a thunderstorm quite as frightening as this.

In an effort to think of something other than the scary storm, Jessica turned her thoughts to Precious's revelation about Fataran Farm. I knew it, I just knew it all along, and she congratulated herself. Nevertheless, what could she do to expose it?

By mid-afternoon, the rain had stopped, and the storm clouds had parted, revealing swatches of blue sky. The calf and Muchengeti's herd, however, were nowhere to be seen, and the dirt track, which had brought them here, had turned into a swirling, muddy river.

Jessica looked over at Patrick.

"They're gone. I'd consider driving around for a bit to look for them," she said. "But I'm afraid we'd sink axle-deep into the mire and could be stuck here for days."

"That's good thinking, Miss Jessica."

Jessica released the foot brake, shifted the Toyota into four-wheel drive, and circled the gomo, heading west back to Kariba.

Their progress was slow. The heavy rain had left deep puddles, gullies, and washouts on the road. Jessica was thankful for the truck's off-road capabilities. Without the added traction, she was sure they would have been bogged down, unable to move. The storm clouds had moved west. Over to the right, they saw the Kafue flowing down from the Zambian hills and into the Zambezi. This morning it had been a trickle; now it was a raging torrent. Up ahead was Mana Pools.

"Patrick, I think we should stay overnight at the Nisbet Safari Lodge. It'll be dark soon and flood damage ahead might be difficult to see."

"That's okay." Patrick said. "My sister works there and I haven't seen her for a long time."

"Then let's do it."

It was dusk when she pulled into a parking space and she and Patrick climbed out.

The lodge brought back sweet memories of her last visit here with Piet, and she was reminded how sorely she missed him. As soon as she had checked in and had entered her room, she picked up the phone and dialed his number. No dial tone indicated the phones were out of order. Perhaps the storm had done it. Sorely disappointed, she replaced the receiver.

Blair joined her for dinner in the restaurant. Gone were his crutches and except for a barely noticeable limp, he seemed to have recovered well after his tangle with Mukuru.

"You are looking so much better than when I last saw you," she said, seating herself in the chair he held out for her.

"*Aye*, lassie, I'm almost right as rain now. What brings *ye* here?" he said, facing her across the table.

"Patrick and I were assisting a team from the Chitora Wildlife Rehabilitation Center release a six-month-old, elephant calf. We'd planned to unite the calf with a particular herd. Muchengeti's group included a young cow who'd lost her calf just days ago. We were hoping she'll adopt the calf and take it on as her own."

"Did she accept it?"

"Darn it, I really don't know. The herd was approaching when we unloaded the calf, but then the storm came and during the deluge we lost sight of both of the calf and the herd."

"That was a helluver storm," Blair said. "It passed over us too. I'll wager that after the rain stopped they found each other."

"Oh Blair, I hope so. I'm so afraid for that little calf. Scared it will either starve to death or be taken by a predator. Pete was really attached to that calf. I'm not looking forward to telling him we lost it."

"Think positive, Lassie," he said. "Where's Piet, by the way?"

"He's with Angus McLaren, flying him around the valley. Do you know Angus?"

"I believe I've run into him a couple of times at Wildlife Protection League meetings."

A waiter walked up to take their order for drinks. They ordered beers and after the waiter left, continued their conversation.

"Angus has been a buddy of Piet's for a long time." Jessica explained. "They were neighbors in Karoi when Piet farmed there. Angus was recently kicked off his farm, so Piet's given him a job with the League."

"That's good to know. I could never figure out how Piet managed everything he does on his own, particularly his anti-poaching activities."

"Yes, he's pleased to have Angus's help."

The waiter delivered their drinks and took dinner orders. Later, during the meal Jessica quizzed Blair about his growing up years in Scotland and his early hunting experiences. He talked about stalking red deer, and game birds like pheasant, grouse, partridge, duck, and geese.

"I've never seen a red deer," Jessica said.

"Genetically, they're not too different from your elk, in America. In fact they can interbreed with them. Although the red deer is native to Europe and the mountains of North Africa, in Tunisia and Morocco, it's been introduced into the USA, Australia, New Zealand, and Argentina."

"Do you have poaching problems in Scotland?"

"*Och aye.* The poaching of deer, hare, and salmon are a big business in Scotland."

She then recounted her conversation with Precious, her comments about her worker, Stanley Matombo, and his revelations about working at Fataran Farm, near Chirundu, hunting elephants. "Remember Piet and I talked about it, here, over dinner after you got out of the hospital."

"Aye, I remember that now."

"Piet and I have flown over that place. It has huge citrus groves, for heaven's sake. Why would they be involved in hunting elephants? But I've had my doubts about it ever since I heard they posted armed guards at the gate. My conversation today with Precious has definitely confirmed my suspicions."

Chapter 30

Tuesday, November 4, 2008

At sun up, Tuesday morning, van Rooyen, Angus, Ananias, Mathias, and Godfrey set off from Kariba with enough provisions to last them for several days. Van Rooyen hadn't seen Jessica since Sunday night, when she'd come over to the houseboat to have supper with him and the McLarens. Because of his and Angus's planned, crack-of-dawn departures Monday and again this morning, he'd spent both nights at the houseboat. He had tried to phone her at home late last night and again this morning, before 5:30 am, but got no reply. Where was she?

Although he felt uneasy about leaving, he had to go. Their anti-poaching patrol would take the team on a grueling, two to three day journey, east along the Zambezi as far as the village of Kanyemba on the Mozambique border. The village was close to the point where Zimbabwe bordered Mozambique to the east and Zambia to the north.

Once they crossed the A-1 at Makuti, van Rooyen discovered that Monday's thunderstorm had left the roads awash with muddy puddles. He shifted into four-wheel-drive. They bypassed the turnoff to the Mana Pools' park headquarters and travelled east, a mile south of the river, slipping and sliding along a dirt trail, taking them through acacia and mahogany woodlands. Cheeky little mopane squirrels darted across the trail in front of them, leaping over puddles and scurrying up tree trunks on the other side. Their tails twitched as they peered down, warily, at the passing vehicle.

"I swear, they're playing chicken with us," Angus chuckled.

At midmorning, they crossed the Sapi River and entered the safari area. From here the landscape changed radically. Behind them, in the national park, were mature trees and dense clumps of thorn thickets, interwoven with game trails. On this side of the river, however, were wide swaths of barren ground, dotted with tree stumps.

"Piet, look at the amount of tree cutting here." Angus commented, pointing at the huge expanse of bare earth.

"It's bad isn't it? Trouble is the people need fuel to cook their *sadza* and what little food they can find. They also need to heat their houses in the winter, and because there's been such a severe shortage of paraffin, they're chopping down trees for firewood. I'm afraid Hector just doesn't have the manpower to police the safari areas outside the parks."

"If it's illegal to hunt and cut wood in these protected areas, why don't the police arrest these guys?" Angus asked. Then he slapped himself. "Sorry, man. That was a bloody stupid question. Why would the police go after wood cutters, when they can't even be bloody bothered to arrest murderers?"

"You got that right," van Rooyen agreed. "Seriously though, it's a fact thousands of wooded acres have been lost since 2000. Check out the number of donkey carts we see on these country roads, nowadays, carrying wood to be sold along the A-1."

Van Rooyen thought about Kigelia Farm, as he had left it seven years before, complete with its expansive orchards of mature fruit trees – citrus, mango, and avocado, all planted by his father in the 1960s. The farm had also boasted several thousand acres of native woodlands and several eucalyptus plantations. The fast-growing gum trees provided valuable timber for fencing and construction, and when the farmer felled a tree, he invariably planted a new seedling to replace it.

He wondered what the farm looked like now. Had all the trees on Kigelia been cut down? What a bloody waste, he thought, and his knuckles whitened from his iron grip on the steering wheel. The unadulterated stupidity of those people made his blood boil. They had no foresight; no ability to see benefits in the long-term. Tragically, his country of birth, once so well endowed with natural resources—wildlife, forests, spectacular scenery, fertile soils, valuable minerals and precious gems—was being totally raped and pillaged.

*   *   *

After enjoying a leisurely breakfast with Blair, Tuesday morning, Jessica strolled out to the parking lot and found Patrick cleaning off the mud-caked, Land Cruiser. He was busily wiping a wet rag across the windshield. She noticed he'd already done his best to wipe down the rear and side windows.

By ten o'clock they had pulled away from the parking lot, headed for Marangora and the A-1. The roads were still slick, but except for the deepest puddles, much of the surface water on the roads had drained away.

"Patrick, I'm going to stop at Fataran Farm on the way home to check that place out. After what I heard from Precious Chitora, yesterday, I know there's something very bad going on there. I've told Baas Piet and Mr. Nisbet what I think. I even told them the story about what happened when your cousin went there to look for a job, but no one seems to believe me."

Patrick frowned but made no comment.

An hour later, they stopped short of the farm's main entrance and turned north down a dirt road that followed a six-foot perimeter fence. They parked in the shade of two large marula trees, just off the main road.

"Lord, this looks like the fence around the Harare Remand Prison. All it's missing is the barbed-wire topping," Jessica commented.

"Eh, Miss Jessica, how do you know this?" Patrick exclaimed in surprise, his eyes wide.

"I've been in there – but just to visit. I went with Baas Piet to see Mr. McLaren."

"It's a very bad place. People die in there all the time."

"Yes, I've heard about the death rate," Jessica said. "In fact there were two of Piet's farming friends arrested and only one of them came out alive. As you know, Mr. McLaren, who survived, is now working with Piet. They left this morning to do anti-poaching patrols in the Chewore and Dande Safari areas." Jessica had hoped they might bump into them today. She missed Piet badly. She hadn't seen him since suppertime on Sunday.

On the far side of the fence was a grove of citrus trees. Around the trees, the ground was infested with tall grass and weeds. Dead branches either dangled from upper limbs or lay scattered on the ground, leaving little doubt that no one had weeded, fertilized, or pruned, these trees in many years. From here, the fence ran north for about one-third of a mile.

"Since everything's so run down, perhaps we'll find a gap in the fence," Jessica said, stepping out of the Land Cruiser.

From the running board, she had an elevated view of their surroundings. The Zambezi was a little more than a mile north. Beyond the citrus grove, less than 200 yards away, she saw a large brick building. Stepping down, she and Patrick moved speedily along the fence line for roughly a hundred yards, until they found an opening large enough for them to climb through.

"Let's take a look around that building," Jessica whispered and they raced for cover in the citrus grove.

Crossing the orchard, they kept their heads down, and scrambled between the rows of trees headed for the brick building. Closer, they heard muffled voices.

"Patrick, can you hear what they are saying?" Jessica whispered.

"Only some words," he said quietly. "I thought I heard a man say '*kudya kwemasikati.*' They're talking about lunch."

"What time is lunch?" she mouthed, pointing to her wristwatch, which showed 11:50 a.m.

"Eh. Maybe twelve o'clock," Patrick whispered. They sat down to wait in the tall grass.

Ten minutes later, the air reverberated with the loud clanging of metal striking metal. Its sharp, rhythmic beat resonated across the farm. Almost immediately, Jessica heard the sounds of footsteps, as men exited the building and hurried away.

"It is the lunch *simbi*," Patrick informed her.

"How long do they have for lunch?"

"Half hour, maybe?"

"We'd better not waste any time, then," Jessica said.

Patrick looked uncertain. "Miss Jessica, are you sure you want to go in? What if they find us?"

"We'll be okay, Patrick," she said with an air of confidence. "But, if you don't want to go in, I'll meet you back at the car."

"I will come," he said. While Patrick wasn't sure this was a good idea, he wasn't about to let her go in alone.

Pushing open the door to the building, they slipped inside. After their eyes had adjusted to the low light, they looked around. They were in what appeared to be a large warehouse and what they saw astounded them.

"Oh my God," Jessica said, with a sharp intake of breath.

*   *   *

By two in the afternoon, van Rooyen and his team had reached the Chewore River at a Kapirinengu, a small village on the Zambezi. Soon afterwards they found their first snare victim—a dead impala, half eaten by scavengers, with the telltale, wire noose still wrapped tightly around its neck. The team removed it and discovered, anchored to tree stumps in the vicinity, half a dozen more empty wire snares, which they picked up.

Next, they found, three miles away, a young female, kudu antelope, still alive, her leg snared in a streambed. She had probably ventured down less than an hour before, to drink from one of a string of pools filled by the recent rain. She startled as the men slid down the embankment to reach her. Her left, rear leg was fastened to a sturdy thorn bush on the bank with a stretch of wire.

Van Rooyen stood a few feet away from her as she struggled frantically to free herself. He grimaced, noting the wire had already sliced through her skin.

"Three of us should be enough to immobilize her, while I cut away the snare," van Rooyen said, motioning to Angus, Mathias, and Godfrey to close in and hold her down. "Ananias," he called out, "As soon as I've removed the snare, bring me the medical kit." To the others, "Angus you take her around the neck and the rest of you hold onto her feet."

The young kudu fought her captors bravely, but she soon collapsed onto the sand under the weight of the three men. Once they immobilized her, van Rooyen knelt and deftly removed the snare. Ananias was immediately at his side with the medical kit.

The tendons and ligaments close to her hoof were still intact so van Rooyen cleaned the wound, sprayed it with fly repellent and injected her with an antibiotic.

"Okay, we're done," he said. "Everyone, back up and let's give her room to get up."

It took the young antelope only a few seconds to realize she was free. She scrambled to her feet and stood eying her rescuers just long enough for van Rooyen to admire her sleek, reddish-brown coat, the black tufted mane over her shoulders, and the unique markings of her species – the eight, vertical, thread-like, white stripes that circled her torso. Then she leapt up the embankment and bounded away.

Van Rooyen picked up what remained of the snare, detached it from its anchor, and handed it to Godfrey.

"This way," he said, pointing south along the streambed. "Poachers obviously set this snare after yesterday's rain. We should find more higher up."

They picked up dozens more along another mile of riverbed and were preparing to turn back and return to the Land Rover, when they heard a low growl coming from around the next bend in the river. Vultures circled above them.

"What's that? Angus said. "Let's take a look."

"Maybe it's a lion, feeding on a snare victim. Watch out!" van Rooyen said, as he followed Angus around a rocky outcrop. While rounding the bend, van Rooyen saw a male cheetah, its fangs bared, pinned up against a large boulder on the opposite bank. A wire noose had entrapped its right front paw.

"Well! This is going to pose something of a challenge," van Rooyen said. "We'll have to sedate the cat, before we can remove this snare." He could have kicked himself. He'd left the dart gun in the truck, which was probably four miles away.

"We have the *muti* here," Ananias said, patting the bag with the medical kit slung over his shoulder.

"But we can't administer it without the dart gun. Any suggestions?" van Rooyen said with a wry face. "We have the drugs, even syringes, but I doubt our little kitty-cat here is going to sit still for me walking up and sticking him with a hypodermic needle."

The men looked at one another with puzzled expressions.

"If we had a tarp, we could throw it over him and hold him down," Angus volunteered. "But, dammit, we don't have a tarp, either."

"Nice try Angus — look at his claws," van Rooyen said. "He'd tear any tarp to ribbons. Nothing for it, I'm afraid. We're going to have to send someone back to the vehicle to get the dart gun. Who's our fastest runner?" he said, scanning their faces.

Godfrey raised his hand. "Baas Piet, I can get there very fast and I can take these to the *motocari*," said the youngest member of the team, who was shouldering the snares collected so far, that day.

Godfrey took off at a fast pace and the other team members settled down in the shade, keeping the cheetah, just a stone's throw away, firmly in their sights. Van Rooyen looked at his watch; it was almost 4:45 p.m.

The cat fixed his stare on the men. It was good he was focusing his attention on them and not on his snared foot, van Rooyen thought. Trapped animals often took extreme measures to free themselves, even if it meant chewing off a body part to secure their release.

Twenty-five minutes later, Godfrey – a little short of breath – arrived back with the dart gun. The men rose, brushing themselves off.

"Good job! Very fast!" Angus said, patting a beaming Godfrey on the back. He turned to observe van Rooyen loading a dart into the gun.

Ready to fire, van Rooyen stepped back and raised the rifle's sights, fixing the cross-hairs on the muscular part of the cheetah's shoulder. He pulled the trigger and the cheetah yelped as the dart hit home. It struggled only briefly to free itself. Van Rooyen and the others looked on as the drug took effect. Three minutes later, the cat was slumped against the rock. The team smiled at one another and hastily followed van Rooyen across a sandbar between the two pools of water.

Van Rooyen handed the gun to Angus and bent down to remove the dart. He tugged lightly on the cheetah's tail to test the drug's effectiveness. The cat moved not a muscle, so he took the wire cutters from his pocket. The snare had lodged an inch or two above the cat's right front paw. He bent over and snipped it off. Taking the animal's paw in his hand, he examined it for any injury. He saw some abrasion, but no deep cuts. The conversation behind him broke his concentration.

"Ker-ist almighty," Angus exclaimed. "There's something bloody, odd-looking about this animal. Look at those spots!"

Ananias, Mathias and Godfrey were, gesturing wildly and talking excitedly in Shona. Van Rooyen turned around, frowning, and muttered, "What in the hell's going on?"

"Baas Piet, look at that cheetah. That's a very special cheetah," Ananias said enunciating his words carefully.

Van Rooyen looked down at the prone animal at his feet. Angus and Ananias were correct. There was something unusual about the cat. Was it? Could it be a rare, king cheetah? He stepped behind the cat, placed his hand under its rump, and moved it to get a better view of the animal's back.

"Damn," he exclaimed. "You're right, Ananias, about this being a special cheetah. It's a king cheetah." He shook his head in amazement. "Incredible! I had no idea there were any king cheetahs left in the wild – anywhere in Africa! Far less, here in Zimbabwe!" His eyes widened.

"Anywhere in Africa? Do you mean that, Piet?" Angus was incredulous.

"I'm almost positive. I'll have to research it after I get home. In the meantime, I need to get measurements and a photo. Damn, I hope my camera's in the truck. Godfrey, go back again as quick as you can and get the camera out of the cubbyhole. Hurry! Hurry! The cheetah will wake up in twenty minutes." He looked at his wristwatch. "No. Maybe in fifteen minutes, Godfrey. Hurry!"

"I go with him, Baas Piet, in case he gets too tired," Mathias said, and raced after Godfrey.

"You've got some good blokes there," Angus commented, then he turned towards the cat. "Piet I saw the odd-looking pattern of spots on this animal, but what makes it a king cheetah?"

Van Rooyen stepped forward and shifted the cat, so Angus could clearly see the three wide, black stripes running down the center of the cheetah's back. "It's caused by a rare mutation which has to exist in both parents. That's what makes it so extremely rare."

"When was it first discovered?" Angus asked.

"I believe the first one was seen in this country in the 1920s."

"Does the cheetah need any *muti*?" Ananias cut in.

"When I cut off the snare, Ananias, I saw nothing more than a slight abrasion. But to be on the safe side, let me check again," van Rooyen said, kneeling next the cat. He lifted the paw, but saw no break in the skin; just a little redness.

"Ananias give me the fly repellent, I'll give it a squirt just as a preventative measure." As he worked it into the hair with his fingertips, he felt a slight movement in the leg.

"He's going to be up pretty soon. I hope they get back with the camera," he said, wanting to kick himself for his stupidity. "Take a lesson here, Angus. Carry a camera wherever you go because whenever you leave it behind, that's when you'll need it the most."

Van Rooyen and Angus, both stared at the cheetah, noticing that one leg after another was starting to twitch.

"We'd better move back," van Rooyen said, and they set off back across the sandbar.

There was a sudden commotion and they heard Mathias's shout, "We got it, Baas." He was running towards them, swinging the camera by its strap.

Van Rooyen retrieved the digital camera and raced back towards the cat. The cheetah was now struggling to his feet. Once upright, he swayed a little from side to side. Van Rooyen had the cat in the viewfinder and pressed the shutter repeatedly. The animal began turning in circles, evidently trying to get its bearings. Van Rooyen captured multiple images from all sides. Then, possibly because his continuous circling was making him dizzy, the cheetah stopped and sat down on his haunches facing away from the camera. Van Rooyen zoomed in, and just as the animal looked back over its shoulder, he snapped several perfect shots of the conjoined spots running down its back. The three wide stripes were the signature markings of the rare king cheetah. Seconds later, the cat bounded off towards the tree line and was soon lost to sight.

Van Rooyen was ecstatic. He couldn't wait to get back to Kariba to tell Jessica of their amazing find and to confirm the sighting with international cheetah experts. He was smiling so wide, his facial muscles ached.

"Hey everyone," he said, "Do you know what we have here? We have found—and there are pictures in this camera to prove it—a one-in-trillion, living, breathing specimen of a king cheetah. It could be the only one in Zimbabwe, maybe in the whole of Southern Africa."

"Are you serious?" Angus said. "That's bloody amazing. I knew the minute I laid eyes on it, it looked peculiar."

"You noticed it first," van Rooyen congratulated Angus. "I was too busy messing with the snare to pay attention to the cat, itself."

Not wanting to be excluded, Ananias chimed in with, "I also saw it was a very special cheetah. It has a powerful spirit. Maybe it will be lucky for us," he said. Mathias and Godfrey smiled widely and nodded furiously.

The sun was sinking fast, spreading its orange glow across the veld.

"I believe we've had enough excitement for the day," van Rooyen said, "let's head back."

When they reached the Land Rover, the sun had dipped below the horizon. They climbed aboard and Godfrey threw the last few wire snares into the cargo area.

"How many did we pick up, Godfrey," Angus asked.

"We got seventy-three, Baas Angus."

"Not bad at all for one day's work," van Rooyen commented. "Let's find somewhere to set up camp and tomorrow, we'll finish off the Chewore and move on to the Dande Safari Area. Hopefully we'll double that number."

*   *   *

Earlier that day, Jessica and Patrick had been standing at the entrance to the warehouse looking around in amazement. Against the back wall, sat rows upon rows of coffins, piled one on top of the other. Others lay open on three workbenches, in the center of the room. In the corner to their left, bales of straw were stacked almost ceiling-high with fragments littering the entire cement floor.

"If this is a morgue, it's the weirdest one I've ever seen," Jessica whispered, as she walked towards one of the open caskets. Patrick followed.

"It smells in here, Miss Jessica, but not like dead bodies," he murmured.

"More like bleach or some other chemical," she commented.

Patrick stood back nervously, as she approached an open casket and peered inside. Neatly packed and cushioned in straw were half a dozen elephant tusks.

"Oh my God! I knew it! I just knew it! Look at this, Patrick," she whispered, hoarsely.

He stepped forward gingerly and looked inside. "I see it, Miss Jessica," he murmured.

Jessica inspected the contents of other open caskets and found they all contained tusks of varying sizes. She picked up a small one, just six inches long. Her eyes moistened in sorrow for the young elephant robbed of more than fifty years of its life. Her sadness rapidly turned into blistering anger.

"Those tusks may have belonged to Narini-Ina's older sister, Narini-Tatu," she hissed.

The poachers' deviousness and guile, in using coffins as shipping containers for the ivory, astounded her. It was diabolical, in fact. From Enos she'd learned of the many African superstitions and fears, which surrounded death. As ploys went, this was ingenious. Unless they were privy to what was contained in these caskets, few Africans would willingly open up and rifle through them. Even Patrick had been reluctant to step close.

The right side of the warehouse was partitioned off into two separate rooms. At the far end, she peeked into the smaller of the two. It was an office with a desk, cluttered with papers, along with chairs, bookshelves, and file cabinets. It had an exit leading directly outdoors. The other room was a storeroom, lined with wide shelves. Piled on them were more tusks. Jessica was examining the ivory, when she heard a door slam. Someone had entered the office. She froze.

There was nowhere to hide. Patrick stood in the doorway, urgently signaling her to follow him. They returned to the main warehouse, preparing to exit the same door through which they had entered. The sound of voices outside stopped them dead in their tracks. Patrick yanked her towards the tall stack of hay bales in the corner and they squeezed in behind them, just as several young men burst through the doorway.

Jessica and Patrick found themselves jammed between a brick wall and a towering stack of hay bales. Jessica's face was pressed against the prickly, bundled straw. It smelled sweet, like fresh cut grass, and it tickled her nose. What if she needed to sneeze? She thought about pulling a tissue out of her pants pocket to cover her nose and mouth, but she didn't dare. Any jostling around would topple the bales and give them away.

Fear clutched at her chest and she felt a sudden shortness of breath. If she and Patrick were discovered, what would happen to them? Ivory poachers were known to be ruthless individuals, particularly when they stood to lose not only their freedom, but huge profits as well, if caught. Jessica was unsure if they would escape unharmed. She had heard countless horror stories about the torturous murders of political dissidents in this country. Even if their battle to save the elephants was not politically motivated, they could certainly suffer the same fate.

Someone had turned on a boom box, tuned into Radio Zimbabwe, and the warehouse reverberated with the pounding music and vocals of popular artists. Jessica was relieved. Now she did not have to worry about a sneeze giving them away. The men continued packing the ivory, speaking among themselves in Shona. There was also much laughter.

"What are they talking about," Jessica whispered nervously to Patrick.

"They are joking about people they say they'd like to put in the coffins," he whispered in reply.

"Like Mr. Mugabe?"

"Oh no, Miss Jessica. Saying bad things about Mr. Mugabe is a serious crime. In Zimbabwe, there are people who will report you. Then the police beat you and take you to prison."

"Did you notice those coffins were made of cardboard?" she whispered directly into Patrick's ear.

"Yes, I saw that. Very cheap stuff. I saw inside the lid, 'Made by Wu Pingsong Packing Co. China.'"

An hour later, at 1: 45, they were still buried in the stack of hay bales. The music blared on monotonously and Jessica felt stiff and uncomfortable. Her feet hurt. She and Patrick were both overheated due to the humidity and lack of air circulation within the stack. Their fear of discovery heightened each time a worker hauled a bale from the pile. Jessica held her breath, praying the stack would not collapse and expose them.

Another hour passed. Her knees were weak and the soles of her feet felt as though they were on fire. She tried relieving the stress by alternately shifting her weight from one leg to the other. She had lost all sense of time, but was too afraid to lift her arm to read her wristwatch for fear she'd dislodge the bales.

They had been concealed behind the stack for more than two and a half hours, when Jessica's right knee collapsed. She fell forward, sending bales tumbling to the warehouse floor. In full view of the workers, Patrick pulled her back onto her feet and together, they made a dash for the door.

Chapter 31

Tuesday, November 4, 2008

Raymond Kaseke returned to his office after lunch, at 12:25 p.m. All morning his men had been packing the ivory. The coffins seemed to work well as shipping containers, and Kaseke was particularly pleased with himself for having come up with the idea. The cardboard caskets were inexpensive, and being imported from China, one of Zimbabwe's few remaining international allies, customs duties were low and officials cleared the shipments promptly. He'd endured several nail-biting delays in securing a shipment date. Finally it was settled that the ivory would be airlifted to Lusaka on Thursday.

Prior to breaking for lunch, he'd checked the men's progress. He was confident they would have the ivory packed and ready to go in plenty of time. Still a nagging concern was the possibility of yet another delay in the plane's departure. For his own peace of mind, he needed to confirm that everything was on schedule.

He dialed Manuel Chipenga's number. After several rings, Manuel picked up.

"*Olá*," he said in Portuguese.

"Manuel, this is Raymond."

"Oh, Raymond, I was just getting ready to phone you. Are you well?"

"I'm well," was Kaseke's brusque response. "I'm hoping you are not going to tell me your plane's broken down again."

"No Sir! She is looking good with her new propeller. I had to get it from

272

America; from a supplier in Griffin, Georgia. None of my African parts suppliers had a propeller available."

Kaseke breathed a huge sigh of relief. "What time will you arrive here on Thursday?"

"The flying time from here, at Chingoza Airport, to Fataran is one hour and ten minutes. I will leave at 1600 hours and arrive at Fataran at 1710 hours."

"That means you are leaving Tete at four o'clock and will arrive here at ten minutes past five?" Kaseke questioned drily.

"Correct. Before you hang up, I need to reconfirm the weight of the cargo. Before, you told me the freight weighed 350 kilos. Is there any change?"

"No change. Weight is the same."

"Não tem problema. No problem, then," Manuel assured him. "I must take off from your farm no later than at 1815 hours, unless you set up runway lights. Is that enough time for you?"

"That will be plenty of time. We will not need any runway lights here. What time will you land at the airstrip, south of Lusaka? I need to let my people in Zambia know when to put up wind socks and set out the fire pots."

"I will get there at 1900 hours; seven o'clock," Manuel said, cautioning Kaseke to have his people check the airfield before dark to remove any obstructions. "They must have the fire pots and wind socks, with lights on them, in place no later than ten minutes to seven," he added.

"What? Are you saying you need forty-five minutes to fly forty miles? What's going on?" Kaseke demanded.

"Raymond, I will not cross over into Zambia anywhere near the border posts at Chirundu. If the Zimbabwean or Zambian authorities detect an unknown aircraft in their sector, they will send their military fighters to intercept me."

"Then what's your alternate route?"

"From your place I will fly due east, well south of the Zambezi, to Zumbo on the Mozambique border," he said, explaining that he'd make a 180-degree turn there, and fly back on a north-west heading directly to the landing strip. "This route," Manuel said, "overflies unpopulated areas in Zambia, where my aircraft won't be detected."

"I will phone my man in Lusaka immediately and give him these times. He, personally, will be there to pick up the freight. George Tembo is his name."

"Tell him also that he must have enough people to unload the plane, *pronto, pronto*. I cannot be on the ground for more than ten minutes, in case the people at Lusaka air traffic control see my aircraft."

"Manuel, I will give George these instructions, and I'll see you here, at Fataran, shortly after five o'clock, on Thursday."

"Yes, Raymond, I'll see you then."

Kaseke smiled as he hung up the phone. For the first time, in weeks, he felt confident he might actually pull this off without a hitch. He made a mental note to have his workers clear the airstrip of rocks and debris and erect windsocks at either end. The field ran west to east, parallel to the river, with its eastern end less than a hundred yards from the farm's perimeter fence.

He heaved his large from behind his desk, and opened the door leading into the warehouse. Music blared from someone's radio, but the men looked to be hard at work. His new foreman, Mason Chickowore, was dragging a hay bale from the stack in the far corner. Kaseke had promoted him after sacking that *benzi*, idiot, Stanley Matombo. He was pleased he got his truck back with only a few scratches, after that bloody *mbavha*, thief, took off with it. Nonetheless, he was infuriated the police hadn't yet arrested him and thrown him in jail. If he ever got his hands on Stanley again, he swore the man would not survive the encounter.

He watched Mason haul the bale over to the men working nearby and approached him.

"How are things going?"

"It is good, Sir," Mason smiled, revealing a mouthful of crooked, yellow, tobacco-stained teeth. "We will be finished before half past four."

"Excellent, excellent," Kaseke said, rubbing the palms of his meaty hands together as he turned and lumbered back towards his office to phone Tembo.

Shortly after 3:15 p.m., Kaseke heard loud voices coming from the warehouse and someone was hammering on his office door.

Irritated, he staggered to his feet, a scowl puckering his face. "*Pinda*, come in!" he yelled.

A young worker, his eyes wide, stuck his head around the door and stammered over the sounds of the blaring radio, "Eish! Sir, we saw some p-people h-hiding behind the b-bales – a b-black man and a w-white woman. Now, they are r-running away and M-Mason and the b-boys are chasing them."

Agitated, Kaseke roughly shoved the youth aside and strode through the warehouse. Outside, he saw two figures sprinting through the orchard towards the fence line, with Mason and his men in hot pursuit.

"*Mahanya*! Run! Catch them! Don't let them get away," he bellowed at the top of his voice.

*   *   *

Panicked, Jessica and Patrick raced between the rows of trees to the gap in the fence line. Behind them, they heard the pounding feet of their pursuers.

"I see the place we came in. Run faster," Patrick shouted, urging her on.

Jessica pushed herself to the limit, breathing so hard her lungs felt they were about to burst. Almost there, but how close were the men? As she looked back, her right shoe caught on an exposed tree root. Losing her balance, she stumbled, falling face down on the hard, packed earth.

"Get up, Miss Jessica," Patrick implored her. "They are nearly here."

"Don't wait for me. You go on." Jessica said, breathlessly. "Go! Go! I'll follow you."

"No, Miss Jessica. Let me help you." He grabbed her arm and helped her scramble to her feet. She cried out in pain as soon as she put weight on her right ankle. She must have twisted it severely. With no time to retrieve her shoe and using Patrick as a crutch, she hopped towards the gap in the fence, just 20 feet away.

They did not make it in time. The men were immediately upon them. Out of the corner of her eye, she saw one of them beating Patrick about the head with a stick. She wished he'd gone on without her. If either she or Patrick were to be captured by these people, she'd have preferred it be she. For reasons, beyond her comprehension, she'd learned Africans tended to be far more ruthless with members of their own race, than they with other ethnic groups – particularly whites.

A man stepped forward and glared at her.

"Who are you?" he growled menacingly, baring a set of uneven, yellow teeth. Behind him, two others hustled Patrick back to the warehouse.

"Jessica Brennan," she said, trying to remain calm, even though her heart was racing.

"What are you doing here?"

"I am an American citizen," she said. "Before I will talk to anyone, I need to speak to the U.S. Ambassador, Mr. James McGee."

The man with the yellow teeth grabbed her arm roughly, pulling her back towards the warehouse. Unable to bear any weight on her injured ankle, she cried out, pleading she could make her own way. She hopped on one leg, moving from tree to tree in the direction of the building. Impatient with her slow progress, Mason ordered two men to drag her the rest of the way. The pain to her ankle was excruciating, as her bare foot bounced along the uneven ground. She gritted her teeth and stoically made not a whimper, refusing to give them any further pleasure from her suffering.

A giant of a man, his face contorted in anger, awaited their arrival outside the building. Evidently, the boss, she surmised.

"Search her, then take her to my office," he ordered the men.

One man grabbed her shirt and fumbled around her breasts, while another emptied her pockets of car keys, a couple of wadded tissues, and a stick of lip balm. He pocketed the keys and threw the other items onto the ground. Her pleas for the tissues and lip balm were ignored.

Later, Jessica found herself bound tightly to a wooden chair in the boss's office, where he interrogated her for more than an hour and a half. From the brass nameplate on his desk, she learned his name was Raymond Kaseke.

"Jessica Brennan, who are you, and what are you doing here?" Kaseke bellowed for the umpteenth time, his eyes squinted in anger.

"Before I answer any of your questions, I must speak to U.S. Ambassador James McGee," she asserted.

"He's not here, so he cannot talk to you. Who is that man with you?"

"I don't know his name. Where have you taken him?"

"You are lying, *handizvo here*, isn't that right? If you don't know him, why do you care where he is now?" Kaseke yelled, pounding his large fist on the desk.

"Because he's a person and all people should be treated with respect," she shot back.

"Then tell me who you are, who he is, and what you were doing here? Maybe then you will be respected."

She closed her eyes. This had been going on for hours. She was so tired of fending off this nasty man's incessant questions. Her head ached and she was trembling all over, deathly afraid of what these people might do to her and to Patrick. She prayed for his safety. The cord tying her forearms to the chair was so tight her hands were turning blue.

"Untie my arms, it's too tight," she complained.

"I will, if you tell me now what you were doing here," Kaseke shouted, jumping to his feet.

She did not reply, so he walked around the desk, raised a hand, and slapped her face. Stunned, she looked up at him and he struck her again. Afterwards he stomped out the door and she could hear him bellowing for someone named Mason. The right side of her face smarted painfully.

The man with the yellow teeth returned, followed by Kaseke, who screamed at him belligerently in Shona. Evidently, Mr. Yellow Teeth was Mason, Jessica figured. When he arrived, he removed the bindings and pulled her to her feet. He then tightly bound her wrists together behind her back and shoved her through an exit, leading outdoors. Nursing her painful right ankle, she limped through the door. Parked outside was a gray, Nissan X-trail, with the familiar Zambian license plates, she and Piet had seen before.

"Get in the back," Mason growled, as he pushed her through the open door. As soon as she was seated, he slammed it shut, walked around the vehicle, and climbed into the seat beside her. He pulled out a long black hood and slipped it over her head.

"What are you doing?" Jessica demanded.

"You don't need to know where we're going," he growled.

The vehicle moved forward, bumping over farm roads. She presumed Kaseke was behind the wheel. Jessica tried to memorize the route. After setting off, they made a left turn, a right, another left, and right again. At this point she gave up, realizing Kaseke was circling, trying to confuse her and perhaps foil such an attempt. They made several more left and right turns and then jerked to a stop.

Mason got out, opened Jessica's door and yanked her from the back seat. She heard leaves rustling and figured the truck was parked beneath some trees. There was a faint scent of oranges. Her captor steered her as she hopped forward and then they stopped. She heard the jingling of keys, a lock turning and a creaking hinge as a door was opened. Mason then shoved her through the doorway, snatching away the hood. Then he backed out, slamming the door shut, and she heard a key turn in the lock.

The place smelled disgusting. She detected odors of mold, mildew, and rat droppings; or was it human excrement? When her eyes adjusted to the gloom in the small, windowless room, she surveyed her surroundings. Only a sliver of fading daylight was visible between the top of the brick walls and the rafters. The place was bare, except for a wooden framework lining the walls, which was fitted with hooks of varying sizes. Perhaps this had been a tool shed or equipment room at one time. Scattered about on the grimy, concrete floor, were a number of empty, wooden crates. She hoped the puddles were just rainwater that had leaked through the roof during yesterday's thunderstorm.

After Mason locked the door and his footsteps faded away, she felt alone and afraid. Needing somewhere to sit other than on the wet, filthy floor, she pushed a couple of crates against the wall. Her cheek still stung and running her hand down her right leg, she felt the painful swelling around her ankle. Looking down at her grimy, bare foot, she wondered if she'd ever get her shoe back. It was an Eastland Newport, a high quality, American made, elastic sided leather boot, one of the most comfortable walking shoes she'd ever owned.

Patrick, where was he? She feared for his safety. While she had appreciated his sticking around to help her, in truth she really wished he'd got away. If he had, he'd be safe and perhaps could have gone for help. How were they both going to get away?

She wondered how long it would be before Piet and Angus got back to Kariba and discovered her missing. How sorely she yearned for Piet. She would have given anything in the world for him to come busting through that door, right now. She needed to see his smile. His smile seemed to promise that all was good and decent in the world and that by his side, she'd always be safe.

*   *   *

Kaseke called Mason into his office. He had been more than a little unnerved by the discovery of that American woman and her Ba Tonga, stooge.

"Who do you think she is? An American spy from the CIA?" he asked Mason.

"I don't know, Sir, maybe. She could have come here with those CITES people from the United Nations. I heard on the radio that they were in Zimbabwe, this week, for yesterday's ivory auction in Harare." Mason replied.

"Eish! That's right, Mason. She could be very dangerous for us."

"What can we do, Sir?"

"We will hold her and that boy prisoner until after Manuel has picked up the ivory. Then I think we should take them for a boat ride down the Zambezi and feed them to the crocodiles."

"Very good idea, Sir," said Mason, nodding vigorously.

Chapter 32

Wednesday, November 5, 2008

After another full day of anti-poaching patrols in the Chewore and Dande Safari areas, van Rooyen and Angus stopped overnight at the Nisbet Safari Lodge. It was after 8:00 p.m., when they pulled into the Lodge's parking lot.

"Are we too late for dinner?" Van Rooyen asked the clerk at the reception desk.

"I'm afraid so, Mr. van Rooyen. The dining room closes at eight o'clock," he replied, "but you can order a light meal from Room Service."

Before going upstairs, they stopped in the bar to see if Blair was around.

"He left a few minutes ago," the bartender said. "He said he wanted to get an early night. Do you want me to give him a message?"

"Not to worry," van Rooyen said, "We'll catch him in the morning. What time does he usually come down for breakfast?"

"He'll be in the restaurant by seven," he replied.

As soon as they entered their hotel room, van Rooyen walked over to the telephone on the table between the two beds.

"I'm calling Jessica," he told Angus. "I want to find out how it went when they dropped off the calf on Monday. I haven't spoken to her since early Monday morning, when I gave her Muchengeti's position." He hadn't actually seen her since Sunday night and he was worried.

"I can tell you've really been bitten by the love bug," Angus chuckled.

Van Rooyen ignored the jibe, but felt a rush of warmth to his cheeks. He turned away. He didn't want to give Angus any more ammunition with which to goad him. The switchboard dialed Jessica's Kariba number and van Rooyen heard it ring. It rang incessantly, so after five long minutes, he hung up.

"There's no reply. I'll try her again in the morning," he said. Disappointment tugged at his heart.

*   *   *

For Jessica, this was her second, hot, stinky, and painfully uncomfortable night propped up on the wooden crate, with nothing but an abrasive, brick wall on which to rest her head. After dark, came the pounding of drums and the raucous, drunken singing and chanting of Kaseke's elephant poachers that kept her awake for hours. She'd spent the past twenty-four hours thirsty, and dry-mouthed, while suffering sharp hunger pangs. Perhaps her ingesting no food or water was a blessing, she thought, since the idea of having to pee or defecate on the floor seemed just too gross to imagine.

*   *   *

At half past five the next morning, before going downstairs for breakfast, van Rooyen tried once more to reach Jessica. Again the phone rang and rang, with no answer.

"I'm really worried now," he announced to Angus. "Crikey, where in the heck could she be?"

"It sounds bloody weird, Piet. Let me give Patsy a ring to see if she's heard from her." Angus gave the houseboat's number to the switchboard operator, and after a couple of rings, his wife answered the phone.

"Hello," Patsy answered groggily.

"Hey Sweetie. Sorry for waking you up so early. I just wanted to let you know that Piet and I are headed home this morning."

Patsy perked right up. "That's good news. Did the two of you catch any poachers?"

"Nope, but we freed a lot of game and picked up nearly three hundred snares. One of the animals we saved was an extremely rare cheetah. It has unusual markings and it's called a king cheetah. Piet's very excited about it. We've got photos to show you."

"That's wonderful, I can't wait to see you, Darling," she replied.

"By the way, Sweetie, have you seen or heard from Jessica lately?"

"No Darling, I haven't. In fact, I expected her to come over for supper last night. We'd agreed to get together while you blokes were out in the bush, but she never showed up."

"Well, she hasn't been answering her phone. Piet tried to get her last night and again, this morning, but still no luck," Angus said.

"Do you want me to go over there?" Patsy asked, her voice filled with concern.

"Never mind, we'll be home in just a few hours," Angus replied. He said goodbye and hung up.

"I'm doubly worried now," van Rooyen said, after Angus had relayed Patsy's side of the conversation. His look was grave and deep lines creased his forehead.

Downstairs, in the dining room, they found Blair digging into a plateful of scrambled eggs and bacon. He looked up when they approached, wiping his mouth with a table napkin.

"Hey lads, you're up early. Come and join me for some breakfast," he said pointing to two empty chairs at the table.

A waiter, who had been hovering in the background, stepped forward with a pot of freshly brewed tea. He set it down on the table and took their breakfast orders.

"Howzit, Blair, you're looking good," van Rooyen said, glancing around for his friend's walking stick. "No stick anymore?"

"I retired it a week ago. I'm in tip-top shape, now," he chortled, looking over at Angus.

"Hey Angus, my mate, Jessica told me *ye'd* been knocking around with Piet. You're not farming, anymore?" Blair asked.

Before Angus had a chance to respond, van Rooyen interrupted with a distraught look, "When did you last see Jessica, Blair?"

"Tuesday morning. Why do you ask?" he replied, surprised by his friend's agitation.

"She's missing. That's why. No one's seen her since Sunday."

"Well, Piet, all I can tell *ye*, is she stayed here Monday night, instead of drivin' home in that big thunderstorm. In fact, we had dinner together that evening and breakfast, first thing Tuesday morning, right before she and Patrick left for home."

"Well, from what we can tell, she never made it home," van Rooyen said brokenly, burying his face in his hands.

Blair stroked his chin thoughtfully. "Wait a *wee* minute," he said. "She might have gone to see Precious. She told me she *didnae* see the calf join the herd because of the storm. Precious *didnae* know that, so she might have stopped to tell her. Another thing, Piet, Jessica was surely in a dither about something. Precious had told her about one of her workers. It was something about his poaching elephants from a farm near Chirundu."

Van Rooyen's gut constricted.

"Was it Fataran Farm?" he shouted, slamming his fist on the table.

"I'm not sure. Why?" Blair replied, startled by his pal's outburst.

"For some reason she's had a bee in her bonnet about that place," Van Rooyen groaned, adding that because he'd heard nothing untoward about Fataran's new owners, he'd given her suspicions little credence.

Overcome by feelings of guilt, he dropped his head onto his folded arms. Why had he disregarded her fears? Had his negligence placed her in mortal danger, just like the time he'd left Sandie and the children alone on the farm?

Angus tried to console him. "Don't kick yourself, Piet. We don't have all the answers yet."

Van Rooyen raised his head, looking at both men straight on, "Well, we damn well know Jessica's missing and that Precious confirmed her suspicions about Fataran Farm. So who's bloody fault is it?" he thundered. "I damn-well should have listened to her, and checked out that bloody place, myself."

"Well Piet, talk to Precious when you get back and see if *ye* can get together with that man of hers," Blair said, patting his friend on the forearm.

Angus murmured in agreement.

Mollified, van Rooyen quietly replied, "That's a start. I'll do that."

The waiter returned with their breakfasts and Angus and van Rooyen hungrily tackled the mixed grills with steak, eggs, bacon and fried tomatoes that he placed before them.

"Angus you never finished telling me why you're no longer farming," Blair broke in.

"Well, Mugabe stole Glengarry right from under my bloody nose, Blair. Piet has been good enough to give me a job, so I'm now helping out with anti-poaching patrols," Angus said with a wry smile, between mouthfuls of food.

"Well, Laddie," Blair said, giving him a wink, "I'm happy to hear that *yer* Scottish heritage is alive and well. *Ye* know it's a fact, nobody can keep a true Scotsman down."

After the meal, Blair took a last swallow of tea and looked at van Rooyen.

"Piet, *dinnae* forget, if *ye* need any help searching for Jessica, Skip and I can lend *ye* a hand. Just give me a ring."

"Blair, I hope I won't have to take you up on that. But if I do, thanks." He and Angus scraped back their chairs.

While driving away, Van Rooyen realized he'd been so preoccupied with Jessica's unknown whereabouts, he and Angus hadn't even told Blair about the sighting of the rare, king cheetah.

Chapter 33

Thursday, November 6, 2008

After leaving Blair at the breakfast table, shortly before eight o'clock, van Rooyen and his team pulled away from the Lodge, and raced back to Kariba. He had to find out if Precious had heard from Jessica since they'd released the calf on Monday.

They dropped off Ananias and the others in town, but before visiting Precious at the Wildlife Rehab Center, van Rooyen drove up to Kariba Heights to Jessica's house. He noticed right away that her vehicle was not in the driveway. While Angus in the truck, he let himself in the front door with the spare key she'd given him.

Inside, the place was deserted. Along with a handful of dirty dishes in the sink were the two wine glasses they'd used Sunday night, after he'd driven her home. The sight of them pierced his heart. Looking around, he found no other sign of more recent activity, so he locked up the house and he and Angus drove away.

They arrived at the Chitora Wildlife Rehabilitation Center a little after 11:00 a.m. and a uniformed guard greeted them at the gate. Recent rains had brought out newly emerged green shoots on the slopes leading down to the lake and a number of antelope and an emaciated zebra were enjoying the bounty. A few of them had bandaged limbs or other visible ailments of one sort or another.

"I gather those are her patients," Angus said.

"Yes, and isn't it telling that so many of them appear to have suffered some snare-related injury," van Rooyen commented.

"Does she go out into the bush to round up all these injured animals?"

"No. It's mostly it's the local farmers who bring them in. The snared animals found by tribesmen—regardless of whether they set the snare or not—will generally end up being eaten. Those blokes will kill them and take the meat home, grateful just to have some protein to eat with their sadza."

Van Rooyen parked the Land Rover outside the Center and when they alighted, Precious was there to meet them. The two men tramped up the stairs to greet her and van Rooyen introduced her to Angus.

"Come in, it's so good to see you," she said. "Let's go sit in my office, where it's cooler."

"I'm very pleased to meet you, *MaChitora*," Angus said, as he followed them through the front entrance. "Piet's told me a lot about you and he's always singing your praises.".

"Eish, he's too kind. Angus, please call me Precious."

As soon as they were seated around the table, she brought out some plastic tumblers.

"You must be hot and tired after that long drive from Mana Pools. I have Coke's and Fanta orange in my fridge," she said. "What would you like?"

They both opted for a Coke. She removed two bottles from a refrigerator in the corner, opened them, and passed them out.

"I know you busy gentlemen didn't come here to socialize, so what can I do to help you today?" she asked, her gaze fixed on van Rooyen's solemn face.

"We're searching for Jessica," he burst out. "She's been missing since early Tuesday, when she and her scout left Blair Nisbet's on their way home."

Precious's normally cheerful face crumpled. "That's bad news. Everything was fine when I last saw her."

"Blair was the last one to see her Tuesday morning, before she and Patrick left for home," van Rooyen said. "Precious, when did you last see or hear from her?"

"Piet, I last saw her on Monday near the Sapi River, where we dropped off the elephant calf," she said, explaining she left there before a bad thunderstorm blew in.

"How come you took off early?"

Haltingly, she explained. "I was afraid to drive in that pouring rain, pulling an empty horse trailer. So I asked Jessica if she would stay there to see the calf link up with Muchengeti's herd. I had no idea she hadn't come back home. I can understand why you must be very worried," she said, her face tightening in sympathy.

"Blair told us Jessica was all excited about something you'd told her about one of your new workers; that this man had told you he'd hunted elephant from a farm near Chirundu. Was he speaking of Fataran?" Van Rooyen asked.

"Let me start at the beginning," she said. "After we unloaded the calf, Monday afternoon, we waited for the herd to arrive. I was telling Jessica about Stanley Matombo, a man who recently came to see me, looking for a job. When I asked him if he had any experience working with wildlife, he told me he had tracked elephants for Fataran Farm."

"Right away," Precious continued, "Jessica became very excited. She told me she'd had her own suspicions about that place; from things Patrick had told her earlier."

"She'd told me the very same," van Rooyen groaned. "I just wish I'd paid more attention. Did she tell you she had plans to go there?"

"No. But from what I have learned about Jessica, it wouldn't surprise me. She's full of courage, that girl!" Precious exclaimed.

"I know she's got spunk," van Rooyen said, ruefully. "Too much, sometimes; enough to get herself into deep trouble."

Angus broke in. "Precious, did you ever report what Mr. Matombo said about the poaching to Zim Parks?"

"No, I didn't. At the time, I wasn't sure if I even believed his story. I thought perhaps he was just trying to impress me so I'd give him a job," she said.

"Where is he now?" van Rooyen asked, his eyes boring into Precious's.

"He's around here, somewhere. He's supposed to be cleaning out animal pens."

"I've got to talk to him right away," van Rooyen said, his jaw tightening. "We have to get the full story. Jessica may be in serious trouble. If the poaching and smuggling stories are indeed true, she could be in grave danger. We should also report this to Hector right away."

"I'll send someone to fetch Stanley," Precious said, getting up and leaving the room.

Ten minutes later, she returned, accompanied by a man in green overalls with 'Chitora Wildlife Rehabilitation Center' embroidered on the back. A native Zimbabwean, he was slight in build and had a pencil-thin moustache.

"Piet, this is Mr. Stanley Matombo," Precious said.

Van Rooyen looked up from the table and said, "Good afternoon, Mr. Matombo. *MaChitora* says you once had a job at Fataran Farm. Is that true?"

"Yes, Sir," he replied, nervously fingering his upper lip.

"You told her you discovered they were involved in the illegal ivory trade and the poaching of elephants. Correct?"

"Yes Sir. They came back from the bush with bloody tusks," he murmured, hanging his head.

"Why didn't you report this to the authorities?" van Rooyen demanded in a stern voice.

"Too afraid, Sir," Stanley whimpered. "The Baas there, Mr. Kaseke, is a bad man. He tried to kill me." Stanley unzipped and stripped off his coveralls, above the waist, to reveal some recently healed scars on his back and sides."

"You'll have to come with us and report everything you know to Mr. Kaminjolo at Zim Parks," van Rooyen said

"Yes, Sir," Stanley said, as he redressed and straightened his uniform.

"But one more question before we go," van Rooyen added. "Do you know of an American woman called Jessica Brennan?"

"No Sir, I've never seen that person."

"Well then, let's go and see Mr. Kaminjolo," van Rooyen said gruffly, as he pushed back his chair and rose to his feet, deeply discouraged that he was still no closer to discovering Jessica's whereabouts.

"Will he put me in prison?" Stanley asked. His brow creased in apprehension.

"If you're willing to testify to all that you've seen, I'll put in a good word for you with Mr. Kaminjolo," van Rooyen assured him.

At the Kariba headquarters of the Zimbabwe Parks and Wildlife Management Authority, Stanley Matombo solemnly offered up his version of the Fataran Farm poaching and smuggling activities. Van Rooyen watched Kaminjolo's demeanor change from one of concern to one of outrage.

"Mr. Matombo," he said angrily, his lips set in a hard line, "Whether you realize it or not, I could immediately have you arrested as an accessory, on charges of poaching and ivory smuggling."

"Yes, Sir," Stanley mumbled, his chin buried in his chest.

"Are you willing to testify in court?"

Van Rooyen felt sympathy for the man. Undoubtedly, he would be top of Kaseke's hit list if he testified in court, so he was surprised to see him glumly nod his assent.

"Because you reported these illegal activities and have expressed your willingness to appear in court as a witness, I will not charge you, for now," Kaminjolo said, placing a weighty emphasis on the final two words.

After dismissing Stanley, Kaminjolo turned to van Rooyen, and thanked him for bringing the matter to his attention.

"We have to get rid of these criminals," he announced forcefully. "I will meet with my rangers, John Chitsaru, Amos Majengwa, and Chipo Kagoro, at quarter past five this evening, on the road to Fataran Farm. We will make a plan to overtake the farm and go in and arrest all the poachers," he said.

"Hector, Blair Nisbet told me to tell you he's willing to offer his support, and it goes without saying you have mine, too. I confess I have a personal interest in exposing the activities at this place."

"Because, why?"

"Jessica and your scout, Patrick, have both been missing and it's possible we'll find them there. They've been gone for nearly forty-eight hours."

"What! I did not know they were missing. Why do you think they are there?" Kaminjolo's draw dropped in consternation.

Van Rooyen filled him in on Jessica's earlier suspicions, based upon the story related by Patrick's cousin, and on her later conversations with both Precious and Blair. He then proposed a course of action.

"Hector, you and your people go on ahead of us and scope the place out? In the meantime, I'll contact Blair Nisbet. He's offered to provide us with automatic weapons. We'll meet there at half past five."

"Okay, Piet. The farm gate is three miles from the A-1. The Tsuro River is halfway. We can meet at the culvert. It's far enough away from the farm to be out of sight of the gate guards, but close enough we can get there in a hurry." Kaminjolo said.

"Good enough! See you there, Hector."

It was 1:30 p.m. when van Rooyen and Angus left Kaminjolo's office. Before leaving Kariba, they stopped to pick up Ananias, Mathias and Godfrey and the five men arrived at the southwest corner of the 360-acre farm complex, approximately three hours later. Van Rooyen stopped the vehicle and after stepping out onto the running board, he surveyed their surroundings through his binoculars. Seeing nothing of interest, they continued driving east. To their left beyond a perimeter fence, they passed a citrus grove, a warehouse, additional fruit orchards, and a large double gate. Behind it was a collection of small buildings, shaded by tall, indigenous trees.

The two armed guards posted at the gate paid them scant attention when they drove by. Since the road led to other farms further on, they were probably accustomed to seeing the odd vehicle or two driving by, van Rooyen surmised. That they carried weapons also did not surprise him, considering Mugabe's followers were still seizing farms.

"Piet, see those buildings over there behind the gate. What's to say Jessica's vehicle isn't parked there out of sight?" Angus asked.

"Possible, but we've no way of knowing," van Rooyen replied.

After covering two more miles, they reached the southeast corner of the fenced complex, and something caught van Rooyen's eye. He stopped the Land Rover behind some tall rocks, left it idling, and looked north through his binoculars towards the river. There, he spotted two men walking beyond the end of the fence line. One carried a *badza* over his shoulder. The other had a sledgehammer in one hand and two white flags in the other.

He described the two individuals to Angus and the three men in the rear. "Got any idea what those blokes are doing?" he asked.

"Can't imagine," Angus replied, peering past van Rooyen to the distant figures. Ananias, Mathias, and Godfrey jabbered among themselves in Shona, shaking their heads.

"It's the flags that interest me. What on earth would a farm need those for?" van Rooyen said.

"Could they be marking a field for fencing or ploughing?" Angus suggested.

"No idea, but I think we should try to get a closer view."

They disembarked and with help from Ananias, van Rooyen clambered up the rocks to the top of the mound. From a height of fifteen feet, van Rooyen could clearly see the layout of a dirt airstrip. Damn, he felt like kicking himself. How could he be so bloody forgetful? Of course, there was an airstrip here. He and Jessica had seen it from the air.

"*Dom kop*, idiot," he castigated himself. "I'd forgotten there was a dirt airfield here," he said with chagrin. "Jessica and I saw it from the air a couple of months ago. The chap with the badza looks to be digging out a tree sapling. They could be clearing the runway. Perhaps they're expecting a plane to come in."

"What's the other bloke doing?" Angus asked.

"He's hammering a post into the dirt. What I first thought were flags, now appear to be wind socks."

"How does any of this involve Jessica?" Angus questioned.

"Other than we both saw the airfield here, I can't think of a thing. However, if there's indeed an ivory poaching and smuggling operation going on here, they could be preparing to fly out a load, shortly. We need to tell Kaminjolo."

They reboarded the Land Rover, van Rooyen spun the vehicle around, and they raced back towards the rendezvous point. This time, the gate guards turned their heads to follow them as they hurtled by. When they reached the western corner of the boundary fence, van Rooyen slammed on the brakes and the Land Rover skidded to a stop. His watch read five o'clock. They still had thirty minutes left before they were due to meet Kaminjolo further down the road.

"Even though we saw nothing when we drove past a little while ago, let's take a couple of minutes to drive down this fence line," van Rooyen said.

"Won't hurt," Angus commented, as van Rooyen swung right and they headed north along a track running alongside the fence, out of sight of the guards.

Between the fence and a long rectangular building to their right, were ten rows of citrus trees, which ran some 500 yards north. They crept along the fence line for about a hundred yards, and then van Rooyen braked suddenly.

"Look! There's a gap in the fence here. If we had more time, we could go in and take a closer look at that building."

Angus peered out his window. "Let's take a minute and look around."

Van Rooyen turned to his chief tracker. "Ananias, let's check this out," he said. "Everyone else stay put, we don't want to stomp all over the ground before he's had time to look."

Ananias climbed down and examined the ground in front of the Land Rover. Angus, head and shoulders protruding from the passenger window, was also studying the dirt.

"Hey! Look, there's a shoe over there," Angus shouted. "Over on the other side of the fence, near the base of that tree. Look, that one, with the broken branch hanging down."

"Plenty of tracks here," Ananias reported. "Many people have gone through the fence. Even children. I see small ones."

"Ananias, let's take a closer look at that shoe, over there," van Rooyen said.

The tracker squeezed though the gap in the fence and retrieved the shoe.

"It is a lady's shoe," he said, climbing back through the gap and comparing the shape and size to some of the shoeprints. "Tracks from this shoe are on both sides of the fence," he announced, handing it through the window to van Rooyen.

While Ananias climbed aboard, van Rooyen studied the brown, leather, right-foot shoe in his hand. He recognized it right away and his heart froze.

"Dammit! This is one of Jessica's shoes," he shouted breathlessly. "She's here! I just know it! Great job Ananias and you too, Angus. Thank you both."

Van Rooyen looked at his watch, opened his door, and leapt out of the vehicle.

"Angus, you and the boys drive back to the rendezvous point and wait for Kaminjolo and Blair. They should be there in less than fifteen minutes. I'm going to scout around that warehouse."

Van Rooyen stepped out onto the road and Angus, looking doubtful, slid over behind the steering wheel.

"Do you have a weapon, Piet?" Angus asked his pal.

Van Rooyen nodded and patted the semi-automatic, 9 mm, in the shoulder holster beneath his shirt. As Angus drove away, he called out, "I'll see you when you get back."

He stuffed Jessica's shoe into the pocket of his shorts and crawled through the gap in the fence.

*   *   *

Kaseke scanned the skies to the east, awaiting the arrival of Manuel in the DC-3. As he leant against the gate of Fataran's fenced complex, just 100 yards from the edge of the airstrip, he took a deep drag on his cigarette to soothe his nerves. The minutes ticked by and he became increasingly agitated. Where in the hell was that Mozambiquen fool? Sunset was less than an hour and a half away and the plane had to be loaded and back in the air before then.

*   *   *

After squeezing through the fence gap, van Rooyen set off ducking and running along a row of fruit trees until he reached the road, running alongside the warehouse, a brick building approximately four hundred feet long, by two hundred feet wide. He scanned the length of it and spied an entrance about half way down. He fingered the shoe in his pocket. It bolstered his courage.

As he approached the entrance, his watch showed it was almost 5:25 p.m. He wondered when Angus, Blair and Kaminjolo were going to arrive. While standing outside a pair of double doors, he heard the drone of an approaching aircraft. Looking skywards, towards the airstrip, he saw a twin-engine, ghost from the past, approaching from the east—a 1935-era, Douglas Dakota, or DC-3 aircraft. As two of its three wheels touched down, the propellers whipped up clouds of dust. As it slowed, its tail gradually sank and its rear wheel met the dirt strip.

Van Rooyen took a moment to study the old plane, whose fuselage was devoid of any markings, except for its official Mozambiquen, C9-CMZ registration. The aircraft no longer wore the livery of any commercial airline or military titleholder. Instead, it was re-painted a dull, olive green. In places, however, where the paint was worn and chipped, its original, shiny aluminum skin showed through. As a vintage aircraft aficionado, van Rooyen knew that as recently as ten years ago, there had been more than four hundred of these grand old birds still flying commercially all over the world.

Turning his attention back to the warehouse, he cracked open the double doors. Minutes later, over the roar of the taxiing aircraft, he heard the crunching of tires on a gravel road. Angus, Blair and Kaminjolo had obviously arrived at the main gate.

Van Rooyen entered the warehouse. Multiple skylights illuminated its interior. Except for, several, empty worktables on a concrete floor littered with pieces of straw and a collapsed stack of hay bales to his immediate left, it appeared empty. Then he heard voices coming from a doorway to his right. He pulled out his handgun and edged closer. As he peeked around the opening, he saw the back of a man dressed in green, camouflage fatigues. Behind him, sitting in a wooden chair handcuffed and chained, was Jessica's scout, Patrick.

"Put your hands in the air and turn around!" he bellowed, as he approached them. The man in camouflage whipped around in surprise and after seeing the weapon leveled at him, he rapidly complied. With his pistol's muzzle pressed against the small of the man's back, van Rooyen patted him down in search of a gun. The man was unarmed.

"Unlock this man's handcuffs and chains," van Rooyen barked.

"I have no key," the man whined.

"He has the key," Patrick said. "It's on the *tambo* round his neck."

Van Rooyen fished around the man's collar, found the cord, and ripped it off.

"Eish!" the man screamed. "You cut me."

"Shut the hell up and remove this man's cuffs and chain," van Rooyen bawled, "or I'll empty the contents of this nine-millimeter in your face."

Trembling, the man released Patrick's restraints.

"Now Patrick, I want you to handcuff this man and chain him securely to that chair," van Rooyen ordered.

Patrick smiled while he complied. With the man safely bound, van Rooyen questioned Patrick about Jessica's whereabouts.

"I don't know where they took her, Baas Piet. But before they found us, we saw those people loading elephant tusks into coffins."

Van Rooyen's heart sank. So now, it was confirmed. This was indeed an ivory poaching and smuggling operation. Jessica was undoubtedly in grave danger. He had to find her.

"We'll find her," van Rooyen asserted, with more confidence than he actually felt. "Reinforcements are on the way—Hector Kaminjolo, Blair Nisbet and their men as well as Mr. McLaren and my three chaps, Ananias, Mathias, Godfrey."

Patrick beamed.

*　　　　*　　　　*

With relief, Kaseke saw the old plane coming in on its final approach at 5:30 p.m. He immediately radioed Mason, ordering him to dispatch the tractor to the airstrip. Parked in a garage closest to the airstrip, awaiting the aircraft's arrival, was an aged Massey-Ferguson, hitched to a trailer loaded with caskets. Mason passed on the order and the tractor rolled out, proceeding through the double gates that opened onto the airstrip."

*   *   *

Jessica had now been held captive for almost forty-eight hours in a musty, windowless, storage shed, less than six feet square. She'd been without food, water or human contact. From the narrow gap, between the top of the walls and the roof, she could tell it was late afternoon again. Her clothes were drenched with sweat and stuck uncomfortably to her skin. Her stained shirt, once white, was now the same dingy color as her khaki shorts. Her mouth was bone dry, her lips cracked and painful, and her swollen tongue felt as though it was glued to the roof of her mouth. Waves of dizziness and nausea washed over her.

She wondered what had become of Patrick. She'd spent hours feeling around the walls and the metal door, in search of a way to break out. If she'd had a crow bar, she could have bashed a hole in the wall, but there was nothing available to her but a few rotten wooden crates.

Her mind had been on Piet van Rooyen, constantly. How sorely she missed him. Did he and Angus get home safely from their anti-poaching patrols yesterday? She knew they faced dangers each time they went out into the bush. It was a miracle Blair survived the elephant charge. When he got home, had Piet wondered where she was? Did he miss her? She regretted not telling him of her plan to inspect this place, fearing he'd try to talk her out of the idea. Now, she could kick herself for her foolishness. She prayed he might learn of her silly idea to come here, from Precious or Blair, and come looking for her.

During her imprisonment, she'd had ample time to grieve the loss of Nkosikaas and her family, whose tusks she believed these men had been packing into those coffins. Her simmering anger for these people festered like an open sore.

Somewhere nearby, a radio tuned to the Zimbabwe short wave station, transmitted from the U.K., was blasting popular tunes. The music was interrupted by a news break and Jessica learned for the first time that Barak Obama had been elected her country's first black president.

"Yesterday the world celebrated the election of America's first African American President, Barack Obama, but in Zimbabwe this significant historic event has received little celebration as millions battle to make ends meet amid the political impasse and the food crisis."

News from home of Obama's victory made her feel homesick, and the tears filling her eyes spilled down her cheeks. The news announcer continued,

"Since Barack Obama has made critical statements about Zimbabwe in the past, local political analysts do not believe the new U.S. administration will soften its stance on African despots, guilty of human rights abuses. An MDC spokesman was quoted as saying that Obama's victory is a victory of hope, faith, change, and a restart of values and dreams which have underpinned our fight as a movement against dictatorship and the neo-fascism of Robert Mugabe."

The radio returned to its musical programming but moments later, someone turned it off and she heard people speaking in Shona. In the background, a farm tractor cranked up, but twenty minutes later, all was quiet again until she caught the drone of an approaching aircraft.

To Jessica, it sounded nothing like Piet's Cessna. Instead, its deep, throbbing tones sounded more like those produced by the big, old fashioned, prop jobs – planes like the old B-17, World War II bombers she'd seen in the movie, *Memphis Belle*. While wondering what kind of plane it was, she heard the tractor start up again. The roar of the plane's propellers, however, soon overwhelmed the rattle of its diesel engine.

Chapter 34

Thursday, November 06, 2008

The vintage DC-3 came in from the east. It touched down on the dirt runway and as it executed a ninety-degree turn to taxi back to the east end of the airfield, its propellers generated a, pulsating, *nyeee-yow*, sound. The pilot swung its nose around to face west, throttled back the engines, and the aircraft's spinning propeller blades slowed to a stop.

The plane came to rest near the farm's northeast, double gates, where Raymond Kaseke had been impatiently awaiting its arrival. After the rear passenger door opened, a man in a khaki flight suit skipped down the steps and strode across the hard packed dirt towards him. The pilot's nametag, pinned below a pair of silver aviator wings, read Captain Manuel Chipenga.

"You're thirty minutes late. What happened?" Kaseke admonished him.

"We were delayed in Tete by a broken down, Linhas Aéreas de Moçambique plane," Manuel replied.

"Well, we'll get your cargo loaded fast and then you can go." And Kaseke thrust an envelope stuffed full of cash into the pilot's outstretched hand.

As Manuel counted the wad of U.S. dollar bills, he stepped aside to let a tractor pulling a trailer loaded with caskets pass by.

"What is this, Kaseke?" Manuel demanded, pointing to the trailer's cargo, his nose wrinkling in distaste. "You didn't tell me your shipment was dead people."

"Manuel, I assure you those caskets contain no dead bodies," Kaseke replied sharply.

"Then what is in them?"

"Ivory."

"Well, I will help them finish loading and then we will take off," Manuel said nervously, stuffing the cash into the breast pocket of his flight suit.

"It's always a pleasure to do business with you, Manuel," Kaseke quipped. "My associate, George Tembo, will be at the air strip in Zambia, before seven, to meet you."

"*Obrigado por tudo*," Manuel said, thanking him curtly in Portuguese. Then he turned, saluted, and walked briskly back to the aircraft.

As Manuel boarded the plane, Kaseke heard gunshots, coming from behind him. Looking at the plane, he saw that Manuel's copilot and the Fataran workers had already lifted four of the six caskets into the plane. Moments later, the two-way radio on Kaseke's belt started to beep. He pulled it from its holster.

"Kaseke here."

"There's big trouble!" It was Mason, and he sounded agitated.

"What trouble?" Kaseke demanded.

"People from Zim Parks have broken through the main gate," Mason shrieked.

"Well, what are the guards doing?"

"I don't know."

"Where are you?"

"I'm in the garage, waiting for the tractor to come back."

"Bring me the keys to the garage and the storeroom, fast!" Kaseke ordered.

Mason reacted swiftly and in less than two minutes, he ran up and tossed Kaseke the keys.

"Now Mason, check to see what's going on at to the main gate, then report back to me."

"Yes, Sir."

*　　　*　　　*

With the guard handcuffed and chained to the chair, van Rooyen beckoned Patrick to follow him as he sprinted away from the building towards the safer environs of the citrus grove. Together, they jogged through the trees to the perimeter fence. The DC-3 had landed six or seven minutes earlier. Now he'd confirmed these people were smuggling ivory, van Rooyen was determined to foil their plan. He prayed he would also find Jessica.

As soon as he and Patrick reached the fence, they heard sounds of gunfire coming from the main gate, approximately a quarter mile away. Confident that Kaminjolo, Angus, and Blair had that situation well in hand, he and Patrick continued on towards the airfield, less than half a mile away. Running along the fence, they passed scores of raised beds, overgrown with weeds, and rows and rows of plastic pots containing lifeless young trees. Evidently, in addition to harvesting and selling the fruit, the farm had once operated a full-blown tree nursery.

What a waste, van Rooyen thought, as anger consumed him. These undeserving benefactors of Zimbabwe's land grab had been the recipients of a fully functioning, citrus farm and nursery, worth millions at no cost to themselves. Moreover, instead of working the farm to produce food to benefit their country and its people, while making a decent living for themselves, they had laid waste to the land, in favor of slaughtering the country's priceless elephant population. It was sickening.

They were approximately two hundred yards away from the plane, when its first engine coughed into life. The motor spluttered for a moment, belching out white smoke until all fourteen of its cylinders fired, setting the propeller blades in motion, followed closely by the second engine.

"Hurry! Hurry!" he shouted to Patrick, "We've got to stop it."

Moments later he saw men beside the plane, preparing to close the door.

*   *   *

As the second propeller began to turn, Kaseke heard shouts coming from his left and saw two men, a white and a black, running towards him. They were a little more than a hundred yards away. Fear gnawed at his insides. First, he'd heard gunfire, and now strangers were approaching. He had to get away.

"Hold the plane!" he yelled, his voice booming across the strip. He started towards it, then hurriedly turned back, realizing he needed a hostage for protection. In fewer than a dozen lumbering strides, he reached the small storage room, grabbed the keys from his pocket, and unlocked the door. Flinging it open, he found Jessica seated on a crate, her hands shading her eyes from the sudden brightness. Seizing her arm, he yanked her out the door and swung her across his broad shoulders. Then with his powerful arms holding fast to a kicking and screaming Jessica, he darted through the gate and started for the plane.

*   *   *

Van Rooyen and Patrick were closing in on the gate, when they heard

Jessica's cries and saw her being dragged towards the DC-3, which stood on the airstrip with its engines idling.

"Jessica, we're coming," van Rooyen hollered, running as fast as his legs could propel him. When he reached the gate, a huge behemoth of a man was shoving Jessica into the plane. He clambered aboard after her. Van Rooyen was almost close enough to touch the fuselage, when the engines roared, and amid a billowing cloud of dust, the plane lurched forward and its passenger door slammed shut.

He grabbed for one of the DC-3's tail fins, but it slipped from his grasp and he found himself scrambling after the plane through a choking cloud of smoke and pulverized dirt. Defeated, he fell back overcome by the suffocating dust and exhaust fumes. Coughing and sputtering, he aimed his weapon at one of the aircraft's tires.

Prior to squeezing the trigger, he envisaged the bullet missing the tire, striking a fuel tank, instead, and the aircraft exploded in flames, killing all aboard including Jessica. He cursed, re-holstered his weapon, and feeling as if he'd taken a heavy blow to the gut, he dropped to his knees.

"I'm sorry that we couldn't stop it, Baas," Patrick breathed heavily, as he ran up.

Van Rooyen rose shakily to his feet and he and Patrick watched the DC-3 lift off, winging its way west.

"Very sorry, Baas, very sorry," Patrick moaned, covering his face with his hands.

Van Rooyen's eyes followed the aircraft as it gained altitude, beginning a wide sweeping turn, back towards the east. As it flew south of the farm, he watched it continue on this heading until it became just a speck on the horizon. Then it disappeared.

In silence, Patrick and van Rooyen trudged back to the gate. As they made their way past the tree nursery, they saw Angus trotting towards them.

"We need to go back to the warehouse," he said breathlessly. "Hector needs our help in deciphering the ivory records in the office."

"We're headed right that way," van Rooyen said. "I managed to free Patrick, here, as you can see, but those bastards dragged Jessica onto the plane. Heaven's knows where they're taking her," he said, adding, "What was all the shooting we heard earlier?"

"The guards at the main gate opened fire on us," Angus replied. "Blair and I returned fire and took them both out. Kaminjolo's people are transporting the bodies to the Chirundu Police Station."

"Did you find anyone else?" van Rooyen asked.

"Hector arrested four blokes," Angus responded. "The one you left handcuffed in the warehouse and a nasty piece of work who identified himself as Mason Chikowore. Two others we found were hiding out in the ablution block. Hector's chaps are also turning them over to the Chirundu police."

"The six who were loading the plane when Patrick and I showed up, ran off into the bush. We may never find them," Van Rooyen frowned.

They continued their trek back to rejoin Kaminjolo. It was almost dark when they reached the deserted warehouse. Angus flicked on the light. Thanks to ZESA, the power was on and a dozen fluorescent strips flooded the huge packing shed. He led them to an office, where Kaminjolo was already hard at work.

After describing Jessica's abduction, van Rooyen asked, "Hector, what's next on the agenda?"

"Piet, your primary mission, I'm sure, is to find Jessica," Kaminjolo said. "We will assist you, of course, but I must first uncover details of Kaseke's poaching and smuggling activities. Perhaps it will lead us to her?"

Van Rooyen found Kaminjolo's words heartening. "I appreciate that, Hector. I've no idea where those bastards took her, beyond the fact that the plane flew east towards Mozambique, and it had a Mozambique registration. Where's Blair, by the way?" he said, looking around.

"He left us a couple of automatics and went home," Kaminjolo replied. "He and Skip have overseas clients coming in tomorrow, who've booked hunting safaris for Friday and Saturday. He said they'd be available next week, if we needed them."

Van Rooyen desperately hoped Jessica would be rescued long before then. He expected, in fact, that he and other members of Kaminjolo's newly assembled team of investigators would find the clues they needed, right here in Raymond Kaseke's office.

The office was dominated by a large wooden desk and captain's chair sitting in the center of the room. Three file cabinets and a bookcase stood against a rear wall, and in the corner a large circular, conference table with six chairs. Everyone sat around the table and at Kaminjolo's request, van Rooyen led the meeting.

"We don't want to scatter papers all over the place, so let's be systematic here," he began.

"What should we be looking for?" Angus wanted to know.

"Most helpful to our investigation, I'd say," van Rooyen replied, "would be invoices, contracts, shipping records, correspondence, work schedules, employee records, address lists, and any journals pertaining to ivory smuggling and poaching. Oh, and don't forget photographs—they could open some doors," he added.

"Who's going to do what?" Angus prompted, as van Rooyen glanced around the room.

"I'll check the bookcase and the desk drawers, while the rest of you each tackle a file cabinet," he instructed.

With everyone assigned a task, they set to work. The four men sifted through books, folders and bundles of papers, pulling out relevant or possibly suspicious documents and setting them out on the table. An hour and a half later, they had set aside a pile of papers and van Rooyen quickly sifted through them, pulling out just two items, he considered valuable.

"Thanks guys. From the stuff you extracted, I believe these two documents will give us a start in tracking the ivory and maybe even Jessica too," he smiled.

Hector, Patrick and Angus looked at him expectantly. Van Rooyen held up a typewritten sheet of paper.

"This is a written contract, dated in January, of this year. The agreement's between Raymond Kaseke of Fataran Farm and a Lusaka man, George Tembo. In exchange for two thousand, five hundred kilos of ivory to be supplied by December 31, 2008, Tembo agrees to pay Kaseke US$200.00 per kilo for a total of US$500,000."

"Eeish," Patrick, gasped. "He must be a very rich man."

"The beauty of this document," van Rooyen chuckled, "is that it identifies both the buyer and seller, and gives us the Lusaka street address for Tembo's business office. Hector, this would be valuable evidence to document the ivory smuggling when you report it to the Zambia police. By the way, Angus and I are willing to go with you to Lusaka."

"Excellent idea, Piet. The police can use this as a basis for issuing a search warrant to seize more evidence at Tembo's place of business," Kaminjolo said, beaming.

Van Rooyen's initial sense of elation at the possibility of immediately locating Jessica gave way to a sense of dread. What if he never saw her again? This wasn't, however, a conclusion he was willing to accept. He was determined to find her.

"Hector, the amount they airlifted today can only be a fraction of the 2,500 kilos contracted for," Angus said.

"No problem," Kaminjolo replied with a smile and a wink. "It's still enough to get both Kaseke and Tembo in a big, big trouble."

"Piet, what was the other piece of information?" Angus asked.

"Just a business card. I believe it identifies the pilot of the DC-3. If we don't find Jessica in Lusaka, we can locate this chap, Manuel Chipenga, in Tete and get him to tell us where he took her," van Rooyen replied somberly.

"Well, I think we've got enough to get started. Let's go on back to Kariba and we'll leave for Lusaka in the morning." Kaminjolo said.

"You want me to come too?" Patrick enquired.

"Yes Patrick, if any of those *tsotsis* were hanging around Fataran Farm, you could help us identify them," Kaminjolo said.

Patrick nodded his assent.

As the men returned to their vehicles, Van Rooyen silently said a prayer, asking God to help them find Jessica. Praying was not new to him. As a child, he was brought up in the strict, South African, Dutch Reformed Church. But in 1990, following his marriage to Sandie Edwards, he'd become a member of the Presbyterian Church. Following the deaths of his wife and children, seven years ago, however, he had turned away from the church, embittered that God had permitted their lives to be so savagely taken. But that night, alone in his room, he dropped to his knees and wept, imploring God to forgive him for abandoning his faith and begging him to protect Jessica and return her to him.

*   *   *

Earlier that evening, Jessica found herself a hostage on a vintage aircraft bound for who-knows-where. Just minutes before takeoff, a man had dragged her aboard, chaining her to an anchor fastened to the cabin floor. When the door slammed shut, the engines roared, and the plane bounced down a dirt airstrip. The bumpy ride smoothed once they left the ground. Through a nearby window, Jessica could see Fataran Farm slipping away beneath them. The aircraft tilted, did an about turn, and leveled out. Below, Fataran Farm was a miniature landscape of tiny buildings, gardens, and orchards. Staring upwards, she saw a group of tiny people and among them, she was sure she recognized Piet. Her throat constricted and her eyes filled with tears.

She looked around the interior of the plane. The cabin was stripped of all its passenger seats. Only one remained—a jump seat on the port side of the forward bulkhead. Occupying it was her captor, Raymond Kaseke. Behind her six caskets, covered and secured with cargo nets. Two days before, she'd witnessed elephant tusks being packed in these caskets. The nets would prevent the heavy coffins from sliding around and crushing her during in-flight turbulence. For that she was grateful. A bumpy ride, however, was the least of her worries. More importantly, where were they taking her and what was her fate?

After the plane leveled out, the co-pilot stepped from the cockpit and walked back to the rear of the cabin to check on the cargo. As he approached her, she looked up at him with pleading eyes. Feeling faint and unable to speak for the dryness in her mouth, she made drinking motions. He evidently understood, because he later returned with a bottle of Coca Cola. She nodded her thanks, hastily unscrewed the cap, and gulped down half the bottle. Since the container's fine print was in Portuguese, she surmised the soda was bottled in Mozambique. While sweeter than the Cokes back home, it didn't taste too bad and it helped quench her thirst.

Her seeing Piet on the ground and her recollections of the frightening events that had occurred in the past three days combined to bring on renewed tears. She covered her face with her hands and sobbed quietly, not only because of what she'd just experienced, but also for a real fear of what lay ahead. Fortunately, her emotional disintegration was drowned out by engine noise and was unseen and unheard by her fellow passenger.

Later, pulling herself together, she brushed away the tears and peered out the window in an effort to get her bearings. In the fading light, she saw the Zambezi River below as it meandered east towards the Indian Ocean. With the setting sun behind them, they were obviously flying to Mozambique. She wondered what plans the man in the jump seat had for her when they reached their destination. Earlier, while he and some other men pushed her onto the plane, she'd caught snippets of their conversation.

While she was far from fluent in Shona, her game scouts, Enos and Patrick, had taught her many of the Shona names for the wildlife they encountered in the bush. A word uttered a number of times by these men was *garwe*. It was one she recognized—crocodile. Were they planning to dump her in a river, to be devoured by these vicious, reptiles. She couldn't imagine a more frightful or agonizing death. Right away, she pushed aside these nightmarish thoughts.

The aircraft dipped its left wing in a steep turn and after it leveled out, she realized they were now flying due west, toward a fading rosy glow above the horizon. Why the turnaround? Was there a problem? Were they going to crash? Or, were they returning to Fataran Farm? If the latter was the reason, she prayed Pete could come to her rescue.

As if in answer to her question about an impending crash, the DC-3 suddenly shook violently as it leveled out from its turn. To Jessica, it felt as though a giant hand had grabbed the plane, tossed it skywards thousands of feet into the air, and then slammed it back down towards the earth. Fortunately, the chain looped around her waist served as a restraint, saving her from injury.

Once the pilot restored level flight, the DC-3 flew on, no worse for wear. They'd just hit an air pocket, Jessica realized, and her hopes that they might be returning to Fataran Farm, were dashed. They were now flying north of the Zambezi and their ultimate destination remained a mystery to her.

*   *   *

George Tembo drove south from Lusaka on the T-2 highway. After travelling twenty-eight miles, he turned left onto a narrow dirt road and for another half-mile, his Mercedes, and the full-size pickup behind him bounced along the rutted, dirt track. It was 6:15 p.m. when he and his four-man crew arrived at the abandoned airstrip. They parked a short distance from the runway.

As ordered, the men installed flashlight-illuminated, windsocks at either end of the landing strip and spaced fire pots along both sides of it. Thirty minutes later, they had the 1,800-foot runway lit. Darkness had swept across a sky now dotted with a million stars and a first-quarter moon was rising.

Tembo peered through his windscreen, searching the dark eastern sky for the green and red navigation lights on the plane's wingtips. He saw nothing. He wondered if the dull roar of traffic, traveling up and down the T-2, would mask the sound of the DC-3's approach. Shortly after seven, he heard the drone of the aircraft's approach. It swung into a low pass over the runway and then disappeared from view. Minutes later, its landing lights reappeared as it descended at the northern end of the airstrip. Its wheels touched down, and then it rolled to a stop.

Once it had landed, Tembo breathed a deep sigh of relief. However, his happiness was to be short-lived. As soon as his men lowered the aircraft steps and he clambered aboard, he came face to face with Kaseke.

"What are you doing here, Raymond?" he growled, a scowl distorting his face.

"We had a problem at Fataran, George. Zim-Parks people showed up just as the plane landed."

"Where's the ivory?" Tembo barked.

"Don't worry. It's here; safely packed in the caskets," he replied with a gleeful smile.

Tembo's irritation subsided, but spiked again the moment he climbed aboard and caught sight of Jessica. "Who is that white woman and what is she doing here?" he shouted angrily, jabbing his finger in her direction.

"We caught her spying on our operation. Would you have preferred me to leave her there to tell stories to the people from Zim Parks? It would not have been a long time before those CITES people would have followed the ivory trail, directly up here to you," Kaseke said.

"So you bring her here? Why didn't you just get rid of her?" Tembo shouted.

The pilot's appearance at the cockpit door interrupted their shouting match.

"Mr. Kaseki, you can talk to this man later. We must offload this cargo right now! I have to take off before the Zambian civil aviation authorities locate me," he demanded, arms spread wide as he steered them back towards the exit.

Kaseke glared at Tembo and said, "Your people must unload this stuff."

Tembo backed off the plane and his four men clambered aboard to carry off the caskets. In less than fifteen minutes, they had loaded and tied them down in the pickup. In the meantime, Kaseke released the padlock keeping Jessica chained to the cabin floor and hustled her towards the exit.

"Where are you taking me?" she demanded.

"Not far," he said, shoving her down the steps.

"Let me go!" she shouted, her face contorted with anger. "You can't hold me here. Take me to the nearest United States Embassy." In spite of her flaying arms and vigorous protestations, Kaseke was able to haul her to the pickup. He fumbled around in the dim light to chain her to a tie-down near the tailgate, and snapped the padlock shut.

"She's all yours," he shouted, tossing the key to Tembo.

Kaseke had turned around and was starting back up the steps into the plane, when Tembo roared, "Stop!" He then ordered three of his men to drag Kaseke away and close the aircraft door.

"You will not leave her here with me!" bellowed Tembo. "You have to stay and take care of this fucking problem, yourself."

Meanwhile, Manuel had started the engines, and the DC-3 was taxiing to the end of the strip. There, it made a 90-degree turn and began its takeoff run.

Tembo tossed the padlock key back to Kaseke. "Put her in the truck and make sure she doesn't get away," he ordered.

"Where are we taking her?" Kaseke asked.

"My driver's going to take you to my warehouse in Lusaka. Hold her there until we can make a plan to get rid of her," he replied.

Kaseke was fuming. The last fucking thing he wanted to do was wet nurse this stupid, American woman. He realized, however, that he had no choice but to depend on Tembo's good graces for his safety. There was no way he could return to Fataran. The place was probably crawling with Zim Parks officials, Mugabe's national police, as well as people from CITES.

Fuck, fuck, fuck, he swore to himself.

Chapter 35

Friday, November 7, 2008

Van Rooyen, Ananias, Angus, Stanley and Kaminjolo, left Kariba in two separate vehicles. They crossed the Kariba Dam wall and cleared customs and immigration at the Zambian border post. As the only certified officer of the law in the group, Kaminjolo was the only one who could take a weapon across the border. The other men had to go unarmed. It was eight in the morning, when they set out on the 115-mile journey to Lusaka.

They drove into town on the Kafue road, and arrived at the local, Zambia Police headquarters at noon. They entered the building and followed signs to the Charge Office. Wooden benches lined the walls of the waiting room and at two of the four customer windows, officers were attending to an elderly woman and a young man in a lime-green tee shirt. The remaining two windows were marked 'Closed.' After the youth walked away, Kaminjolo, in his official Zim Parks uniform, stepped up to the window. The three chevrons on the policeman's shoulder boards showed he held the rank of sergeant.

"Sergeant, I am here to report a kidnapping. I also have evidence of illegally poached ivory, being smuggled into Zambia," Kaminjolo said.

"Sir, your identification?"

Kaminjolo pulled out his wallet and pushed both his Zimbabwe driver's license and his Zim Parks identification card through the open slot in the glass.

"Welcome to Lusaka, Mr. Kaminjolo," the Sergeant said. "First, who was kidnapped?"

"Sergeant, her name is Jessica Brennan. She is an American elephant researcher and she was captured by a Zimbabwean, Mr. Raymond Kaseke, after she discovered his poaching operation."

"Where was she kidnapped?"

"At Fataran Farm near Chirundu, in Zimbabwe."

"Why is this of any concern to the Zambia Police?"

"Because we witnessed men capture her and load her and the ivory onto a plane yesterday. We have reason to believe the plane landed somewhere near here last night."

"What makes you think the plane landed in Lusaka? I can, of course, check with air traffic control at Lusaka International Airport to get a list of flights that came in from Zimbabwe."

Van Rooyen stepped up to join Kaminjolo at the window. "Sergeant, we seriously doubt the plane landed at the airport," van Rooyen said. "It's an old prop job, a DC-3 that can land and take off from a dirt runway, anywhere."

"Who are you?" The officer said, glaring at van Rooyen, his eyes owlishly magnified through his spectacles' thick lenses.

Kaminjolo broke in. "This is Mr. Piet van Rooyen. He's assisting me in the investigation."

"Okay, carry on Mr. Kaminjolo."

Van Rooyen handed Hector the ivory contract they'd discovered in Kaseke's office the night before.

Kaminjolo continued. "When we searched Mr. Kaseke's office, we found this agreement between him and a Mr. George Tembo, of the Tembo Travel and Tourism Agency. This agency is located here in Lusaka, at the Holiday Inn on Independence Avenue. We believe Mr. Tembo is the person who received the ivory, and who may have knowledge of Miss Brennan's whereabouts." He pushed the typewritten document under the glass partition, along with the snapshot of Jessica that van Rooyen handed him.

The police sergeant took his time to study both the document and the photograph, and then he turned back to Kaminjolo. "If you will take a seat, I will arrange to get a search warrant from the magistrate's court to search the premises at Tembo Travel and Tourism Agency."

"Thank you," Kaminjolo said, and he and van Rooyen joined Ananias, Angus, and Stanley on benches in the waiting room.

*　　　　　*　　　　　*

Jessica had spent an uncomfortable night stretched out on a concrete floor in this new place. She hadn't seen that dreadful man, Kaseke, since her arrival last night. She was thankful the other men had removed the handcuffs and had been decent enough to permit her to use the toilet before they departed for the night. Someone had even left her a water bottle. They had restrained her with the same heavy, padlocked chain, wound tightly around her waist, and anchored to a second tether looped through a crossbeam, supporting the legs of a hefty wooden table. In the darkness, she had no idea of her surroundings, but could detect the deep, pungent scent of wood shavings.

She slept fitfully, and in the morning when light flooded through a high window, she sat up and looked around. She appeared to be in a store room-cum-workshop, its floor littered with wood chips, and shavings, hence the smell. She estimated that the rectangular room measured at least sixteen feet in length and about half as wide. Suspended from hooks on a wall-mounted pegboard were a variety of woodworking tools, and stacked four feet high below the window, were fifty or more logs, many with the rough, tree bark still covering them. The ever-present, six caskets, sat in a row perpendicular to the opposite wall. There was also a brass key, on a hook closest to the door. She felt a brief surge of excitement, thinking it might fit the padlock chaining her to the table, until she realized it was way beyond her reach.

Once on her feet, she examined the table. It had an enormous, electric-powered, miter saw mounted on it. Other power tools sat on the floor around the room, including a chain saw. Her stomach twisted at the sight of the diabolical tool that Piet had described seeing the poachers use to hack off the elephants' tusks. She looked over at the coffins and her thoughts fell into a deep well of sadness. She knew that inside them were tusks belonging to matriarch, Nkosikaas, and her family.

Her mind wandered back to times when she had observed the activities of this feisty, fifty-two-year-old, elephant cow with the tell-tale, four-inch tear in her left ear. Nkosikaas had led her fourteen-member family, which included her three adult daughters, Narini, Njiva, and Ndoro, and their offspring, on countless journeys crisscrossing thousands of square miles of the Zambezi Valley. Of the three matriarchs she had studied, Nkosikaas had been most famous for her earth-pounding, mock charges, replete with enraged rumbles and ear-piercing, trumpets. Her frightening performances had led even the most experienced hunters to quake in their boots.

She thought about the sole survivor of this clan, Narini-Ina, the orphan calf she and Precious had released just days ago with Nkosikaas's sister, Muchengeti and her family. Jessica had fond memories of the antics of the little orphan's cousin, Ndoro-Tatu, who as a yearling, would race around with his comical, loose, floppy gait. Then he'd shake his head, flap his ears, and head-butt his indulgent mother and older siblings. His tiny tusks, just stubs, were also in one of those coffins. Her anger toward the men responsible, together with her never-to-be-forgotten memories of the noble creatures they had massacred, brought a torrent of tears spilling from her eyes.

At 7:30 a.m. she heard voices emanating from somewhere close by. Men and women were conversing in a local dialect, interspersed occasionally with a man's shouts. She didn't recognize any of the spoken words, so she figured they were speaking in a language other than Shona. In the background, she heard sounds of continuous tapping, along with sharp clinks and thuds. She wondered who they were, and what they were doing.

Several hours passed. She had long since consumed the contents of the water bottle, and her mouth and lips were raspy dry from thirst. She called out to attract someone's attention.

"Help!" she shouted. The chatting and tapping continued unabated. "Hello. Can someone help me?" she cried out even louder.

Finally, the door jerked open and Raymond Kaseke appeared. His face wore an angry scowl.

"What do you want?" he growled. "This is Mr. Tembo's place not mine."

Her heart fell. This was the last person she'd hoped to see. She hadn't forgotten how badly he'd treated her at Fataran, and on the plane coming here. She wondered if Mr. Tembo was the man driving the Mercedes, last night.

"I need to use the toilet. Can one of the ladies out there take me to the toilet?"

"No, and shut up!" he thundered, swearing under his breath as he started for the door.

"Please, Mr. Kaseke, I also need something to drink, and I haven't eaten in days," she pleaded. The words stuck in her craw. She hated having to seek favors from this detestable man.

Ignoring her entreaties, he walked out, leaving the door ajar.

Through the gap, she was able to sneak a quick peek into the adjoining space. It looked like a workshop. Men and women, at workbenches, were using hand tools to cut, slice, and whittle away at wooden figurines of elephants, giraffes, and buffalos that were all in various stages of completion. Closest was a wizened, old man in a soiled tee shirt, who was working on a foot-tall, intricately detailed carving of a black rhino. The quality of his work was impressive, but from his bedraggled appearance, he looked to be someone who was poverty-stricken. Evidently, this Mr. Tembo paid these talented artists paltry wages.

A short while later, Kaseke returned with a water bottle and some food—a small bowl of *sadza*. Grateful, she thanked him.

He ignored her expression of gratitude and headed out the door. Before she had a chance to raise the toilet issue again, he returned, reached around the door, and deposited a smelly, metal bucket, setting it firmly on the floor beside her.

"Toilet," he said in a gruff voice, as he left the room again. He swung the door closed, but she didn't hear the sound of the latch seating itself.

For the moment, she ignored the bucket, and focused instead on the food. He'd supplied no spoon for her to eat the *sadza*. However, she'd seen it eaten often enough by people out in the bush, so she picked out a glob with her fingers, rolled it into a ping pong-sized ball, and took a bite. It was surprisingly tasty, even without the usual gravy. It tasted like a thick, cornmeal porridge, minus the sugar. She was famished so she finished the entire bowl and gulped down half the water.

At midday, the sounds of the carving ceased for a while, and then continued throughout the afternoon. She hated having to use the bucket, but admitted the alternative would be worse. The stink was atrocious. It brought to mind Angus's stories of life in the Harare jail. At five o'clock, the sounds emanating from the workshop ceased. Jessica wondered how long it would be before any more food and water came her way.

After a while, a slight breeze cracked open the door. The added airflow alleviated some of the odor, and Jessica felt some relief. Her eyes kept focusing on the brass key, on the wall near the door. She wondered what Kaseke had planned for her. The uncertainty of her fate was terrifying. She had to get that key. But how?

*　　　　*　　　　*

The police sergeant called out Kaminjolo's name at 1:30 p.m. and motioned him up to the window.

"Mr. Kaminjolo, Police Sergeant Mabenge and Detective Sergeant Rusere will be leaving shortly to serve the search warrant on the Tembo Travel and Tourism Agency. They suggested you meet them there, because they may have some additional questions for you.

"Thank you Sergeant," Kaminjolo said. "We're on our way."

Outside the police station, van Rooyen conferred with Kaminjolo.

"Hector, follow us. We have a street map, and can find the Holiday Inn. The agency's office is directly off the hotel's main vestibule."

"Good Piet. Ananias and Stanley can ride with me and we'll see you there."

When they arrived, they found a police cruiser parked in front of the hotel. As they climbed the front steps, leading to the revolving door in the front entrance, they spotted a tall, powerfully built black man, in a business suit, dashing from around the side of the building. He raced past them, and leaped into a black Mercedes, parked in a reserved space beside the hotel.

"Where's the fire? That fellow is in a terrible hurry," Kaminjolo remarked.

"He certainly is," van Rooyen agreed, as they stepped through the revolving door into the hotel lobby. He wondered if that was George Tembo.

The Tembo Travel and Tourism Agency's glass-fronted entrance opened up into a large alcove containing two workstations. Seated at one of them was a young woman with a name badge, identifying her as Lucy Mukoko. She wore a green, tailored business suit with the agency's initials, T. T. T., embroidered above the Zambian flag on her jacket's breast pocket.

"May I help you?" she asked, glancing nervously behind her.

"We're here to assist the police in their investigation," Kaminjolo replied.

"They're back there, through that door," she said, pointing to a doorway to the left of several travel posters mounted on the rear wall. The colorful posters depicted local Zambian sights and tourist activities—Victoria Falls, Lake Kariba and wildlife in the Lower Zambezi National Park.

The five men filed through the door, which opened up into a hallway. From there, they followed the sounds of voices, taking them into one of two private offices. Police Sergeant Mabenge and Detective Sergeant Rusere were already hard at work, flipping through documents in a filing cabinet.

"You can check those papers on Mr. Tembo's desk, his e-mails, and the documents in the trays on his desk," Detective Sergeant Rusere said.

Van Rooyen gathered up the papers scattered over the desktop, looked them over, and then checked Tembo's e-mails and files on his desktop computer. Kaminjolo, meanwhile, sifted through the 'In Box,' while Ananias and Stanley checked the 'Out Box.'

"Angus, go through everything in the rubbish bin, and then check the bookcase," van Rooyen said.

"Here's something interesting," Detective Sergeant Rusere said, holding up a file folder stuffed full of papers. "It is labeled 'Shubo Gu' and it has a lot of e-mail printouts and correspondence about production orders and deliveries. The letters came from a Mr. Shubo Gu, Chinese Embassy, United Nations Avenue, 7430, Lusaka, Zambia."

"That may well prove to be quite significant, Detective Sergeant," van Rooyen said. "I'm collecting everything needing further investigating in this tray," he said, pointing to the empty, wooden file tray.

"This Gu bloke must be a character of high stature," Angus said, lifting an intricately chiseled, three-foot-long ivory carving of a train of eight elephants, from the top of the bookcase. "From its patina, I can tell it's a valuable antique.

Look at this inscription. It says: 'To George Tembo, in gratitude for past favors, Shubo Gu."

Angus replaced the ivory carving on top of the bookcase and picked up a small frame sitting behind it. It contained a color photograph of a tall black man and standing beside him a shorter, white-haired, oriental man, wearing heavy black-framed glasses. He handed the picture frame to van Rooyen.

"Do you think these two blokes are our possible suspects?"

"I don't know," van Rooyen said, passing the frame to Sergeant Mabenge. "Sergeant, do you recognize either of these men?"

Mabenge studied the photograph for a few moments, then handed it back. "No, I don't know them," he said, shaking his head.

By three in the afternoon, the investigation had turned up nothing more than Tembo's place of employment and evidence that there was a business connection between him and a man called Shubo Gu.

"I'm sorry gentlemen, but we see no evidence here that George Tembo was involved in poaching or ivory smuggling," Detective Sergeant Rusere said. "Anyway, even if we had proof that Mr. Gu had smuggled ivory out of the country, the man's a diplomat with diplomatic immunity, so we can't touch him."

Van Rooyen's heart sank. After such promising leads, they were still no closer to nailing Tembo, or finding Jessica.

Kaminjolo shook hands with the two sergeants, thanked them for their efforts, and apologized for wasting their time.

"It's okay," Sergeant Rusere replied. "Phone us if you find any new evidence that we can investigate." The two officers then saluted sharply and left the room.

"So what's the next step?" Angus said, looking around at his glum companions.

"Hey Angus, give me that picture," van Rooyen said. "The lady out front can probably identify these men." He took the frame and hurried out towards the front office.

"Miss Mukoko," he said cheerfully, noting her nametag. He handed her the picture frame and bent down to whisper. "I have a bet with a colleague back there, that these gentlemen are two famous American actors, Samuel L. Jackson and Jackie Chan. Am I right?"

Lucy Mukoko gave a shy giggle, and then tried to disguise her laughter by covering her mouth.

Grinning, van Rooyen asked again. "Am I right? You have to tell me. We're betting the cost of a dinner, here at the Holiday Inn."

"Oh no, Sir," she said, as spurts of laughter escaped her lips. "This is a picture of Mr. Tembo and Mr. Gu."

"Oh dear, never mind. But thank you Lucy," he said with a fake frown. "Darn it! I was obviously mistaken, and now I'll have to pay for lunch!"

He strode back and announced to the group, "Yup, these blokes are indeed Tembo and Gu."

"And so? What does that mean?" Kaminjolo asked, raising his eyebrows.

"My recommendation," van Rooyen began, "is that we wait outside the Chinese Embassy until Gu leaves the building, and then we tail him. It's possible he'll lead us to where the ivory is stored and I just pray to God that we find Jessica there too."

Chapter 36

Friday, November 7, 2008

They arrived at the Chinese Embassy, at 3:45 p.m. Van Rooyen and Kaminjolo parked facing one another, on opposite sides of United Nation's Avenue, just half a block down the street. Kaminjolo had picked up this old, law enforcement trick somewhere along the way, and it had worked well in the past. Regardless which direction the suspect fled, one of two chase vehicles would always be facing the right way to take up the pursuit.

Van Rooyen and Angus maintained surveillance on the embassy's gated driveway. The wait seemed interminably long.

"Trouble is we don't even know if he's in there," Angus said. "Don't you think one of us should go in? We could be sitting here till midnight."

"Not a good idea," van Rooyen replied. "I'll bet he has a private office. It's unlikely he works in view of the public. That means we'd have to ask a receptionist, and that could raise suspicions."

"I suppose you're right."

Today, business at the embassy was slow. For the entire hour they'd been sitting there, only two vehicles had driven through the gate into the building's parking lot. Foot traffic had also been sparse. Fewer than a handful of pedestrians had walked in off the street.

"I suppose there aren't many tourists clamoring for travel visas today," Angus commented.

The weather was blistering. Even with the windows open, they were sweltering. Trickles of perspiration ran down his chest, soaking his shirt. A row of Flamboyant trees stood behind the embassy. Soon brilliant red blossoms would cover their branches. He remembered his and Jessica's discussion about these trees when they drove into Harare to visit Angus in the prison. Although it was only last month, it seemed so long ago, now. He missed Jessica. Lord, how he missed her and feared for her safety. Today, the thought of losing her was overwhelming. There was nothing for it—he had to find her.

By 5:00 p.m., the activity around the embassy was beginning to pick up. Once more, Van Rooyen and Angus studied Shubo Gu's likeness in the photograph. He had typical oriental features: broad cheekbones, a small nose, full lips, and on his head a mop of short, straight, snow-white hair. Cars were exiting the gated embassy car park.

"Here," van Rooyen said, handing Angus a pair of binoculars. "You check the drivers and I'll keep an eye on the front door."

Ten minutes later, Angus spotted a small, white sedan exiting the gate.

"That's him in the white car! Just like the photo. He's got white hair, and glasses with black frames. Follow him!" Angus cried out.

Van Rooyen drove forward, pulling into the left lane, behind the white car. Kaminjolo made a quick U-turn and fell in behind. The car turned left onto Haile Selassie Avenue and at the first roundabout, turned onto Independence Avenue. Their route, continuing north, took a left jog at the Supreme Court building, a tall, imposing, red stone structure whose six lofty, white marble columns stood in front of the court's recessed entrance. Topped with a parapet surrounded by short Grecian columns, the structure, probably constructed in the 1950s, appeared more than a little worse for wear—its paint chipped and faded.

At the next traffic circle, Gu turned right onto Cairo Road, and after five blocks took another right onto Mumbwa Road. They followed the small white car across two more intersections, but when it turned off into a narrow street, leading to a long, rectangular commercial building, they continued straight ahead.

Looking around, van Rooyen could tell they were in an industrial area. He doubled back at the next cross street and half way down the block, pulled off onto the verge and stopped, across from a row of Jacaranda trees. The street Gu had turned onto was approximately a hundred yards in front of them. When Kaminjolo drew up behind him, van Rooyen walked back to speak with him.

"Let's leave the vehicles here and walk the rest of the way," he said.

*   *   *

Jessica was determined to free herself. She was not going to sit back, to await an unknown fate. She had to get that key. At 5:15 p.m., all was quiet. The place seemed deserted. She eyed the small brass key hanging from a hook closest to the door. To reach it she'd have to move the ponderous saw table at least five feet. She positioned herself behind the table and gave it an almighty shove. It hardly budged. Dismayed it had taken all her strength to move it less than an inch, she was determined to do better.

The table, with its thick legs and support struts, was likely made of mopane, one of Southern Africa's heaviest timbers. For her second attempt, she stepped back as far as her bonds permitted and forcibly threw her entire weight against it. The table shifted a couple of inches closer. Mentally patting herself on the back, she threw herself at the table once more, straining mightily against it. This time she gained another three inches. Although the exertion left her breathless, she doggedly continued moving it a meager three inches at a time, until she was finally able to reach the key.

*   *   *

Gu had received a phone call from George Tembo earlier that day, informing him the ivory had been delivered last night and was now in storage at his Mumbwa Road premises. They agreed to meet at the warehouse at 7:30 p.m. In his eagerness to see the shipment, however, Gu left for the warehouse, as soon as the embassy closed its doors at five o'clock. After all, he had waited weeks for this delivery, and had tired of the repeated delays. Tembo had made him too many promises about its imminent arrival and Gu had run out of patience. He was sick of having to deal with his frantic Beijing customers who had been telephoning and e-mailing him for weeks, demanding news of their orders.

Gu parked his small, white Hyundai under a jacaranda tree beside the entrance. Before exiting the vehicle, he opened the glove box and removed a small, Norinco 9 mm, semi-automatic, and three spare, 14-round magazines. He dropped the magazines into his right, trouser pocket and slipped the weapon into an inside pocket of his vest. Because the ivory trade attracted so many undesirables, Gu never conducted business without his trusty, Chinese-made pistol.

He found the front entrance locked. Hoping Tembo's workshop manager was still there to let him in, he knocked on the door. Getting no immediate response, he rapped several more times. A few minutes later, the handle turned and the door opened. Gu then found himself looking up at the biggest man he'd ever seen.

"What do you want?" Kaseke said in a gruff voice.

"I come to see Mr. Tembo," Gu said.

"What's your name?"

"Shubo Gu. I come from Chinese Embassy; Mr. Tembo's number one important customer."

Kaseke stepped aside to let him pass, following him through the deserted front office.

"Why are you here?" Kaseke said.

"I come to inspect my ivory shipment. Mr. Tembo tell me it come last night. But I never saw you before; what is your name? "

"Raymond Kaseke; I brought your ivory shipment up from Zimbabwe."

"Fataran Farm?" Gu quizzed him.

"Yes, that's my place," Kaseke replied.

Gu had heard Tembo speak of this man. He had often called him problematic and unreliable. With Kaseke on his heels, Gu made his way into the workshop. It was deserted; the artisans must have already gone home. Then he turned into the shop's storage and supply room. He was not surprised to see the six caskets sitting side by side, perpendicular to the wall. Tembo had alerted him about the new shipping containers, ahead of time. He walked over, lifted each lid, and saw elephant tusks of varying sizes stacked lengthwise, between bundles of straw. He smiled, pleased that Tembo had actually come through this time.

"Those coffins were my idea," Kaseke beamed, and he gave a deep belly laugh that jiggled his flabby cheeks.

*   *   *

She grabbed the key off the hook, and as she inserted it into the padlock, she heard the sound of approaching footsteps. Moments later, a white-haired Asian man, followed by Kaseke, trooped past the partially open door. Still chained to the table and unable to run, she yanked the key out of the lock and dropped it into her pants pocket. She stood motionless, praying she hadn't attracted their attention.

She was crouched behind two large, empty cardboard boxes, sitting underneath the workbench when the sound of their footsteps returned. When she'd moved the heavy table, the boxes had been dragged along with it. She hoped Kaseke wouldn't notice the table had been moved since last night. The two men entered the storeroom and walked directly to the caskets. She peeked through a gap between the boxes and saw the white-haired man opening the lids of each of the caskets.

After examining all six caskets, both men turned to leave. As the Asian man passed by, he caught sight of her.

He turned to face Kaseke, demanding in heavily accented English, "Who is this woman?" Then he marched up to her. "What are you doing here?"

She looked at him and responded in a quiet, matter-of-fact, tone.

"This man kidnapped me," she said pointing an accusing finger at Kaseke. "I told him to take me to the United States' Embassy, but he's held me prisoner here, illegally, for the past 24 hours."

Gu seemed confused at first, but then his face reddened.

"Who brought you here?" he said in a clipped tone, his lips forming a thin line.

"That's him, right there, Raymond Kaseke. He kidnapped me at Fataran Farm, in Zimbabwe, and then dragged me onto an old plane. It was a real old prop job, badly in need of new paint. Seriously, it looked like something out of that aviation salvage yard in Tucson, Arizona," she babbled nervously. "May I have something to drink, please?"

A tall man in a business suit appeared in the doorway.

"He was there too," Jessica announced, pointing at Tembo.

The Asian man walked over to the new arrival. He was seething, waving his arms about angrily.

"You are a stupid fool, Tembo; you and Kaseke. Who is this American woman, and why you tie her up here? It is no good. You put my business in danger."

Jessica had to assume his business was smuggling ivory. If so, then these three men were undoubtedly bad news. She realized she had blabbed too much, and had likely placed herself in extreme jeopardy. She needed to make a run for it at the earliest opportunity.

"What are you doing here Gu?" Tembo demanded.

Jessica could see from the man's bulging eyes and taut sinews in his neck, that Tembo was incensed

"You were not supposed to be here until later," he bellowed. "Our meeting was for half-past seven. You have no right to barge into my place of business, uninvited."

"When I come Mr. Tembo, this man let me in," Gu replied angrily, stamping his foot. "You have bad security. People could steal the ivory."

"I agree Mr. Kaseke had no business letting you in. But, Mr. Gu, let me assure you the ivory was perfectly safe. If you understood our African culture, you would know that people here do not monkey around with the dead. Nobody would dare to open a casket and let out all the bad spirits," he fumed.

Tembo's face took on a menacing grimace. He stamped his feet, and began gyrating in a demented fashion as if to emulate an African spirit dance.

Jessica found his performance frightening.

"Okay, okay!" Gu blustered. "What about this white woman? You bring her here. So stupid!"

"Calm down, Mr. Gu. You need to hear what Mr. Kaseke has to say." He pointed at his supplier. "Raymond, tell him."

Kaseke stepped forward to face Gu.

"She was spying at Fataran, so we took her prisoner. When the Zimbabwe parks people showed up to raid the place, I did not want to leave her there. So when the plane came to pick up the ivory, I took her with us."

Jessica listened attentively. So it was Piet she'd seen at Fataran when they were taking off. Her heart warmed at the realization that he had indeed been searching for her.

"What you do with her?" Gu challenged Tembo shrilly, pointing to Jessica, who was standing next to the work bench.

"We will dispose of her in one of the rivers—the Kafue, or the Zambezi," Tembo said.

"What if somebody finds her body?"

"Oh no, Mr. Gu, there won't be anything left. The crocodiles make sure of that."

The thought of a crocodile devouring her, sent deep chills running through Jessica's veins. It made the fine hairs on her arms stand erect.

Gu walked along the row of caskets with Kaseke and Tembo at his heels. He glanced over at Jessica and she stared back at him with a defiant look. She felt in her trouser pocket for the key. She knew she had to wait for just the right moment to unlock the padlock and flee.

The three men looked down at the six caskets. Gu spoke first.

"George, put ivory in proper boxes for diplomatic air freight."

"Bring me the embassy labels, Mr. Gu," was Tembo's curt response. "After you have transferred the American dollars into my bank account, I guarantee your shipment will be delivered to the embassy in the proper containers."

Jessica had heard enough. It was time to go. She pulled the key from her pocket and with shaking hands, unlocked the chain encircling her waist. Then slowly, carefully, she let it slide silently to the floor. The men were still hovering over the caskets, when she turned and raced towards the warehouse, hoping to be able to exit the building though a rear door. In her haste, she slipped on the sawdust-coated floor and almost fell. Recovering, she ran on.

Her near fall alerted the men and they took off in pursuit. Behind her, she could hear their pounding feet getting closer. She sped into the darkened warehouse, racing down the center aisle past rows of tall, shelving racks that almost reached the twelve-foot ceiling. Between the rows, walkways on both sides, labeled from A to H, gave access to the shelves. Ahead in the gloom, she could see the rear warehouse door.

She had bolted a mere twenty feet into the warehouse when she heard two deafening blasts, and bullets whizzed over her head. Panic-stricken she screamed, ducking left into Aisle D. As she raced on in the darkness between rows of shelves, her bare foot struck something heavy that was sitting in her path. Her toes smarted painfully as she hopped forward. All at once, ceiling-mounted, neon strips flooded the warehouse with light. She looked back over her shoulder. She saw a tipped-over, gallon-sized can, and a widening puddle, which was spreading across the walkway and under the stacks. She detected a strong odor of turpentine, or some other flammable liquid. Feeling totally exposed, she whipped around in search of somewhere to hide.

*   *   *

Van Rooyen and the others crossed the street, and moved swiftly along a worn path beneath the row of Jacarandas. As they closed in on the street where Gu had turned off, they heard several explosive sounds of gunfire emanating from the building to their right. After the shots, they heard a woman's scream, and they took off at a dead run.

*   *   *

Tembo had led Gu and Kaseke into the darkened warehouse. He'd thrown the light switch to bathe the entire facility in bright, fluorescent light, and then the three men had paused in the center aisle, their ears pricked for any sound of movement. While Tembo's eyes had been roaming around for any sign of the fleeing woman, Gu had blindly fired off two shots.

Tembo was furious. "Mr. Gu, what in the fuck are you doing? That was very stupid!" he shouted. "You wasted your ammunition, and shot fucking holes in my walls." He then called out in a booming voice, "Miss Brennan, come out and give yourself up. You have no other choice; there's no other way out." He received no response.

Minutes later, with no sign of the woman being willing to surrender, they pulled out their weapons and split up to search the warehouse. Each man examined a row of shelves, peering around the stored items, shifting objects to expose pockets or spaces large enough to conceal a person. Tembo had worked his way along several rows and had found nothing. He was moving along Aisle C, when he heard some shots and then saw flames shooting towards the ceiling just one row ahead. He darted into the center aisle to see Gu, pistol in hand, running towards him, sheer panic on his face.

"I saw her running...tried to stop her," he said, panting heavily.

*   *   *

Jessica, her heart hammering, squeezed herself between some rolls of carpeting on a lower shelf, left of Aisle E. While she was thankful the shooter had such a lousy aim, it didn't quell her feeling of sheer terror. She had overheard Tembo admonishing the oriental man, but it brought her no comfort. She was positive all three of them were bloodthirsty killers. Tembo was now calling for her to give herself up. What was he thinking? Still foremost on her mind was their threat of feeding her to the crocodiles. She was positive a bullet would be quicker, cleaner, and far less painful than death-by-crocodile. Therefore, instead of resting her fate in their hands, perhaps she'd be better off deliberately putting herself in harm's way. She had no time to decide. Footsteps were approaching.

Seconds later, more shots rang out. The blasts assaulted her ears and she felt the sharp sting of grit peppering her exposed skin. Then came a mighty whoosh, and she felt the intense heat. In the aisle just behind her, flames shot upward, forming a column of fire. She muffled her screams and shielded her face from the scorching fire. The heat was intolerable, so she crawled out from between the rolls of carpeting. The flames took hold and spread like wildfire on both sides of the aisle where the turpentine had spilled. She heard men shouting.

As the fire continued to burn, she heard explosions from aerosol cans and other combustibles. Meanwhile thickening, dark, acrid smoke swirled around her and burned her eyes and throat. She dropped down onto her hands and knees, and crawled towards the back door. She tried to open it, but the door held fast.

*   *   *

Seeing the raging fire, Tembo raced for a fire extinguisher mounted on the wall next to the entrance. Rather than searching for the American woman, the protection his property was of greatest importance to him now. Just as he reached for the extinguisher, four men burst through the double doors.

*   *   *

Earlier, when van Rooyen and company reached the parking lot, they had found two vehicles parked there, Shubo Gu's white Hyundai and a large, black Mercedes.

They found the entrance unsecured, so van Rooyen and his four companions barged in. Almost immediately, they heard a second volley of gunshots, and fanned out, sprinting through the silent workspaces and utility rooms. Kaminjolo searched the workshop, Ananias and Angus headed for the office's supply room and the toilet areas, while van Rooyen and Stanley entered a fair-sized storage and utility room.

Van Rooyen glanced around the room. He saw an empty water bottle and a metal bowl, its sides encrusted with dried sadza. Both were sitting on a sturdy equipment table, supporting a heavy-duty power saw. Against the far wall, he noticed a stack of wooden logs, and beneath the workbench, was an open padlock and key, laying on the sawdust-covered floor

"Someone must have been tied up here? Maybe it was Jessica," Van Rooyen whispered to Stanley, who was pointing to his left. Van Rooyen's gut twinged when he caught sight of the six caskets he'd last seen being loaded on the aircraft at Fataran. He walked over and his hands trembled as he cracked open one of the lids.

"Damn, damn!" He cursed at himself. Why had he so quickly dismissed Jessica's suspicions about that place? If anything happened to her, he knew now that he'd be the one to blame.

Ananias, Angus, and Kaminjolo joined them, reporting that the supply room and toilet areas were clear. Wordlessly, van Rooyen pointed to the caskets. All three looked towards them and grimaced.

Van Rooyen's eyes were starting to burn, he could smell smoke, and he noticed the air in the room was becoming hazy.

"Jessica has to be here somewhere, I know it. We've got to find her; can't waste another minute. Let's check out that warehouse."

Kaminjolo ordered Ananias to guard the ivory, and van Rooyen and the ranger slammed open the double doors and rushed in, followed closely by Angus and Stanley. Once inside, van Rooyen found himself in a huge warehouse, partially engulfed in smoke and flames.

He stood in the center aisle between rows of tall shelving units, and through the haze, he saw a wall of flame and dense clouds of rising smoke that curled down from the ceiling. Just twelve feet away, stood Gu and a large man he was unable to identify. Stanley grabbed his arm.

"Baas, the black man is Kaseke."

Suddenly, from behind them came a booming voice. "Who in the hell are you and what are you doing here?"

Van Rooyen spun around to see a man in a business suit, leveling a gun at them. Right away, he recognized him. He was the man from the photograph—George Tembo.

Then he heard a second voice, "George, it's Zim Parks—the people who attacked us at Fataran."

Van Rooyen's eyes bored into Tembo. "Where is Jessica," he demanded.

With a smirk on his face, the ivory trafficker shouted, "She's in there," and he waved his gun towards the wall of fire.

In fury, van Rooyen charged him.

Tembo fired his weapon, but a fraction of a second before the bullet left the chamber, van Rooyen received a violent blow to his shoulder, knocking him sideways. As he staggered to keep his balance, he saw Angus collapse and his heart stopped when he realized his close friend had taken the bullet intended for him.

Overcome by rage, he leapt over Angus's body and tackled Tembo, pinning him to the wall. He grabbed for the weapon and they both crashed to the floor.

*   *   *

Kaseke had observed the fight between the two men. He'd tried aiming his weapon at the white man, but was never able to keep him in his sights long enough to get off a shot. Perhaps now was the time to get away, he thought, and he turned and took off towards the rear of the warehouse. He lowered his head and raced through the burning wall of flame. On the other side, he slapped at his clothing to snuff out a few smoldering spots. He found Jessica huddled next to the door. He tried to open it and failed. He then gave the door some strenuous kicks, but despite the weight and power behind the blows, the door held fast. He then turned to Jessica, grabbed her by the hair, and jerked her to her feet.

*   *   *

For more than five minutes, Van Rooyen and Tembo rolled around on the concrete floor, kicking and grunting as they grappled for the gun. When the gun discharged with a loud crack, the struggle was over and both men lay spread-eagled and unmoving.

Kaminjolo rushed forward. "Piet, are you okay?" He bent down to touch his shoulder and van Rooyen stirred. He then slowly rose to his feet, leaving George Tembo's motionless form stretched out on the floor, the gun still clutched in his hand. Blood pooled on the warehouse floor.

Van Rooyen and Kaminjolo immediately turned to check on Angus. He was still alive, but on the right side of his chest, blood oozed from a bullet wound. He didn't respond to their voices, however, and his breathing was labored.

"All I can think to do is stop the bleeding," van Rooyen said, and ripped off his shirt. Together, he and Kaminjolo wrapped it tightly around Angus's chest.

*   *   *

Kaseke grasped Jessica around the neck, holding her up as a shield between him and the fire, and frog marched her ahead of him back through the flames. When they emerged on the other side, he brandished his firearm in his free

321

hand and headed for the entrance to the warehouse. Over her screams, he yelled, "Move out of the way! Let us through, or I'll shoot! His adversaries stepped aside.

*　　　　　*　　　　　*

Van Rooyen was tending to Angus when he first caught sight of Jessica. His heart leapt, but his elation quickly turned to a mind-numbing feeling of helplessness. He felt powerless knowing there was no way he could take out Kaseke, without harming the woman he loved. Their eyes met, and she began kicking, punching, and thrashing about to escape his grasp. She struggled so fiercely that Kaseke feared losing his grip on her. He brought his other hand and arm into play to secure his grip on her and his weapon dropped to the floor. Van Rooyen immediately leapt forward, kicked the gun out of the way, and grabbed for Jessica.

Kaseke dropped her and dove for his weapon. As he reached for it, Kaminjolo bellowed, "Don't touch that firearm! Put your hands behind your back!"

Van Rooyen was lifting Jessica to her feet, when Kaseke's hand closed around the handgun. Within seconds, there was an ear-piercing blast, and Kaseke slumped, lifeless, to the floor. Van Rooyen turned to see Kaminjolo standing several yards away, his gun in his hand, down by his side. Then he saw Gu emerge from the smoke, run past with Stanley in pursuit.

Except for clumps of singed hair, and a few burn marks on her clothing, Jessica appeared to be in good shape. He untied her, and they hugged briefly.

"We have to get Angus out of here," he said, hurriedly pulling himself away.

"What happened?"

"He saved my life; took a shot meant for me."

The smoke had advanced and was now inundating the entire warehouse. All three of them were coughing and choking.

Van Rooyen sent Jessica ahead and he and Kaminjolo carried Angus outside. Miraculously he was still alive, though seriously wounded.

The sun had already dipped below the horizon and it was getting dark. They found Stanley waiting for them in a section of the parking lot, furthest away from the burning building. He had Gu shackled to a chain link fence. Noticing Ananias was missing, Van Rooyen ran back inside to find him. Five minutes later, they both returned carrying a casket full of ivory.

"Thought you might need it for evidence," he told Kaminjolo with a wink. "And by the way, amazing, but the telephone in there was still working, so we phoned for an ambulance and called the police."

Angus was regaining consciousness. His eyes opened. "Where am I," he said, turning his head to look around.

Jessica crouched down beside him. "You were shot. Piet's called an ambulance and they'll be here very soon."

Minutes later, a fire engine approached, red lights flashing and siren wailing.

"Eish! That was quick. Who called the fire station?" Kaminjolo asked.

"We didn't call them," Ananias replied, and the others shook their heads.

"Perhaps someone from around here saw the smoke," van Rooyen volunteered.

The fire engine pulled up, squelched its siren, and four firemen wrestled down hoses and connected them to a hydrant near the row of jacaranda trees. With water gushing, they went in to fight the fire.

Now that the panic was over, van Rooyen swooped Jessica into his arms and for several minutes, they clung to one another. Only when the sounds of whoops and cheers interrupted their reverie, did they break apart. With an arm clasped tightly around her shoulders, Van Rooyen scanned the four smiling faces around them and looked down at the woman by his side.

"Jessica! Oh, thank God! I had the nightmarish notion we might never see you again," he said tenderly, swiping his free forearm across his eyes. "And, I have to tell you that if it hadn't been for these chaps, we might not have found you in time."

With tears of joy streaming down her face, Jessica thanked everyone. "Honest to God, you all saved my life and I'll never forget that." Then she stepped away from van Rooyen, and approached each man, in turn. Beginning with Kaminjolo, she hugged each one of them.

Afterwards, while they sat beneath a streetlight, to await the arrival of the police, Jessica described everything she had experienced after Kaseke nabbed her at Fataran.

"Jessica, I'm so sorry. If I had taken your hunch about Fataran seriously, you would have been spared all that," van Rooyen said afterwards wearing a hangdog look on his face.

"Hey Piet, don't beat up on yourself. Let's look at the positive side," she said, as she stroked his forearm gently. Her eyes scanned the group. "Thanks to you guys we put a major ivory poaching and smuggling ring out of business."

Shortly after 7:00 p.m., a Zambian police van drove up with Police Sergeant Mabenge and Detective Sergeant Rusere. Behind them, was an ambulance and a small white pickup with a camper top, bearing the local medical examiner and his assistant.

The EMTs moved Angus onto a stretcher and loaded him into the Ambulance. They sped off to the Lusaka Hospital. Meanwhile, the local medical examiner and his assistant took body bags into the now-smoldering building to collect Tembo's and Kaseke's remains.

Kaminjolo greeted the police officers. "You gentlemen work very long hours," he said.

"We were intrigued by this case, Mr. Kaminjolo," the detective said. "Do you have any new clues in the kidnapping and ivory smuggling cases you reported this morning?"

"I do, Sergeant Rusere," Kaminjolo replied. "In fact, we have witnesses and all the evidence you need."

"Who are the witnesses?"

Under the single streetlight's muted glow, Kaminjolo motioned for Jessica to step forward.

"Sergeant, this is Miss Jessica Brennan, the American who was kidnapped in Zimbabwe and flown into Zambia the other night. She will testify that she was kidnapped by Mr. Raymond Kaseke, and held prisoner here by Mr. George Tembo of the Tembo Travel and Tourism Agency. Mr. Piet van Rooyen and Mr. Stanley Matombo are here and can testify that I was forced to shoot Tembo and Kaseke, after Mr. Tembo shot and wounded Mr. Angus Mclaren. Mr. McLaren is the man who just left in the ambulance. Mr. Kaseke held us all at bay until he dropped his gun. When he retrieved it, I was forced to shoot him."

After hearing Kaminjolo's story, Sergeant Rusere spoke to Jessica. "Good evening, Miss Brennan. I am glad to see you are well and we will need to get your statement, when we return to the station."

Jessica nodded.

"Where's the evidence?" Sergeant Mabenge enquired.

"We have some in this coffin, right here, and once the fire's out, there may be more inside," Kaminjolo replied, pointing to the building.

Kaminjolo threw back the lid. "It is okay to open this coffin, gentlemen. There are no dead people or spirits lurking inside—just the evidence, as you can see. Elephant tusks! According to Mr. Gu, here," he continued, pointing to the Chinese ivory merchant shackled to the fence, "the weight of these tusks, when added to those still in the building, totals 260 kilos."

Sergeant Mabenge was barely able to contain his astonishment. "I have never seen such a thing," he said, as he contemplated the coffin and its contents, his hands on his hips.

Afterwards both he and the detective burst into peals of laughter, and with the exception of Shubo Gu, everyone looked on, amused.

*   *   *

Attempting to contain his mirth, Sergeant Mabenge continued, "Of course, I will have to hold the evidence at the station, until the case is closed. When we leave here, I will also need everyone to come and give their statements," he announced.

Gu, meanwhile, demanded angrily to be afforded his diplomatic immunity and be released immediately.

Van Rooyen realized that Gu was not worried in the slightest about being prosecuted. Nor was he concerned about upsetting his boss, the Chinese ambassador. While Gu might sustain some financial loss, it was his reputation with his Chinese customers that would suffer the most.

Turning to the detective, Kaminjolo handed him the framed photo of Tembo and Gu.

"This photograph is of Mr. Tembo and Mr. Gu," he said. "It was on display in the travel agency at the Holiday Inn. Mr. Gu is an attaché at the Chinese Embassy here. Unfortunately, his diplomatic status protects him from being tried for any crime. We held him here to testify, specifically, about his partnership with Mr. Tembo in the smuggling of ivory from Zimbabwe. There is a document that proves Mr. Gu purchased the ivory directly from Tembo, to ship to his clients in the People's Republic of China."

The detective looked at Gu with distaste. "Mr. Gu, you will come with us to the police station to make a statement. Only afterwards will we release you to your embassy."

Gu's face fell when Sergeant Mabenge replaced his plastic wrist restraints with a pair of steel handcuffs and bundled him into the police van.

Jessica, her lower lip trembling, looked down at the tusks. Speaking to Kaminjolo and the others she said, "I'm positive these came from Nkosikaas's family. I recognize a lot of the nicks and other marks on them." She pointed to a small tusk with a broken tip. "For instance, I know this one belonged to Narini-Tatu, a five-year-old bull calf. I was there when he lost the tip in a tussle with his twelve-year-old cousin, a bull calf, Njiva-Piri."

Overhearing her comment, Detective Sergeant Rusere expressed surprise. "You saw this?" he said, staring at her with a dropped jaw.

"I did," she replied. "I have been studying these elephants for more than three years. When I first saw that little guy, he was only two years old," she said, tears glistening in her eyes.

"We need to take all the evidence to the station now," Police Sergeant Mabenge said. All witnesses must follow us to the station, so we can prepare their statements."

Using the medical examiner's gurney, Kaminjolo and van Rooyen, assisted the Zambian authorities in retrieving the singed caskets from the building and wheeled the evidence to their van.

The four vehicles departed for the police station. When they arrived, police constables transferred the caskets into secure evidence lockers and the witnesses filed into the charge office to give their statements.

At almost 11:00 p.m., the detectives gave Kaminjolo and his group permission to leave.

"If we need any further information from you, Mr. Kaminjolo, we'll contact you at your Kariba office," Detective Sergeant Rusere said.

Before they departed, van Rooyen said, "I don't believe we should attempt the four-hour drive home, tonight." He proposed, instead, they stay overnight at the Holiday Inn and leave for home first thing the next morning.

The exhausted group nodded in agreement and piled into their two vehicles for the short drive to the hotel. Before setting off, van Rooyen turned to Jessica in the passenger seat. He smiled and squeezed her hand, feeling a sudden, overwhelming rush of emotion that almost took his breath away.

"What happened to your shoes, my love?" he asked, looking down at her bare feet.

"Oh, I lost one of them at Fataran, while they dragged me back to the building. I have no idea where I lost the second one."

"Well, here's the one you lost at Fataran," he said, removing the shoe from the pocket of his shorts. "I picked it up there on the road near the fence line," he said. "Before we leave Lusaka tomorrow, I reckon we should stop and buy you a new pair."

The next day, before leaving Lusaka, they stopped at the hospital to check on Angus. He was sitting up in bed with an oxygen tube up his nose and other tubes draining his chest.

"Patsy's on the way," he told them. "She should get here any minute. By the way, don't anyone dare make me laugh. It hurts like a bitch."

Jessica gave his hand a squeeze and van Rooyen said, "You're not looking so good, *Shamwari*. Thanks for saving my hide, by the way. If you hadn't jumped in and shoved me out of the way, I would have been a goner. I owe you."

"What damage did the bullet do?" Jessica wanted to know.

"I was bloody lucky, Jess. The slug collapsed my lung, but the doctors fixed it. Luckily, the bullet didn't hit any other vital organs. It's still in here" he added, gingerly patting his chest. "The good news is I can go home in a three or four days. But tell me, Piet, what happened after I got shot.?"

Van Rooyen had filled him in, and afterwards Angus commented, "I have to say those Zambian cops were a bloody breath of fresh air. If this had happened in Zim, the buggers would have told us, first off, they had no petrol, so no help. Then, because whites were involved, they'd have told us they couldn't respond because it was 'political'. And in the end, we all would have been arrested on some trumped up charge."

"Too true, Angus," van Rooyen said. "We can only hope that one day it will get better."

Chapter 37

Friday, November 14, 2008

Van Rooyen spoke into the mike in his headset, "Kariba Tower, this is Cessna one-five-zero, Whiskey-Kilo-Bravo. Request permission to taxi, departure to the east." Jessica had meanwhile buckled herself into the copilot's seat.

The propeller on the Cessna's nose spun and Jessica looked on with pride as her man scanned the instruments in front of him while performing his pre-flight system checks. Through the earphones in her headset, she heard the tower's reply.

"Roger, Whiskey-Kilo-Bravo; taxi to runway zero-niner zero, and hold short."

The engine roared and the plane taxied towards the runway. While passing by the terminal building, Jessica noted with interest that the Air Zimbabwe, sixty-passenger, turboprop, Xian MA60 had been moved away from the front apron and was now parked on the right side of the terminal.

After receiving the tower's clearance, van Rooyen pushed in the throttle and Whisky Kilo Bravo began her take-off roll. Once in flight, Van Rooyen leveled the plane at three thousand feet and radioed the tower the direction they planned to take. Instead of following the Zambezi, he had turned away from the river towards the woodlands on the southern, upland and escarpment areas.

Now the rains had come and water was available inland, they searched for the elephants further south. Jessica pressed her forehead tightly against the window. Only ten days ago, the landscape across the Zambezi's southern alluvial flood plain had been dusky brown and dry as a bone. Today it was covered in a carpet of emerald green and large herds of buffalo, wildebeest and zebra dotted the verdant slopes of the Hurungwe Safari Area. The scene was so magnificent; it brought a lump to her throat.

"Piet, thanks for flying me out here today. Just a few days ago, I feared I'd never again be able to see scenes this stunning. It seemed almost too hard to bear."

Van Rooyen fixed his eyes on her, and took her delicate hand in his. "For me, it was the thought of being without you for the rest of my life, what was really too hard to bear."

His admission made her heart soar. She hoped he didn't think that she wouldn't have missed him any less.

"You can't know," she said, "how good it felt, looking out the window of that old plane and see you down there on the ground; knowing, in my heart that you were out there, looking for me. Just believing that was what kept me going during some exceptionally dark days and nights." She smiled at him, her eyes bright with tears.

She'd asked him to fly her here today in hopes of discovering if the orphan calf had become a part of Muchengeti's family. They spotted their first elephants after they reached the veld, well south of Mana Pools. Van Rooyen throttled down and they dropped to a thousand feet. Trudging along in single file were five bulls. Jessica spread her loose leaf binder across her lap and after retrieving the binoculars, she looked down.

"Fundisi's down there," she said. "He's always the easiest to pick out. At 44, not only is he the oldest and the biggest bull in the valley, but his crossed tusks always give him away."

Van Rooyen dropped the starboard wing, eased on the left rudder and side-slipped the Cessna to give Jessica a closer view. Then she spotted Mukuru, the 40-year-old bull with the fist-sized hole in his left ear.

"Mukuru's there too, and whoop-de-doo, he's still wearing his GPS collar!" she cheered. "Since his entire family was culled in 1983, I'm so happy to see he's still around."

She also saw Ngomo, Nkosikaas's first born. "I'll have to tell Hector, when we get home. I have him to thank that Ngomo's still with us, today."

"You're right about that," van Rooyen agreed.

She spotted two younger bulls who were hanging out with the others. Studying them carefully and comparing them to sketches in her binder, she confirmed they were Chimuti and Chiripi-Poshi, both related to Chembere's family.

They left the bulls behind and Van Rooyen leveled out and they continued flying due east. To the south, the rugged, granite hills of the escarpment rose above them. They crossed the Chewore, as it meandered through the hills on its way to join the Zambezi. After the rains, the dry sandy riverbed had morphed into a lush watercourse, its banks thick with tall reeds and grasses.

"Look! There are more over there!" Jessica called out in excitement, pointing to where the river widened.

Van Rooyen turned Whisky-Kilo-Bravo in the direction Jessica was pointing. As he got closer to them, he lowered the right wing and brought the Cessna into a wide circle. Below, paddling in the water, near the riverbank, Jessica counted thirteen elephants. The largest, a cow with a broken left tusk, lifted her head, and pointed her trunk skywards to take in the scent of the large, noisy bird circling overhead.

"It's definitely Muchengeti and her family," Jessica said. "I'm looking for the calf."

Through her binoculars, she was able to pinpoint Umsizi, the bereaved mother of Rufaro and the stillborn calf, Mazukuru.

"See the calf?" van Rooyen asked.

"Not yet, but I've spotted the foster-mom."

Fearful of the noisy contraption buzzing above them, the elephants jostled around bunching up together. Had she been down there on the ground, Jessica knew she'd be hearing the rumbles and trumpets as the mothers nervously reined in their calves. Van Rooyen continued to circle, while Jessica's trained her eyes on the elephants.

"I think I see a little trunk sticking out from under Chikoma's belly. Go around just once more, Piet."

The Cessna circled the herd several more times.

"Chikoma, Umsizi's daughter, is definitely caring for a calf," she said. "And while I can't guarantee it's little Narini-Ina, common sense tells me it couldn't be any other. I'm so thrilled," she added, beaming across at van Rooyen, "and I can't wait until we get home tomorrow, so I can break the news to Precious."

Van Rooyen brought the Cessna around, and they headed north-west towards the Nisbet Safari Lodge.

*　　　　*　　　　*

At 3:30 p.m., they landed Whiskey-Kilo-Bravo on the rutted, dirt airstrip at Mana Pools. As van Rooyen brought the plane to a stop, he commented, "This runway never seems to improve. With the amount of traffic coming in here, bringing all those tourist dollars, you'd think the government would tar it, or at least grade it, van Rooyen remarked.

"Oh hush, will you? You say that every single time we land here," Jessica laughed.

"Perhaps there'll come a day when I won't have to."

Sulemon must have heard the plane, Jessica thought, because as soon as they landed, he drove up in the minivan sporting the Nisbet Overland Safari, logo.

"Hi Sulemon," she said with a happy grin, as she walked over and warmly shook his hand. "You're looking well." She felt great affection for Blair's tracker-cum-overall, number one guy. She'd never forget how ably he'd handled everything the day Mukuru charged Blair.

"*Masikati Baas Piet na Miss Jessica*," Sulemon greeted them, wishing them both a good afternoon.

"Good to see you again," van Rooyen said, jovially slapping him on the back.

"How was your flight?

"It was good, thank you Sulemon. The rains are here and everything looks so green," van Rooyen replied, as he pulled out their overnight bags.

"Oh yes, Baas Piet. There's lots of new grass for the animals," Sulemon said cheerfully, as he loaded their bags into the back of the minivan.

As they drove away, Sulemon looked over his shoulder at Jessica in the back seat. "Baas Blair will be very happy to see you, Miss Jessica. We are glad you are back."

Fifteen minutes later, they arrived at the Nisbet Safari Lodge.

"I'm always impressed by the beauty of this place," Jessica said, looking up at the lodge's natural stone façade against its wild Zambezi River backdrop.

"It has some outstanding views," van Rooyen said, pointing to groups of giraffe and zebra drinking at the water's edge.

After they'd checked in, the desk clerk smiled and whispered, "There's no charge, Mr. Nisbet told me you were his quests." She handed them two room keys.

Jessica looked across at van Rooyen with a knowing smile. She was certain they wouldn't use the second room, this time. Nonetheless, it would feel awkward for them to refuse the second key.

"And Mr. Nisbet asked if you would meet him for dinner at seven o'clock this evening."

"Of course, we'd love to," Jessica replied.

The porter had already taken their overnight bags from Sulemon and was marching towards the lift. Van Rooyen and Jessica followed him.

"You have rooms, twenty-five and twenty-six," he said, opening both doors with a master key.

The same rooms they'd slept in last time, Jessica noted. "Just put both bags in this room," she told the porter. "We'll sort them out later." She handed him an American, five-dollar bill. He nodded his thanks and backed out the door.

In deference to Jessica, van Rooyen selected the room without the crocodile murals. They entered and he closed the curtains to block out the bright, afternoon light. Taking Jessica in his arms, he enveloped her in a heart-hammering embrace. Then gently lifting her chin, he brought his lips down on hers and they kissed sensually, open-mouthed. His kiss made her body quiver. Locked in each other's arms, they danced to unheard music, while sashaying towards the bed.

As he kissed her, his hands worked feverishly to unfasten the buttons on her blouse, exposing her taught breasts with their hardened nipples. He fondled and kissed them and she moaned softly. Pressing her body against his, she moved her hands up and down his back, caressing him through the fabric of his shirt. She could feel his manhood pushing hard against her and, with an urgency that was hot-blooded, passionate, eager, and wanting, they made love as never before. Later, bathed and dressed for dinner, they trooped downstairs, arm-in-arm.

"We've still got thirty minutes till dinner. Let's have a drink on the balcony," van Rooyen said, steering her towards the door. With no other guests around, they chose a table overlooking the river. The clouds in the west burned a fiery red as the sun dipped towards the horizon.

A waiter approached to take their order. "Bring us a bottle of your finest champagne," van Rooyen said.

"Champagne? What's the occasion?" Jessica smiled, her eyebrows raised quizzically. "I just feel like celebrating this day with you," he said, as he covered her hand with his.

"Well, Pete that's real sweet of you," she teased. "I'll be happy to toast whatever it is you have in mind to celebrate this evening."

Looking looked down towards the river, they spotted a large, tuskless matriarch accompanied her ten family members, plodding in single file down to the water's edge.

"Look Piet, it's Chembere and her group. We'll celebrate their joining our party."

The waiter arrived with a champagne bottle in an ice bucket and two champagne glasses. Piet paid him. The waiter then popped the cork, pouring a sample of the sparkling, white wine into a glass for van Rooyen to approve.

He took a sip. "Excellent," he told the waiter, who poured the champagne into both glasses, replaced the bottle in the ice bucket, and then walked away. Van Rooyen leant forward and took both Jessica's hands in his. He had deadly serious expression on his face.

For a few seconds Jessica tensed, as a feeling of uneasiness washed over her. Was there something wrong? However, when he smiled she relaxed visibly.

"Jessica," he said, "Last week you were taken from me and I felt as if my whole world had collapsed. It made me realize how much I need you in my life, and how meaningless my existence would be without you. Will you marry me?"

Jessica's heart almost leapt from her chest, and tears of joy filled her eyes. She paused for a moment to clear the lump from her throat and to recover her composure.

"Oh Piet! What do I say? Yes? Of course. Oh, darn it. Listen to me blabbering. What I'm trying to say is I can't think of anything in the world I'd want more than to be your wife," she said, leaning towards him across the table. His mouth gently drew her lips against his and they shared a lingering, soft kiss.

They drew apart and van Rooyen fumbled in his trouser pocket, to produce a small, blue velvet box. He opened it, and Jessica gasped when she saw the diamond solitaire ring, sparkling brightly in the late afternoon light.

"It was my mother's, Jessica. I've had it reset, and I know she'd be honored for you to have and wear it."

"Oh wow! It's so beautiful, Piet," Jessica said breathlessly, as he placed it on her finger. The fit was perfect and she held out her left hand to admire it, while brushing away tears of happiness with the other.

Down at the riverbank, as the sun's brilliant, red-orange afterglow hovered above the western horizon, Chembere and her family cast long, gray shadows along the Zambezi.

Jessica and van Rooyen toasted one another and at five minutes to seven, holding tight to one another, they made their way, hand in hand, to the dining room.

"Isn't Blair going to be surprised?" she said, squeezing his hand.

THE END

Afterword

Despite van Rooyen's hope that one day "things will get better," in real life the plight of elephants has worsened considerably in Zimbabwe, and throughout the entire African continent. At time of publication, the October 2012 issue of *National Geographic Magazine*, in its investigative report, *Blood Ivory*, claims that poachers kill at least 25,000 elephants each year, worldwide, and that "the slaughter is massive and accelerating."

Meanwhile, in Zimbabwe, senior ZANU-PF officials and army commanders seized the Save (pronounced Sa-veh) Conservancy in August 2012, the largest private wildlife sanctuary in the world. Environmentalists believe they grabbed the wildlife jewel, home also to the critically endangered black rhino, to line their own pockets through the sale of lucrative, hunting concessions.

The Conservancy lies in the southeastern, Lowveld of Zimbabwe, and covers approximately 3,400 square kilometers, or 1,312 square miles.

Glossary

AK-47	Kalashnikov automatic rifle. A model of a 1947 weapon originally made in the Soviet Union.
AKA	Also known as
BBC	British Broadcasting Corporation.
BMW	Bavarian Motor Works. German automobile manufacturer.
Br.	British.
CAMPFIRE program	Communal Areas Management Program for Indigenous Resources. It compensates the public for damage inflicted by wildlife.
CIO	Central Intelligence Organization, Zimbabwe's secret police.
CITES	Convention on International Trade in Endangered Species of Wild Fauna and Flora.
EMT	Emergency medical technician.
ETA	Estimated Time of Arrival.

ABBREVIATIONS
Contd.

FN rifle	The Fusil Automatique Léger ("Light Automatic Rifle") or FAL is a self-loading, selective fire, battle rifle produced by the Belgian armaments manufacturer Fabrique Nationale de Herstal (FN).
GDFW	Global Defense Force for Wildlife, a non-profit environmental group.
HAFAC	Humanitarian African Food Assistance Corporation.
NOCZIM	National Oil Company of Zimbabwe.
OJ	Orange juice.
Ph. D.	Doctor of Philosophy (Doctorate degree).
R.L.I.	Rhodesia Light Infantry.
RPG	Rocket propelled grenade.
UH-1D	U.S. Army Bell UH-1D Iroquois (AKA Huey helicopter).
ZANU-PF	Zimbabwe African National Union - Popular Front.
ZESA	Zimbabwe Electricity Supply Authority.
ZNSPCA	Zimbabwe National Society for the Protection and Care of Animals.
ZPWMA	Zimbabwe Parks and Wildlife Management Authority.

AFRIKAANS

Ja	Yes.
Boerevors	A sausage created from a traditional Dutch recipe. Popular in South Africa.
Braaivleis	Barbeque, cook out.
Domkop	Idiot.

AFRIKAANS Contd.

Knobkerry	An African cane with a knob at one end. Used for throwing at animals in hunting or for clubbing an enemy.
Kopje	Small hill.
Skellum	Rogue
Veldskoens	Shoes made from untanned leather or soft rawhide.

GERMAN

Ja doch	Of course.

PORTUGESE

Linhas Aéreas de Moçambique	Mozambique Airlines.
Oh meu Deus	Oh my God.
Obrigado	Thank you.
Obrigado por tudo	Thanks for everything.
Não tem problema	No problem.
Pronto	Quick.
Tchau	Goodbye.

SCOTTISH GAELIC

Afore	Before.
Aye	Yes.
Ye	You.
Cannae	Can't.
Dinnae	Don't.
Didnae	Didn't.
Och aye	Oh yes.

SHONA

Badza	Short-handled African hoe.
Chipemberi	Rhinocerous.
Eh, amai we!	Oh my! (Literally, Oh my mother)
Eh, waka pusa iwe	Oh you stupid idiot.
Endai	Go.
Fambai zvakanaka	Go well.
Gomo,	Hill.
Gukurahundi	The early rain, which washes away the chaff before the spring, rains. (Euphemism for ethnic cleansing)
Handizivi	I don't know.
Handizvo here?	Is that not so?
Hapana	Nothing, not a single thing.
Hapana basa	No jobs.
Hatina ma U.S.	We don't have U.S. dollars.
Hazvigoni kutendeka	I don't believe it.
Hokoyoi,	Be careful.
Hongu	Yes.
Kudya kwemasikati	Lunch.
MaChitora	Mrs. Chitora.
Madala	Elderly, old.
Mahanya	Run.
Mahorokotoi	Congratulations.
Mangwanani	Good morning.
Manheru VaChitata, makadini	Good evening, Mr. Chitata. How are you?
Masikati,	Good afternoon.
Masikati, makadini,	Good afternoon (Polite - to a senior)
Mazvita.	Thank you.
Mbavha	Thief, robber.
Motocari	Motor car, car, personal road vehicle.
Muchenjere	Tall reeds.

SHONA Contd.

Muchitendai	Don't mention it.
Mudhara	Old man.
Mukuru	Big, large.
Murambatsvina	Drive out the rubbish.
Murungu	White person.
Ndakutadzira	I'm sorry.
Ndinoda nyama	I want some meat.
Ndiripo kana wakadini	Traditional polite response to a greeting.
Nherera	Orphan.
Pambere ne ZANU-PF	Up with ZANU-PF.
Pane foni yenyu	Phone's for you.
Penga	Mad, unbalanced, crazy.
Phasi ne murungu	Down with the white man.
Pinda	Come in.
Rori	Lorry (Br.) truck.
Shamwari (s)	Friend (s)
Simbi	Iron, metal.
Tafa nenzara	We are dying of hunger.
Tambo	Leash, rope, string or cord.
Teerera	Listen.
Tiripo kana, makadiniwo	I'm fine, and you.
VaKaseke	Mr. Kaseke.
VaZanunga,	Mr. Zanunga.
Zvakanaka, ndatenda chaizvo	I'm well, thank you.

ZIMBABWE SLANG

Braai	Short for Braaivleis.
Chuffed	Pleased.
Eeish!	An exclamation.
Howzit	Hello, how are you.

ZIMBABWE SLANG
Contd.

Kapenta	A sardine imported from Lake Tanganyika.
Mealie meal	Corn meal.
Medem	Madam
Mozzies	Mosquitoes.
Mushi	Good, nice, good looking.
Mushi bird	Good looking woman.
Simbi	Sound made to alert workers to start and end of workday, by drumming on a suspended plow disk, using an iron pipe.
Ya	Yes. Phonetic derivative of Afrikaans 'Ja.'
ZESA	Power. E.g., ZESA's been off for twelve hours.
Zim Parks	Zimbabwe Parks and Wildlife Management Authority.
Zim	Zimbabwe.

OTHER

Ba Tonga	An ethnic group of people from Northern Zimbabwe and neighboring Southern Zambia, and to a lesser extent, in Mozambique.
Bredie	Stew, gravy.
Brochette	Pieces of meat on a skewer.
CIA	United States Central Intelligence Agency.
Chibuku	Chibuku beer is consumed in southern Africa—a thin fermented porridge, usually made from sorghum.
Daga	Soil, earth, dirt.
Flog	Sell. British slang.
Green Bombers	ZANU-PF youth militia. Named for their green uniforms.
Hanky	Handkerchief.

OTHER Contd.

Huey helicopter	U.S. Army Bell helicopter (UH-1D Iroquois) Introduced during the Vietnam War.
JAG	Justice for Agriculture. JAG is a non-profit organization dedicated to serving commercial farmers and farm workers affected by Zimbabwe's 'Land Reform' program.
Knobkerrie	Short, heavy wooden club with a knob on one end, used by native peoples of South Africa for striking and throwing.
Necropsy	Animal autopsy.
Mashonaland	A region in northern Zimbabwe. The home of the Shona people.
Matabeleland	A region in southwestern Zimbabwe. The home of the Ndebele people.
Musth	A bull elephant in musth is primed to mate. He has high testosterone levels and is usually aggressive. Musth bulls produce thick secretions from their temporal glands, and continuously dribble urine.
Nom de guerre	Pseudonym used in wartime.
Panga	Machete.
Samoosa	Stuffed Indian pastry, popular in Zimbabwe and South Africa.
Shona huts	Traditional, circular pole and daga, dwellings with a thatched roof and floors of pounded cow manure.
Zambezi Beer	Brewed in Harare of malt, maize, hops, and water.
Vundu	Largest catfish in the Zambezi river system.

Author Biography

Diana M. Hawkins was born, and grew up, in Zimbabwe. She moved to the United States as an adult, where she pursued a career as a journalist and environmental writer. Her narrative nonfiction pieces, **Crackers: Wildlife Rescue Dog** and **Nyaminyami** were included in a hard cover, short story anthology, entitled *Mansovo: Tales and Trails,* illustrated by world-famous, wildlife artist, Craig Bone. She also published a children's picture book, **Lumpy the Elephant. Shadows along the Zambezi** is her first novel.

Endorsement for Shadows along the Zambezi

I was most honored when Diana Hawkins asked me to write a recommendation for her book, **Shadows along the Zambezi**.

When she first approached me with her request for me to write a review, and not having read the book, I assumed she was a born and bred American. I began reading it with some skepticism because I wondered how a person who had never lived in Zimbabwe could accurately convey the situation in this country. After reading the first few chapters, however, I realized she in fact had an intimate knowledge of Zimbabwe, because she had captured the true feeling of my home country.

I found **Shadows along the Zambezi** *thoroughly enjoyable and easy to read. Although it is a work of fiction, it could very well be a true story since much of what Diana has written about has actually happened in Zimbabwe. It is an action-packed adventure with all the necessary elements to make it a bestselling novel. I especially loved how she gets "up close and personal" with the elephants and her vivid descriptions of the Zimbabwean countryside and weather.*

I could really identify with this story because, in my capacity as Chairman of the Zimbabwe Conservation Task Force, I have often been on anti-poaching patrols and have had close contact with wild animals. Diana gives a very accurate account of the dangers, elation, and heartbreak that accompanies this lifestyle.

One word of warning, once you start reading this book, it is very difficult to put down.

Johnny Rodrigues
Chairman, Zimbabwe Conservation Task Force
Harare, Zimbabwe.

Johnny Rodrigues

Johnny Rodrigues formed the ZCTF, in 2001, with the blessing of the Minister of the Environment. Its mission was to assist the Zimbabwe Parks and Wildlife Management Authority in conducting anti-poaching patrols, and to raise funds to assist the cash-strapped, agency in carrying out its wildlife conservation responsibilities.

Despite the non-profit's early successes, the government soon withdrew its support when it came to light that government officials, including individuals in the Police, Army, and National Parks, controlled the primary poaching rings. Even though this revelation frightened off many of Rodrigues's volunteers and supporters, he carried on undaunted.

In spite of death threats, home break-ins, efforts to force his vehicle off the road, and other tactics employed to intimidate him, Rodrigues has saved countless animals. He and his volunteers work tirelessly to remove snares, prevent fires from burning critical wildlife habitat, and repair pumps that bring water to dried-up water holes. Without their labors, many more animals would suffer slow, agonizing deaths from thirst, starvation, drowning, or strangulation. The Zimbabwe Conservation Task Force accepts donations at http://www.zctfofficialsite.org/

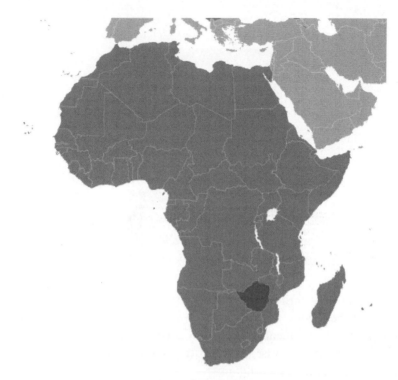

Map of Zimbabwe

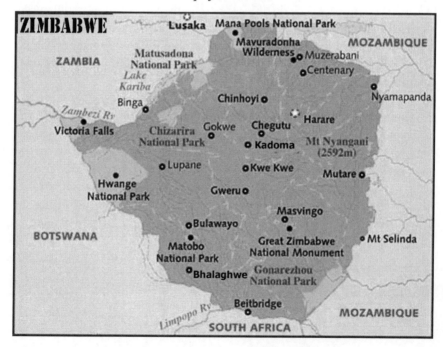

Printed in Great Britain
by Amazon.co.uk, Ltd.,
Marston Gate.